LOVE ME TO
DEATH

LOVE ME TO
DEATH

MARISSA CLARKE

Entangled Publishing, LLC
2614 South Timberline Road
Suite 109
Fort Collins, CO 80525

Visit our website at www.entangledpublishing.com.

Edited by Liz Pelletier
Cover design by Libby Murphy

Paperback ISBN 978-1-62266-391-0
Ebook ISBN 978-1-62266-392-7

Manufactured in the United States of America

First Edition October 2014

10 9 8 7 6 5 4 3 2 1

For Liz

His wings are gray and trailing,
Azrael, Angel of Death,
And yet the souls that Azrael brings
Across the dark and cold,
Look up beneath those folded wings,
And find them lined with gold.

~Robert Gilbert Welsh

THE PROPHECY OF THE UNITER:

FROM THE ASHES OF DEATH, THE UNITER SHALL RISE.
AWAKENED BY WARRIOR'S BLOOD TO RESTORE BALANCE.
WITH THE POWER TO DETHRONE TYRANTS AND ANOINT KINGS.
GUARDIAN OF THE BRIDGE BETWEEN SPECIES
ABOVE AND BELOW THE VEIL

CHAPTER ONE

This couldn't be happening; things like this happened to *other* people.

The skinny guy in the black baseball cap leveled the gun at the clerk behind the counter and without a word, pulled the trigger. Elena dropped to the floor between the candy shelves and car care products, ears ringing.

She studied the man's reflection in the circular convex mirror above the beer cooler as he rummaged through the cash register, stuffing his pockets with bills. His reflection was distorted, but she could still make out enough to give a description to the police. It was impossible to tell how tall he was, but he had black tangled hair and unnaturally pale skin. His blue flannel shirt was filthy and torn. More animal than human, he cocked his head to the side in a swift, jerky motion, then stared into the mirror. His eyes were...*red?*

The slam of the cash register drawer made Elena flinch. In horror, she watched through the mirror as the killer stalked to the far side of the store, passing the milk cooler one aisle over from her. Without a sound, she slid out of the center of the aisle, flattening up next to the metal shelves of candy, hoping he wouldn't spot her in the mirror. He paused, met her eyes in the reflection, and laughed. It was a hideous, feral laugh that made her body tense in a terrified rigor. She'd never heard anything like it. Almost metallic, it sounded like more than one person laughing. In the mirror, she watched him round the corner of her aisle.

Run, her body screamed. Elena leapt to her feet and flew for the door. *Run!* As she skidded around the corner at the end of the aisle, a gunshot rang out, followed by a searing pain as if her shoulder blade had exploded. Her knees gave way, and her head hit the floor with a sickening crack.

Footsteps. A pause.

"Get up!" the man growled in his unnatural, metallic voice, shoving her with his foot.

Play dead. She remained on her belly, eyes closed, breathing shallowly. *Please, let him think I'm dead.* Blood from her shoulder oozed under her cheek. He kicked her ribs, and she groaned.

"It's a shame I've already had dinner," he said.

Bang.

Oh God. He had shot her again, and pain raged through her body like fire radiating from her shoulder blade. His leisurely footsteps were followed by the tinkle of the bell on the door.

She was *going to die.*

For twenty-six years, Elena Arcos hadn't even really lived, and now it was over. Always waiting for something to change, something to give her purpose, someone to take her away. But that had never happened. She had lived her life under the radar, trying to not make waves. Trying to conform. Waiting. Waiting…for *what?*

For nothing.

She was going to die, dammit. Right here, on the filthy floor of the Corner Quick Mart. Just another news headline with no backstory whatsoever.

"Roll over and look at me." The male voice was deep, calm, and tinged with an exotic accent she'd never heard before. The timbre and confidence of the voice commanded compliance, but Elena found herself unable to move.

The bell on the door hadn't jingled again. This was someone who was already in the store—but she had been the only customer.

"I said, roll over."

"C-can't." Just the mere attempt to speak caused such intense pain she was certain she would faint.

"Bullshit. Your act worked on that worthless, thieving bastard, but it won't work on me."

Act? Undoubtedly, this was a death-experience hallucination. The power of his voice combined with his thick accent made her want to obey his order and roll over so she could put a face with the voice. She placed her palm on the floor in order to push up, but it slipped out from under her in the slick pool of her blood spreading across the grungy vinyl tiles. She whimpered as her chest slammed painfully back to the floor.

His voice rumbled near her ear. "Weak, pathetic creature."

She cried out as she was yanked roughly onto her back.

"Open your eyes!" the deep voice commanded. "Do it. Stop wasting my time."

Dressed in black, a magnificent tower of a man with ebony hair stood astride her, hands on his hips. He was scowling—eyes narrowed. He leaned closer and stared. Surely, this beautiful male creature was the angel of death, come to release her from the pain.

She looked into his gold eyes, glad this would be her last memory. She would leave life with the image of this perfect face in her mind and his forceful voice in her brain. Even through the mirage-like haze of pain, she noticed the well-developed muscles in his arms as he reached behind his head and drew out a long, brilliant sword from a sheath behind his back. He held it over his head like a knight from Arthurian Legend, the glimmering tip of the blade pointing down at her chest.

The pain felt like it was far away as she focused on his beautiful, fearsome form. Elena found herself calm rather than frightened as she stared up at the amazing creature preparing to plunge a sword into her heart.

She had never envisioned death like this. She had always assumed it was a horrible, shattering experience. This was... almost pleasant.

"I'm ready," she whispered.

A puzzled expression crossed his face. "I can't understand you. If you have last words, spit the blood out of your mouth so you can speak."

She closed her eyes, beginning to slip away under the surface of unconsciousness. Strong fingers on her jaw jerked her head to the side.

"Spit!" he ordered.

She smiled at the memory of the beautiful face of her angel of death as she succumbed to the darkness.

CHAPTER TWO

The lights were bright enough to shine pink through Elena's closed eyelids. *No pain.* Certainly this was heaven.

"Miss Arcos?" It was a woman's voice. Alto. Sweet.

Elena felt too good to open her eyes. The last thing she remembered was the searing pain of the gunshot wounds, and then his golden eyes. "Mmm hmm?" She remembered a sword...

"Miss Arcos, are you awake?"

"Mmm hmm." *And the body of a god.*

"There are two investigators here to talk to you about the robbery."

Nope. Not heaven. She opened her eyes to find a woman staring at her from the end of the bed. She was in her midfifties, wearing cranberry medical scrubs with her short, brown hair pulled back with barrettes.

Elena shot bolt upright. *The hospital. Damn.* She marveled again that there was no pain as she reached behind her to pull the open back of the gown together.

Maybe she had dreamed the whole convenience store robbery—gorgeous, golden-eyed death angel and all.

When she reached up to run her hands through her hair,

her fingers got tangled. She pulled her blood-matted curls over her shoulder to examine them. Her blonde hair was darkened with sticky, dried blood. She could hardly find her voice. "What happened?"

The nurse shifted nervously at the foot of the bed. "You've been unconscious for a while."

"What happened to me?"

"Well, that's what the investigators are trying to find out. May I bring them in? They've been waiting a long time to talk to you."

Investigators? The last thing she needed was to be interrogated. What in the world had happened anyway? If she wasn't dead, then *she* was the one who needed answers, not them.

The nurse pushed a button on the side rail, raising the head of the bed so that Elena was sitting up. She pulled the covers up to her neck as the nurse left to summon the police investigators. As she replayed the robbery in her mind, she could find no explanation for what was happening.

She was dead.

There was no way she could have lived through the second shot. And if she had, she certainly wouldn't be pain-free like this. But she was covered in blood—at least her hair was.

She had to get out of here. She looked around the room in an attempt to figure out which hospital she was in, but it was just a typical ER exam room. Could have been any one of the Houston Medical Center anchors.

Ah ha! A Central Hospital OSHA protocol was plastered to the cabinet in the nurses' station—just like the one that hung on her lab door at work. She could see the poster through the glass wall at the end of the room. So private—like a fish tank. At least she was in the hospital she worked for.

Elena jerked the rough sheet higher under her chin. Through

the glass wall, she saw the nurse leading two men toward her room. They joked and laughed with each other until they reached the door, where they became somber and businesslike.

Both of them were somewhere between forty-five and fifty. As if they had planned their outfits in advance, they both wore short-sleeved button-downs and tan slacks. The shorter one with sandy-colored hair spoke first. "Miss Arcos, my name is Jack Knowles, and this is Edward Gonzalez. We're investigators with the HPD Robbery/Homicide Division. May we ask you a couple of questions?"

Elena crossed her legs under the covers. "Um, sure." Why, she wondered, did she feel like she'd done something wrong? She should be glad these guys were trying to find the asshole who had shot her and the store clerk. Instead, her instincts were screaming that she should be wary and guarded. She shook her head to clear it. These were the good guys, right?

Detective Gonzalez walked around to the other side of her bed, so that she was flanked on either side, like they were setting her up for a game of keep away. Her heart raced as Detective Knowles placed a laptop computer on a tray table near her bed and slid it in front of her.

"What happened to you in the store?" the dark, stocky Detective Gonzales asked as he flipped open a small notebook like something out of a dime-store detective novel. His brow furrowed as he studied her.

She got the distinct feeling these guys thought she was a part of the robbery. The instinct to remain guarded flared again.

"I don't really know what happened. There was a guy with a gun," she muttered, closing her eyes.

"Do you know the man with the gun?" Knowles asked.

The computer drive whirred to life. "No."

Gonzalez's voice came from the other side. "How did blood

get in your hair and on your clothes?"

She kept her eyes closed. She was right; with one on each side, they were playing verbal keep away—or at this pace, ping-pong. She didn't want to play. She was dead.

"Miss Arcos?" It was Knowles. "How did you get covered in blood?"

"I've no idea. I thought he had shot me, but I guess I was wrong." Her answer was feeble, and she knew it. Telling these guys about the sexy death angel would guarantee her a trip to the funny farm—at the very least a heavy-duty psych evaluation, which would delay her discharge from the hospital. She kept her eyes closed in some kind of denial of reality

The nurse's voice came from across the room. "Detectives, the test results are back. It is human blood on the patient's body and clothes, and it matches her blood type."

Elena assumed Gonzalez was speaking because the voice came from his side of the playing field. "Miss Arcos. We need to get some answers from you. Please open your eyes and cooperate."

How did you explain the unexplainable? She had been shot. *Twice.* She should be dead. Maybe if she cooperated, they would go away. *These are the good guys*, she reminded herself. She opened her eyes and looked at the detective named Knowles. She gasped.

Sitting on the counter behind him was her angel of death from the convenience store. He was wearing black jeans and a black leather vest with no shirt. Strange markings covered his arms, neck, and chest, like tattoos in an alien language or something. The gold hilt of his sword peeked from over his shoulder. Maybe he had failed the first time and was here to claim her.

From his casual perch on the counter, the death angel gave her a smile. The impact was devastating. Elena's heart ripped into hyperdrive. It wasn't a "hey, good to see you" kind of smile. It was a devious, "I know something you don't know" smile. He was dangerous—and she knew it. Dangerous and irresistible. Her body came to life as if electrified. She shifted uncomfortably on the hard hospital bed and recrossed her legs.

The detectives seemed oblivious to the sword-wielding man's presence mere feet from them. In fact, Detective Knowles set his notepad on the counter inches from the death angel's thigh. He was invisible to them.

I'm crazy. There was no other explanation.

"Miss Arcos, why don't we start with some basic information," Detective Knowles suggested, clicking a ballpoint pen.

Elena answered questions about her age, address, contact numbers, and other personal information, while the detective scribbled on a form on a clipboard. "How are you feeling?" he asked as he flipped the page over.

"Like I want to go home."

The man with the sword was no longer on the counter. She scanned the room and couldn't find him. She chewed her bottom lip as Knowles inserted a disc in the laptop on the tray table in front of her. Out of nowhere, the death angel appeared at her shoulder, causing her to flinch and whack her knees on the table drawn across her bed. He leaned forward, studying her mouth, only inches from her face. She stopped chewing her lip and drew her mouth into a tight line. Oh God. What was that smell? It was *him*. He smelled as good as he looked, like leather and something else—some kind of cologne or soap.

She stared at the death angel's scowling face. Gorgeous, angular, with a day's growth of beard dusting his jaw line. "Who are you?" she whispered.

Detective Gonzalez patted her hand. "We're investigators. We're trying to figure out what happened to you in the store."

She found herself unable to draw her eyes away from the dark stranger who had backed up and was now leaning against the wall. Why couldn't they see him? He had a smirk on his face, which made her heart hammer. "I want to go home," she whispered.

"After we watch the disc from the surveillance camera in the store, we'll leave you alone. We're hoping you'll be able to clarify what's happening as we watch it," Detective Knowles said.

The man with the sword moved to the end of the bed. He appeared to be looking at her eyes. Not into them, like someone would if they were trying to communicate. No. He was looking *at* her eyes, as if he were studying a pinned bug specimen. Elena squirmed like that bug as she managed to pull her eyes away from the death angel.

Detective Knowles punched some keys on the laptop, and the disc began to play. There was no audio. On the screen, she watched herself enter the store. The camera had filmed from the corner where the mirror was mounted. She watched as she walked straight to the candy aisle. Detective Knowles paused the disc.

"It looks like you are familiar with the store. Why were you there?" Knowles asked.

"I was getting a Milky Way bar."

Gonzalez smiled. "Do you do this often?"

It was obvious he thought she was lying. "Yes. I have hypoglycemia—low blood sugar—I need candy when it gets bad."

It was Knowles's turn to lob the ball across the court. "So, you've been to this store before?"

"Yes."

"How many times?" Gonzalez seemed to enjoy the game more than Knowles. Grinning, he leaned against the bedrail, close enough for her to smell cigarette smoke clinging to his clothes.

"Um. Pretty much every day for the last three weeks."

Knowles's turn again. "Why for three weeks?"

She groaned. If only she knew. "My blood sugar has been out of whack since I started working at the hospital," she explained, smoothing the top of the sheet into a neat, straight fold. "The store is the first place to buy chocolate on my way home."

Gonzalez asked, "What do you do at the hospital?"

"I'm a research biologist in the hematology lab."

Gonzalez must have forgotten it wasn't his turn in the keep away game, because he continued the questioning. "What is your job in the lab?"

"I have a Ph.D. in Biology. I'm working as a research scientist on a cancer drug protocol. I study blood anomalies."

Deep laughter filled the room. Elena had been so distracted by the detectives she'd forgotten the death angel, who had moved to the glass wall when the questioning began. "That's perfect," he said in his deep voice. "Absolutely perfect. The fox in the henhouse."

What was that accent, she wondered. German? No, Russian, maybe. Whatever it was, the effect of his voice on her body was as profound as his smile. Her insides clenched.

Knowles spoke next. "So you've been going to this convenience store every day to get a candy bar after work."

She nodded but continued to watch the death angel, who chuckled as he stared out the window into the ER hallway. Like something out of a really great dream, here stood a huge guy with sexy markings, deep voice, and a sword—and for some reason, she was the only one who could see him. Physically, he was too good to be real. Maybe he *was* a dream. *Don't wake up, Elena*, she urged, trying to memorize every detail of his magnificent body. But she knew it wasn't a dream. She had died and was stuck in some kind of freaky purgatory.

"Miss Arcos, are you okay?" Detective Knowles waved his hand in front of her face.

"Uh, sorry, yeah," she mumbled, reluctantly drawing her eyes back to the computer as Knowles restarted the surveillance disc. On the screen, she watched herself pick up a Milky Way bar. The robber walked into the store and spread his hands out on the counter. The clerk behind the cash register dropped the tabloid he was reading and stood up. She watched the small laptop screen as the robber pulled a gun out of the front waist of his pants under the flannel shirt and shot the clerk, who collapsed behind the counter. Everything was exactly as she remembered it. The guy cleared out the cash register and then walked down the aisle beyond her to the back of the store. He turned on her aisle, and she bolted. He leveled the handgun and shot her in the back on the right shoulder. She hit the floor. The guy shoved her with his foot and then kicked her. Calmly, he aimed the gun at the middle of her back and fired. Blood spread out between her shoulder blades. As if he had not just shot two people, the guy strode nonchalantly out of the store.

Detective Gonzalez stopped the disc. "So, Miss Arcos, what happened next?"

Elena held her breath in an attempt to control her panic. No way was she going to talk about her imaginary death angel, who had disappeared from the exam room sometime during the review of the surveillance recording. More unnerving than his presence was his absence. "I don't remember."

Detective Gonzalez started the disc again. Neither he nor detective Knowles watched the computer; they watched Elena, who could feel their gazes as she concentrated on the black and white images on the screen. After the robber left the store, the death angel appeared out of thin air. She gasped, and then looked at the detectives, who were oblivious.

In the recording, the death angel spoke and then shoved her over onto her back effortlessly, as if she were a rag doll. He stood over her and withdrew his sword. Grabbing her chin, he forced her head to the side. She remembered he had told her to spit the blood out of her mouth so that he could understand her. Elena in the recording went limp.

She watched the laptop screen, mesmerized, as he lifted the sword to plunge it into her chest, but stopped short. He resheathed the sword and squatted down over her, opening her eyelid with his thumb and finger. Then he parted her lips and examined her teeth. He turned her head to one side and then the other, as if he were checking out her neck.

He ran the back of his fingers over her cheek. When he withdrew his hand, he balled it into a fist and punched the metal shelf next to her, causing an avalanche of candy to cascade to the floor. He appeared to shout as he stood up. Pausing a few times to look at her, he paced like a fierce, caged animal. Elena was glad there was no sound to the recording, because from the look on his face, she was sure his words were as aggressive and dangerous as his movements.

He stopped pacing and returned to her unconscious body. He pulled out a cell phone, punched some numbers, and put it to his ear. After speaking only a few words, he shoved it into his back pants pocket. As if he were afraid to touch her, he rolled her onto her stomach. He placed his palm over her shoulder blade and slowly pulled his hand away. When he turned his palm over, it looked like something was in his hand, as if he were a magnet that had attracted something. The bullet? *No way.*

Not breathing, she watched the computer screen, as he repeated the process over the middle of her back. Again, something stuck to his palm. *Damn.* It *had* to be the bullet.

He put whatever it was in his front pocket and stood up. After staring at her for a moment, he shook his head and disappeared.

A woman entered the store and covered her mouth. It was clear she was screaming. After some time, men came and put Elena on a gurney. Obviously paramedics. The next stop would be the hospital. End of story. She wasn't dead. Death had saved her instead.

Detective Knowles stopped the recording and closed the laptop. "So, um, explain that please, Miss Arcos."

"Explain what?" she mumbled, half buying time, half testing to see if they had seen the death angel.

Knowles put his hand on her shoulder. "Miss Arcos. It looks like you were shot, but there are no bullet wounds. We expected it to be fake blood, but you heard the nurse; it appears to be your blood. How is that possible?"

A sexy death angel pulled the bullets out? "I can't explain it."

Gonzalez spoke while Knowles packed the computer up. "Miss Arcos. We need you to cooperate here. Something about this isn't right."

No shit.

Gonzalez sighed as if his patience grew thin. "Do you know the man who shot you?"

"No."

"Can you describe him for us?"

The death angel reappeared at the foot of her bed before she could answer. He put his finger to his lip indicating she should be silent. His nearness caused her heart to fire into hyperdrive again. She swallowed and took a deep breath, hoping her voice wouldn't tremble like her body. "Um, well, I didn't really get a good look at him. I was pretty freaked out. I don't remember anything, actually."

Gonzalez leaned close. "Miss Arcos, the cashier died. If it

turns out that you are somehow involved in this crime, you will be an accessory to murder. You need to tell us the truth."

Why wasn't she telling them the truth, she wondered. Crazy was better than guilty of murder. She stared at the man with the sword who had lost his air of ease. He seemed to sense she was considering coming clean about what had really happened. He took a step toward her. The sword made a metallic *shing* sound as he pulled it out of its sheath.

"If you remove the Veil, I will have to kill them. Your fate is already sealed. Reveal nothing, or they are dead as well." His unusual accent punctuated the danger in his words.

As well...

"Miss Arcos, you won't like it in jail," Gonzales said.

At that moment, a tall brunette woman wearing a lab coat strode into the room. She looked from Gonzalez to Knowles to Elena. "I beg your pardon. I'm Dr. Williams. This is my patient. Is there a problem, gentlemen?"

Elena was shocked when the drop-dead gorgeous woman that looked like a supermodel said she was a doctor. She was charged to know that this woman would choose a profession that used her brain when she could have struck gold with a career using her perfect body and face. Her long white coat gapped open at the front, revealing a tailored navy blue business suit with a red silk shirt underneath. Both of the detectives seemed completely stunned by her. Their professional airs dissolved into the countenances of nervous high school freshmen.

Knowles awkwardly zipped up the computer bag. "No, doctor. There's no problem. We were just showing your patient a video of the robbery."

The doctor nodded. Gonzalez stuffed his notebook back into the pocket of this shirt. "Dr. Williams, the nurse said that the blood was a match for Miss Arcos. With no wounds, how do you explain that?"

The doctor shrugged and gifted them with a perfect, full-lipped smile. "It was a hell of a nose-bleed, I guess. Right now, I need to examine the patient. I will be happy to talk to you in the hallway. There are chairs in the waiting area just past the nurses' station." She gestured to the door.

The detectives took the cue and left the exam room, looking over their shoulders as they shuffled out.

The doctor closed the door and drew the curtain across the wall of glass. Her demeanor changed completely when she turned around. "What the hell do you think you're doing, Nikolai? Have you lost your mind?"

The death angel, sword still in hand, crossed to where she stood near the door. Even though the woman was tall, he towered over her, and with the sword, he looked deadly. "No, Aleksandra. I have not lost my mind. There has been a mistake."

The woman didn't appear intimidated by the death angel at all. She had the same accent and was matching his aggressive body language exactly. "You bet there's been a mistake. Otherwise, you would never have called me. Why does she still live?"

"She's human."

The woman gave his shoulder a shove. "Like hell she is." To Elena's horror, the woman strode to her bed and grabbed her by the hair. "Can you hear me? See me?" She gave Elena's hair a painful jerk. "Can you feel me, creature?"

Elena cried out, terrified.

Aleksandra released her hair and gave a disgusted snort. "You're an idiot, Nikolai. She can see me. I lifted the Veil for the idiot cops, but I replaced it when they left. If she's human, explain that."

"I can't," he conceded.

Elena's heart thumped so hard she could hear it in her head.

"She sees us, Nikolai. She is not human. She must die. Now." Desperation tinged his voice. "No. She isn't one of them. Look at her. Look at her eyes, Aleksi. She hasn't embraced the Underveil yet. I'm not permitted to take a human soul."

Aleksandra pulled a dagger out from under her lab coat. "Not all of us are as pure of purpose as you, Niki. Allow me to help you out here." She stalked toward the bed where Elena huddled. For some reason, Nikolai with a sword turned Elena on, but this woman with a dagger was terrifying.

Before Aleksandra reached the bed, Nikolai grabbed her by the shoulder and spun her to face him. "No! Her soul calls me. There has been a mistake. She's…she's…" The huge man appeared defeated by his own words. "This is a mistake."

Elena was amazed by Aleksandra's reaction—she laughed. She threw her head back and laughed. "Aw shit, Niki. That's impossible. You're just thinking with your dick. You've been too long without, that's all. One good night in bed with a strong, hungry woman, and this creature's pitiful call will be as inconsequential as her species…and just as easy to conquer."

Nikolai shifted his gaze and the tip of the sword to the floor. Aleksandra ran her fingers across his cheek. She pointed at the sword. "Are you going to use that, or are you just showing off?"

He glared at her with his gold eyes. "Fuck you, Aleksandra."

She laughed again. "You'd like that, but nope, little Niki, it's not permitted."

"You're sick, you know," he said as he slid the sword into the sheath behind his back.

She stowed the dagger back under the lab coat. "That's why you love me so much." She placed her hands on either side of his face. "Niki baby. You had a direct order. The minute she embraces the Underveil, kill her. If you don't, you know the punishment for disobedience. You have to do this." She brushed her fingers across his lips. "I couldn't bear losing you. Don't fail. Fydor wants you to screw up."

Elena found herself almost growling at their intimacy. She was...jealous? *Aw, for God's sake.* She couldn't possibly be jealous of some blood-hungry woman who was stroking the face of the man who was going to kill her. Kill her with a sword, no less. What was wrong with her? She'd gone crazy. *Yep.* Certifiable.

"I won't fail. I never have," he said. "I'll call you when it's done."

The woman kissed his cheek. "I love you, you know. I'll go deal with the detectives. Since the Underveil wasn't exposed, I don't have to kill them. I'll just take their notepads and computers and screw with their memories." She laughed. "Yeah, I think maybe I'll make them remember going to a topless bar instead of the hospital. That should give them something to think about when they go home to their wives." She winked at Nikolai. "I'll tell the techies at headquarters to hack into the hospital system and erase her medical records." She grabbed the patient chart from off the counter where she had laid it. "I've got this." She gave Elena a pointed glare. "Poof! Like magic, little girl, you're gone. You never even existed. None of your kind will exist when we're through." She trembled as Aleksandra chanted some strange words and disappeared into thin air with the chart.

She pulled her knees to her chest and bit her lip, fighting the urge to cry. Unable to bring herself to look at Nikolai, she closed her eyes and laid her chin on her knees, waiting for him to carry out Aleksandra's orders.

Nikolai stared at the diminutive, blonde woman with blood-soaked hair, curled up in a ball on the hospital bed. So fragile—not at all what he had expected. Vampires were fierce, calculating warriors, and this one was the daughter of Gregor Arcos, one of the most notorious vampires of modern time.

Gregor had killed Nikolai's father two decades ago, instigating the bloodiest war in the history of the Underveil.

Fydor, Nikolai's uncle, had sent him on this mission so that he could personally avenge his father's murder. Eager for closure, he'd accepted the assignment readily, anticipating a worthy opponent.

A pitiful human was not at all what he had expected.

He had spent the last two decades preparing for this moment by killing every rogue vampire he could find in an attempt to alleviate some of the pain, but the void in his heart was just as empty. Even Aleksandra couldn't fill it.

Certainly no gratification would be derived from reaping the soul of this tiny creature. Tiny, but not inconsequential. When he had stood over her in the convenience store, ready to end her life, something had happened—something more frightening than death itself: He had felt the pull of her soul. A distinct tugging at his own, calling him to join with her.

No. Impossible. Aleksandra was right. He was nuts. Maybe he *had* been too long without a woman. He shook his head and sighed. The girl in the bed shuddered, her head still on her knees and her eyes closed.

Something foreign in him wanted to calm her but knew it was the wrong thing to do. He was a Slayer—a terrifying being created to patrol the Underveil and execute immortals who broke the laws. He wasn't a wimp who consoled unconverted vampires before he killed them. *Grow a pair.*

But what if Fydor was wrong? His messages had been odd recently, consumed with finding Arcos's offspring and executing her as soon as possible, insisting she was planning an attack on the royal family to avenge her father. He'd devoted a huge amount of resources to the task and insisted Nikolai be the only one to carry out the mission, which had suited him fine. Killing anyone related to his father's murderer seemed apropos. But now that he'd met her, something seemed way off. What if she wasn't a menace to the Underveil? He couldn't execute her until he knew for sure. He had to take her somewhere they could have privacy for a while. Some place Fydor and his soldiers had not been so that they couldn't teleport in unannounced. Someplace even he had never been that was close enough to not use a ton of energy in transit. He intentionally infused his voice with hatred, more to motivate himself than to frighten her. "Get up, parasite. We need to get out of here."

Instead of obeying him, she squeezed her legs tighter to her chest. *Damn.* He was going to have to do this by force. He yanked the sheet off her and grabbed her arm. "Listen to me. We can do this the easy way or the hard way. Get out of bed, or I will drag you out. Do you have any powers?"

"I don't understand."

Shit. "Can you teleport or read minds or do anything unusual?"

She reached down and pulled the covers back over herself defensively; her blue eyes flashed anger as they met his. "I don't know what you're talking about. I don't have any powers. I'm just a regular person who had a regular life until you came along and screwed everything up."

Her surprising defiance caused a wave of adrenaline to roll through him. "Kiss your regular life good-bye, princess." He ripped the cover back down and grabbed her ankle. "Get out of that bed, or I'll make you wish you had."

She glared at him, eyes narrowed. For some reason, she didn't seem as frightened of him as he thought she should be. Most of his victims practically soiled themselves in terror from his mere presence.

His hand was enormous on her pale, narrow ankle. The skin

on her leg was smooth and soft. He was suppressing the urge to run his hand up her calf. In fact, he was suppressing the urge to do a lot of things. He cursed as he noticed her slender form was completely visible through the sheer cotton hospital gown. He raised his gaze to her face, focusing on her soft, full lips. Big mistake.

Nikolai had expected to have to fight the urge to torture the progeny of his father's murderer, but he had never anticipated fighting the urge to fuck her.

Maybe he should just kill her here and now. She wasn't really human. She could see through the Veil, right?

Before he could withdraw the sword, Elena got out of bed. She slid out on the side opposite him, clutching the back of the gown. "Okay," she whispered. "You said we needed to get out of here. I'll go. But I don't have any clothes. They must have cut them off me. I'll have to wear this hospital gown."

He ran his eyes up and down her body, amazed at how she affected him. She was not his type at all. He liked stronger women who could play rough. This creature was too breakable for his tastes, but his body didn't seem to concur with that assessment. "You don't need clothes. You'll be invisible to humans," he said.

"Where are we going?"

"To your home."

"Why?"

"We'll wait in private for you to embrace the Underveil, so I can kill you."

CHAPTER THREE

Elena almost lost her nerve when Nikolai stormed across the ER exam room. His sheer size was terrifying enough but he grabbed her with such force she was certain the bones in her wrist would break.

Pull it together, she warned herself, *don't let him see your fear.* There had to be a way out of this situation. She just needed time to figure it out, and going with him would give her more time than hanging out here, as evidenced by his tendency to yank out his sword and threaten her. Digging down deep, she found the remaining vestiges of her courage and her voice, which, to her relief, didn't squeak.

"There's no need to bully me. I said I'd go with you." She jerked her arm in an ineffectual attempt to loosen his grip. "You're hurting me."

He leaned down, putting his face on her level. "You don't know what pain is."

"And I don't want to. I'll cooperate. Please…just lighten up a little."

To her relief, he relaxed his hold. With his free hand, he reached into his front pocket and pulled out a long silver cord. "Move and die," he warned, releasing her wrist.

She knew without a doubt he meant it. She stood still as stone while he looped an end of the cord around her wrist and then, wearing a deep scowl, fastened the other end around his own, muttering some incantation in a bizarre language.

The thin cord shimmered as if liquid mercury undulated within. A slight current emanated from it. Energy traveled from his body to hers. Mesmerized, she marveled at the waves of color traversing from her wrist along the length of reflective surface. "What is that?" she whispered.

The deep, masculine timbre of Nikolai's voice pulled Elena out of her stupor. "A soul bond forged by light elves, parasite. It's a tendril of your soul you see moving through it. If it breaks, you die."

She stared into his mirthless, golden eyes. "Why are you doing this?"

"Beats the hell out of handcuffs. Now, let's get moving before the Underveil is exposed. We need to get to your home so I don't have to kill you here. It would be messy. Too many humans, and since you are unconverted, your body would be visible to them."

From the look on his face, she could tell he was absolutely serious. She was going to die. Why did it bother her so much, when she had accepted death at the convenience store?

Nikolai began chanting in an odd language. Her body felt strange, like she was lighter or buoyant, somehow. He stopped chanting and looked into her eyes. "Think of your home." He put his large, warm hands on either side of her neck. "Close your eyes and picture it. Picture both of us there."

She considered screaming. Maybe the detectives would hear her and help. The thought was fleeting. By the time they could react, she'd be dead. They were no match for this guy anyway. If he could pull part of her soul out of her body and hold it hostage in a silver chain, what else could he do? Her death was inevitable. Might as well do it where nobody else got hurt.

"You know what I am and what I do. Don't defy me, creature. No tricks. Imagine your home."

She had no clue what he was, but she knew killing was a big part of it. Resigned to limit casualties to herself, she closed her eyes and pictured her living room with its tattered furniture, out-of-date wood paneling, and worn-out carpeting. Nikolai resumed his chant. A rustling behind her broke her concentration. She opened her eyes to see a nurse opening the curtain on the hallway wall of the exam room.

His hands tightened around her throat. "Little parasite, if you piss me off, you will suffer a death so slow and horrible, you will *beg* for your life to end."

She couldn't breathe. "Please," she managed to croak. "Worried about nurse seeing us." Out of the corner of her eye, she could see the nurse cleaning up the room in order to get it ready for the next patient as if Elena and the death angel weren't in the room, and as if he weren't choking the life out of her.

Nikolai loosened his grip, and she gasped for air. He balanced the tips of his fingers on either side of her neck again. "We are under the human Veil. She cannot see or hear us. Now, concentrate on your home and us in it." He repositioned his hands to the side of her neck. "And don't fuck with me."

Don't fuck with him... The sad thing was that instead of serving as a threat, his words caused a warm flush to roll straight through her body. Though his word choice was not what she would have used, that was exactly what her body wanted to do. It had to be the result of near-death trauma. Elena closed her eyes and envisioned the tattered, velour sofa in her living room.

As she created this mental picture, Nikolai ran his fingers over the sensitive skin of her neck and started chanting again. His incredible smell filled her nose, and as she pictured the sofa, she imagined herself lying over him while he used those long fingers to do something other than murder her. She was certain she was going insane, because even though she knew this guy was going to kill her, she wanted him.

There was a whooshing sound and a flash of heat. With a hard slam to her senses, Elena found herself exactly as she had envisioned: on her sofa, astride Nikolai, wearing only her hospital gown. Heat seeped through his jeans, warming the bare skin of her thighs.

He groaned, eyes closed.

She adjusted slightly, centering the hard ridge of him just... there...

He hissed air through his teeth and froze. His golden eyes flew open, and then narrowed. "What kind of magic is this?" he growled. "You have picked the wrong man to provoke."

He shoved her off of him onto the floor as he sat up. She landed on all fours and scrambled backward until the silver cord pulled taut. She sat back on her heels and tucked the gown closed behind her. Pulling deep, she calmed herself with her father's words. *Do not ever let your enemy know the extent of your fear or what it is you desire the most.* Expanding her lungs with a deep breath, she forced her body to still and waited for his next move.

His hateful glare was terrifying. "What is it you want, parasite? Do you think you can bargain for your life with your body? Think again. I'm not that weak." He jerked the cord. "I could snap this and kill you right now, but unlike your pathetic species, I don't kill humans, and I don't fuck my enemies." He turned sideways as if looking at her were painful.

Elena took a deep breath and willed her heart to stop racing. What in the world had just happened? He seemed to think she had intentionally provoked him—that she wanted to hurt him, somehow. He considered her his enemy, yet she didn't even know who he was. Hell, she didn't even know *what* he was. He kept talking about species and weird things she knew nothing about as if she were a part of some alternate dimension. Nothing made sense anymore. The only thing she knew for certain was that making him angry wouldn't keep her alive. And right now, Elena Arcos wanted to live.

Perhaps a more docile demeanor would work better. "I'm sorry," she whispered, shifting to her knees on the wood floor. She pulled the back of the hospital gown together and tucked it under her backside. "I don't know how these things work, and didn't know you were going to replicate my vision. I can't even imagine why I thought of us like that. Really, I'm sorry."

Nikolai paced the length of the room, trying to wrap his head around her words. Vampires didn't offer excuses, and they never apologized. Never. Yet, this woman had just given a plausible explanation and an eloquent apology.

She was an utter enigma. He had never wanted a woman like he wanted this one, which was why he had reacted so violently when he found her on top of him. As he invoked the spell to move them, he was imagining her in that exact position. Perhaps she had lied about her powers and could read minds after all. Or maybe it was just that she felt the pull, too.

Wanting her was in complete opposition to his nature and purpose. Killing her would be the final act in avenging his father's death. It had to be done, and he had to be the one to do it.

As soon as he could carry out justice, he would begin

fulfilling his father's last request. He would be free to find the Uniter and stop the war that was brewing.

Diminutive and frail, she remained on her knees next to the sofa. As he watched her tremble, something in his chest caught, as if he had been pinched on the inside. *What the hell?*

"Are you okay?" he asked reflexively, kicking himself internally for being so weak.

She didn't look up. "No. I'm hypoglycemic. I'm going to faint."

"What does that mean?"

Her voice was barely above a whisper. "My blood sugar is too low. I need sugar."

He stood. "Where is your kitchen?" She didn't even look up. "Hey. Look at me." His voice was softer than he had intended.

She looked up, her eyes full of tears. *Oh shit.* Women's tears undid him.

"How can I help you?"

She shrugged her shoulders. "Why do you care?"

"I don't want you to be uncomfortable. I'm not here to torture you."

Her eyes narrowed. "No, you're just here to *kill* me."

She was right, and for some reason, it made him feel like shit. For the first time in his centuries of life, doing the right thing didn't seem like the right thing to do.

Just moments earlier, she had been full of fire, and now she was an empty shell. He needed to get her to eat, but couldn't go unless she came with him because of the cord.

"Can you stand?" he asked.

She didn't react, but stared listlessly at the floor, still shaking.

He pulled her up by the shoulders. Eyes glazed, she teetered slightly. He scooped her up into his arms before she collapsed. He didn't know anything about her condition, but she said that food would help. She had told the detectives that she had gone to the convenience store because her blood sugar had been low. That was hours ago.

He strode toward a door to the right of a boxy, old-fashioned television. "Can you die from this?"

Her eyes were closed. "Why do you care?"

He wished he knew. He pushed the door open with his foot. Bingo. It was the kitchen. Still cradling her in his arms, he opened the tiny refrigerator and pulled out a carton of orange juice, trying to avoid whacking her head on anything in the process. When he set her on the Formica countertop, she was able to keep herself upright, so he headed for the cabinet next to the refrigerator, which seemed like the right spot for a glass. The cord on his wrist jerked, and he spun around just in time to catch her before he yanked her off the counter. He had forgotten he had bound her soul.

Growling a stream of profanity, he righted her and grabbed the juice carton. As he opened it, she leaned against his shoulder and sighed, which caused that uncomfortable pinching sensation in his chest again. He needed to get the juice in her before she passed out. He held the carton to her lips. "Come on, drink this. It will make you feel better."

"Screw you." Her voice was slurred and weak. Clamping her lips tight, she shook her head.

He growled in his throat and grabbed her lower jaw, pulling down to pry her mouth open. She shook her head again and jerked her jaw from his fingers. "You just want me strong so it's more fun to kill me."

"Slayers do not kill for fun." It was his job. His duty to keep the Underveil controlled and contained. She believed him some kind of monster, and for some reason, that bugged the shit out of him. He shook his head. What should he care what a vampire thought of him? "Listen to me, Elena Arcos, you will—"

Ding-dong.

"Are you expecting someone?" he asked.

"No." From the startled look on her face, he knew she was telling the truth.

Ding-dong.

She appeared to be holding her breath.

"Elena?" A woman's voice called from far away. "You okay, darlin'?"

"Who is that?" he asked.

"My aunt Uza."

"Is she human?"

Her eyes narrowed. "God, I'm sick of this batshit crazy human/nonhuman business. Of course she is."

"Elena, honey, I know you're in there," the voice called from the outside of the house.

He grabbed her by the shoulders and pulled her from the counter to her feet. "Get rid of her." Practically carrying her, he guided her to the door. "Fuck it up, and I'll kill her too."

"What a charmer." She leaned against the front door. "I'm fine, Uza. Going to bed. See you tomorrow, okay?"

There was a considerable pause, then a chuckle. "Hottie-totty didn't waste any time then, huh?"

Elena's startled gaze swung to his.

"And drink the juice, honey. You're gonna need it," she called. "Have fun!"

Have fun?

Elena teetered, and he tightened his grip just in time to keep her from hitting the floor. *Shit.* She'd fainted. *Now what?* Nikolai scooped her up and looked though the peephole in the front door. An old woman wearing a floral mu-mu hobbled down the sidewalk in front of the house. Abruptly, she turned around as if she could see him through the door and gave a thumbs-up.

"The hottie-totty didn't waste time?" What the hell did that mean? He stared down at the fragile woman in his arms. Maybe it was customary for her to bring men to her home and the old woman knew it. Like lightning, rage bolted through his body. Surely, the sexual habits of his enemy—his soon to be *dead* enemy—should be of no relevance to him.

He carried her to the kitchen and grabbed the orange juice. He had to revive her in order to…what? To kill her? But she was painfully human. Humans were not within his jurisdiction.

His phone buzzed in his pocket. He set the carton on the counter and shifted her from a cradle hold to where she balanced over his shoulder, then pulled out his phone and read the text from Aleksi. "Confirmation squad departing from local hdq in 5. You have 30 mins max."

Shit, shit, shit. Fydor's men were on the way to confirm the execution had been carried out. He had to get out of there. Panic and fear were not part of his composition, yet both took a strangle hold on him as he tried to formulate a plan. They'd never felt the need to confirm his kills before. Why now? And how did they know where he was?

Human still over his shoulder, he paced a small circle. In all honesty, it was a stupid idea to bring her here. Of course Fydor would figure it out. They kept tabs on all of their enemies. Fortunately, since none of them had been here before—at least he hoped they hadn't—they could not just teleport in unannounced. They'd have to do it the old-fashioned way.

He shifted her higher on his shoulder, and her open-backed hospital gown gapped even further, exposing her entire ass. He squeezed his eyes shut and shook his head to clear the image from his mind. Maybe he should just return to the fortress with the girl and wait there to kill her. Fydor could even do it himself that way. Something in Nikolai screamed in protest at that idea. Something wasn't right about this whole thing. His instincts had always been flawless. That's why he was a superior Slayer. Until he figured this out, he had to keep the girl alive.

And then it happened. The worst possible thing ever. As if confirming his decision to cut and run, a fragment of his traitorous soul traveled down the cord and entwined with hers in a brilliant display of blue and silver sparks.

He shouted his anguish to the empty house in what came out as a primal roar. His soul had confirmed what his body had screamed but his mind had denied from the moment he laid eyes on her: this harmless, weak, pathetic human was his. His true mate—and the fact his soul had crept down the cord to meet hers meant that if the cord were broken, not only would the girl die, he would as well. He'd been ensnared in his own trap.

CHAPTER FOUR

A horrible, animalistic growl jerked Elena from oblivion. Her head throbbed, probably from the double-whammy of her low blood sugar coupled with the fact she was being toted caveman-style over the death angel's shoulder.

From this angle, she could see that she was still in her kitchen and that Nikolai had a truly fine ass. *Wait. What an absolutely absurd thought.* He growled again. Something had upset him. Oh God. She had passed out. What if Aunt Uza had come back?

"Put me down," she said.

The pacing stopped so abruptly her chin slammed into his lower back. He stooped and placed her feet on the floor. It was then she remembered she was bare-ass naked for the most part. She pulled the gown closed behind her as he steadied her by the shoulders.

"We have to leave," he said.

"Nope. Not happening. Kill me here, or not at all. I've had enough."

He jerked the cord, causing her to tumble forward into him. Heat rolled off his chest into her palms, and she resisted the urge to run her hands over the smooth leather of his vest. *Wrong, Arcos. Wrong in every way imaginable.*

"Listen to me and listen well. You will do two things in the next three minutes. You will drink enough orange juice to make you stable, and then you will find something you can wear in public and not be noticed." He punctuated his order with another sharp yank on the cord.

Public. That sounded promising. Surely he wouldn't kill her in public. Still, she wasn't ready to go so easily. Perhaps he had realized she was not a vampire or whatever it was he thought her to be. Maybe he would let her go.

"Why should I cooperate? What's in it for me?"

He took a step away and leaned down to where his face was level with hers. "I'll put it to you this way. I'll tell you what's in it if you do *not* cooperate: torture. Horrible, painful torture at the hands of six or so of my kind coming to insure I carried out my orders." He ran his forefinger in a line from her throat, between her breasts all the way to her navel, then back up in a path that almost made her faint again. "And after they've all had you, and broken you, you will understand why you should have cooperated with me. Believe me when I tell you I'm the lesser of the evils."

Stubborn? Yes. Stupid? Hell, no. She picked up the carton of OJ and took a guzzle, then another, and another, until she couldn't hold any more.

"Let's go," she said, heading toward the kitchen door. When the cord pulled taut, she gave it a jerk to get him to follow, which he did, all the way to her bedroom. "What kind of clothes? Where are we going?" She stopped short when she saw the suitcase on the bed. She popped the latches and found it packed with everything from a Parka to red lace lingerie.

The death angel snorted. "Sorry to alter your previous vacation plans."

"What? No. I didn't do this."

His eyebrow shot up. "Perhaps one of your lovers packed for you. An unexpected trip, maybe?"

She stared at the suitcase full of enough clothes to last a week in any climate. There was also cash. Lots of it. What was going on? The only one with a key to her place was Uza, and she was usually too out of it to even organize for a trip to the grocery store.

He slammed the suitcase closed and snapped the latches. "You'll just have to disappoint him. Now find something to cover yourself." He pulled her to the closet by the cord.

She held up her wrist. "This is going to make it tricky."

"There's nothing I can do about that. You are a clever girl. Figure something out." He pulled out his phone and checked the time. "Now."

She yanked a halter-top sundress off the hanger and stepped into it, then pulled the cord to get more freedom of movement. "Help me out here," she said. "I can't do it one handed."

He moved closer to give her use of both arms. She hated him being this close because it made her body go stupid. Really stupid. *He plans to kill you.* At least that's what he said. He could off her so easily, yet he hadn't. Something was holding him back. Her heart beat a tad faster as it filled with hope. Maybe she could escape before he made good on his threats.

"Please turn around," she said once the dress was pulled to her waist under the gown.

"For God's sake, woman," he growled, turning away. "I've seen your body all day. Don't flatter yourself."

His words stung, which was beyond ridiculous. She yanked the hospital gown off and pulled the halter up and tied it behind her neck. "Fine. Done."

He put the suitcase on the floor between them and extended the handle. "Hold this and don't let go."

Bossy jerk. She grabbed the handle.

He placed his hands on the side of her neck and then started that unintelligible chant he had done at the hospital. The tingly warmth from his fingers emanated through her body.

"Think of a hotel in another city where you have stayed that you can picture well. In your mind, recreate the lobby or the parking lot, if possible. Do not imagine yourself in any position other than standing next to me." He arched an eyebrow. "Are we clear?"

A loud crash and men's voices downstairs caused her to jump. "Yes."

"Imagine it now." He closed his eyes and chanted.

The air warmed, and she felt as though she were dissolving—or more accurately, evaporating. Then, like before, it was as if her entire body were slammed by pressure from all sides at once. When everything stilled, she opened her eyes to find herself in the lobby of a Texas hill-country resort she had visited last summer. She and Nikolai stared at each other in the dark corner where they'd landed, suitcase clutched tightly in her hand between them.

He nodded. "Well done."

She fought the urge to smile. God, she was pathetic to respond to his praise.

"You look terrible," he said.

So much for praise. "Thanks."

He balled the cord in his palm, then placed her hand over his, concealing it for the most part. To anyone else, it looked like they were simply holding hands. A huge, sword-wielding, bare-chested god with a scrawny chick. "Wait. You can't just go prancing around with that thing strapped to your back."

"Number one, I never prance. Number two, I'm concealed by a partial human Veil. What they see is me in a business suit."

"What do they see when they see me?"

"You. Exactly as you are." Grabbing the handle of her suitcase in his free hand, he pulled her to the gift shop near the registration desk and plucked the first baseball cap off of a souvenir display and passed it to her, dropping her other hand. "Put it on with your hair hidden underneath."

She read the cap out loud. "Ride 'em cowgirl?" *Classy.* She twisted her hair on top of her head and slipped the cap over it while he paid. A disguise, maybe? No telling. The guy was unpredictable.

He balled the cord up and pressed his palm against hers again. "Do as I say and follow my lead. Do not act out or let on that you're unwilling, or I will not only kill you, I will kill everyone in this room. Are we clear?"

Giggles erupted from two little girls getting their faces painted at a table across the room near the door.

"Clear."

He sauntered to the desk with Elena in tow as if he owned the world—and her, too, for that matter—and requested a room for the night. He paid in cash and took the card key from the girl who all but openly propositioned him from behind the counter. *Holy crap.* He probably got this all the time. Elena looked him up and down trying to imagine him in a business suit. Were the situation different, she would probably be drooling just like the clerk who told him to call her if he needed anything. Emphasis on *anything.*

The room was decorated in Texas rustic style with a huge king-size bed that seemed to scream "ride 'em cowgirl," just like the freaking cap she wore. The death angel's eyes were locked on the bed as well. Maybe he was tired... He adjusted himself. Maybe she was an idiot.

She caught a glimpse of her reflection in the mirror over the desk and gasped. She still had blood smeared on her face and neck from the shooting. It seemed like it had happened ages ago. No wonder he had her put her hair in a cap. It was caked with blood. She shuddered.

"Are you cold?" he asked, pushing the handle down on her rolling suitcase.

"No. I'm grossed out."

He looked around the room. "It doesn't meet your approval?"

"No. I'm grossed out by me. I'm disgusting." She pulled the cap off, and her blood-caked hair tumbled down over her shoulders. "I can't believe you didn't cloak me in a magic spell or whatever it is."

"Vain, are you?"

"Hardly. I just don't like going around looking like I bathed in blood."

A dark look crossed his face. "Isn't that your wildest dream, vampire?"

Her stomach churned at the hatred in his tone. "I'm not a vampire. I never will be one, so if that's what you're waiting on, settle in, buddy. You're going to get to feel all superior dragging me around looking like you rescued me off the street for a looooong time."

He blanched at the acid in her tone. "I didn't cloak you because it takes energy to hide a human in the human world. The energy caused by teleporting dissipates, but cloaking leaves, for lack of a better description, a trail. Simply cloaking my clothes will leave a weak signal. Cloaking you would leave a much stronger one."

That made sense, she supposed, but she still hated it...and him. She looked around the room again and spotted the open bathroom door. She really needed to use the restroom and take a shower. Surely he'd untie her for just a moment. "I swear I won't run. Please untie me so I can have some private moments in the bathroom."

"No."

"So I can't even pee?"

"Of course you can. You may do whatever you wish. Shower, relieve yourself. Hell, pleasure yourself for all I care. The cord remains."

"Until I'm dead."

"Yes."

She really didn't have a choice. Unless he killed her in the next two minutes, she was going to pee herself.

"Let's go." She entered the bathroom and realized the cord was long enough for him to remain outside while she used the toilet. She closed the door in his face with a slam and stifled a grin. A small victory, but a victory nonetheless.

He would have to come in if she were going to shower. Though it probably wouldn't be that big a deal. Even though it was obvious from the perpetual bulge in his pants he was male and she was female, he had made it clear he hated her—or he hated whatever it he thought she was. Tears stung the back of her eyelids. Clearly he considered her beneath him.

Nikolai leaned his forehead against the closed door. He wanted to have this woman beneath him. His body all but screamed it out loud. He had to have her. No more games. No more waiting. She was his, and he would make it so.

He stared at the pulses of his soul as it traveled the exposed inches of the cord before disappearing behind the closed door. There had been fireworks when their souls collided on the cable between them. There would be fireworks when their bodies met as well.

She had flushed minutes ago. He knocked. "My turn."

There was no response. He tried the door to find it locked. What the devil was she up to? He reached into his back pocket, pulled out a lock pick, and popped the door on the first try. He found her sitting on the closed toilet lid, knees drawn to her chest, sobbing and trembling all over. He crouched in front of her, but she buried her face in her arms.

"Hey." His voice was barely above a whisper. "You okay?"

A choked laugh came from her. "Am I okay?"

He ached to see her like this. "Yes. That was my question."

She lifted her head and met his gaze directly. "No, I am not okay." She unfurled and sat up straight. "I can't believe you have the balls to ask me that. How can you even imagine I would be okay?"

Nikolai swallowed the lump in his throat. "I simply wanted to—"

"To what?"

He could hardly believe it himself. "Calm you."

"Calm me? What, before you kill me?" She pushed to her feet, and Nikolai stood as well. The air was charged with her anger. "Because that's what all of this is about, isn't it? Killing me."

He didn't know what to say. That was how it started, certainly, but things had changed.

"Let me tell you about my day, and you tell me if I'm okay," she said.

He moved to sit on the toilet lid and give her free reign to rant. Perhaps, like Aleksandra, letting it out would make her feel better.

She held up a finger. "First, my asshole boss berates me for not being productive enough, which is total bullshit, but tells me he'll look the other way if I go out for drinks with him." She switched the finger she held up to her middle one, making a crude gesture. "Right. Drinks my ass. My ass is what he wants. Not a chance." She straightened her forefinger again, leaving two fingers up. "Second. I have a hideous blood sugar attack and stop to buy a candy bar, but get killed by some freak instead. You'd think that would be the happy ever after ending, but no. I get revived by..." She gestured to him. "Whatever *you* are, taken to the hospital, interrogated by cops, assaulted by a crazy lady, transported to my house to be murdered, then moved here to be murdered instead, all the while being insulted and degraded." She stopped and took a deep breath. "Oh yeah. I'm just great. Any other questions?"

There was so much power inside this tiny human. He wondered what she would be like if allowed to come into her immortal powers. He stifled a smile. She would be a force to be reckoned with, for certain. But his orders were clear. He must destroy her, which hardly seemed just since she had no involvement with his father's murder whatsoever. Fydor's intel could not have been that faulty. Why had he lied to him?

While she caught her breath, Nikolai watched the blue and silver threads of their souls dance along the cord. What a cruel trick of fate that they were bonded. If only there were a way to release himself from her and release her from her execution. He must find a way.

She dropped to her knees at his feet. "Please. Please let me go. I'm not what you think I am. I'm just a human trying to make a living and get by."

He wished he could set her free, but severing the cord would mean death for them both. "No. And you are not human. Not entirely. You see under the Veil. I think you will become something else with the right trigger."

She slumped back onto her heels. "Like what?"

He pulled a dagger out of his boot, and she scooted as far away as the cord would allow. He pricked his thumb with the tip, and her eyes grew large, and then her pupils dilated to the point where they filled her irises completely. She never took her eyes off of the drop of blood balanced on the pad of his thumb as he rose and approached her. He wiped it on her lower lip and stepped back. She resisted at first, but eventually, darted her tongue across it. He pulled her to her feet to look at her herself in the mirror. "Like that."

Elena gasped at her reflection. Her eyes were red. Only for a moment, but still red—just like the guy who'd shot her in the convenience store. *Shit.* The bathroom walls closed in a bit. Surely this wasn't happening.

Wait. Nikolai said her dad had been a vampire. His eyes were never red. Maybe it was the freakish death angel blood that did it. Maybe it would make any human's eyes red.

"It's a trick," she said. "It's your wacked-out blood that did that, not my physical composition."

"No." He almost looked sad. "No trick. Biology and genetics. Your father was a vampire. So are you."

"Dad's eyes were brown."

"He wore lenses in your world. They were blood red at court."

"At court?"

"Your dad was a powerful man. He was the ambassador and ruler of the vampire nation until its collapse. He lived dual lives because he had a human to protect."

"My mom."

"Yes. A foolish move on his part. And in the end, he couldn't protect her anyway. Like you, she was frail and weak. Her humanity was his undoing."

Nothing about her mother had been her father's undoing.

They adored each other. "He loved her. Some things are worth dying for."

"Many things are worth dying for. Love is not among them. Love is a fabrication of humans to glamorize and rationalize desire."

"You're wrong."

"I'm not. Lust and desire alone drive us, regardless of species. The lust for power..." He ran his hands down her arms, and she trembled. A smile pulled his lips as he placed them next to her ear. "The lust for pleasure..." His breath tickled as his wicked hands moved to her waist and slowly traveled up her sides, around the swell of her breasts, and rested on her shoulders, leaving her a trembling mess. "Pure lust and desire. Nothing else. Love does not exist."

Elena struggled to control her ragged breaths and slow her misfiring heart. His simple touch made her lose control. She was on fire, and it made no sense. None at all. She opened her eyes and met his in the mirror.

He leaned down to her ear again. "Is what you are feeling right now love?"

"Of course not." She was relieved her voice came out solid and not breathy.

"Most humans would confuse what you are feeling with that tender, fictitious emotion." He bit her earlobe, and she swayed a bit. His grip on her shoulders tightened. "What exactly are you feeling, Elena Arcos?"

It was bad enough he was going to kill her. Torturing her was beyond sporting. She straightened and lifted her chin, meeting his eyes directly in the mirror. "Lust. Pure, unadulterated lust."

He grinned.

"But not lust for you. Lust for a shower, you asshole. Take your hands off of me."

His grip on her shoulders tightened.

A spike of fear shot through her. Perhaps being a bitch wasn't the way to go. "Get your hands off of me, *please.*"

He chuckled and lifted his hands. He knew. He knew what he did to her, and it was infuriating.

They stared at each other in the mirror a long time. The top of her head barely reached his shoulder. The top of her *blood-encrusted* head. Yuck. She shuddered and shot a longing look at the shower. He pulled the curtain aside and gestured for her to enter.

"By all means. Slake your lust, vampire."

To her surprise, he didn't try to get in with her. He stayed outside the curtain like a gentleman. Ha! A gentleman executioner. She shampooed for a second time, reveling in the steam and scent of the hotel soaps. It felt so good she wanted to moan, but knew that would be a mistake. She'd seen that look before. He may hate her, but he wanted her. Her boss got that look every freaking day. She dropped the empty shampoo bottle with a bang and reached for the conditioner. The cord checked her an inch or so short of it.

"I need some slack, please," she said. His hand appeared around the curtain, and she stilled. It was so large. She shook her head and picked up the conditioner. "Thanks. I got it." The hand disappeared. She slicked conditioner through her hair, rinsed, and turned the water off. Before she could ask, a towel appeared from around the curtain. "Um, thanks."

What now? It was going to be awkward getting dressed while tied to him. Before she even stepped out, though, he climbed in fully naked except for his vest, which he couldn't take off because of the cord. Naked and wow—glad to be there. *Oh God.* She spun around, squeezing her eyes shut, trying to block out his deep chuckle.

"I'm lusting for a shower as well," he said. "Please hold this."

To her relief, he nudged his vest into her hand. He'd slid if off, but it was restricted by the cord, so he'd shoved it across to her. She shrugged it on, inside out, and then scurried out of the tub before he asked her to hold something else.

Elena tried to put on her dress while he showered, but with her on the outside of the tub and the cord only ten or so feet long, she was jerked by the wrist every time he raised his long arms. It was almost like he was doing it intentionally. Then, a rhythmic *tug, tug, tug, tug* on the cord began, and he moaned.

No! No, no, no. This was not happening. She squeezed her eyes shut and held her breath, refusing to let her mind go there. She'd seen way too much when he stepped in the tub. Dang. Way too much and there was a lot to see. And he was...

Tug, tug, tug, tug, tug.

Crap. She slumped to the floor and waited...and waited. She leaned her head back against the wall, trying to block out the delicious smell of leather and spice coming from his vest wrapped around her. Oh, come on. How long could one guy...

Nikolai stepped from the shower expecting to find the vampire clean, frustrated, and needy. Huddled on the bathroom floor, she leaned against the tub, sound asleep. It made sense, he supposed. She had died today, after all.

Perhaps he should have left her dead in the convenience store. At least her end would have been quick and peaceful. Who knew what would happen to her now, especially if his uncle Fydor got his hands on her.

He scooped her up in his arms and carried her into the bedroom.

No. Letting her die would have been wrong. Fate had

stepped in, he was sure of it. There was more to this girl than met the eye. Not human, not immortal, somehow she balanced on the sharp, dangerous edge between worlds.

He laid her down in the center of the bed and brushed the hair from her face. Who was she really? The daughter of his enemy, but she was an enemy to no one. Still, she had power in her. He felt it.

He had to come up with a plan. The first thing he needed to do was get the cord removed. The only way he knew to do that was to go to its place of origin, which was dangerous business not only for a human, but for a Slayer as well. The truce between the light elves and his people was tenuous at best and relied solely on his successful retrieval of the Uniter.

But first things first. Before he could accomplish anything, especially a complicated teleport, he needed rest.

CHAPTER FIVE

Elena woke in a tangle of arms and legs. Large ones. Not moving or even breathing, she shuffled through her memories and sorted out where she was and whose legs she was playing pretzel with. Ah. The death angel. The last thing she remembered was waiting for him to finish…yeah, *that*.

Okay, so now what? She was still in her dress and other than a headache and extreme hunger; she felt no worse for wear. So far, so good. The light peeking around the hotel blackout curtains indicated it was well past sunrise.

Like a human game of Pixie Sticks, she carefully slid an arm free, then a leg. But before she could free her other arm, Nikolai shifted position and trapped her all over again, pulling her in so close she could hardly breathe. She sighed and relaxed. Even if she had gotten loose from his grip, she was still bound to him by that damned cord.

Somewhere down the hall, the elevator dinged.

He mumbled something in another language and pushed against her, causing her to gasp. He was hard. And large. And so there. Thank goodness she had her dress on, or even in his sleep, this was a done deal.

Men's voices rumbled in the hallway, and the hair on the

back of her neck prickled.

"Hey," she said. Maybe waking him while he was like this wasn't a good idea. But he *always* seemed to be like this and something in her had warning bells going off. "Wake up."

More mumbling in that foreign language. Then a crash from outside.

As if electrocuted, Nikolai grabbed the sword next to him and sat bolt upright in bed.

"What is it?" she whispered.

He covered her mouth.

Another crash and loud voices speaking a language she couldn't understand from the hallway.

"They know we're here. We must leave now." Sword still in hand, he pulled her by the wrist to the bathroom where he grabbed his pants from the floor. "Help me," he said, stepping into the jeans. She grabbed the waistband and pulled while he jerked up on the other side. Not bothering to zip up, he stepped into his boots just as the door to the room crashed in. He pushed her behind him and bolted into the main room, swinging wide with the sword.

There were three of them. All with red eyes like the guy from the shooting. Vampires. They hissed like snakes and scattered to avoid the swing of his sword.

"Hunted by my own people and now fucking parasites?" Nikolai growled. "Who sent you?"

The tallest one answered. "Give us the woman."

Nikolai backed up several steps, putting Elena within reach of her suitcase. "How did you find me?"

The three vampires closed in.

She knew he was about to zap them out of there. She wrapped her fingers around the handle and gripped it tight. The cash could be useful, especially if she could escape from Nikolai.

The vampires were only ten or so feet away now, just out of blade-striking distance, but they were eyeing one another as if they had a plan. Right when one reached for his waist, Nikolai swung. Elena closed her eyes. There was a grunt, then a crunch, and then a thud.

"Who's next?" Nikolai said.

She opened her eyes and screamed when her eyes met the red ones staring up at her from the severed head on the floor. Blood oozed out, and she found herself no longer freaked, but transfixed, fighting the urge to run her fingers through the thick, crimson puddle. Hell, she wanted to *roll* in it. She shuddered and held tight to the suitcase. Holy shit. He had been right. She was turning into one of them.

"I'll ask again, and if you tell me, I'll spare you." Nikolai shot a quick glance over his shoulder at her and nodded when he saw she still clutched the luggage. He took a step toward the two remaining vampires, who didn't look as cocky as they had before their buddy's head had been lopped off. "Who sent you and how did you find me?"

Elena peeked around Nikolai's considerable mass and studied the vampires. She couldn't allow herself to become one of those things.

"Time's up." He lifted the sword over his head, and before the vampires could sufficiently react, he came down on one, hitting it in the shoulder, the blade cutting its torso almost in two vertically. Blood splattered out, nailing Nikolai all over and Elena in the face and arm. Blood. It was everywhere, and her body buzzed with need and hunger.

No! She would not give in to this. She would *not*. She let go of the suitcase long enough to wipe her face off on the bottom of her skirt.

"And then there was one," Nikolai said. The last vampire backed toward the door. "No you don't. Talk or die."

The man no sooner than reached for the door than Nikolai lunged, dragging Elena with him, stabbing his sword through the vampire's neck, skewering him to the door.

"Oh my God," she said, covering her mouth. There was blood on her hand. The metallic, salty smell filled her nose. Irresistible. She could almost taste it. She *wanted* to taste it. "Oh my God," she said again, running toward the bathroom only to be jerked to a stop by the cord on her wrist. "Help me. Please help me. Not this… Not them."

It was painful for Nikolai to watch her battle. How horrible it must have been for her to have a soul in opposition to her reality.

He moved near her so she could make it into the bathroom in time to throw up, which yielded nothing but dry heaves. She had no food in her at all.

"Get it off me," she screamed.

She turned on the shower full force and stepped in, clothes and all—even his vest. She grabbed the bar of soap and frantically scrubbed her face, arms, and even the front of her dress. Then she ripped the dress from under his vest and off her body in one hard tug. "Get it off," she cried, this time more a whimper than a scream.

A foreign part of Nikolai wanted to take her in his arms and hold her. To tell her it was okay, but it wasn't okay. She was simply becoming aware of what she was, and even if she didn't know it yet, it was inevitable. Like a fatal cancer, her vampirism lurked, waiting for the opportunity to consume her.

She slumped down into the tub, water still pounding down

on her. She tucked her knees in and rocked. He took the hand towel from the sink and held it under the spray, then wiped his face and chest free of blood. After rinsing it in the sink, he wiped his arms down as well. There was no time for the luxury of a shower.

The blue waves in the cord pulsed. Even knowing what she was, his soul still reached for her. He had to end this.

"We must go now," he said, turning the water in the shower off. He reached into the holster in his boot and pulled out his dagger to cut the leather vest from her body, leaving her completely bare. He'd never seen anything quite like her before. Her skin and form, though undersized, were flawless. Perfect, actually. Pale, delicate, and feminine.

He put his knife back in its holster. Fate was cruel. He had to find a way to release them from the cord. He understood deep down that she would have to be destroyed before she succumbed to her true nature, but he also knew he would never be able to do it himself.

First things first. He wrapped her frail, trembling body in a towel and led her back to the main room. "We need to search the bodies to see if they have any clues as to who sent them or how they found us. Vampires cannot track energy trails."

Her eyes were unfocused and trained only on the gyrations of color in the cord binding the two of them. She was probably in shock. Witnessing decapitations was bad enough, but combined with the realization she was genetically destined to become evil must have been too much for her frail human mind.

Nikolai searched the headless body first. Nothing. Not even a cell phone. Only the gun he had been reaching for when Nikolai struck. The vampire he had split almost in two yielded the same result. When he plundered the pockets of the one spiked to the door, however, he found a strange device—an electronic component of some kind.

"What do you make of this?" he asked Elena.

No response. She might have actually snapped. Trembling, she watched the cord, clutching the towel to her, eyes vacant.

He shoved the device into his back pocket and yanked his sword from the door, and the guy attached to it slumped to the floor. He wiped the blood off the blade onto the bedspread and grabbed the sheath from the bed and strapped it on, then slid his dagger in his boot. He needed to get them out before there were any more surprises.

He guided Elena to her suitcase and pulled the handle out. After wrapping her fingers around it, he placed his hands on either side of her neck. Her numbness was okay at this point. He knew exactly where they needed to go, and only he could get them there. "Don't let go of the suitcase," he said. "We might need the money, and you will need clothes. Are you ready?

She didn't respond.

If only things were different. If only there were a way to save her from her destiny. Perhaps the elves would have a solution.

"Stay with me now. Gregor Arcos's daughter does not just check out or give up."

But she had given up. When the pressure of teleportation receded, she simply stood next to him like a mannequin, unblinking in the dappled sunlight twinkling though the forest canopy.

"Descendant of Azrael, your presence in our domain is forbidden. What brings you here?" The voice was lovely, almost like music, but it grated on Nikolai like the scream of a banshee.

He kept his eyes lowered, knowing the light elf was too bright to look at directly. "I seek your help and advice."

"You brought a human. The penalty is death. You know that."

"Not human entirely, and I did not actually enter your forest. I stand at the edge. Again, please hear me. I beg your help."

Nikolai lifted his eyes enough to see the golden, shimmering hem of a garment swirling around a woman's bare feet. The fabric glimmered, and light undulated from within the fibers, just like the cord tying him to Elena.

"Reveal your request before I carry out justice on this spot."

"We are bound by a cord of your people's creation. I need to untie this woman—to set her free. How do I do this without killing us both?"

The creature's amused laughter held no mirth. With smooth strides, she approached, bringing a wave of floral scent with her. Elena's eyes remained closed as the elf lifted her chin.

"She has power," the woman said.

"I know," he answered.

"What is she?"

"I have no idea."

She released Elena's chin. "Her aura is strong. Far brighter than any creature I've seen outside the elven world, yet her flesh is human." The woman ran her fingers over Elena's collarbone above the towel, and she shivered. "And she's starving. Truly starving to death."

"How do I help her?" Nikolai asked.

"Isn't your job to destroy? To kill? To eliminate?" Hatred dripped from the elf's tone.

"I... Yes." He took a deep breath. "Just tell me how to break the cord without killing her."

The shimmering creature waited a long time before answering. "I cannot help you. That cord was forged by Aksel. Only he can untie it before its time."

"Where do I find this Aksel?"

A sigh that sounded like the ocean wind preceded her

words. "If only we knew. He was cursed centuries ago and has not been seen since."

"Cursed by whom?"

"Our troubles are not your concern."

A growl entered his tone. "Well, it's my trouble, too. I need the guy."

"You are lucky I don't kill you on the spot, Slayer, for bringing a human to our forest. We gave your people use of our cords in exchange for finding the Uniter to put an end to this war. As with all in the natural order, using something for a purpose other than its intended one is risky and foolish. If you are too dense to see the answer, I cannot help you."

Leaves from the forest floor whirled and fluttered against the bare skin on Nikolai's arms, neck, and face as the elf retreated back into the woods, leaving no trace except her sweet, floral scent.

He dropped Elena's hand and glared at the cord. Fucking elves. Stuck-up, worthless creatures. Intended purpose? Well, what the hell was the thing intended for? It bound souls, for fuck's sake.

It was bad enough being bound to a vampire, but now she was catatonic. Perfect. A vegetable vampire.

If only he hadn't tied himself to her… *That's it!* He needed to go back before it happened and take a different course. He needed a Time Folder. He needed Stefan Darvaak. But Darvaak hated him. Hell, everybody hated him for that matter. It wasn't him in particular—it was what he was. Nobody loved the physical embodiment of death. Not even an immortal like a Time Folder, who literally could not be slain by any outside means.

Nikolai's job had never bothered him before. Ridding both planes of evil immortals had always seemed like a noble cause. Now, it felt anything but noble.

CHAPTER SIX

"We need to teleport again. Keep a grip on your bag, okay?"

Nikolai wrapped Elena's fingers around the suitcase handle. She didn't even bother to open her eyes anymore. And she looked so pale and weak. He needed to feed her. He'd had no idea she was starving. He should have, though. She'd ingested nothing but orange juice for two days, and she was having blood sugar issues when he found her. His face flushed hot from shame. First, he needed to get out of the elves' forest.

She was cold to the touch when he placed his hands on her neck this time. Her shoulders relaxed, and she sighed at the contact.

"Hang in there," he said. "I'm going to get you some food."

He knew it was a risky move without contacting the Time Folder first, but he had no choice. There was no one else he could turn to, so he teleported them right into the guy's living room. At least he hoped it was still his living room. It looked the same, all black and white and chrome and glass. Slick son of a—

"Mr. Itzov. To what do I owe this unannounced and unexpected pleasure?"

Nikolai turned toward the voice slowly so as not to appear

aggressive. The Time Folders were a strange lot—almost pacifist in behavior unless you angered them; then they shocked the shit out of you. Literally. And at this point, Nikolai was not up to a jolt.

"Ah, and you brought a naked human. How...appropriate?"

Nikolai snatched Elena's towel from the floor and wrapped it back around her body, tucking it in under her arm. "I seek your help."

Darvaak leaned casually against the doorframe through which he'd appeared. "I've never heard that from a Slayer before. Not since yesterday, anyway." He walked to the wet bar and pulled the stopper from a crystal decanter of what appeared to be Scotch and poured two glasses. "I said no then, too." He handed Nikolai one of the glasses.

The Time Folder looked Elena up and down.

"Pretty." He took a sip of Scotch. "Not of the Underveil." He cocked his head to one side, gaze still locked on her. "Not human entirely. She's in the middle of a conversion, yes?"

"I believe so."

"Why are you dirtying up my living room, smelling of sweat and vampire blood with a naked woman, Nikolai Itzov?"

He held out his wrist. "I need this restraint removed."

Darvaak shook his head. "You need a lot of things worse than you need that. First, you need a shower. But more importantly, that woman needs food. Protein especially. She smells diabetic."

He was relieved the Time Folder hadn't kicked him out yet, but his superior attitude begged an ass kicking. And the heightened sense of smell had always bugged the crap out of him.

"I'm not sure I can get her to eat. She's pretty out of it."

"So I see. Though, I can't say that I blame her, considering the company she's keeping." He took another sip of his drink. "I'll wager I can get her to eat."

"Yeah, yeah, I know. You can get women to do anything. Even eat out of your hand. I remember." Losing that bet still rankled.

He laughed. "It was a long time ago that I made that claim, Itzov."

"Only a century."

"Let's hope *this* woman will eat out of my hand. She might be dying, which by the looks of that cord and your own soul's presence in it, would be terrible news for you. Congratulations are in order, I suppose." He shook his head. "Poor woman. Does she know?"

Nikolai consciously uncurled his fists. Fighting with the arrogant prick wouldn't serve his purpose, no matter how good thrashing him would feel. "No. She doesn't know, and I'd like to keep it that way."

The Time Folder placed his half-empty glass on the bar. "Wise. If she knew, chances are she'd never come back to reality. I mean, centuries with…" He flippantly gestured to Nikolai and then leaned casually against the bar. "Fortunately, Slayers can survive if their mate does not, and humans potentially have multiple mates. Depending on what she converts into, she could escape this fate yet, yes? Well, as long as you free yourself of the soul-bonding cord."

They could escape it, but they had to stay alive first. "Yes."

Darvaak gestured to a leather chair to his right. "Please sit and put her in your lap if you don't mind."

Nikolai did as he asked. Then, he downed the Scotch in one gulp and set the empty glass on the table next to him.

"Wrap your arms around her to keep her from hurting herself."

Hurting herself? "What are you going to do?"

He crouched in front of them. "A simple transference of

energy. Similar to electroshock therapy, only my way is safe and effective."

Nikolai tensed at his words. He was going to shock her.

"Be calm, Slayer. I won't hurt her. She appears to be in a trance state of some kind, retreating into her mind like someone who has been through severe trauma." His gaze traveled up and down Nikolai. "From the look and smell of you, I would venture to guess she saw you butcher someone or several someones?"

Nikolai said nothing. Time Folders not only had superior senses, they had fantastic analytical capacity as well. The guy didn't expect a response. He already knew the answer.

Darvaak put his hands on either side of Elena's head. "Sweet girl. You need to come back to us now. We want to help you."

He closed his eyes and bowed his head as if praying, but Nikolai knew he was acting like a conductor and summoning a charge to send through her. Nikolai gritted his teeth and prayed it didn't hurt her too much. He'd been shocked by one of these creatures, and he hoped to never experience it again.

Darvaak exhaled slowly, and Elena's body jerked. Then she gasped, and her eyes flew open.

"There you are, I'm so glad you decided to join us," the Time Folder said with a smile.

E lena had never seen a man this beautiful—well, except Nikolai, but they were different. This man was the exact opposite of her death angel. He was gentle with a soft voice. His blonde hair framed a fine-boned, angular face that featured crystal clear blue eyes—eyes that were eerily pale and intensely focused on her face. He was speaking to her, but it was difficult to isolate words. He was talking about food.

Food. She was hungry. She tried to stand, but something

constricted her. Turning, she bumped noses with Nikolai. His gold eyes locked on to hers as if he were trying to see straight inside her. "Steady," he whispered. "You're safe."

Safe. Nothing in her felt safe. The tangy smell of blood was all over his skin. Images of the evil creatures that invaded the hotel room flooded her head. She was one of them. "No!"

Nikolai's arms banded around her like steel. She needed to get away. *Had* to get away.

The man with the gold hair put his hands on her shoulders. "Shhh. Be peaceful. You are under no threat."

Not from outside, but what about the monster inside her? The one with red eyes she saw in the hotel mirror. She struggled to free herself. She had to get away from the smell of blood. "Let me go!" Her voice sounded faint and distant.

Nikolai released her, and she leapt off of his lap and skittered as far away as the blasted cord would allow. "You have to let me go." She covered her nose and mouth. "The smell."

The blond man stood. "See? You didn't take my word for it. You stink, Itzov."

"Shut up and help her," Nikolai shouted.

The guy walked to a marble-topped bar and picked up a drink. "Why, Nikolai Itzov, if I didn't know better, I would think the great Slayer had a weakness after all."

"My only weakness was in my judgment—to think that coming here was a good idea. Thinking that you could help us."

The blond man drank the contents of the glass in one shot. "I can."

"Then do it, dammit."

He set the glass down gently. "There's a price."

"There always is."

The two men stared at each other. Nikolai with a heated glare. The blond man with amusement. Both were equally beautiful and terrifyingly powerful. Elena held her breath.

"One moment, please," the blond man said, disappearing into another room. He returned quickly with a covered bowl. "Follow me."

The bathroom was enormous. Big enough for a party. The man set the bowl on a counter and picked up a remote control. After pushing a few buttons, the lights dimmed and water gushed from a wide spout into a huge, sunken tub in the center of the room.

"I hate to see you roughing it like this, Darvaak. Compensating, perhaps?"

The blond man simply smiled. "Life is good."

"Where is your mate?"

He picked up the bowl and uncovered it. "I said life it good, not great."

"Did she ditch you already?"

Elena held her breath as the man Nikolai had called Darvaak approached. He exuded confidence and power but didn't seem to take offense at Nikolai's obvious taunt. He reached into the bowl and pulled out a strawberry. "My life-mate hasn't met me yet." He held the strawberry in front of Elena's lips and smiled. She couldn't help but smile back. "Open please," he whispered.

She did. It tasted delicious. God, she was hungry. It was all she could do to not grab the bowl from the guy and shove her head in it like an animal at a feed trough. The image made her giggle.

The man's smile broadened. He selected another strawberry. "Again, please," he said.

Nikolai's voice sounded unnecessarily harsh. "How is that possible? I thought your species wilted and died like delicate flowers if separated."

"Please sit here." The man gestured to the side of the tub.

Elena, still holding the towel in place by clamping her arms tight to her side, lowered herself to the marble ledge.

He smiled as encouragement. "You appear sufficiently recovered to manage this yourself, now." He placed the bowl of strawberries in her lap.

She took a bite of another berry as he turned his pale eyes to Nikolai and his smile faded. "Being apart from my life-mate is painful. It would not be my first choice of strategies, but it's my only option at this time. Revealing myself to her would put her in danger." He stuck his hand under the running water, testing its temperature. "I'm nothing if not patient."

Elena looked down to discover she had almost emptied the bowl. Still, she was famished. She took a deep breath, feeling much closer to normal. She needed to relax and let her body process the sugar and stabilize her insulin.

The blond man picked up a bottle of blue liquid and poured some of the contents into the running water. Bubbles frothed over the surface, emitting an intoxicating smell that covered up the lure of the blood coming off Nikolai's skin.

"You don't expect me to bathe in that, do you?" he asked.

The blond man smiled. "Will you wilt like a delicate flower?"

Nikolai growled.

The guy shook his head. "It's for her, Slayer. It's to cover your stench and…" He looked directly at Nikolai's crotch. "And spare her from the sight of other undesirable aspects of you."

Nikolai growled again.

The tub was almost full and covered with iridescent bubbles. Darvaak punched a button on the remote, and the water stopped. "In you go, Itzov," he said, and then turned to Elena. "You, my dear, might want to look the other way until your stomach is more settled."

Feeling much better now, she smiled. The man's teasing was

entertaining. Nikolai didn't seem to think so, based on the dark look he shot the guy.

"I'll be back with more food in a moment. And I'm going to call my tailor. Your situation calls for some creativity. You can't run around half-dressed until you're free of that cord."

And with that, they were alone.

Nikolai sat on the marble ledge next to her and pulled off a boot. He opened his mouth as if to say something, but clamped his lips shut and pulled off his other boot. He sat for a moment, looking defeated, and her heart pinched.

"I'm..." He took a deep breath and lifted his wrist bound by the cord. "We'll find a way out of this. I promise."

Obviously, getting away from her was a high priority, not that she could blame him, but the cord was the least of her worries. Not becoming a monster was foremost in her mind.

"You should have killed me back in the store," she said.

He stood and slipped off his pants. She didn't even pretend to look away. At this point, what did it matter? Her fate was sealed. There was no way she could allow herself to become one of the red-eyed demons. She might as well take in the sights while she still could. And the sights were mighty fine.

"You were already dead when I found you." He stepped out of his pants and froze...well, except for the part of him that obviously approved of her stare. It practically waved and shouted "Howdy!"

"For God's sake, get in the water, Itzov, before you make the girl throw up. We're supposed to keep food down her, remember?" The blond guy stood in the doorway with a tray in his hands. "Here you are, Elena." He set the tray next to her while Nikolai stepped into the tub. "Shall I feed you?"

"No!" Nikolai said.

The blond man ignored him totally. "Now that you are

feeling better, let me introduce myself." He held out his hand. "I am Stefan Darvaak. Welcome to my home."

She took his hand, and a slight electric current jumped through her, causing her to jerk her hand back quickly.

"Only those under the Veil can feel my energy. What are you?" He sat next to her, both of them with their backs to Nikolai, who was submerged in the bubbles up to his neck. "Or rather, what are you becoming?"

Tears filled her eyes. She wiped them away with her fingers.

"I'm sorry," Stefan said. "I don't fully understand your situation." He stood. "Just call if you need anything." He put the remote next to her. "The red button will alert me." He paused before exiting. "Be nice, Itzov." He held up his hand and wiggled his fingers. "Electricity and water don't mix."

Nikolai slid completely underwater, disappearing beneath the blanket of bubbles, leaving Elena alone with the tray of food that looked like a dream. Nuts, cheese, more fruit, and what appeared to be sliced turkey. Yep. Turkey. Her stomach growled as she chewed. Then it dawned on her that Nikolai hadn't eaten either. In fact, he hadn't even had any of the juice. He had to be starving.

He broke the surface with a splash and wiped his face with a washcloth.

She gestured to the tray. "Want some?"

He nodded and opened his mouth. She turned to give him access to the tray.

Bubble-covered hands emerged from the water. "Help me out here."

She selected a slice of turkey and rolled it up. Like a baby bird, he opened his mouth and bit off a piece. *That mouth.* Her face got hot, and she turned away. After a moment, he cleared his throat, and she turned to find him eyeing the other half of rolled turkey slice in her hand. She raised it to his open mouth, and he grabbed her wrist, taking the bit of turkey and her fingers into his mouth, too. His lips and tongue were so warm. She squirmed as pulses of excitement bolted through her as he sucked on her fingers. This should not have been so stimulating. He was her captor. A man sent to kill her. A man who *should* kill her, seeing how she was about to turn into a monster. How long would it take before her eyes turned red and her soul black? Not long enough, she realized, looking at the gorgeous man with his lips wrapped around her fingers. Not nearly long enough.

N ikolai saw it in Elena's eyes: lust, pure and simple, just like that coursing through him. She wanted him. There was no doubt about it. And he needed her. Like he needed to breathe, he needed this woman.

"Join me." His voice was barely a whisper—more of a prayer, actually.

Her pupils dilated slightly, but her knees clamped together and she stiffened and then turned away. Her mind was battling with her body.

He relaxed back against the marble, willing her body to win the war. "I won't touch you. I promise. The water is perfect."

She looked at him over her shoulder, and he almost shouted "Hallelujah." She was close. He knew it.

"I didn't violate you last night at the hotel. I promise not to touch you now…"

She jerked around, leaving her back to him again. Her shoulders rose and fell with rapid breaths. So close.

"Unless you want me to."

Her breathing stopped. He had no doubt she craved his

touch, but he also knew she was stubborn and scared. Her world had changed completely in the last two days. He wished they could have met under different circumstances—just a man and a woman with no barriers between them.

"And if I don't want you to touch me?" she whispered, still facing away.

"Then I won't."

She swiveled to face him. "I don't."

Liar. "Very well."

She set the tray down and stood, clutching the top of the towel wrapped around her. "Please turn around."

"*You* didn't."

Her face flushed red.

God, she was beautiful. He almost couldn't stand it. He had to find a way to help her—to save her from her fate. Hell, to save *him* from her fate. There had to be a way to trick biology. He turned away to give her privacy. When he heard the gentle splashing as she entered the water, he almost groaned. When he met her eyes, he did.

A startled look crossed her face, and she slumped lower in the water until the bubbles were up to her neck. "You promised."

Unsure of how his voice would come out at that moment, he simply nodded.

"This tub is like a swimming pool," she said after a few moments. "Huge." She ducked under, and he offered her a washcloth when she surfaced. She wiped her face. "Exactly what is… um…?" She pointed with her thumb to the door.

"Stefan Darvaak?"

"Yeah, Stefan. What is he?"

"A pompous asshole."

She wiped her hands on the cloth and grabbed a piece of

cheese, exposing the side of her breast as she did. Nikolai let his head fall back against the tile with a thud.

She settled into the water. "Seriously. He's not a Slayer, obviously. And he's not a vampire. What else is there?"

Nikolai closed his eyes to prevent going crazy at the sight of her. "You name it, it's out there. Conjurers, sorcerers, channelers, vampires, shifters, Banshees, Skin Jumpers, demons of all kinds, and even Time Folders like Stefan Darvaak."

"Time Folder," she repeated.

Something brushed his lip, and he sat up and opened his eyes with a start. She smiled and waved the piece of cheese. He opened his mouth, and she dropped it in, pulling her fingers away before he could suck on them again.

"So what does he do?"

He shrugged. "Besides piss me off? He makes an obscene amount of money."

She rolled her eyes. "Why is he called a Time Folder?"

"Because he folds time…if you pay him enough."

She sat forward, and for a moment, he thought her breasts would rise above the bubbles. Correct that. He *hoped* they would, but they didn't. God, he wanted to touch her. She was only a foot or so away from his hands—and other parts of him for that matter.

"He folds time. What does that mean?" Her color had returned, and she sounded more like the Elena he enjoyed. The feisty one that had had told him to kill her then and there because she would not go with him. Thank goodness he hadn't and she *had*.

"It's hard to explain, but he can manipulate time and travel back via limited parameters to observe. It's very useful to the Slayers. He can be an eyewitness to crimes."

She scraped some hair from off her forehead. "It's a good

thing I'm not going to be around long because I'd never get this stuff straight."

He leaned forward. "What do you mean, 'not be around long'?"

She grabbed his shoulder, desperation clear in her touch and expression. "You have to promise me something: Don't let me become one of those creatures. I can't live like that. You have to promise to use that sword and end me before it happens." A tear ran down her cheek, and he brushed it away with his thumb. "Promise me," she insisted.

He shook his head. "Humans don't just change over into vampires. They replicate by killing humans, draining their blood, and replacing it with some of their own. You were born of one, not bitten and turned by one. It's unprecedented."

"Promise, Nikolai, or I'll kill myself before it happens."

Seeing her fear made him ache. If a promise would make her feel better, he would give it, even if there was no way he could carry it out. He reached under the water and grabbed her ankle, then gently tugged her closer from her side of the tub. "I promise you, Elena Arcos, I will kill you."

"Aww. Isn't that romantic?" Stefan said from the bathroom door. "Sweeter words have never been uttered. I bet you are a real winner on Valentine's Day, Slayer."

Elena could feel Nikolai's tension through his grip on her ankle, but he said nothing.

"My tailor and his assistant are here when you two lovebirds decide to leave the nest. I hope you don't mind, but I took the liberty of selecting some things from the suitcase to be adapted to accommodate the cord, Elena. You're going to be a bit more of a challenge, Itzov. They brought some items that might fit, though." He winked at Elena. "No rush. They won't be ready for a while." This time, he shut the door.

After he'd been gone a moment, Nikolai loosened his grip on her ankle and stroked circles with his thumb as he stared into space. She cleared her throat. "I can't decide whether he likes you or hates you."

His gold eyes met hers, thumb still making lazy circles. She'd never been drawn to anyone with this kind of intensity, and it unnerved her. Then he moved his face within inches of hers, and she forced herself not to lean in. "How about you, Elena? Do you like me or hate me?" he asked. His gaze darted to her lips, then back to her eyes.

And she was lost.

What did she have to lose? She was as good as dead anyway. She'd seen the monster in the mirror herself. How long before it won? Months? Weeks? Hours? And still, his thumb circled as his hand slid past her knee to her thigh, shooting delicious sparks up her spine.

She closed her eyes and breathed in. There was no more lingering smell of blood, only fragrant bubbles and the distinct odor of Nikolai, which at this moment was like a drug she could get hooked on if she did it even once. But she might be dead any hour now, and once might be all she could ever have.

"You tremble," he whispered against her mouth.

"You scare me."

His hand had stilled. "I swear to not hurt you. I could never hurt you."

She was afraid to open her eyes and see his face. He sounded so sincere. "Except when you kill me."

"No pain. Only pleasure."

And then, he slid his hand up and gently stroked across her as his lips met hers. She gasped at the effect of his touch. It was as if every nerve ending in her body were exposed. Her body jerked, and he smiled against her lips.

"Easy," he whispered, trailing his fingers up her abdomen to the swell of her breast. He deepened the kiss, twining his tongue with hers and his fingers into the hair at her nape . "Relax," he murmured, but nothing in Elena could relax.

More. She needed more of him and his velvet tongue and his talented fingers that moved from one breast to the other, torturing her until she thought she might scream. Relax? Not a chance. This was wrong and dangerous, and honestly, downright stupid, but she'd never wanted anything like she wanted Nikolai. And, God, what he could do with his hands…

"Time's up," Stefan called from the other side of the door, jarring them to reality with several hard knocks.

"Shit," Nikolai growled.

He pulled away, and she whimpered. Panting, she stared at him as he held her at arm's length. Wide shoulders covered in those strange, and at the moment, painfully sexy markings—everything about him turned her on. But it shouldn't.

He closed his eyes and took a deep breath, then let it out through his teeth. "I might have to kill a Time Folder."

"You wouldn't," she said, half believing him from the look on his face. He was a killer after all.

He shrugged and then smiled. "I can't. They can only destroy themselves, which is lucky for him."

As she came back down to earth and the magic faded, she was grateful for the interruption. This man, Slayer, whatever he was, was dangerous. And even though her body disagreed vehemently, sex with him was a bad idea.

He stood and wrapped himself in a towel, but not before she got an eyeful of what he'd had under those bubbles. What in the world would she have done with all that? There was no way it would have worked out logistically, much less any other way.

She stared down at the cord that bound him to her—the

one that held her prisoner. They were enemies. He had said so himself. She would need to keep her horny dying wishes to herself. Some things just weren't meant to be. She stood and wrapped up in a towel as quickly as possible.

What had she been thinking? This guy was death. Death and sex didn't mix. She had to keep herself under control and not let this ever happen again.

CHAPTER SEVEN

Fucking Time Folder. Nikolai glared at the back of Stefan Darvaak's head as he introduced Elena to his tailor, a probable rodent shifter of some kind, who looked to be eighty in human years, which meant he was probably five centuries old. He and his assistant, a frail-looking woman in tinted glasses with dark skin and hair, had altered some of Elena's clothes to accommodate the cord by buttoning on top of the sleeve since she couldn't put her arm through.

He knew he should be grateful Darvaak was helping them, but still... He had been *this* close to having her, and he was certain the asshole had interrupted them on purpose. Shifting in the chair didn't minimize the resulting ache, but he did it again anyway, keeping the bath towel tight at his waist.

Elena smiled as the Time Folder whispered something in her ear and Nikolai fantasized beating the living shit out of him.

"Perfect," Darvaak said while she set the newly altered shirt to rights.

The little shiny jewels sewn onto the back pockets of her blue jeans winked in the light. Yeah. As if Nikolai needed something else to draw his attention to her ass. He shifted again.

The Time Folder threw a pair of jeans to him, and he caught

them in his fist, wishing they were the guy's neck.

Smiling, Darvaak sat in a leather chair. "I suppose we should get down to business now that it's clear your charge is not going to die at any moment, leaving me with two bodies to dispose of."

Nikolai pulled the new jeans on. Perfect fit. Of course, they were; Darvaak always got details right. One more reason to hate him. He tugged on one of the boots he'd carried in from the bathroom.

"Two?" Elena asked, sitting on the sofa next to Nikolai, who yanked on his second boot.

"Oh." Darvaak grinned. "Oops. I forgot. The Slayer didn't tell you. If you die, he dies. If he dies, you die."

Her face clouded.

Forgot? Time Folders never forgot anything. He was provoking them, the bastard. He loved stirring things up. All of them did. Maybe knowing everything got boring. Well, Nikolai could make his life less tiresome. He could make the Time Folder *wish* he were dead even if he couldn't outright kill him.

Her eyes narrowed on Nikolai's face. "You lied to me."

"A Slayer lie?" Darvaak gasped, then grinned and leaned back to watch the inevitable show he had just breathed to life.

Nikolai stood, and the tailor scurried from the room. His assistant pushed her glasses up on her nose, but kept her head down, needle weaving in and out the shoulder of a black T-shirt furiously.

"I haven't lied to you, Elena."

"You did. You said you'd…" Her eyes flooded with tears.

Dammit, dammit, dammit. No tears. Nikolai lowered himself back onto the sofa to keep from taking her in his arms.

She drew a deep, shuddering breath. "You said you'd kill me before I turned into a monster. You lied. You can't kill me or else you kill yourself. You *knew* that."

He couldn't kill her anyway. Ever. He was certain of that now. Even if she became a vampire, he would never be able bring himself to do it.

"What kind of monster do you think you will be?" Darvaak asked.

Her voice trembled. "The worst kind. A heartless, soulless murdering vampire."

The woman working on the shirt stilled for a moment and then continued her sewing.

The Time Folder cleared his throat and recrossed his legs, smoothing an imaginary wrinkle at his knee. "And how do you know this?"

Her eyes shot to Nikolai, and then she shrugged. "I know. Trust me."

Darvaak leaned forward. "I trust you implicitly, Elena. Itzov, not so much."

Nikolai stood. "That's enough. Let it go. We need to get down to business."

"You are in my home, enjoying my hospitality, asking me for favors, yet you have the audacity to behave as if you are in your own domain?" Darvaak's voice remained level and his body eerily still. "The rest of the Underveil might fear you, Slayer, but I don't. And right now, I'm caught up in a situation where I believe a human has been taken hostage, which by your own laws, is a crime, is it not? Shall we summon a tribunal?"

Nikolai sat down. A tribunal would mean certain death for both of them.

Darvaak leaned back again. "I thought not."

"I'm not his hostage." Her voice was barely above a whisper.

The Time Folder's eyebrow arched. "No?"

"He saved my life, actually. I need his help. He…he's helping me."

"By promising to kill you?" He folded his arms over his chest. "To keep you from becoming a vampire…"

She nodded. "It's kinda screwed up, huh?"

"Immensely."

Nikolai opened his mouth to speak, and Darvaak held up his hand. "Not yet. I'll shock you into unconsciousness and alert them as to where you are if you even utter a peep, Itzov. You've involved me in something I'm not happy about, and you'll indulge me a moment more."

Nikolai couldn't believe this man was besting him. The Time Folders were notoriously meddlesome, but also considered rational and fair. He was hoping for a glimpse of the latter attributes. At least Darvaak was calm, as opposed to his counterparts. Over the last two centuries, the only other pair of Time Folders on the planet had become unpredictable at best, as evidenced by the shock he received from a female Time Folder named Hestia the last time the Slayers used them to witness a crime. Stefan Darvaak was the only stable one left—and right now, Nikolai wasn't so sure about that even.

Darvaak turned his icy eyes to Elena. "So, I only have one more question for you. You fear turning into what you call a heartless, soulless, murdering vampire. Exactly how many vampires do you know?"

"None."

"So you got this idea from…"

Nikolai fisted his hands to keep from charging him. He was still fucking with them. "Get to the point."

Elena sighed. "I was shot by one, and we were attacked by three more. They were horrible. My eyes went red when I ingested some blood. I crave it when I smell it. I'm doomed to be a murderer just like they were."

The girl sewing on the shirt paused again and laid her

needle down.

"When did you ingest blood?" Darvaak asked.

Nikolai cut in and answered. "I ran a little test at the hotel. It was only a drop. Her body reacted. There's no refuting the evidence."

"I need to see it. Can you replicate it?"

"No!" she cried.

Darvaak placed his hands on her shoulders. "I am trying to help you. I can't do that until I'm certain what we're dealing with. Please. Just one time."

Elena took a deep breath. "Fine."

She turned her huge, tear-filled eyes to Nikolai, and his heart hammered. The poor woman was terrified, not of him, but of herself. He forced down his uncustomary sympathy and straightened his shoulders. Bit by bit, she was breaking down his resolve, and he knew it would mean his doom. Before her, it was so easy. Vampires were all bad and had to be destroyed. Now, every single solid truth he had held seemed made of gauze, like the flimsy garments of the elves.

"Quit staring at me and just do it," she said, squeezing her eyes shut.

As Nikolai pulled the dagger out of his boot, he noticed the woman at the table near the back wall was stone still, watching him. Hands in lap. "Perhaps we should be more private about our business."

Darvaak shook his head. "My employees are completely loyal. That or they are dead." He held his hand out, palm up toward Nikolai. "Please, allow me. I'm testing a theory."

Nikolai placed the dagger hilt in his hand, and Darvaak sliced the tip of his forefinger, then handed the weapon back. "Open your eyes please, Elena," he said as he got on his knees in front of her. "Yes. Now your mouth."

She obeyed, and he placed his forefinger on her tongue and then withdrew it.

Nikolai's body went rigid everywhere as he imagined that tongue on his own fingers...or in his mouth...or on his... A growl rumbled deep in his chest. He was going to kill Darvaak, plain and simple.

"Easy, Slayer," he said. "It's just an experiment, not a challenge. Look. No reaction."

Nikolai met Elena's deep blue eyes and loosened his grip on the dagger hilt. The Time Folder was right; her body hadn't reacted to the blood.

"Now you, Itzov," he said, returning to his chair.

Nikolai, never taking his eyes from Elena's, pricked the end of his thumb and noticed she had clamped her lips shut. Was it him she rejected, or was it that she suspected, as he did, that it was his blood specifically that affected her? He held his thumb up, and she shook her head. Instead of forcing her mouth open like he wanted to, he simply repeated what he had done at the hotel and wiped his thumb across her bottom lip. There was more blood than last time, shimmering like macabre lip gloss. He held his breath, stunned by the revelation that he *wanted* his blood to affect her.

"Please, Elena," Darvaak said. "I understand he repulses you, but we need to know."

Repulsed her? The man was as good as dead. Truly immortal or not, Nikolai would find a way.

Her tongue darted out, and she covered her face. Her shoulders shuddered, and a sob escaped her. The girl in the tinted glasses scooted to the edge of her seat as if to rise, but Darvaak held up his hand. "Let's have a look, and then it will all be over."

Elena lowered her hands and then slowly opened her eyes—her piercing, crimson eyes—and all of Nikolai's blood shot straight to his cock. God, fate was a sick, twisted bitch. *Doomed.* He was certainly and absolutely heading straight for the fiery pits of hell, he realized, as he lusted for his sworn enemy, the vampire.

After an almost unendurable few moments, the red faded, leaving her irises the wild, stormy blue of the ocean.

Nikolai could breathe again.

"It's species related," Darvaak said, appearing totally at ease. "Perhaps even more specific than that."

Me. Let it only be me, Nikolai's subconscious screamed to his horror. He sat back against the sofa cushions, trying to appear nonchalant. He deserved an Oscar for this performance.

"And just how did you come to be a vampire?" Darvaak asked. "This is very important, Elena."

"I-I was born this way."

"Her father was Gregor Arcos," Nikolai said, hoping to put an end to the fifty questions game.

Both eyebrows shot up then. Darvaak uncrossed his legs and scooted to the edge of his seat. "Father as in your maker, or father as in insert tab A into slot B?"

Nikolai shot to his feet. "It's not a fucking joke."

The Time Folder stood as well. "It damn well isn't, Slayer. Sit down!" For a moment, he was sure Darvaak was going to zap him, but then he returned to his customary composed demeanor. "Please."

Nikolai sat, but everything in him rebelled against it. He hated not being in control, and at that moment *everything* was out of his hands: Elena's safety, the secrecy of their location, even his own life. All of it rested in the well-manicured hands of this smartass Time Folder. What a fucking mess.

"Her father bred with a human."

"Ah. Now we're getting somewhere." Darvaak stood and

paced down the long glass wall overlooking the tops of pine trees outside the high rise. "I didn't know human/vampire progeny were possible."

"They're not," Nikolai said.

Darvaak stopped his pacing and stood behind Elena. "Yet, here she is. Proof yet again that nature…or the unnatural finds a way." He strode to the woman who had set her sewing aside and took her hand. "Before we get to the issue of the cord binding the two of you, I'd like to introduce you to someone, Elena." He escorted the tailor's assistant to stand right in front of her. "This is Margarita Juarez. Margarita, it is my pleasure to introduce you to Elena Arcos." The woman took off her tinted glasses. Stefan Darvaak stepped back and smiled. "And now, Elena, you can say you know one."

CHAPTER EIGHT

Elena stared into Margarita's blood-red eyes and nearly fainted. Dear God. All the awful things she'd said about vampires. "I'm…" Her breath caught in her throat. "I don't know what to say. I'm sorry… I—"

Margarita held her hand up. "It's nothing I haven't heard before. Our species has its bad apples, just like humans— because all vampires were humans first." The woman's red eyes bored into Elena. "You don't have to choose violence. I don't. Your father didn't."

Her breath caught. "You knew him?"

Sliding her glasses back on, the vampire shook her head. "No. I know *of* him. Everyone does. Things were better when he was alive."

No kidding. Elena's rib cage felt like it would shatter if she so much as took a breath. She had been very young when he died, but still, she missed him so much—even though what she remembered about him seemed distorted now that she knew what he had really been.

Margarita returned to her sewing while reality hovered just out of Elena's reach. She stared down at the cord. She was turning into a vampire, and Nikolai couldn't kill her. And that, coupled with the fact all vampires weren't evil as he had portrayed them to be, certainly put a new twist on their relationship. Had everything he told her been a lie?

She stared at Stefan, who studied her with his eerie, pale eyes, and then at Nikolai. He'd been no more than ten feet from her for the last two days, but she felt like they were miles away from each other. Even when he'd had his mouth and hands on her, they'd been worlds apart.

She sat again and turned back to Stefan. "Please find a way to free me from this—from *him*."

"I certainly appreciate your desire, but I can see no way that I can be of help other than seeing you clothed and fed. That cord is elven-forged. Only the artisan can break it without killing you. It's too late for me to help you."

"The elf who made it isn't available. And it's not too late," Nikolai said. "You can go back in time before I tied it on her... us." The desperation in his voice matched her own. "Please," he continued. "Fold time to before I bound her and take the cord away. I know you can do this."

The tailor shuffled back into the room and gathered his supplies. He moved so strangely, and his eyes were brown, not red. If Margarita was a vampire, what was he, Elena wondered. He took the shirt from Margarita and handed it to Stefan, not even looking at Elena or Nikolai.

"Send a bill," Stefan said, and the man bowed and backed away, then scurried straight for the door, followed by his assistant carrying her sewing box. Stefan rose and placed his hand on a black pad by the door, and it clicked and swung open.

Margarita paused just inside the door and removed her glasses. "Your father believed that vampires are not unfortunate victims of fate. He told us that we are creators of our own destiny. His words became our motto: 'With wise choices, we are destined for greatness, with poor choices, oblivion.'" Her red eyes never wavered from Elena's, as if trying to memorize her. "My people are close to complete oblivion. Make wise choices, Elena Arcos."

She left, and all of them stared at the closed door for what felt like forever.

"Wow," Elena said, finally.

Stefan leaned back against the door. "Nothing like a light-hearted farewell."

Nikolai scooted to the edge of his seat on the sofa. "Go back in time and remove the cord from my possession," he said, as if fate and salvation from oblivion had not just been bandied about.

Perhaps to him, Margarita's words weren't relevant, but to Elena they were. *We are creators of our own destiny*. She closed her eyes and ran the words through her head several more times. Her father's words. *Wise choices*. She had a choice. She didn't have to become a monster. If she had to become one of these creatures, she could be like her father instead.

"I cannot manipulate the past," Stefan said, returning to his chair. "I can only be an observer. You know that, Itzov."

"You can't, or you won't?"

"I won't." Stefan sat. "It can produce disastrous effects. World-altering effects."

"Just eliminating the cord?"

"Yes. We never know the full impact of a seemingly insignificant event."

"Then I'll approach the others of your kind to help me. They're less…conservative."

Stefan's eyes narrowed. "That would be unwise."

Nikolai leaned even closer to the Time Folder. "Is that a threat?"

"A statement of fact. *Think*. I know it's hard for you, Slayer, but really think. If your soul hadn't gone down that cord to claim her, would she be alive? Would your impression of her be different? Knowing she's your mate had to impact you somehow. The result of eliminating it would have the exact effect you are trying to avoid. She'd be dead, and we both know it."

Every red flag in the universe shot up and blew in the wind of Elena's mind. "Whoa." She held her hands up. "Stop. Back it up." What else had Nikolai had lied about? "What's this 'mate' business?"

Nikolai groaned and covered his face.

Stefan grinned. "You. Him. Destined to be together forever…literally. He's known from the start."

She wanted to scream. Instead, she kept her voice level. "Stop screwing with me, both of you. I deserve to know exactly what's going on." She yanked the cord to get Nikolai's attention. "Tell me now. Tell me everything going on without edits or omissions."

Nikolai crossed his arms over his chest, pulling her wrist when he did. "Or what?"

She yanked back. "Or I'll find a freaking way to kill you in your sleep."

To her chagrin, he smiled.

"You think I'm kidding?" she shouted.

His smile widened. "I hope not. It would be exciting to see you try it."

Stefan laughed. "Logic is wasted on him. Threats? Now, you're speaking his language."

Elena was so angry she didn't even know how to react. Nikolai was maddening. It was like her needs and feelings didn't even matter at all. He had threatened her, insulted her, made her feel inferior, and now she was his mate for freaking *ever*?

She wanted to cry, but there was no way she'd let this brute get to her. Never again. She gripped her knees and met his golden eyes. "Mate? Never. Screw you."

His smile grew wider. "Now you're *really* speaking my language."

"Figuratively. Never ever literally."

Nikolai jerked the cord so hard it yanked her body across his, noses almost touching. Her heart hammered as she flattened her palms over his warm, smooth, bare chest. It took every ounce of self-control to not run her hands over those muscles. Damned traitorous body. Whose side was it on anyway?

He jerked the cord again. "Now you listen to me, vampire. Your execution order came from the Slayer king himself. Your life was forfeit the moment the kill order was signed. It is by my grace alone you live at this moment."

"Or the grace of this cord," she said, shoving her bound wrist between their faces. "You would have already offed me if it weren't for the fact it would kill your sorry ass as well."

"I wonder…" Stefan cut in. "What about her caught the king's eye?"

"Her father was Gregor Arcos."

"And?"

"And…"

Stefan leaned closer. "There's more to it than that. More to *her*."

There *was* more to her. That was clear to Nikolai. Why would his uncle be so adamant she be destroyed? She was human and had been unaware what her father really was. It didn't make sense.

She slid off him and covered her face with her hands. She'd been through a lot in the past two days. More than the average human could bear. But she wasn't the average human, was she?

She scratched her collarbone and then covered her face again. Nikolai wanted to help her—to free her from her grim fate. But he didn't know how.

She scratched again and made a whimpering sound.

"Is something in the fabric irritating you?" Darvaak asked.

"It feels like something crawling under my skin. Like ants." She pulled the neckline of her shirt out and looked down. "Oh, wow." She pulled the neckline down enough to reveal her neck and part of her chest just under her collarbone. "Look at this."

But before Nikolai could get a closer look at what appeared to be a splotchy rash, shrill sirens broke out, causing her to jump to her feet and cover her ears. Nikolai grabbed his sword from the side table.

Darvaak bolted to the room off the kitchen and the alarm stopped, and then he strode back in with his phone to his ear. "How many?" His gaze shot to Elena. "How much damage did they do?" He pulled the top off the crystal decanter at the bar and poured some Scotch in a glass and tossed it back. "Did you take any of them alive?" He poured another splash of Scotch. "We'll meet you in the basement."

Nikolai held his breath as the Time Folder set his phone down and swirled the gold liquid in the glass.

"It appears we have underestimated how badly your Uncle Fydor wants her dead. It's hard to fathom he would send soldiers to invade my building. A huge risk, yes?"

Yes, it was. Slayers needed Time Folders. Without them, innocent people could be executed. Also, it was unclear just how much power these freaks of nature had. Time Folders were from a world other than this one, and little was known about them. There was a hands-off policy between the two species. Slayers would also never risk exposing the Underveil by marching on a building such as this, inhabited by humans.

Even though humans couldn't see them unless they desired it, they would see damage done to the structure or environment, since it was a human dwelling and not masked by the Veil. He knew Darvaak didn't seek a response, and honestly, he didn't have one.

Darvaak turned his pale eyes on Nikolai, abandoning his drink. "It is fortunate only two of your kind have ever been in my flat, or we would be in a far less advantageous situation. They got no farther than the parking garage. I'll need to rethink my guest list in the future to keep Slayers from just popping into my suite."

Darvaak had mentioned he had turned down a request from another Slayer only yesterday. "Who is the other?" Obviously, that Slayer hadn't been with them, or they would've made it into this posh suite and not just into the parking garage.

"My business is always conducted in complete confidentiality." He walked to the door and put his hand on the pad. The door clicked and swung wide. "Shall we?"

The elevator opened to a small alcove with metal double doors. A huge man in a security guard uniform, a bear shifter, no doubt, judging by the shape and size of him, opened the door, his beefy fingers wrapped around the throat of a Slayer female Nikolai didn't recognize.

"Welcome to my home, Slayer," Darvaak said, bowing as if she were not an invader.

The Time Folders had always been a mystery to Nikolai. In direct opposition to his own nature. So polished and slick it irked him. Based on the woman's smirk, he wasn't alone in his feelings.

"I'm sorry my hospitality does not extend to my suite. Blood in the carpet is a pet peeve of mine."

Like all women of Nikolai's species, she was tall and well

muscled with dark hair and gold eyes. Blood coated her arms up to the elbows. Next to him, Elena flinched and turned away.

The Slayer held up her arms and wiggled her fingers. "Right in the middle of a blood bath. Care to join me, Elena Arcos?"

Elena shuddered.

"Who sent you?" Nikolai asked. "How did you find us?"

When she lowered her arms, blood dripped from her hands and splattered onto the perfectly polished concrete of the basement. She hadn't dipped herself in an adversary's blood; it was her own, running from long slices carved into her forearms.

"Aleksandra asked me to tell you something, Niki baby." The guard's fingers still around her neck, she motioned Nikolai closer with a finger. He approached and stopped a foot or so away. The woman grabbed him on either side of his face with her blood-soaked hands and pulled him to her, dragging his mouth to hers and planting a hard, openmouthed kiss. He kept his lips sealed tight, and she growled. He shoved her away right as the security guard yanked her back. And then he smelled it—the bitter, sickening smell of almonds: cyanide, mixed with the floral scent of an elven elixir. It was fatal for Slayers, but the concentration had to be strong. In fact, it took so much of it to kill a Slayer, it could never be ingested accidentally or slipped into a food without being noticed. It was taken by his kind deliberately to avoid capture. This woman's blood flowed with poison, and she would die soon.

"Come on, Arcos," she taunted as the guard snapped a collar around her neck that was attached by a chain to a ring in the wall. Good old-fashioned dungeon hardware. Nikolai's estimation of the Time Folder went way up.

The woman strained against the chain, reaching for Elena. "You want it. It's right here. Just waiting." Drips splashed to the floor. "Yum!"

Slayers were never taken alive. This explained why she hadn't destroyed herself instantly before capture. She was trying to poison Elena. Fury flooded Nikolai's body.

"Come on, vampire. Do what you were designed to do." The woman's grin was maniacal. "Dinner time! Come and get it!"

"Enough," Darvaak said, pushing the elevator button. The doors slid open, and he stepped inside.

Nikolai wanted to question this woman before she died and find out why she had mentioned Aleksandra. Surely Aleksi wasn't part of this. He'd left her at the Fortress where she'd be safe. He leaned close to Elena's ear, and she flinched. It pained him that she feared him. "Can you stand it a moment more? Her blood is poisoned. Does it tempt you? We can leave if it does."

She shook her head. She was so strong. Stronger than most immortals he knew.

Darvaak rolled his eyes and stepped out of the elevator. "She won't talk. She is a tool and nothing more. They used her to get to Elena. She has no value."

"Where is Aleksandra?" Nikolai asked her.

She leaned against the metal wall and grinned. "In Fydor's bed."

Rage flared like a match had hit kerosene in his veins. Nikolai grabbed her by the hair and slammed her head back against the wall. "Liar!"

Elena cried out and moved away to the extent the cord would allow. *Shit.* He'd pulled her too close to the Slayer's blood. He backed up several feet, and Elena scooted with him.

The woman laughed, eyes unfocused. "You idiot. She's sacrificing herself to buy you more time. Just like your mother did." A shudder passed through her. "Destroy the girl now before he kills Aleksandra. Before he kills us all..." Her eyes rolled back in her head, and she slipped to the floor.

Aleksandra.

Nikolai's breaths came in quick gulps. His mother had married Fydor to buy him time? Time for what?

She had to have been lying. He needed to return home. Now.

CHAPTER NINE

Elena's skin burned and itched. She reached up and scratched her collarbone for the billionth time while Nikolai scrubbed the woman's blood from his face in Stefan's bathroom sink. The *dead* woman's blood. She shuddered.

He hadn't said a word since the woman slumped in a heap on the concrete floor at his feet. He'd acted like he didn't know her, but he certainly knew the woman she had mentioned: Aleksandra. That was the name of the doctor at the hospital—well, the woman pretending to be a doctor. The one who kissed him and called him Niki… His lover, obviously.

She rubbed her burning chest. Images of the dark-haired, supermodel-gorgeous woman clouded her brain. Compared to Aleksandra, Elena knew that she was exactly what he had called her repeatedly: weak and pathetic.

"Hey." His wet, warm hand stilled hers. "What's going on?"

She stopped scratching and dropped her hands. "Nothing." But something *was* going on. She was upset because he pre-ferred some Slayer woman to her. That should thrill her. Make her the happiest human—well, mostly human—on the planet. They'd get out of this cord, and she'd be free of this bossy, lying, miserable man.

But somehow that wasn't as appealing as she'd like it to be. Something in her sought his approval. Longed to be with him. Wanted to help him... A freaking *sick* part, and it had to be tied to ingesting his blood. *No. Just, no.* She must rein in her hormones or libido or whatever this was until he removed the cord.

"What's wrong with you? You keep scratching and rubbing your chest."

Oh, that. Yeah. There had been strange splotches on her skin. She'd barely glimpsed them before they'd gone down to interrogate the woman. "It's nothing."

He picked up a hand towel and dried his face. "We need to leave here as soon as possible. You should eat again first."

"And we should find out which one of you is carrying the transmitter," Stefan said from the door of the bathroom.

"Do you ever knock?" Nikolai asked.

"It's my house, my rules."

Nikolai picked up the shirt the tailor had left. "What transmitter?"

"The one that brought your people down on me. My affairs and location are all but invisible to the Underveil since my energy trail is different. Only you and one other even know where I live because I chose foolishly to allow it." He held up an electronic device. "And we found this on one of the dead Slayer males in the parking garage. It appears to operate like a tracking device."

Nikolai stilled partway through pulling the shirt up from where he had stepped into it. Like Elena's, the shoulder over the arm with the cord buttoned, so it had to be pulled on from below, rather than over the head. "The vampires that attacked us had one, too." He nodded to his discarded, blood-splattered pants still lying where he had abandoned them for his bath. He pulled the shirt up the rest of the way. "It's in the back left pocket."

Stefan eyed the pants in a heap on the floor, face placid. "I'll take your word for it. The transmitter is most likely inside one of your cell phones."

"Elena doesn't have a phone with her. My phone is in the pants."

"I recommend you allow me to dispose of it. I have several prepaid cell phones I use as what my assistant, Bridgette, likes to call burner phones when I don't want to be tapped, recognized, or tracked."

What on earth would he do that would be so underground as to need a phone like that? Elena resisted scratching, but pressed her palm to her chest to quell the burning.

Nikolai grabbed her wrist. Then, he reached up with his other hand and pulled the neckline of the shirt down several inches before she could react or knock his hands away. His eyes widened. "Holy shit."

She almost screamed when she followed his gaze. Inky markings similar in style to his stretched across her chest. Tingles of dread tickled her spine, and she was slammed by an overwhelming urge to vomit. "You did this," she said, jerking away from his grip.

"I had nothing to do with it." Nikolai held his hands up in surrender.

"May I see?" Stefan's touch was gentle and tentative, as opposed to Nikolai's grab-and-yank style. She couldn't help but glare at Nikolai while Stefan examined the skin just below her collarbone. Her captor was behind this somehow—he and his wacked-out Slayer blood. Maybe it would go away like the red in her eyes did… If only *he* would.

"It's in the ancient language, just like your markings, Itzov," Stefan said. "I've only ever seen them on you. Other Slayer markings are in Elven."

Nikolai said nothing.

"Who marked you?" Stefan asked. "Very few speak or read the old tongue anymore. How came you to know the language of the elders?"

"I don't. I don't even know what my markings say exactly, but I've been told it's the Prophecy of the Uniter."

Stefan smiled. "So it seems."

Nikolai crossed his arms over his wide chest. The T-shirt the tailor had modified hugged his muscles and made him look practically edible. *Crap!* Elena shook her head to clear out the hornies and replace them with common sense.

"Oh, and I suppose you're fluent in the ancient language, Darvaak," Nikolai said.

"I am. That and several hundred others, both human and otherworldly." When there was no response from Nikolai, Stefan continued. "I've been reading your way-too-naked skin since you popped in here unannounced. You're like a billboard; you can't blame me. Although I'd never heard of this prophecy before, it's proclaimed all over your body."

Nikolai said nothing; he simply stared at Stefan.

"Aren't you going to ask me what your markings mean exactly?" Stefan asked.

Nikolai's eyes narrowed. "No."

No? Elena couldn't believe it. No way was she was going to be kept in the dark because of some one-upsmanship pissing match between these guys. "I want to know what mine mean."

Nikolai's gold eyes narrowed. "We must go now. It's critical."

"So is this," she said. "It's critical to me, anyway."

Stefan turned her to face the mirror and pulled the right side of the collar of her blouse down far enough to expose part of the markings. "The ancient language is written similarly to Egyptian hieroglyphics, with images representing items or concepts rather than letters of an alphabet. This" — he trailed his fingers over a shape that looked like a curved talon or blade — "is a symbol for the beings of earth. Humans, if you will."

In the mirror, she watched Nikolai's fists ball up.

Stefan then reached across and exposed the marking on the left side. "This is indicative of the creatures *not* of the earth. Those under the Veil."

Elena stared at a curved marking similar to the one representing humans. It looked almost the same, except that where the human symbol had serrations on the inside of the curved shape. This one had jagged edges on the outside.

Nikolai shifted foot-to-foot, and for a moment, Elena thought he was going to make Stefan stop. Instead, he took a deep breath and lowered his eyes, "Please hurry."

"And this last shape in the middle where the two symbols intersect is the glyph for light." His eyes met Elena's. "It sounds similar to your name. It's pronounced E-lee-nee."

Her father had always called her his little light. Her name even meant light in Romanian, her father's native tongue.

"So, you see, the light joins the two together." His eyes met Nikolai's. "The light unites them, yes?"

"We're leaving. Now." Nikolai grabbed her by the wrist and yanked her into the living room. "Grab your suitcase," he ordered, pointing to where it sat next to the sofa.

Screw him. She'd had enough of his ordering her around. "No."

"No?"

"No." She thought for a moment he was going to lose it, but the look in his eyes was fear, not anger. He wasn't just afraid, he was terrified. He backed away a few steps, studying her, trembling. Oh crap. He was afraid of *her*.

Nikolai shook his head to clear it. This wasn't possible. It had to just be another pointer or manifestation of the prophecy. She could not possibly be...

No.

The Uniter would be a man, a strong one, capable of great deeds. According to the prophecy, the Uniter would dethrone tyrants and anoint kings. This woman couldn't even sufficiently feed herself, much less defeat a tyrant.

"There's more," Darvaak said.

"There's not." Nikolai needed to gain control of the situation. He had to get away from here and find Aleksandra.

"What?" Elena said. "What more?"

Fuck. He needed to make sure of things, lots of things before she heard any more of this craziness. First, though, he needed to talk to Aleksandra. "Nothing more. I have something urgent to do right now."

She ripped her hand from his and pulled as far away as the cord would allow. "So do I."

She defied him? No one defied a Slayer. Reflexively, he placed his hand on the handle the sword.

Her eyes didn't even widen. No flinch. No fear. "Do it. Go ahead. I've got a death wish and a damned good reason to have one. Do you?"

After at least ten solid, lung-filling breaths, he relaxed. Reaching for his sword had only been instinct resulting from centuries of training. He couldn't kill her. Not a chance. Not even if he were free of the cord.

She crossed her arms over her chest. "I thought not."

He didn't dare look at the Time Folder. If he had a smug smirk on his face, Nikolai would be obliged to pound it off him, and then it would take even longer to get to Aleksi. "Tell her whatever you know so we can go." He turned his gaze out the window. If Darvaak touched her again, he might lose control.

"There are symbols underneath the larger glyphs. They, like the ones I described, are similar to those on the Slayer. Not identical, though."

Nikolai ground his teeth so hard he thought they might crack. So, she had the symbol for the Uniter on her. So what? She probably had part of the prophecy as well, just like he did. Most likely cast by the same conjurer to proclaim the coming of the man who would save both worlds and build a bridge between them. It meant nothing other than she truly wasn't of the human world and he had been sorely remiss in thinking she was. Aleksi might die because he had not carried out the orders.

"The writing says, 'From a warrior's blood, I rise.'"

That's not what *his* markings said. Not at all. His said that from a warrior's blood, the Uniter shall rise. Not "I." Nikolai met Darvaak's eyes.

The Time Folder lifted an eyebrow. "I believe that answers why your uncle has such extreme interest in her, does it not?"

"No. It does not." He reached out and pulled Elena to him. So close her body touched all the way down. "I appreciate your help, Darvaak. I will compensate you, of course."

"Of course you will." The Time Folder walked behind the sofa and around to the suitcase. "Are you going to your home?"

"Yes."

He popped open the case and pulled out Elena's parka. He slid the sleeve over her free arm, then ripped open the Velcro that would allow it to be secured over her other arm. "You are accustomed to fending only for yourself, Slayer. You must change your mindset. Anticipate her needs—like food for example." He opened the small case wider to show Nikolai a stash of protein bars. "She will be of no use to you or any of us dead."

And suddenly, Nikolai felt like a total prick. The Time Folder was right. He hadn't taken her needs into account at all. It would be cold in his homeland. She was still weak and would need nourishment. It was time for him to pull his head out of his ass and start thinking clearly. Even if the markings meant nothing, this woman was in his care—at least for the time being.

Darvaak closed the suitcase and wrapped Elena's fingers around the handle. "Despite misgivings on both of your parts, Itzov, you should consider turning her completely. Her odds of survival would increase dramatically." He slapped Nikolai hard on the shoulder. "So would yours." After moving several steps back, he bowed to Elena. "I've no doubt we will meet again. You are welcome in my home anytime. I wish you luck and wise choices, Elena Arcos."

Enough of the sappy farewells. They were running low on time if he was going to make it before the sun rose over the Carpathian Mountains. Nikolai placed his hands on either side of Elena's neck and began the chant that would invoke the transporting spell.

CHAPTER TEN

When the pressure of teleporting faded and the ground finally solidified under her feet, Elena opened her eyes…and screamed.

Nikolai clamped a hand over her mouth. "Silence or we're dead."

Crap. They were dead anyway. The stone wall they stood on was no more than two feet across, which would seem plenty wide except for the fact they balanced at least five stories up and it was snowing like crazy.

Her eyes locked on what appeared to be a frozen moat below with miles of forest stretching out beyond. *Holy crap.* They'd landed in a scene from *Lord of the Rings* or something.

"Don't look down."

Right. Too late.

He reached down and took the suitcase from her hand.

Damn, she was sick of this—sick of being terrified, sick of being ignorant and helpless, sick of depending on him for everything. But right now, she had no choice because he'd landed them like a couple of birds perched on the freaking wall of a castle or something a billion feet above the ground in the middle of a snowstorm.

Then it occurred to her that he could only teleport to places he'd been before. Why had he ever been *here?*

"Hold on to me," he whispered.

She grabbed his belt loops on the back of his jeans. He had no coat on over his T-shirt. He had to be freezing, since her teeth were chattering and she wore a parka. Served him right.

She shuffled along behind him, keeping the same foot forward until they reached a huge window in the building at the end of the wall. He pulled his dagger out of his boot and jimmied the lock until the window swung open inward. He paused, holding his breath as if listening, then stepped over the sill and into the room, turning to help Elena. Once inside, he silently closed the window behind them.

A blow came from behind Elena's knees, sending her to the floor right before a heavy crack filled the blackness.

"Aleksi," Nikolai whispered.

"Niki?"

Then the sound of a match striking. The tiny orange flame grew as it took hold on a candlewick. The unmistakably perfect form of Aleksandra, dressed in something so sheer she might as well have worn nothing at all, waivered in the flickering light. "Why are you here?"

Nikolai rubbed the back of his head. "To have my skull cracked, obviously."

She ran to a basin on a small table and retrieved a wet a towel before returning to him. "Here, let me clean it off."

Elena remained on her knees but covered her nose and mouth. The smell of his blood was unlike anything else. It was a magnet pulling every molecule in her toward him. She rolled in a ball on her side to prevent her body from crawling to him on its own. She gulped a breath of air through her mouth to keep from smelling it, but she could *taste* it.

"You hurt her," Nikolai said as Aleksandra wiped the blood

from the back of his head.

"No." She rinsed the rag in the basin and put it back on his head. "She can't possibly be that fragile. If she is, we're all dead."

Nikolai grabbed her wrist. "Meaning what?"

"We can't talk here. Go to the forest—to the big tree where we played as children." She grabbed a huge brown fur from her bed and placed it in his arms. "Go now, Niki, before they come." She pulled Elena to her feet and shoved the suitcase at her. "I'll follow soon."

He pulled her back out through the window and leaned against the building. She kept her eyes on his face, rather than look down this time. The sun was rising, softening the harsh lines of his face. He drew her near, hands on neck. "We can't teleport in or out of the fortress. It's magically protected to prevent it."

So close she could taste him, Elena weaved on her feet as Nikolai chanted. Then, with a slam, she knew she had been teleported again. Eyes closed, she breathed deep through her nose, taking in the rich, coppery perfume of Nikolai's blood, no concern as to where they were. Hell, they could be up on another wall for all she cared. It was as if his blood had rendered nothing else relevant. Her whole body hummed with the scent of him as she dropped the suitcase and wrapped her arms around his waist, pulling him as close as possible.

A deep, masculine rumbling sound rolled through his chest, reverberating through her body as he reciprocated and ran his hands up her back, entwining his fingers in her hair. "Elena," he whispered.

Yes. This was what she wanted. She lowered her hands and rubbed over the hard ridge in the front of his jeans, and he groaned again. She needed him with her, against her, in her. She needed to…bite him?

No!

She shoved as hard as she could against his chest, sending him sprawling in the snow.

No.

"What game is this?" he asked, rising to his feet.

Still shaking off the blood-induced trance, she took a step back. There was only an eerie hint of light slanting low through the trees, accenting the angular planes of his face. He'd never looked more beautiful to her—wild and angry, surrounded by the surreal beauty of the untouched forest.

What was happening to her? This was all wrong. She took several more steps back. This wasn't like her at all. She was attracted to order and convenience. Security and predictability. Not some wild, primitive immortal death angel in the middle of a forest who knows where. A death angel who hated her.

It had to be his blood making her crazy. And every minute she was with him, she found herself more vulnerable. *It's only his blood,* she assured herself. She could beat this.

Nikolai stood and brushed the snow off, then grabbed the bearskin and shook it. It was only his blood she craved, and for some reason that bugged the shit out of him. Why should he care at all? She was a vampire, and even though their souls met on the cord, he knew it would never work. Perhaps it was simply the rejection that burned. He'd never been denied by a female before, and it stung. Yes, that was it. It was only his pride. She meant nothing.

"We need to get moving," he said, wrapping the bearskin over his shoulders, then grabbing the suitcase and tucking it under his arm. Fortunately, they were very close to the meeting place. "Come."

He struck out for the destination but the cord jerked him

to a stop.

"Come!" he repeated.

"I'm not a dog you can command."

He could see the defiance in her eyes, and it aroused him. So strong. But as much as he admired her will, they didn't have time for this right now. They could play who's on top later.

"Elena. We must—"

The sound of motors cut him short. *Shit.* They'd been discovered, and teleporting again this soon was iffy, especially since there were two of them. Besides, he needed to take care of this because he couldn't just let Aleksi teleport right into a trap or ambush. Best to face whatever was bearing down on them and hope it wasn't Slayer Elite Forces.

"Listen to me well. You must not move no matter what you hear, do you understand?" She was mortal and could get hurt so easily.

She opened her mouth to speak, but he cut her off.

"If they see you, they'll kill you. Get on your belly in the snow, now. Lay perfectly still no matter what."

She nodded and dropped to her hands and knees. At least she was compliant when it was essential. Once she was flat, he spread the skin over her. He would need to stay in one place to be effective. If he were within their striking range, they'd be within his as well. He pulled the cord to give himself the most length possible. At least it wasn't on his sword arm. He positioned himself over the skin, one foot on either side of her. No blade would find her. Not while he was alive.

The first of the snowmobiles crested the berm, and he almost shouted out with relief. The next two were no different. They were manned by wood elves, the easiest of the Underveil creatures to defeat. Why would they be defending the Slayer fortress?

Though equipped with rifles—probably to kill or injure Elena—the elves were also armed with swords. Bullets would do nothing to him, but a good slice with a blade would slow him down, though not kill him, even if forged by the light elves. He would have to be burned to ash or decapitated by a Slayer sword to be defeated, and the chance of a wood elf doing that was zilch. Still, they could kill Elena easily, which was his primary concern as the first snowmobile rocketed toward him.

Sword in front, ready, he waited...and smiled. This is what he was best at—what he was made for: combat.

Before the elf could even get his sword around in a full swing, his head hit the snow in a black, sticky mess. The snowmobile continued down the hill to a ravine, headless body dumped before it rolled.

"Next?" Nikolai shouted.

Ah, two at once. Bring it. Feet still on either side of Elena's body, he brought the sword over his head and swung in a full arc, slicing the torso of one, and causing the other to swerve wildly, losing control of his vehicle, which rolled several times before smashing into a tree.

The one with the slice through his middle came to a stop and dismounted the vehicle. He yanked the rifle from his snowmobile, grin visible in the rising sunlight. Shit. He'd figured out Elena was under the fur.

A quick glance revealed the third guy who had wrecked was limping toward his vehicle, probably to get his rifle as well.

Shit, shit, shit. If only he weren't tied to her. Heart pounding, he focused on his opposition. They'd try to immobilize him with bullets most likely.

The wood elf engaged the magazine with a sharp click, and Nikolai snatched the dagger from his boot. As the gun tip rose, aiming right at the vulnerable human between his feet, Nikolai drew the dagger back and allowed all his well-trained muscles do the work. Landing hard, he held his breath as the shower of bullets began.

Forever, the sharp staccato of gunfire rang in his ears, as every nerve ending fired with pain. The woman under him remained motionless. If she died, so would he. Hopefully, his body would absorb it all, and none of the bullets would pass though him into her.

A shrill, familiar scream echoed through the forest, and then the gunshots stopped.

"The bastard!" Aleksi shouted from somewhere nearby. "Wood elves?"

He groaned and lifted his head to find her storming toward him, gold eyes flashing.

"Honestly," she continued, helping him roll off Elena. "Is there no one with whom Fydor will not ally?"

Elena flinched as Aleksi ripped the fur off her. Relief flowed through him like warm water. She had survived. He wanted to sit up and check her for wounds, but was unable to move.

"Are you shot?" Aleksandra asked her.

"I—I don't think so."

"Well, then get up."

She rolled to her side and tried unsuccessfully to push to her feet.

Aleksi, sword covered with black tree elf blood, crouched over where Nikolai lay sprawled on his back in the blood-soaked snow. She placed her hands on either side of his face. "Hang in there. I'll get the bullets out as soon as your human baggage makes herself useful."

Elena tried to stand again, but fell back on her back. "I can't. My legs are frozen or asleep or something."

"Then crawl. I need your help."

She crawled the several feet through the bloody snow to his side, covering her nose and mouth with her hands. Obviously, the smell of his blood was affecting her.

"Hold out your hands," Aleksandra ordered. "I can't leave evidence that he has been healed. You must take the bullets with you."

Elena held out her bare hands and placed them together. One, by one, for what seemed like forever, Aleksi moved her hands over his body, removing bullets with a pain that rivaled being shot in the first place. Fuck, it hurt. And still, they kept coming. *Clink, clink, clink.*

"You'd better be worth it, little human," Aleksi said, finally sitting up. "There. I got them all. Niki, are you still with us?"

"Yes." His voice was strained, but at least he could still talk.

"You need to teleport now. Right now. Can you do that? I know you're hurt. Has a sufficient amount of time passed?"

He nodded, which was the best he could do with his body ripped full of holes.

"More will come if we remain here, and they might not be simple wood elves. Go to the cabin. It's very close, so you won't have to use a lot of energy to get there, and no one knows of it. Teleport there and heal. I'll come to you when I can."

Again, he nodded.

"Where is your dagger? The one I gave you?"

His eyes searched the area and stopped on the body of a wood elf with a jeweled knife hilt protruding from the gray skin of its throat.

"It's how they've been finding you. I overheard Fydor bragging about it to a guard. He altered it and put a device in the handle so they could track you." She walked to the body of the creature, ripped out the dagger, and wiped the black sticky blood off it onto its jacket. "And it's how they'll find me." She stood on the bearskin that had covered Elena, raised the blade, and plunged it into her own belly. "Shame on you for stabbing me like this." Her face contorted in pain. "I love you. See you soon."

Mouth open in a silent scream, Elena, still holding the bullets, trembled as Aleksi crumpled over in the snow.

With a grunt, he pulled the suitcase to them and popped it open. Aleksi's plan was good, but only if they could get the hell out before more of Fydor's men came. "Put the bullets in here. If Fydor is really trying to have me killed, we can't leave evidence she helped me." She dropped them in a shower into the bottom corner of the suitcase. "Now hold this and we go."

She gripped the suitcase tightly.

"Lean close." He stared into her blue eyes and put his hands on her neck. As he chanted, the familiar pressure of teleportation began.

Once solidified, he leaned against the wall for support. He'd thought the worst of the pain was over when Aleksi finished removing the bullets, but teleporting proved him wrong. Just because bullets couldn't kill him didn't mean they didn't hurt like hell. There must have released two dozen rounds into his body. Damned wood elves.

He straightened and took a ragged breath. He hadn't been here since his father's death over twenty years ago. They'd used to camp here when hunting bear and boar. The cabin looked exactly as he remembered it, sparsely furnished with only two beds, a stove, and rough-hewn beams on the ceiling. It seemed like only yesterday he was staring up at the knotholes in the beams as his father told him stories of his people and the species under the Veil.

Swallowing hard, he brushed away the ghosts of happier times. His father was dead. And now that he knew Arcos's offspring was not complicit whatsoever in that murder, he was discharged from avenging his death. Or was he? Maybe the rumblings and rumors had some merit. Maybe something more complicated than the two kings killing each other in a swordfight had caused his father's death.

His uncle had planted the location device in his dagger. Why? Aleksandra made it sound like he was behind all these attacks. Well, until he found out what was really going on, he would trust no one. The only thing he was really sure of was that this woman was paired with him by fate, and Uniter or not, he'd protect her.

Judging from the dim light coming in the windows, the tiny cabin was completely snowbound. Good. They would be all but invisible. He needed to be sure they stayed that way.

Elena had moved as far from him as the cord would allow. Her eyes were dilated. She lusted for his blood. If only she wanted *him* like that. Well, it was probably a good thing she didn't at this point because he hurt too much to do anything to relieve her if she did.

"I have no spare clothes," he said. "I can do nothing to eliminate the blood and make you more comfortable until I heal."

"How long will that be?"

"I have no idea. I haven't eaten in a while and am weakened. Usually, the wounds close in less than a day, so probably by this time tomorrow."

She groaned and slumped to the floor, covering her face. "I'll never make it."

"That bad?"

"That good. You have no idea how good you smell."

Well, part of him didn't need healing and sprang to life at the husky tone of her voice. "How good?"

"So good, I don't care that I can't feel my feet anymore."

Shit. He'd done it again. Thinking of himself and not her. Dammit, she might have frostbite in those silly tennis shoes and blue jeans. "Take off your pants," he ordered.

"Look, I said you smelled good. It wasn't a green light."

"Woman," he said, jerking off her shoe, "be silent." He removed her other shoe and wrapped her toes in his warm hands. "Can you feel that?"

"Yes. It hurts, so cut it out."

It was imperative to get her dry and warm before frostbite set in. He reached up and unbuttoned her jeans.

She gasped and grabbed his wrists. "I said—"

"Say nothing." He hadn't intended his voice to be that gruff, but if she lost her feet, they were screwed. He yanked her wet jeans down to her knees, then pulled them the rest of the way off from the ankles. How could he have been so stupid as to have buried her in the snow in such clothes? Humans were not like Slayers and other Underveilers. They succumbed to the elements so quickly. He threw the wet jeans aside.

"Well, way to bypass foreplay all together," she said. "Figures you'd be selfish, just like you are about everything else."

He grabbed a bearskin from the floor and wrapped it around her. "I'm not ripping off your clothes to fuck you. Not that I don't want to, because I do. And I will. But not until you ask me to…and I want you to be able to walk afterward, which you can't do without feet. So just be quiet for now." If she lost her feet, he'd never forgive himself.

Mouth open, she stared at him as he reached under the fur and wrapped the balls and toes of both her feet between his large hands.

She stared over at the iron potbelly stove. "Can't you light a fire to warm it up?"

He shook his head. "Not in the daytime. The smoke will be spotted. No fires in the daytime. No lights at night." He cupped his hands and breathed warm air on her toes. "Move your feet for me." She did, and he sighed with relief. "I don't think you were cold long enough, nor is the temperature so low you will have lingering effects."

He stood and picked her up, every wound in his body screaming. Mercifully, the entire width of the cabin was hardly more than the length of the cord, so his walk was short. Holding his breath so he wouldn't groan in pain, he lowered her gently on one of the two beds.

Then, he pulled the suitcase over and popped it open, relieved to find flannel pajamas and thick socks for her under a piece of red lingerie that made his mouth go dry. He grinned when he saw that Stefan had also included another pair of jeans and a shirt for him as well.

He shivered and the gunshot wounds answered with searing pain. He was wet, too, but with blood, not melted snow.

He tossed the pajamas and socks to her. "Can you manage these?"

"My feet are back, but they're not happy about it."

"I am." He pulled out two protein bars and set them on the tiny table between the beds, then peeled off his bullet-perforated, blood-soaked clothes. Using her wet blue jeans, he wiped as much blood off his body as he could, wincing as the rough fabric scraped across the entry holes. To his relief, many of the wounds had begun to close and were no longer bleeding. Still, they hurt like hell. He needed to dispose of the clothes, but couldn't do it yet. If someone came across the discarded items, they would know they were still in the mountains. He could teleport somewhere, but it created a trail and also took a ton of energy, which he needed in order to heal. For now, she would just have to endure the smell.

He opened the potbelly stove and shoved the clothes inside. That should buffer the odor of blood somewhat. He turned back around to find her staring. She had put on the pajama pants and socks and was still in the parka, eyes wide as they traveled up and down his body. Dammit, what shit timing to have his gut full of holes. Fate was a heartless bitch.

Chapter Eleven

Elena almost fainted when Nikolai leaned over to shove the clothes inside the stove. Never had there been a more perfect body on the planet, she was sure of it, and his backside was just as delicious as the front. Her mouth watered, and as much as she would have liked to blame it solely on the blood lust, she was certain it was more than that.

Here was a man who had to be in excruciating pain, caring for her first. He'd taken off the bloody clothes. Though, based on his pained expression, it almost killed him to do it. He had done it for her. She'd totally misjudged him.

"Eat a bar," he said, wrapping himself in a blanket from the other bed, teeth chattering.

She reached over, picked one up, ripped it open, and offered it to him. "You too."

He took it and smiled, which cause her heart to soar. Such a beautiful smile, punctuated with a dimple on one side. Why had she never noticed that before?

"Your hair is wet," he said between bites. "Is your coat wet?"

She chewed and swallowed before answering. "A little. I'm afraid of being colder if I take it off."

"Being wet is the worst thing in a situation like this." He shuddered from cold and dug through the suitcase again. "Layers are the most effective." He pulled out several garments, but none had been altered to accommodate the cord with the exception of the pajama top she already had and one other T-shirt. "Take off the parka and your blouse if it's wet, and we will let it dry. Put this on under the pajamas."

Then, to her surprise, he turned his back. She stripped off the parka and found her shirt dry underneath. After putting on the other items, her teeth were chattering.

"I'm sorry we can't start a fire," he said, "but we must stay hidden."

She took another bite of protein bar and pulled the brown fur all the way up to her neck, settling back on the pillows. "Where are we exactly?"

"We are in the Carpathian Mountain Range near the Romanian border. This was my father's hunting cabin." He settled into the tiny bed across from her and pulled up the thin quilt, cord stretching between them like a child's jump rope.

She sat up. "Won't they know to look here?"

He shook his head. "No. No one has been here in over twenty years, and I doubt my uncle Fydor even knows it exists."

A shiver racked his body, and he winced. It must have hurt to have his muscles contract when he was riddled with bullet holes—bullets he had taken to protect her. His unselfishness was humbling. She'd thought so poorly of him, when perhaps it was only his nature and not his actions she'd taken into account. Even though he'd been a jerk about vampires and her weakness, he'd always protected her. And even though it was clear he wanted her in the hotel, he hadn't pushed himself on her. She was also certain that the only reason he approached Stefan was because he knew she would benefit from it—again, he had put his comfort aside to see to hers.

And as far as his lying to her, though she didn't like it, she kind of understood it. How well would it have gone over if he had told her, "Hey, you hate my guts, but I'm your mate for life"?

And she *had* hated him. Part of her still did, but it wasn't him, per se; it was what had happened to her life since she met him, but that wasn't his fault. Hell, his life was just as screwed up as hers since their meeting. Finding out his mate was a vampire couldn't have been great news, and now his own uncle was trying to kill him.

He shuddered again from the cold.

"It's warmer over here," she said. "I have the fur thing and more blankets."

It was clear from his furrowed brow that he was uncertain whether she was genuine or not. Perhaps he thought she was taunting.

Could she stand being that close to him while he still smelled of blood? Yes. She could. Look what he was enduring for her. He had to be in horrible pain.

"Please come over here. We'll both be more comfortable."

He rose and walked to her bed. "Are you sure? I'm still bleeding."

She lifted the covers. "I'm positive. It'll just be like being in a candy store while on a diet. I have tremendous self-control."

If only it were just the blood. It was *him* she craved. But he was hurt. This was safe.

He slipped under the covers behind her and spooned against her body, pulling her close. Immediately, she felt warmer. Infinitely warmer, especially in a few select places. Holy shit, he smelled good. Edible. Maybe this wasn't going to work after all.

Nikolai shifted slightly so as not to press his erection against her. The combined body heat was a great idea, and he didn't want her to regret it because one part of his body was more grateful than others.

Her hair still smelled like the bubble bath at the Time Folder's house. His mind drifted to the way her flesh felt in the bathtub, and he got even harder.

She took a deep breath through her nose and squirmed. He was sure if he reached down inside those pajama pants, he'd find her wet.

He fought off a groan.

No. He couldn't do that. He had to respect her wishes.

What were her wishes? Right now, he knew she wished she could have his blood—she wanted it so badly she was aching. Perhaps if he helped her with the ache, it would help the blood lust as well.

He reached between them and adjusted himself to no avail. The thought of getting her off was almost enough to drive him over the edge.

"I need to touch you," he whispered in her ear.

Her body tightened. Other than that, she didn't respond, nor did she breathe.

"Let me touch you, Elena. It will help with the craving you feel." And it would help distract him from his pain to bring her pleasure.

She let her breath out slowly, not answering either way. Still, she hadn't said no. Perhaps she was embarrassed to say yes. Humans were odd that way.

"You can stay fully dressed. I swear I will not... I won't..."

Still, she didn't answer, but she pushed back against him and gasped when her ass met his erection. He suppressed the urge to push back. He'd never wanted anyone like he wanted this woman, and here he was in bed with her, too full of bullet holes to do what his body demanded. Still, he could do enough if she'd let him. Her slender body squirmed in his arms, and that was sufficient invitation.

Her back was still to him, pressed tightly against his body. Slowly and deliberately, he slid his hand over her side, and the air rushed out of her lungs in a whoosh. He stilled, fingers just dipped inside the waistband. "With only my hand and your mind, okay? We can make you feel so much better." She whimpered, and he moved his fingers only fractionally lower. "Do you trust me?"

"Yes," she said, finally, and he almost came at the mere word. He wasn't sure if it was the fact that she'd given him permission to touch her or that she admitted to trusting him that pleased him the most. Suddenly, he wasn't cold anymore. He was warm everywhere.

Elena thought she would die when he traced his fingers along the line of the elastic at the top of the pajama pants, then slipped them just underneath and stilled. *No. No, keep moving.* He was asking for her permission.

"Yes." She had no other possible answer. Her body was screaming for his blood, for his touch, for anything he'd give her.

His lips grazed the skin of her neck, and she trembled, thrills shooting through her, pooling low in her body. And then he moved his hand, pausing right at the top of her curls, then tracing lightly back up in a maddening, erotic retreat. He smiled against her neck as she shuddered.

"So responsive," he said. "You're going to come so hard. You need to come hard, don't you?"

Holy crap. How was she supposed to answer that? "I…"

Nikolai's hand glided down again, this time dipping all the way between her legs, and her body jerked at the contact. Current buzzed through her. He paused and simply pressed his hand against her. "Just one hand this time, but imagine how it will feel when I use my whole body."

She bit her lip and groaned at the image his words produced. The pressure was perfect, and she rocked against his hand. She'd never felt like this, not that she'd had tons of experience, but she'd had enough to know this wasn't normal. She rocked against him again, and he chuckled. He thrust his erection against her backside and made a low, rumbling sound deep in his chest, causing her to nearly reach her breaking point.

Too much. It was too much. But not enough, somehow. Then he trailed his hand lower and slid a finger between her folds, then deep inside her. This time she groaned along with him.

"Imagine my tongue right..." He slid his finger out and straight to her most tender spot. "Here." Then he applied pressure, making small circles.

Tiny electric pulses shot through her, and she gasped for air.

His lips tickled her ear as he spoke. "One hand and your mind is all it takes—your brilliant, inventive mind. Imagine what our bodies could do together. Think of the possibilities, Elena."

But she couldn't think of anything. She was so close. She could only feel his talented fingers between her legs, his big body at her back, and his warm breath on her neck.

Relentlessly, he circled with his fingers until she thought she might scream, and then he pressed his palm against her as a finger slid deep inside, and out, again and again. Then another finger joined the first, and he pushed deeper.

"So wet," he whispered.

She pushed back against his hand, setting a tempo that he followed perfectly, keeping just the right amount of pressure.

He was too much. His voice, his words, his touch. Too much.

The rhythm of his breathing matched hers, and it thrilled her to know he was turned on, too. She increased the speed as she bucked into his hand, his fingers filling her and his palm pushing hard against her, causing the most amazing friction. And faster still.

"So close," he whispered. "It's right there. You're ready."

And she was.

"You need this," he said. "Come for me now."

And she did, shattering into a million pieces as she screamed his name.

Nikolai had dreamed about what his fated mate would be like since he was a boy. Before his father's murder, he had always imagined she would have the attributes of his mother: beautiful, loving, and fiercely loyal. Loyal? No. His mother was the worst kind of traitor.

For twenty years, he'd pushed his mother out of his mind and his heart. She had no place there now. Not when he held Elena in his arms. His mate, who exceeded all expectations.

He couldn't pull her any closer, but he tried. He wanted to melt into her limp body, still quaking with aftershocks, and become one with her—a sentiment he'd never had in his many centuries of life. But this was how it was supposed to be with the mate fate had assigned. Human. Vampire. At this moment, it didn't matter. She was his—even if she didn't fully know it yet.

He kissed her shoulder and then pulled the bearskin up to her neck. "Better?"

She nodded.

She'd called his name out in passion. No greater aphrodisiac existed. He wanted to bring her to climax all over again if for no other reason than to hear her cry his name again. But there were other reasons. He wanted to please her. To see her happy.

She rolled in his arms to face him, placing her hands on his chest. He could feel her intent before her muscles contracted, and he placed his hand over both of hers. "No. Just enjoy the moment." Her brow furrowed. "Sleep in my arms. That wasn't intended to prompt an act in kind."

"But I want…"

He placed his finger over her lips. "I know. And the fact that you *want* to touch me is enough for now." The look of disappointment in her eyes tugged at his heart. "I want to be whole when we're together. I need to heal."

She sighed and rolled back over again, and more than ever he regretted the circumstances. He finally had broken through and now had to put it on hold because somehow the wood elves had allied with his uncle and had blasted him full of bullets. He kissed her neck and draped his arm across her body. "Sleep. When night comes, I'll light a fire, and we can talk."

"What about?"

He had no fucking idea, but there was nothing more interesting in the world to him than this woman. He wanted to know everything about her. What she liked to eat, her favorite music, the sounds she would make when he was finally deep inside her. Everything. Needing to feel her silky skin, he slid his hand under the hem of her shirt. "Does there have to be an agenda? Can't we just talk?" She trembled as he cupped her breast. "Do you need to come again?"

She shook her head.

"I'm sorry that I'm injured."

"It's my fault," she whispered.

He nestled into her hair and consciously relaxed, willing his body to heal. "No. We're in this together. No fault." Hand still molded over her breast, he reveled in the warmth of her body and the strength of her spirit. Perhaps fate wasn't such a bitch after all.

Chapter Twelve

It was pitch black when Elena awoke with a start. She lay perfectly still, waiting for the fog of sleep to clear so she could orient herself, which seemed to be harder to do each time she woke.

Nikolai's big body was wrapped around her still. She smiled at the wicked things she knew he could do with that body. "Imagine the possibilities," he had said. *Yeah, and yum.*

He made a hissing sound though his teeth and stirred, which caused him to groan. He must have been in pain. Well, of course he was. He'd been shot full of bullets. She'd only been shot twice, and it had been unbearable. She couldn't even imagine dozens of wounds. Why hadn't Aleksandra healed him as he had healed her? Perhaps she needed the power to heal herself, or maybe it would leave an energy trail. He groaned. Poor Nikolai.

Poor Nikolai? What a strange turnaround. Her captor had become the object of her sympathy. How messed up was that?

"Elena," he murmured, then rolled to his back, sound asleep.

He'd said her name. Was he dreaming about her? Imagining all the things her mind had conjured that they could do together?

"Elena," he said again.

A rush of power filled her. She rolled over to face him in the pitch blackness, tucking in close to conserve heat.

Tentatively, she placed her hand on his chest, and his even, rhythmic breathing stopped. "It's only me," she whispered. Still, he held his breath.

She ran her hand gently across his chest, grazing a nipple with her fingertips, and he inhaled sharply. He was awake. She smiled even wider.

Her near-death experience, well, experiences, had weighed in and taught a powerful lesson. Take advantage of opportunity while you have it, and what an opportunity this was—a naked god of a man was in bed with her. A man who had made her see stars the last time he touched her. What kind of fool would pass that up? Not Elena Arcos, for sure, she decided, trailing her hand below his sternum toward his navel.

His muscles tensed under her touch, which made her one step short of insane. His warm, hard body, in combination with the lingering scent of his blood, made him more irresistible than Aunt Uza's dark chocolate brownies—and she could eat a whole plate of those.

This level of pure desire shocked her. Sure, she'd experienced a tingle now and then with her ex, but this was absolute raw need, and it caused her whole body to feel electrified and achy.

She trailed her hand lower and traced the trail of crisp hairs leading to…

"Stop," he said, gently placing his hand over hers.

No. Just, no. "Why?" She wished she could see his face so she could read his emotions, or at least get a glimpse of them. Why would he reject her?

He took a deep, shuddering breath. "I'm still healing." He slipped out of the bed, and she felt cold all over, inside and out.

Tucking into a ball, she bit down her hurt. He didn't want

her. Of course he wouldn't. She would eventually be a vampire, which repulsed him. But then, why had he…?

The match he struck over at the stove seemed as bright as a lamp, which gave her a clear view of an impressive erection indicating she didn't repulse him. Nope. Not at all.

He opened the door to the Franklin stove and held it to some twigs he had placed in there earlier along with some logs over the wet and bloody clothes. With a slight brightening and a crackle, one ignited. He closed the front of the stove, plunging them back into blackness.

"No light at night. No fire during the day. We'll get it warm enough to sustain us through another day if Aleksi doesn't come before then."

Aleksi. Of course. That's why he stopped her even though it was obvious he wanted her. When asleep, he might call Elena's name, but awake, he was Aleksandra's. Elena felt like someone was standing on her rib cage.

"How are you feeling? How is the blood lust?"

And that, too. He didn't want her to bite him. "Inconsequential."

"That's too bad." He opened the door to the stove, revealing a nice, bright fire and the fact that he was still sporting a huge erection. He closed the door and then slipped back into bed with her. His movements were stiff and his skin cold.

"Too bad?" she repeated, squeezing her eyes shut against the sting of tears. He hated vampires. Turning into one would repulse him. Why was losing the blood lust bad?

He grabbed her by the middle and pulled her against him under the thick blankets and fur. "Terrible. I was hoping to distract you again."

What the hell? He was the most confusing person ever. He could touch her, but she couldn't touch him? Wow. A jolt of thrill shot straight between her legs. *Shit.*

What was it about opportunities she had learned? Oh yeah. To take advantage of them.

"It would warm us up," he whispered, gently nipping her earlobe. "By the time the fire heats this room, we will be throwing off covers." He slipped his hand under her pajama shirt. "What do you think?"

She took in a deep breath and held it.

His warm hand slid over her rib cage and lightly skittered over a breast, causing her body to contract. "Oh yeah. You think it's a great idea." He trapped her nipple between his fingers and pinched just enough to set her on fire, then chuckled as a pitiful squeak erupted from her, despite her best efforts to contain it. "You think it's the best idea in the world, but this time, I use only my mouth."

Holy crap.

"Does that appeal?"

She squeaked again, and he laughed. Perhaps his goal was to drive her completely mad. All he had to do was talk and she was lost.

He moved his hand to her other breast and pinched the nipple, and she gasped. He put his lips to her ear. "Sorry. I had to be fair and not leave that one out. Hands-free from this point on, okay?"

She almost whimpered when he pulled away. The complete darkness made it so that she couldn't really tell what he was doing, which added an element of surprise—like she needed any more surprises. The man was a living, breathing study in the unexpected.

He remained completely still, not touching her, which caused her to squirm. "Now, were it warm in here, Elena, I would go about this in a completely different manner. I would start and end the same way, though."

She found herself breathing so hard she was sure she'd hyperventilate.

His deep voice felt like fingers on her body, tickling over her skin until she had to squirm. "Do you want me to tell you about it?" he asked.

God. He said he'd only use his mouth. Surely he didn't mean by talking…though, at this point, she was so worked up, it might do the trick. "Yes."

"Well, it would start by my kissing you until you begged me to—" She scooted closer, wedging up against him, and he backed away to where they weren't touching. "No, no. My mouth only. Be still."

This would kill her—all one hundred trillion cells in her body would kick off simultaneously if he didn't touch her. She was sure of it.

"Now this first part, the kissing, I can do even with it cold in here."

Thank God.

She felt him shift. She was pretty sure he was kneeling near her elbow, but the infuriating lack of light kept her uncertain, which increased her excitement even more. Her nipples tingled and her breasts ached with every breath—well, with every pant. She crossed her legs and clamped her thigh muscles tight to alleviate the building pressure.

"Please," she whispered.

He made a *tsking* sound. "Oh, Elena. You're doing this all out of order. First, I kiss you, and *then* you beg."

"Then *do* it!"

He chuckled and the bed shifted again. She could feel his breath on her lips. And then his tongue—only his tongue as it swept over her lips like lipstick. Or crack. Dang. The guy was a drug. She needed him. More of him. She wove her fingers through his hair and pulled his mouth down hard to hers and he froze.

Shit. What now?

"What was our strategy, Elena?"

For someone who couldn't catch her breath, her voice was plenty breathy. "Strategy?"

"I told you how this would happen. I would bring you pleasure using what?"

She was certain she'd die before his strategy ever came into play. She recrossed her legs with the other one on top and squeezed hard. "Your mouth."

He took her hand in his. "And this is?"

"Not your mouth."

After kissing the top of her hand, he turned it over and kissed the inside of her palm, making her mind run crazy circles with images of where else he might put those lips. "Clever girl." He reached over her and felt down her arm in the darkness and took her other hand in his. "I'm going to help you now, so we're not interrupted again by things that are *not* my mouth." Then, he bound her wrists together with...the cord? "Keep your hands above your head or I stop, do you understand?"

Her heart leapt into hyperdrive. Not from fear, but from raw, undiluted desire. She needed this man so badly it hurt. "Yes."

"Where was I? I was going to kiss you first, which would have been my plan whether it was warm enough to throw off all of these blankets or too cold to be naked, like it is now."

Somehow, it didn't seem too cold to be naked anymore. In fact, her skin felt hot.

Again, he traced her lips with his tongue, and she fought to keep her bound arms above her head. Not being allowed to touch him, coupled with not being able to see him was maddening.

He pulled away for a moment as if testing to see if she'd break his rule, and then his lips met hers with none of the gentleness he'd just shown. His mouth crushed hers. Possessed it, their tongues tangling in a tempo that reminded her of the rhythm he used with his hand the last time. When he pulled back, he was breathing heavily, too.

"Is this where I beg?" she asked. "Because I'll totally do that. This is going to kill me."

"You do realize that the orgasm is also referred to as the 'little death,' don't you? Saying this will kill you is almost a statement of fact. A prediction even. And here, I thought you didn't have any special powers."

"Do you always talk this much?" For a moment, she was worried she'd offended him, but to her relief, he kissed her again until she was breathless.

"Yes, I always talk this much, because what goes on in your mind contributes as much to the experience as what I do to your body. I want you right here with me, mind and body."

"I'm here."

"Good. Would you like to hear what I would do to you if it were not cold and I could strip that bearskin from you and have you naked?"

A thrill at the image of him ripping the covers off shot through her body. She shuddered.

"Mmm. I'll take that as a yes," he said, slipping back in under the covers but not touching her. "First, I'd kiss my way down from your neck to your breasts, which need a lot of attention, don't they?"

She couldn't lie still, and suddenly the cord around her wrists was a burden. She bent her elbows.

"No. Arms stay up, Elena. I'd be working on your breasts

right now, and your hands would be contrary to my mouth-only rule." He chuckled when she growled. "And then, I'd move lower, down your ribs, across the beautiful, smooth skin of your stomach to your belly button. I'd have to stick my tongue in your belly button of course."

"Of course," she said, running the image through her head. Her whole body tightened and thrummed with desire. Thank goodness she hadn't died in that convenience store or she'd have missed this.

He eased out from under the covers again, and the cord tugged at her wrists as he moved to the extent of its length. "And that is where the two plans converge and end the same way."

She had no doubt how it would end. This amazing, masterful, talented man was going to take her to the absolute height of ecstasy. With only his mouth. She groaned as he pulled the covers up from the bottom of the bed only as far as her knees and sat at the foot.

"Do you want me to tell you about it?" he asked.

"No! I want you to do it!" When he didn't move, she thought she would cry. "Please, Nikolai."

"I'm still a bit sore from the bullets and can only use my mouth, so I need your help."

"Anything."

His weight left the foot of the bed. God, she wished she could see him.

"If you would please, keeping your arms over your head, scoot all the way down to the end of the bed. Ordinarily, I would wrap my fingers around your beautiful ass and pull you down here myself, but rules are rules."

What should have been a mood-killer ended up being incredibly stimulating as the rough fabric of the sheets rubbed against her, and she imagined his fingers digging into her backside as she scooted all the way down to the foot of the bed using only her legs and torso, hands still bound above her head.

"You know the torture is as exquisite for me as it is for you, Elena." Cool air swirled around her legs as he pushed the covers higher. "I want to touch you and run my hands all over you. I want to shove myself inside you and completely fill you up until you scream my name like you did when you came for me before."

Had she done that? Really? She'd been a little distracted, like she was right now. He pulled her pajama pants down to her ankles. She started to pull a foot free, but he stopped her. "A little restraint is good sometimes."

The goose bumps prickling along her thighs could not possibly be from the cold air in the cabin. She felt so hot she was sure she'd burst into flames like flash paper any second.

His knees thumped on the floor. "Relax, Elena. Open for me."

She took a deep breath and exhaled, letting her legs fall apart.

"Yes. Perfect."

He kissed the inside of one thigh and then the other, and she whimpered, not even caring that she sounded so desperate. She was.

His breath was warm on her skin as he spoke. "I predict that when I am healed and I truly take you, you will come before I am even fully inside."

No doubt. But right then, what she needed was... *Yeah. That.*

She almost screamed as he ran his hot tongue from the bottom of her all the way to the top, and then paused and circled in just the right spot to make her scream for real. She needed this.

Before he'd even touched her, she was so aroused she thought she might explode. Now, she knew she would. He repeated this over and over: bottom to top and circle until she was writhing and pulling against the cord at her wrists, and then he placed his whole mouth over her.

Nothing had ever felt this good. She was sure of it. And for an indeterminate amount of time, it was as if the world outside— the dangers, the freaky creatures that wanted them dead, even the things about themselves that made this impossible— became insignificant. All that mattered was the way his mouth moved against her. She arched her back and moaned as her body heated and buzzed with mounting pleasure.

God, the things he could do with that tongue—things that caused stars behind her eyelids and spasms that shook like an earthquake rattling her bones apart. Things that took her to the top of the cliff and let her soar. And all the while, she screamed his name.

CHAPTER THIRTEEN

Elena leaned against the headboard, tucked her knees up, and chowed on a third protein bar as Nikolai told her another tale from his childhood. They'd talked and laughed for hours in the dark until the sun penetrated the cocoon of snow over the cabin, and dim light glowed through the two tiny windows.

Nikolai's every word entranced her. He was fascinating and intelligent and had been just about everywhere on the planet. She'd never even left her home state before. The two of them were so different, yet, she felt an intense connection to him, as if they'd always known each other.

"Well, Darvaak proved useful after all," he said. "I do have more clothes than the ones I burned."

She took another bite and watched him lift a pair of jeans from the suitcase and pull them on. His movements were less stiff, and most of his wounds had closed completely. *Soon.* He'd said, as soon as he healed… Thrill shot through her, and she scooted up higher in the bed, hugging her knees to her chest.

He looked over his shoulder at her and smiled. "Again?"

"I'm fine. I'm just thirsty." And horny as hell after watching his reverse strip show, but she needed to get some control.

His grin revealed that he knew she was lying. "After you've

slept, I'm going to take care of every need you have."

She scanned him from head to toe in the dim light piercing the snow, from the top of his head to his bare feet and every hard, muscled part of him in between, and her mouth watered. "And you'll let me touch you?"

"I'll let you do anything your imagination can conjure."

Amen.

"First, I'll take care of your thirst." He grabbed one of the metal tankards from the shelf near the stove and slid the window open. He scooped some of the snow that buried the house into the mug, then closed the window. "Even though I put the fire out, the stove should still be hot enough to melt it." He placed the tankard on top of the stove.

The markings on his body were mesmerizing. Her own didn't itch at all anymore. It must've only been an effect of them rising to the surface. "What is the prophecy you and Stefan talked about?"

He pulled a gray T-shirt from the suitcase and unbuttoned the shoulder. "It's just an insignificant legend. Nothing more." He stepped into the shirt and pulled it up.

"You're lying to me again."

Both pain and anger flared momentarily in his golden eyes as he buttoned the shirt over his shoulder, and then he picked up the tankard and swirled it. "Almost melted." He set it back down. "Where the hell is Aleksi?"

And here she had been all cozy and practically drooling over the prospect of getting to touch him at last, and he had to bring up his lover. *Perfect.*

She settled back down in the bed and rolled with her back to him. When would she learn? They'd whiled the hours away talking, and she'd discovered so much about him…about herself, and here she was thinking he actually liked her. He was simply killing time until Aleksandra arrived. *Perfect.* Freaking cord.

She needed to escape him as soon as possible before her heart followed her body and melted every time he looked at her. Hell, it might already be too late.

Eventually, pretending to be asleep transitioned into the real thing—her only way to escape him until the problem of the cord could be solved.

Voices pulled Elena from the greatest dream ever, in which Nikolai had healed fully and was making good on his promise. Making good in ways she didn't even know were physically possible.

"What took you so long, Aleksi?" Nikolai's voice asked. "I've been stuck here for over twenty-four hours."

Stuck here? Elena didn't move, pretending to still be asleep. Well, good-bye dream euphoria and hello, hell.

"The dagger had a bit of elf ore in it and took forever to heal. Fydor never left my side," Aleksandra's voice answered.

"Well, isn't that romantic?"

"Fuck you, Niki."

"Not me. Him. Isn't that what you're doing?" God. He sounded so mad.

Elena cracked her eyes open, but the room was pitch black. It was nighttime again. And cold.

Aleksandra sighed. "I'm doing what women have done from the beginning of time. I'm protecting someone I love. He's on to you, and he wants you dead."

His voice trembled with rage. "And giving him your body will change that?"

Footfalls came from the foot of the bed as if she were pacing. "It's irrelevant. You can shout at me about it later. I can't be gone long. We need to talk about your human."

His human? Like a possession? Elena's body rebelled against her command to remain perfectly still.

"Let's get this straight now. I'm not killing her. No one is killing her." The tone in his voice was deadly. Elena suppressed a shudder.

"Well, of course not. Fydor believes she's the one, and he wants her destroyed while she's still human. On the off chance he's right, you need to get her to a safe house as soon as possible."

"How would you suggest I accomplish that? I'm not welcomed by any of the vampires, and I doubt the Time Folder will take me in again."

Exasperation tinged Aleksandra's tone. "I'm talking about her, not you. The vampires would protect her for sure. Deliver her to them and be done with her."

"You're forgetting an important factor, Aleksi: we're bound by an elven cord. We're a package deal."

"I have the solution. It's another reason it took me so long to come to you. I went to the elves and found out how the cord works."

"They told you? They wouldn't tell me anything other than only the one who made it could cut it."

"Of course they didn't tell you. They think you're an asshole, and they hate you."

"The feeling is mutual."

Her voice softened and came from closer to where he was. "Don't you even want to know what I found out?"

"I'm sorry. Yes. Please tell me."

"Its real use is for elf bonding ceremonies. It's where the humans get their hand-binding traditions. The elves wind it around the wrists of both partners, and if the partners' souls are suitably paired, which yours are because they touch on the cord, it will fall away once the union is consummated."

Her news was greeted with absolute silence.

After a few moments, she continued. "It's like when the bedsheets were checked the morning after the wedding in other cultures to be sure the deed had been done, only much more civilized."

"Nothing about the elves is civilized," Nikolai answered. "They just cover everything in sparkle and glitter and call it refined. They are blood-hungry killers just like the rest of us."

"Leave the hate aside, Niki. Are you hearing me? Getting rid of the cord is easy—well, if you can tolerate sex with a human, it's easy. Personally, I couldn't do it. But look on the bright side: because she's human—or a human derivative—you can't get her pregnant or catch any diseases. Then, you need to make sure she becomes immortal. If she's really what Fydor thinks she is, it would benefit us all if you turn her as soon as possible."

Elena swallowed and took a silent, deep breath. Good God. What was she? How could her becoming immortal benefit a bunch of beings that were nothing more than assassins? She wouldn't do it. Never.

"Actually, now that I think about it, you should turn her first. Sex with a vamp would be as bad as doing a human, but at least she'd be hardier and a lot more fun, right? Well, as long as you didn't let her bite you."

Nikolai didn't respond.

"Don't tell me you've become attached to her. Surely you're not that weak."

"I'm not weak, Aleksi."

Elena's heart sank. Being attached to her was *weakness?* Stupid brutes. Loveless, horrible creatures.

"Well, then do what you have to do," Aleksandra said. "Turn her, fuck her, and get rid of her."

Nikolai sat on the bed across from Elena in the total darkness for a long time after Aleksi teleported out. Fydor suspected Elena was the Uniter. Why then, would he want her destroyed? The Uniter would end the war that was brewing... Surely Fydor didn't *want* the war. Surely...

He stood and paced in a small pattern between the beds. It was essential to turn her in order to make her safe. Could he do it? He'd never witnessed a human change into an immortal of any kind. He didn't know the first thing about it. Only that his blood triggered not only her eyes to change but also the markings to come to the surface. His blood was the catalyst. *He* was the catalyst.

The words were branded on her very skin. "From the blood of a warrior I rise." *His* blood.

Could Elena be the Uniter? It certainly looked that way. Perhaps it wasn't physical power that was needed to save the Underveil. Maybe it was inner strength, and in the limited time he'd had with her, he'd come to discover she was more powerful than anyone else he knew.

She would become a vampire. The very thing he'd sworn vengeance against. The species he'd hunted and slaughtered every time he caught one breaking the law. And yet, somehow that didn't make a difference at all to him. He wanted her. Needed her no matter what she became. She was his.

Sitting on the bed, he laid his hand on her, getting oriented in the dark. She was on her side, facing away. He smoothed his palm over her shoulder to her neck, then leaned over and kissed her jaw. She didn't react. "Elena?"

He ran his fingers over her cheek and found it wet. Tears.

"Are you okay?"

"Just do it." Her voice waivered, and it felt as though his insides had crumbled.

Perhaps she assumed he still planned to execute her, or maybe she was emerging from a bad dream. "Do what?"

She jerked away and shuffled to the top corner of the bed. He reached for her through the darkness and found her crouched on the mattress against the wall, trembling.

Night had fallen long ago, and he had failed to even light the fire. He needed to see her. He reached over and pulled the matches from the bedside table and struck one. The look of horror on her face froze him in place. "Do what?" he repeated. The match burned down to his fingers and snuffed out, leaving the smell of charred flesh.

"What you have to do to break this cord and free me from you," she said in the darkness. "Just do it and get it over with."

Something was up. Something bad. "Exactly what is it I'm supposed to do to break the cord, Elena?"

When she didn't answer, he struck another match and lit a lantern hanging on the wall. Surely, a tiny bit of light just for a few moments wouldn't give them away. The cabin was buried under feet of snow, and no one knew of it other than Aleksi, and he was sure she'd been careful to not be observed when she had teleported in. Since his mother's traitorous marriage to his uncle, she was the only person he could really trust…well, aside from Elena, but right now, he wasn't even sure of that, based on the look she was giving him.

"Talk to me," he whispered.

"You're the talker. *You* talk."

So hostile. Not like her at all. Then the problem dawned on him. "You were awake when Aleksi was here."

No response.

Shit, shit, shit. "Elena, I'm trying to help you."

"Oh, yeah, sure you are. It all makes sense now. Get the worthless, weak human off a few times so you can, what? Oh yeah. *Turn her, fuck her, and get rid of her."*

His chest caved in on itself. "Not my words."

"But a great plan, and you're a big one for plans, aren't you? Let's see. Your first plan was to use only your hand, then only your mouth to get me off." She crawled to the end of the mattress and stood at the foot of the bed. "Well, I make plans, too. See, I can do the same thing. Only, I'm going to use only my hand and my mouth to tell you to fuck off." She flipped the bird at him right as the helicopter roared overhead.

Nikolai instinctively grabbed his sword. They'd been discovered. And if it was Fydor's Elite Team, they were as good as dead.

CHAPTER FOURTEEN

Nikolai knew the Slayer Elite Team would have night-vision goggles, poison bullets in long-range rifles, and elven-forged Slayer swords.

He and Elena were like fish in a barrel unless he had enough strength to teleport them out. His injuries had taken a toll, and he had no idea how far he could get them before his energy waned and they landed…anywhere.

Perhaps the snowmobiles were still where the wood elves had attacked them several miles away. Surely, he could get them that far.

"Put on the parka," he instructed, unlatching the suitcase. "Quickly."

"Are you kidding me?" she replied. "I'm not going anywhere."

He didn't have time to argue. By now, the soldiers were riding down zip lines, landing all around the cabin. He turned the lantern up all the way, slipped into his boots, shoved several stacks of cash from the suitcase into her parka pockets and then the rest into his own, threw the parka over his arm, and grabbed her by the neck.

"No way!" Tears streamed down her face as he started the teleportation chant. A slam against the heavy wood door was followed by another. Just as his molecules began to break apart and the pressure began, the wood of the door cracked. Three of them slammed through the door as his vision faded and they were transported to another location out of reach.

The cold air scorched Elena's lungs. The forest was tinted an eerie blue by the low moon. It looked like the same place where they had been attacked by the things with black blood. Yep. It certainly was, she realized as Nikolai led her down a hill toward an overturned snowmobile. The bodies of the creatures were gone. He turned the vehicle upright and pushed down on the choke and cranked it to life with a rumble. "Get on, Elena." He handed her the parka.

She had seen the things that broke into the cabin. He was certainly the lesser of the two evils. She slipped on the parka, Velcroed it over her arm bound by the cord, pulled up the hood, and straddled the seat behind him. Because she had no choice, she wrapped her arms around his waist, angry with herself for feeling better for it. With a lurch, the snowmobile jerked forward and then zoomed up the hill. Elena tucked in behind his big body, glad for the wind protection. He had no jacket, she realized, entwining her fingers in the T-shirt.

It felt like they were going a million miles an hour as they zipped through the moonlit night up a snow-covered incline and then followed what was probably a frozen riverbed through the forest. With her head against his back, she could actually hear his teeth chattering. It was a good thing he was immortal. A human wouldn't be able to endure this without a coat.

Aleksandra's words ran through her head. *Turn her, fuck her, and get rid of her.* Elena couldn't let that happen. If the immortals planned to use her somehow once she was turned, she would have to be sure she stayed human—at least that way, she could escape them through death. She would die before she allowed herself to become a tool or weapon of some kind.

And as far as the "fuck her" part went, it might be worth it to get free of him, but there was no way in hell she'd let him take advantage of her again. She'd been so stupid. She'd actually become fond of him. *Shit,* she was falling in *love* with him. Thank God she saw his true colors before it was too late. Still, it would be nice to be free of the cord. Was she willing to go there? To let him touch her again? *No.* Her heart wouldn't take it. There had to be another way.

But Aleksandra had told him to get rid of her. That made no sense. If she was useful somehow, why get rid of her? Why dump her in a safe house with vampires or the Time Folder?

Her hands stung and the tips of her fingers were numb even though they were under his T-shirt. He must be half-frozen because he didn't have a body blocking the wind for him like she did. Still, he raced along toward who knew where. Her teeth clacked together as he steered the snowmobile over a rough patch and up an embankment. Snow fell silently around them, and below, a smattering of tents and carts littered the clear space inside of a ring of trees. A fire burned in the center.

"Perfect," Nikolai said, steering the snowmobile toward the camp. This time, he didn't race, though; he slowly chugged down the hill. As they got closer, men emerged from tents and carts, armed with rifles. He stopped the snowmobile in the center of the camp and remained perfectly still on the seat. "Do not look at any of them in the eye," he whispered. "Stay quiet and keep your head down. They must think I am human and we are lovers."

"Fat chance on both counts," she whispered back. His rib cage expanded with a deep breath under her freezing cold hands. The men closing in seemed to be human. Maybe they could help her escape.

One of the men shouted to them in a foreign language. Nikolai got off the snowmobile and answered as he helped Elena off. There was more conversation, which seemed pretty tense, and then one of the men shook Nikolai's hand. Two others pushed the snowmobile under the trees.

The snow had picked up, and she could barely see the ring of tents circling the fire, which had died down significantly in the last couple of minutes.

"Fate is on our side at last," he said quietly. "The snow will cover our tracks."

Her teeth chattered. Nikolai looked her up and down. His gaze stuck at her feet—or where her legs disappeared into the snow. "You wear only socks."

She nodded.

He said something to one of the men and then picked her up in his arms. She started to struggle to get down, but he clamped his arms tight like vises, reminding her how inhumanly strong he was and how completely human she was—and completely at his mercy, which was not what she wanted at all. She gave another twist, and his grip tightened even more.

"Stick with the plan. Appearances matter right now."

She stilled. The man struck out, and they followed him to a tattered covered wagon. The man shouted something, and an old woman stuck her head out from the canvas at the back. She cocked her head and stared at Nikolai and Elena, then pulled the flap open and gestured for them to enter.

He lifted her into the back of the cart, which was carpeted with blankets and animal skins, then climbed in. He nodded to the woman, who had backed up to the other side of the space near the small oil lamp hanging from one of the arched ribs holding the canvas in place.

Nikolai wordlessly ripped Elena's socks and wet pants off. When she opened her mouth to protest, he pinned her with a glare so menacing she snapped her lips closed and yanked a blanket over her legs. In all sincerity, she felt much better out of the wet clothes, but it would have been nice if he hadn't manhandled her in the process. Part of the show, she assumed.

The woman took the wet clothes and hung the over a line at the front of the wagon, then stared at the cord binding them. She studied Elena's face, then Nikolai's, and then she spoke. Her voice was raspy and weak, but Nikolai didn't seem to have any trouble understanding her. He responded several times and even smiled once.

This freaking cluelessness was driving Elena insane. She had no idea where she was, why she was there, or what they were saying.

He took his sword off and laid it down against the wooden side of the wagon. The woman's gaze followed it and stayed on the jeweled hilt.

"She's going to kill you in your sleep for it," Elena said. "You spoke of lust to me once. That's it."

"It's why I'm not sleeping," he said, stretching out near his sword. "Please join me."

"Go to hell." She adjusted the blanket around her legs, suddenly feeling a little bare without her flannel pajama pants.

His eyes narrowed. "If you do not do as I ask, you are jeopardizing your safety. I made a bargain out there, and if you continue this, they will change their minds. Get over here and lie next to me now so that I can warm you up, or I will come and get you."

The old woman was watching them intently with her black eyes. There was more going on here than his wanting to conserve warmth.

"What bargain did you make?"

"I asked for their hospitality, and they wanted something in return. They wanted you. I told them we had run away together and that your father searches for us. I told them you belong to me, but that they could have the snowmobile."

"I don't belong to you."

He sat up, and before she could react, he grabbed her by the arm and pulled her into his lap. She gasped and grabbed the blanket, covering her bare half below the parka.

"Well, you'd better make it look like you do unless you want them to ride *you* rather than the snowmobile."

Asshole. She slid off his lap, keeping her back to the woman, who watched them with open fascination. Elena used a tone that, if you did not speak the language, sounded like she was flirting with him. "What am I expected to do to make it look like I belong to you?"

"Act like you don't hate me."

She rolled her eyes but maintained the sweetness in her voice. "I do hate you."

"Act like you want me."

"I don't."

He leaned very close. So close his nose touched her ear. "Act like you did when my tongue was inside you."

She didn't move as she replaced the unwanted jolt of excitement with anger so deep it limited her breath. It took everything in her to maintain her flirtatious tone rather than the threatening one she wanted to use. "It's a good thing you're not going to sleep, because I'd use that sword of yours to cut your tongue out."

He leaned back and an eyebrow shot up. "You make me hard."

"You make me sick."

"I want you so bad, Elena."

"Only because it serves your purpose."

His intensity and sincerity startled her. "You have jumped to an erroneous conclusion based on someone else's words. What you heard does not express my thoughts or feelings. Not at all."

Feelings? What feelings? He didn't have any. He said so himself. He felt desire. He had told her that love was a myth fabricated by humans to justify lust. Well, she had plenty of that. As mad as she was, her body still screamed for him. Well, it could scream until it was hoarse. She would never capitulate. If she had to go along with his charade, so be it, but it was only a show.

"Don't fight me," he warned, leaning toward her. "She's watching. They are all waiting for her report."

Surely, he was joking. But when his gaze shot to the woman behind her, then back to her face, she knew he wasn't.

"I'm going to kiss you, and you're going to act like you like it." He moved closer, as if testing her. "In fact, you *are* going to like it, because no matter how mad you are, your body knows and wants me."

His lips touched hers, but the contact was as light as the flutter of a butterfly's wing.

She drew back to speak. "You can talk all you want, Nikolai, but neither my body nor my mind is listening. That ship sailed and it left without you. The minute this cord is gone, so am I."

Nikolai knew she was dead serious. She would leave the minute the cord no longer bound them. Well, as much as it pained him, perhaps he should see to it that the cord stayed in place a while longer. At least until he could win her over. Because no matter how fucked up it was, fate had put them together, and despite the misgivings and obstacles, he planned to keep her.

He leaned in to kiss her again, and she pressed her lips in a thin line. Good thing the woman watching could only see the back of Elena's head because the look on her face was that of a person who had just swallowed a bug.

After repeated unsuccessful attempts to get her to kiss him back, he lay down, pulling her with him, and covered them with several thick furs. She tried to turn her back to him, but he pinned her in place, facing him, with his hand on her pelvis. "Relax, Elena." He ran his hand over her perfect, bare, round ass, and he groaned.

"Take your hands off me," she whispered so quietly he could barely hear it.

If only he had known she hadn't been asleep when Aleksi had come to the cabin, he could be deep inside her now. How could he have been so careless?

He kept his hand wrapped around her cheek, but stilled. The old woman watched them from the corner of the large covered wagon. These nomadic family groups were notoriously suspicious of outsiders. It was important he convince her they were lovers running away, which was damned hard to do if one of the lovers was rejecting the other.

"Stop fighting me," he whispered. "We need these people to house us for a day or so until I can teleport again. They won't do it if they think I lied. We need their cover and trust." And he needed Elena's trust. He craved it even more than he craved her body.

He slid his hand up to rest benignly at her waist, and her muscles relaxed slightly. "Just go along with me. Kiss me once to make it look like you are not here against your will."

"I am."

The old woman cleared her throat. "She doesn't want you, eh?" she asked in Romani.

"She does," he assured with what he hoped was a believable grin. "She is worried about her father. And like all good women, she wants me to work for it."

The woman laughed. "In my day, I would have made you work for it, too."

She settled in as if going to bed, but left the lantern lit so she could watch them. Nikolai gritted his teeth. All it would take to set this woman's mind at ease would be one kiss. One kiss, and they could hide among these people until he was back at full power. Fydor would never think to search for him among humans.

He looked down into Elena's eyes and ran his hand from her waist to her thigh and back again. "Kiss me once. That's all it will take. A real kiss."

"It's not going to happen."

Yes, it was. Nikolai bit the inside of his cheek, just enough to taste the coppery tang of blood. Only a drop, probably, but it might to the trick. "Then, I'll kiss *you*."

He kept his hand on her waist and pressed his lips to hers. She remained still as death while he swept the seam of her mouth with his tongue. Then she inhaled sharply though her nose. Her lips parted and her tongue met his. *Yes! Finally.*

She growled low in her throat and angled her head to deepen the kiss and then pushed him on his back. Nikolai fought for self-control as he looked into her red eyes. He wanted her and didn't even care if they had an audience. But, being human, she would. And even that tiny bit of blood had driven her out of control, he realized as she swung her leg over him and climbed on top.

Reaching under the parka, he clamped down on her hips to still her. The woman grinned and reached up for the light. After extinguishing it, her rustles indicated she was finally going to bed.

He could have Elena right now, and he'd never wanted anything more in his life, but he knew that when her blood lust faded, so would her lust for him. She would regret it, and he wanted their first time together to be perfect—not a blood lust–induced quickie in front of an old Romani woman in the back of a cart. "Easy, baby," he said. "That was sufficient to convince her."

His cock was straining so hard against his jeans he was sure it would bust the zipper. He had no idea she'd react this aggressively. Imagine if he had really bitten down hard, releasing more than a mere drop of blood. He grinned. That would be the plan later, after she cooled off from what Aleksi had said.

Still straddling him, Elena's body tensed. "You bastard."

"Don't move," he said, hands holding her immobile. "Just relax against me until she falls asleep."

"You did that on purpose. You slipped me a roofie!"

He was glad he couldn't see her face in the darkness. If it matched her tone of voice, it was deadly. "I'm sorry. I did what I had to do."

She climbed off him, intentionally kneeing him in the chest as she did so. Had she no self-preservation instincts at all? They could be kicked out in the cold. and she wouldn't last through the night.

The old woman struck a match and lit the lamp.

"I have to pee," Elena said. "I'm also thirsty and hungry. Just because you're an immortal, chauvinistic badass doesn't mean you can ignore my needs. I'm sick of this, Itzov. I'm sick of *you*."

CHAPTER FIFTEEN

Elena uncurled her aching fingers from fists when they returned to the wagon. Their little visit with Mother Nature had been less than ideal logistically, but at least Nikolai had been a gentleman about it. Maybe he knew how angry she was and didn't want a scene in front of an audience.

The woman shook her head when Elena tugged off one of the fur-lined boots she had loaned her. Well, at least someone gave a crap about her comfort. "Thank you," Elena said. The woman nodded and handed her a bottle of clear liquid.

"That's not a good idea," Nikolai warned.

"Was it your idea?" Elena asked, pulling the top off the bottle.

His brow furrowed. "No."

"Then it's probably a good one."

He sat back against the wall of the wagon, dark eyebrow arched. "Suit yourself."

She took a sniff. *Vodka. Good.* She liked vodka. She raised the bottle to her lips and took only a small sip. It tasted nothing like what she'd had on the occasions she'd had vodka before things went all weird. Still, after the burn wore off, it left a warm trail all the way down to her stomach, and right now, after traipsing in the snow, warm was good.

She took a larger sip and glared at Nikolai. Biting his lip had been the lowest blow ever. He'd used her weakness to manipulate her. It was mortifying to think her body snatched the steering wheel away from her and was ready to spin off for a joy ride on its own.

She took another swallow from the bottle and closed her eyes while the warmth spread from beyond her throat into her whole body.

She had to get away from Nikolai. Being helpless sucked beyond anything she'd ever experienced. She was not a possession. This was going to end, and it was going to end now.

She opened her eyes and met his. An electric jolt shot straight through her at his intense gaze, zapping through her body to all those places he'd set on fire in the cabin. *Shit.*

Aleksandra's words ran through her head. "Turn her, fuck her, and get rid of her." *Like hell.* She took another gulp of vodka. She'd had enough of being manipulated. It was time to turn the tables. She would be in control for once.

The only way to be really safe was to become immortal so these assholes out to kill her would have a harder time of it. Margarita had said she didn't have to be evil. She had a choice in the matter, just like she had a choice right now. And the choice was pretty appealing. She smiled and Nikolai smiled back.

He took the bottle and drank from it. She watched with fascination as his Adams apple moved with each swallow. The lamplight played across his unshaven face, making his skin gold, like honey.

She would become immortal and free herself. Her smile broadened. He tipped the bottle to her in salute and drank again.

Freeing herself from the cord might be the best part of this whole deal. Two could play this manipulation game. She could do a lot worse than having to screw a hot, talented death angel to free herself, right?

Right.

But then what? She had to get away, and she was in the middle of nowhere. She doubted the people in this camp would help her, but there was always the snowmobile hidden in the trees.

First things first. She'd figure out her escape once she was immortal and free from the cord. Nikolai wasn't the only one who could make plans. And her plan had six easy steps.

Step one: get rid of the audience. She smiled at the old woman, and her smile was returned. Elena placed a hand over her heart, and the woman nodded. Then, she jerked her head toward the back of the wagon in the universal gesture for *get lost*. The old woman wrapped her shoulders in a quilt and chuckled, then made her way to the back of the wagon. She said something to Nikolai before leaving, but he didn't respond. He simply stared at Elena until her blood heated and her pulse hammered in her ears. Big, sexy brute of a man. Just his gaze made her wet.

Step two: become immortal. This was trickier and a bit horrifying. She didn't have the luxury of doubt, though. It had to be done, regardless of her complete and total ignorance of the process and potential discomfort involved in the transition. To be successful, she had to get him to agree to be the blood donor. She crawled over to him, blanket still tied around her waist. His eyes narrowed. "What's going on in your mind, Elena?"

"Your mouth is on my mind." Her eyes fell to his lips, and she remembered how soft they were and how good he tasted. As if he were a magnet, she drew closer.

He tilted his head, expression wary.

"And my mouth," she whispered, only inches away from him. "Together."

He held her away by the shoulders.

"What?" she asked, enjoying the boldness brought on by the plan and assisted by the vodka. "You don't like my plan?"

"I approve wholeheartedly of your plan...in execution," he said, still holding her shoulders. "It's your motivation that concerns me." His grip loosened slightly. "And the timing. You've gone from cold to hot."

"Hot, yes." She reached out and ran her hands over his hard chest. "Very hot."

The words were true. It was the first time in a while she hadn't felt cold. The wagon was cozy, and she'd had just enough alcohol to warm her.

"Relax, Nikolai. I won't bite you," she whispered. But she would. There was no going back. She could never return to her old life. All she could do was follow her destiny and make wise choices. So far, she'd made *no* choices...until now. She was not going to put her fate in anyone else's hands again. Even if those hands could make her see stars.

"Kiss me, Nikolai. Not as a show for some woman spying on us. Kiss me for me. For you. For real."

And the kiss *was* real. Too real. So good, she almost lost her nerve.

"Elena." Her name from his lips drove her wild, and she pressed even closer.

Step three: get him so aroused he wouldn't care if she bit him. So far, so good.

She ran her fingers through his hair, massaging his scalp.

He groaned and rolled her beneath him.

"You're not so talkative tonight," she teased, running her hands down his back and up again.

"I'm slightly overwhelmed."

"Only slightly?" She slid her hands under his shirt and

scraped her nails down his back, and he thrust against her.

"Okay. More than slightly." His voice was deep and raspy, which caused her lower body to tighten.

She scraped her nails back up to his shoulders. "You want me."

He placed his forehead against hers. "God, yes."

She reached between them and unsnapped his jeans. He grabbed her arm and pinned it above her head, then did the same with her other hand. This is not what she had planned. She needed control in order to achieve her plan. But this big, powerful man had a different scenario in mind.

"Not now. Not here," he said. "Not like this."

What the hell? He was saying no? She'd have none of that. She wrapped her legs around him and thrust up, and he groaned. He released her arms and grabbed her face in his hands and lowered his mouth to hers in a deep, consuming kiss. That mouth. That delicious, talented mouth.

She wrapped her arms around him and reveled in the intimacy. Several times, she almost bit him, but couldn't bring herself to do it. It would be so sneaky—wrong, like what he had done to her. Yeah... *He* had done it with no thought as to her wishes. So be it.

She took his bottom lip between her teeth and bit down. Hard.

He hissed in pain, but then groaned as she rocked up against him and sucked.

The result was instantaneous and shocking. His blood filled her mouth, and she went crazy. *More.* She needed more of it. Of him. *Now.*

"Elena," he said when she pulled away to swallow. "My God, what you do to me."

Like super high-octane gas, his blood fueled her. She no

longer felt hungry or thirsty or tired. She felt powerful. Strong. Strong enough to push him over onto his back. She straddled him and kissed him again, drawing deep on his lower lip as he cupped her breasts over her parka.

She needed his hands on her. "Clothes off," she ordered, ripping the parka from her body. Damned Velcro on the sleeve. She couldn't get it off fast enough. Then she removed the pajama top.

She looked down at Nikolai who gazed up in wonder, blood glistening on his lips. "Beautiful," he whispered. "Extraordinary." He reached up and skimmed his fingers over her breasts, causing warmth to pool between her legs. "Perfect."

"I need you naked." She unbuttoned the shoulder of his shirt and pulled it down to his waist. She climbed off him and tugged his boots off, then unzipped and yanked his jeans down, shirt right along with them, and tossed them away. Kneeling at his feet, she paused to enjoy the view. He was the most beautiful thing she'd ever seen. Every inch of him was powerful, and his skin flickered gold in the lamplight. Yes. She wanted this. All of him, and his blood coursing through her made her strong. She needed more.

"I need to bite you," she said, crawling back over him wearing only the boots, centering her core right over his erection.

"I know." He placed his warm hands on either side of her face. "Open. Let me see." She opened her mouth, and his erection pulsed under her. "You're changing." He placed his thumb against a tooth. He withdrew, showing her a puncture wound with a drop of blood swelling from it.

Holy shit. She ran her tongue over her top teeth to find two elongated and very sharp canines. A pang of fear stopped short and melted immediately when he grinned.

"And your eyes are red. Deep, beautiful, passionate red,"

he whispered. "I love it."

Her chest pinched inside. Slayers didn't believe in love. And there was no way the most distinguishing features of vampires—her red eyes—appealed to him. *Focus on the plan*, she reminded herself.

"Bite me, Elena." He ran his hands from her throat across her breasts, circling the nipples, then lower, down her belly to where her body met his. "Tell me what you need." His fingers found just the right spot, and he applied pressure, causing her to grind down on him. "That's it. Tell me with your body and your words."

She groaned. The blood had made her strong, but she needed more. She stared down at the beautiful man beneath her. He hated vampires, but he was encouraging her to drink his blood. Desire, fear, and confusion swirled through her in a volatile concoction. She couldn't back out now. She had to do this to stay safe. To stay alive, she had to become immortal and free herself from him.

"Talk to me," he said. "Tell me what you need."

Him. She needed him. More than just his blood or the pleasure he offered with his playground of a body, she needed *him*—and that was far more terrifying than becoming a bloodsucking monster.

Blood still glistened over the bite on his lip. She leaned down and licked it off, and he ran his hands over her back, urging her on.

"Do it," he whispered, sweeping his hands over her skin, making her body thrum. "You can't hurt me."

But he could hurt *her,* and now that she had his blood flowing through her, she felt even more bonded to him. The goal was to escape. *The plan. Return to the plan.*

Step four: drink enough blood to become immortal.

Instinctually, her body ground against his, forward and back. It was difficult to focus with his thick erection so hot and hard underneath her. Just a few inches forward, then a shift in angle, and a hard press down, and she could have him inside her. That's what she wanted. And she'd heard Aleksandra say she couldn't get pregnant. Diseases didn't even transfer between different species. Perfect. She threw her head back and continued to rub over him.

No. She'd gotten off schedule. Blood first, then Step Five. She kissed his shoulder.

"Yes," he whispered. "Do it. Make yourself strong and safe. Bite me. Drink from me."

Running her tongue over his skin, she could feel his pulse. He was alive with what she needed. His blood would save her life and make her immortal. It would enable her to escape.

"Do it, Elena." He swept his warm hands over her back.

Breaths coming in shuddering gasps, she paused at the area between his neck and shoulder and pressed her lips to him. She could feel the blood right under the surface. So close she could almost taste it.

He thrust up against her. "Yes. There. Now."

Her teeth cut through the flesh easily, and evidently painlessly, because his body bucked and he moaned with pleasure as she bit down. Rich, sweet blood filled her mouth, and she clutched him in desperation. She needed something else. More. More than his blood. She needed his body. She needed Step Five.

Not withdrawing her mouth, she scooted forward to where the head of his erection pressed against her entrance.

He took himself in hand and rubbed up and down against her. She was slick and so ready.

"Now?" he asked, wrapping an arm around her waist.

Yes, God, yes. Now. Unwilling to pull away from his neck, she pushed down, and he groaned. Barely there. Just the head of him was inside her now, and she thought she would die from the overwhelming pleasure. She swallowed and lifted her head, power surging through her as her body hummed with change and need.

"What did I say in the cabin?" he asked.

She took a deep breath and pushed down several more inches. Moaning, she reveled in the fullness as he stretched her. So large. So right. She paused as his blood and body filled her.

He reached between them and rubbed his thumb against her core. "I made a prediction, did I not?"

She couldn't answer. She could only survive, as she struggled to breathe and the pressure built from the fullness and the relentless circle he made with his thumb. His blood filled her with electricity and his body with the promise of spectacular release.

"I said you would come before I was fully inside you. You're there. Let go," he whispered, pulling her down, forcing himself farther into her, massaging her with his thumb.

She gasped for breath as her body hummed with pleasure. So perfect. So right. Just there. *You will not call his name this time. This…exercise is for the sole purpose of escape and survival. Follow the plan.* Then, he increased the pressure of his thumb, and she tumbled over that edge, escape and the plan completely obliterated momentarily by pleasure.

Nikolai almost spilled when she convulsed around him, ecstasy on her face as she came silently in wave after wave, but he held on. She deserved more.

And she was tight. So impossibly tight. As her climax receded and her body relaxed, he pushed a little farther into her and she moaned. It was almost more than he could stand. Perhaps it was because it had been so long, or maybe it was because the blood sharing was programmed in his body to be mind-blowing, but part of him suspected it was because it was *her*. And he needed her so badly.

This was not how he had wanted their first time to be—rushed and in a caravan in the middle of nowhere. He had wanted to pamper her and make it perfect, but fate had decided otherwise and stopping now was impossible. His body and soul screamed to truly claim her and not hold back. His was on fire to the point of near mindlessness, which was bad.

But she was immortal now. She could take anything. Still, he didn't want to hurt her. He grabbed her pelvis and pushed her up to where he was barely inside, and she gasped, and then, using every ounce of self-control he possessed, he pulled down gently, gaining more entrance. She moaned. Just a little more and he'd be fully inside.

Arm tight around her waist, careful not to get the cord tangled on anything, he rolled her under him. She planted her feet and pushed up. *Yes.* She wanted more. He pulled out, then slid back in. Almost there. "Okay?"

She opened her blood-red eyes, and it was all he could do to not lose it. So hot. So...

He thrust hard and she gasped. Then she smiled. So he did it again and again and again. He was fully seated now, and she met him thrust for thrust—harder and harder until he was mindless from the feel of her, wet and tight around him. His body slammed against hers in a fast and steady rhythm until he thought he couldn't hold on anymore, and then she pulled him down and bit him on the other side of his neck.

And that was it. The minute she pierced his skin, she came.

He stilled as she clenched around him, squeezing him while she drew from his neck. The pain was so right. Everything about her was exactly right. He thrust into her one last time, and in a resplendent burst of light, he found the release he'd longed for since he met her. Complete, total, and absolute release.

Once he came back down to earth, he rolled to his side and pulled her against him. The cord had been right. She was his. For the first time ever, he could envision spending his life with someone. She was powerful, and smart...and his.

Still breathing hard, she shifted and held up her right arm. "It worked. The cord is gone."

"Not really." He buried his face in her hair and pulled a blanket over them. "We're bound, you and I. I won't ever let you go. You're mine."

A pained expression crossed her face and a tear slipped from the corner of her eye. "Step six," she whispered.

And just like that, Nikolai found himself alone in the wagon with nothing in his arms but the empty air.

CHAPTER SIXTEEN

Nikolai shot bolt upright. What the hell had just happened? He shouted Elena's name as he yanked his jeans on. It was as if she had just disappeared. *No. Not as if.* She *had* disappeared. He picked up his shirt from off of her parka. *Shit.* She was still naked, wherever she was.

Fully dressed, he bounded from the back of the cart. "Elena!" he shouted. He put his arms through the straps of his sword sheath and called her name again. Nothing answered but the wind through the snow-laden trees.

She could teleport in her immortal form, *dammit.*

A sickening churn filled his gut as Aleksandra's words slapped him in the face. Elena had followed them to a tee. She'd used him to turn, fucked him, and gotten rid of him.

She was gone.

He leaned back against the wagon and closed his eyes. She'd left him and he might never see her again. No more of her smartass comebacks, no exquisite come-ons. Nothing.

The snow coated his lashes and stung on his bare arms. A few of the men, awakened by his calls, emerged from their tents to see what was going on.

"It's nothing," he told them. "Go back to bed. I'm sorry I

disturbed you. Everything is fine."

One by one, they disappeared, except for the old woman. She poked him in the chest as she passed to climb the steps back into her wagon. "You don't strike me as one who just gives up. Sometimes you have to make fate bend to your will." And with that, she lifted the flap and disappeared inside her home.

Nikolai stood shivering for several moments. The woman was right. He'd just had mind-blowing sex with a woman who made him think of forever. No way in hell was he just going to let her leave him. He wouldn't. She couldn't. She was his.

He had to find her.

*W*ow. It had worked. After she'd bitten Nik the second time, Elena had known she could teleport. She'd even seen images of herself standing right here, like a premonition, so she gave it a try. She'd pictured where she wanted to be, and then, *poof*, there she was. After a few disoriented moments where her body felt like it was shrink-wrapped a little too tightly, she grabbed a bath towel from the bar next to Stefan's enormous tub and wrapped it around herself. Her body still thrummed with Nik's blood and felt as if it were stretching from the inside out, probably as a result of her changing into a whatever-the-hell-she-was. Not painful, but not comfortable, either.

"You're mine," she repeated out loud. "What kind of misogynistic crap is that?"

She wiped the tears from her cheek and grabbed the remote that operated the tub and pushed the red button to call Stefan. He'd told her she was welcome anytime. Hopefully, he meant it. She pushed a green button, and the lights came on full. She squinted and cursed, pushing a different button that caused the exhaust fan to whir to life.

"Technical difficulties?" Stefan asked from the doorway.

"Oh. Hi. Sorry to just burst in like this. I, uh…was just going to…"

He took the remote from her. "I assume you want a bath. You smell like it's been quite an adventure." He pushed several buttons, and the water poured from the tub spout, the lights dimmed, and light classical music piped in from the ceiling. "Dirt, blood, vodka, and sex, yes?"

That pretty much summed it up.

He tilted his head in that odd manner he had. "And look at you all grown up and immortal. How do you feel?"

She turned and gazed at her reflection in the mirror. A total stranger stared back. Her hair was a tangled mess, her skin pale, and though more muscled than she had been, she looked thin. And her eyes—they were tinged with red like the blood she'd consumed. She was real monster now. "I feel like crap."

"You need food."

"Do I?" She thought she'd be stuck with a blood diet.

"What sounds good? Pasta? Garlic bread?"

It all sounded good. "Yum."

He took her hand and pinched the skin of her forearm. "And you are horribly dehydrated." He held her hand between his. "And cold." His icy, pale eyes narrowed. "I'll kill the prick."

"Take a number." Her voice sounded as tired as she felt.

"First things first. Remove whatever those things are on your feet and get clean and warm." He poured bubble bath in, then handed her the remote. "As you know, the red button calls me."

After he left, she stepped into the warm, frothy water and relaxed against the sloped wall of the tub. Warm and safe, she was no longer a prisoner. She had gotten here on her own. She dunked under and rinsed the grime from her hair, then shampooed three times.

Stefan brought her food and a pitcher of water with a stemmed goblet. Everything was perfect and elegant, just like the man. So *not* like Nikolai. *The brute.*

She stood and scrubbed her legs. "I'll never let you go," she mimicked in her best Nik-like accent. "You're mine." She sat and washed her feet. "His *what?* His freaking lap dog?"

"I beg your pardon," Stefan called from the next room.

"Sorry. Just talking to myself." She washed her face one last time, then finished off her fourth goblet of water.

He appeared in the doorway. "You are highly agitated. What did he do to you?"

She lifted an eyebrow, bubbles up to her neck.

"I don't need a play-by-play. I just want to know what drove you here." He held a towel out for her. When she hesitated, he continued. "Elena, as lovely as you are, I have no interest whatsoever in you sexually. I am biologically designed to desire only one person. She was...born twenty-three years ago. The minute that happened, my sexual appetite turned off like a light switch, only to come back on recently when she came into power—and only for her." He shook the towel he had stretched between his hands. "Come on. I'm a one-woman man. Lose the human modesty. It has no place in the Underveil. Enjoy what you are."

She stepped from the tub and allowed him to wrap the towel around her. "What am I?"

He smiled. "I have no earthly idea."

"I thought I was a vampire."

He took another towel and squeezed her long hair to dry it. "Not like any I've encountered."

"My eyes are red."

He shifted the towel to another spot and squeezed. "Yes, but part of your original eye color is there as well."

She moved to the mirror and looked closely. Sure enough, there were blue flecks in them. She opened her mouth and ran her forefinger across her top teeth. "The fangs are gone."

He pulled a brush from a top drawer. "You must not need them anymore. Or perhaps they retract? Teleport to the living room for me, please."

She closed her eyes and pictured the sofa of his living room, wishing to be there, and before she could take a breath, she *was* there.

After a few moments, he strolled in with the hairbrush and a bathrobe. "See? You have powers and are definitely of the Underveil, but you are not a vampire. And you ate food. Vampires lose all appetite for it the minute they taste blood."

The pasta had been delicious. "No blood for this girl, thank you." She grinned and Stefan grinned back.

"He didn't break your spirit at least."

Nikolai hadn't broken anything really, except her heart. She took a deep breath and accepted Stefan's help into a silk bathrobe. How odd it was to have a man cater to her. Nikolai would never have pampered her like this.

"Is there a reason you have a woman's robe at hand?"

He stilled for a moment and then tied the sash. "For years, I have prepared for my mate to join me. I have a full wardrobe for her at all my residences."

His sadness was palpable. She wanted to ask him about it, but held off.

He traced his fingers across the markings just under her collarbone. "The Uniter. Right here in my living room."

"What does that mean?"

He turned her facing away and ran the brush through the ends of her hair, working up through her wet tangles. "I'm not exactly sure, but I know the prophecy, if you want to hear it."

"She doesn't." Nikolai's voice rumbled through her like an earthquake. It was as if his blood had made her a tuning fork that vibrated with his words. She should have expected this. Of course he would look for her here. She spun to face him.

Clean-shaven and wearing fresh clothes, he was delicious. He looked so civilized compared to the man she had been chained to. She wanted to run to him, and that repulsed her. Why would her body be such a traitor? Sexual attraction did not a healthy relationship make. This guy was bad news.

Stefan handed her the brush and turned to face Nikolai. "I will give you to the count of three to leave my home, or I will shock you into unconsciousness, Itzov. You are not welcomed here."

"She's mine."

Bitchin' bad word choice, asshole. She crossed her arms over her chest and glared.

Stefan looked from Nikolai to Elena, then back again. "She appears to be a free agent. One with tremendous power potential, so you'd best mind your manners. I leave it to her whether you stay or go."

Nikolai's gold eyes locked on hers. "Elena, please. We need to talk."

There was no way this man would change. He was too entrenched in his way of thinking. In his possession and domination. A relationship of any kind with him was impossible, no matter how much she wanted it. What was left of her heart shriveled to nothing. "I'm sorry, Nikolai. I've nothing to say to you. I want you to leave."

Stefan took several steps toward Nikolai, who took one step back. The Time Folder must have packed a real punch to back Nik down. "I'm going to have to ask you to leave, Slayer. You've done your part. You raised her from the ashes. You empowered her with your blood. Now it's up to her to do the rest."

The desperate tone in Nikolai's voice made her heart ache. "Please. Please just talk to me."

She held up her hand before he could say any more and weaken her resolve. "Just go."

The look of betrayal on Nikolai's face brought tears to her eyes.

Stefan touched her shoulder. "Could you give us a moment, Elena?"

Something about leaving these two men alone worried her. Stefan patted her shoulder and Nikolai nodded. Okay, maybe they wouldn't destroy each other, but there she went again allowing herself to be out of the loop and helpless. *Dammit.* She hated men. All of them.

Nikolai held his breath even after Elena shut the bedroom door behind her.

"I should kill you, Itzov." The Time Folder casually lowered himself to the couch. "Imagine my surprise when a hypothermic, dehydrated, starving, newly-turned immortal showed up in my bathroom naked with the exception of some worn out footwear of questionable origin."

"I—"

He raised his hand. "You were supposed to take care of her. Your stink was all over her, so you obviously took care of yourself."

Nikolai drew a deep breath and reminded himself that the Time Folder was a necessary ally. He needed this man and was grateful he had taken care of Elena, even if he was a know-it-all, elitist, self-righteous asshole with the nose of a fucking bloodhound. "You've got this all wrong."

Darvaak crossed his legs. "I hope so. For her sake, I really do."

The two men stared at each other for several moments. Nikolai always wondered about the extent of these creatures' powers. Sometimes they seemed to have seer talents, but it could just be the analytical abilities of their bizarre alien brains. Freaky bastard.

"Here's what I'm going to do for you, Slayer." He stood and moved to the bar. He poured two glasses of Scotch and offered one to Nikolai, who joined him and downed the drink in one gulp. He needed about ten more of those.

Darvaak leaned down behind the bar and straightened up with a phone and a charger in his hand. He punched in some numbers and then handed the device to Nikolai. "I've programmed my number in there. It is a disposable, untraceable phone, so your dear uncle Fydor will not be able to locate you. I will call you if she wants to see you. You will call me if you decide you are no longer an arrogant, selfish bastard." Darvaak put the charger in his hand and then wiggled his fingers. "Taa taa, Itzov."

Fucking Time Folder. He had no choice. Elena wouldn't talk to him.

Well, at least she was safe with this guy. He thought of the close call with the vampires and wood elves and even Fydor's Team. Hell, she was safer with the Time Folder than she was with him, for sure. "Okay." He shot a longing look at the bedroom door.

Darvaak placed his hand on Nikolai's shoulder, and a slight jolt of current ran down his arm. "Give her time." He gave Nikolai's shoulder a squeeze and retreated to the bedroom, leaving him alone.

"Give her time," he repeated. Time he had. Patience, not so much. This sucked. He stepped behind the bar and poured himself another glass of Scotch. Well, no better place to wait it out than right here, he supposed. He strolled to the kitchen and opened the refrigerator. *Jackpot.* If nothing else, the Time Folder lived well. So would he until Elena came to her senses.

"He's still out there," Elena grumbled for the zillionth time. "What does he want?" She stopped pacing long enough to set the hairbrush down on a dresser by Stefan's bed.

He smiled and put his arms behind his head on the pillow. "He wants my Scotch."

She took in the long, relaxed body of the man lying on the bed who acted like there wasn't a barbaric, sword-wielding caveman in his living room.

"And he wants *you.*"

She shook her head. "He doesn't want me. He wants to control me."

"All relationships are power plays. You just need to get the rules straight, which he's not ready to do yet. He not only has to overcome his Slayer's genetic drive to dominate, he has to deny his control-driven society's upbringing. You, on the other hand, need to realize these things are part of his composition, and allow him a little control. The two of you come from very different worlds. Give him time."

"Time!" She threw her arms up. "He had plenty of time while he was dragging me all over hell's half acre in the snow like I was some dog on a leash he could command. Sit! Stay! Roll over."

Stefan lifted an eyebrow and smiled.

She sat on the edge of the bed. "Yeah, well, the roll over part was pretty good, but the rest…"

He sat up. "Since he's not leaving, why don't we?"

"We'd have to walk by him on our way out, and I'm really

not up to dealing with him."

Sliding out of bed, he smoothed his shirt. "You are thinking like a human."

"I *am* a... Well, guess I'm *not* a human. I'm a...whatever-I-am."

Stefan disappeared into a closet and returned with woman's jeans, a shirt, and some sandals. "Whatever you are, you can teleport, and I suspect you can take me with you." He placed the clothes on the corner of the bed. "These will be a little long for you, but they should fit otherwise. Have you ever been to Hobby Airport?"

"Yeah, why?"

"Because most Underveilers who have the gift can only teleport to places they've been before. I do not have this gift, so if you could please teleport us to Hobby after you get dressed, there's a plane waiting to take us away. I arranged everything while you bathed."

"So you already bought our tickets?"

"No. I bought a plane."

"That's a bit excessive, don't you think?"

His grin was beautiful. "Not at all. I wanted a new plane, and this was a great excuse to add one I'd had my eye on."

"Like a new pair of shoes." She hoped her sarcasm came through loud and clear.

"Precisely. Go put some on."

After grabbing up the stack of clothes, she headed to the bathroom, shaking her head. Good thing she was immortal because getting used to this kind of thing was going to take a long, long time.

CHAPTER SEVENTEEN

Elena took another sip of her daiquiri and stared over the turquoise ocean. Stefan's private island off the coast of the Dominican Republic was paradise. So beautiful, in fact, it didn't seem real—but then, neither did anything that had happened to her since she'd been shot in that convenience store. Especially the moments she'd spent in Nikolai's arms, which she was trying really hard not to think about.

Taking a deep breath, she reclined her lounge chair and closed her eyes, focusing on the soft sounds of the ocean lapping the shore and the sea birds overhead. No matter how hard she tried to empty her mind, she always saw the same thing: Nik, with his strong, hard body and brilliant smile. And his voice, and his words, and the way he…

Shit. No. Just, no. She wouldn't allow herself to go there. He was an ass who had yanked her around like a dog on a leash. She could not be owned.

"Screw him!" she grumbled. *Yeah, if only…*

She'd slept for twenty hours after Stefan had introduced her to his staff, and then had done nothing for an entire week but lie around on the beach, but still she was tired and at the same time, restless. She constantly felt like she had lost something, but was too exhausted to look for it. Maybe it was the conversion into being a…whatever-she-was that had worn her out. Or maybe it was the fact Nikolai had starved and dehydrated her.

Or had he?

Maybe he just hadn't known her needs. Her species was different than his. Maybe she should have been more vocal. He'd always tried to make her comfortable when he knew things weren't right.

Stop it. Stop making excuses. She was done with him. Period. She'd hang out here until things settled down, and then she'd go back home and try to simply live a normal life—well, as normal as possible considering she was some kind of blood-powered freak of nature now. Obviously, after a couple of weeks of no-show, she'd lost her research job in the hematology department. Ha. She'd probably want to snack on the samples anyway. Her goofy grin at her own silliness faded. No. It would only appeal if it were Nik's blood, wouldn't it?

"Lovely sunset," Stefan said, sliding into the lounge chair next to her. He wore linen slacks and a light cotton shirt rolled up at the sleeves, buttons open half way down his chest. The tangerine and magenta sunset tinted his skin, making him look like a bronze statue. So beautiful, yet, he did nothing for her. Only one man made her feel like her body was on fire, and no matter how hard she tried to douse it, the flames smoldered under the surface, waiting to be fanned. It was like she had to be near Nik in order to feel right, which was just…wrong. Surely the hunger would pass in a few more days. She just needed to wait it out.

"How are you feeling?" He tapped his bare feet on the side of his lounge chair to knock the sugary sand off.

"Much better," she lied.

"Bridgette tells me you skipped breakfast and lunch today."

She adjusted the back of the lounge chair so that she sat upright. She had been a little freaked out by his housekeeper's intensity over the need for food. "Yeah, I really wasn't hungry."

He tilted his head and lifted an eyebrow. "Are you hungry now?"

She shook her head and watched a gull scoop something up from the water and took another sip of her drink.

He crossed his legs at the ankle. "I've been trying to sort out what exactly is going on, but am not able to get a clear picture. My sources have provided all the pieces of the puzzle with the exception of few crucial ones."

Another gull snatched the prize away from the first and flew away screeching.

"Well, you're way better off than I am, because I know squat," she said.

"Here is what I know: Both yours and Nikolai Itzov's fathers died in an incident rumored to be combat resulting in the death of both, yet no one witnessed it. Your father's death destabilized the vampire nation, leaving it in chaos, causing a large number of them to go rogue and feed on humans. That sparked the execution of thousands of vampires at the hands of the Slayers, which resulted in a rebellion that divided the vampires into two factions."

The whole thing sounded like a plot for a scary book. Elena folded her legs up and shifted in her chair to face him. *This craziness is real,* she reminded herself. *I'm not going to wake up from this.* But she wished she could—she wished she could forget the whole thing…well, maybe with the exception of a few hot encounters with a Slayer. Those she never wanted to forget. Heat shot through her at the mere thought. *Dammit. Stop.*

Stefan stared over the water as he spoke. "Fydor, the newly instated Slayer king, replaced Nikolai's father and immediately married his mother."

"How did that go over?"

"Fydor marrying Tatiana Itzov was a good move politically. She was loved by their people and gave him validity. According to my sources, the marriage was not well-received by Nikolai, who moved out of his family's compound the day the engagement was announced."

Poor Nik. They had talked for hours in the cabin, and he'd never mentioned any of this. He'd kept it light and funny, probably to make her comfortable. Just like he'd done with his body. He'd eased her fear and discomfort. Maybe she'd misjudged him more than she thought. And as much as she tried not to, she worried about him.

"Fydor vowed to cease all executions if the vampires swore allegiance to him as their king, as long as the feeding on humans was discreet and had a low mortality rate," Stefan continued.

Low mortality rate? Humans shouldn't die at all if there were other options. Elena could hardly believe it.

"The ones who did not swear allegiance to Fydor appointed a new vampire king and are considered rebels. They stay true to your father's dictates, feeding only on willing immortals."

"Like Margarita."

"Yes. In fact, her brother is the Arconian leader."

"Arconian…"

"As it sounds, they took your father's name."

Well, no wonder Margarita was all up in her business that day. She smiled as another piece of the puzzle slipped into place.

He leaned down and brushed some sand off his recliner. "Nikolai, unaware of the agreement between his uncle and the vampires that allowed them to predate humans, continued to kill the violators of the laws of the Underveil while searching for you."

"For me?"

"For the Uniter, who appears to be you." He gave a half laugh. "I would love to have seen his face when he figured that out."

No kidding. Finding out the person he sought was enemy number one, and a woman at that, must have been a shock to his big, bad, misogynistic Slayer system. "It wasn't pretty, I'm sure." She took another sip of her drink. "So, not knowing Uncle Dearest had given the vamps the green light to drain humans, Nik slayed them."

"Well put." How could a guy that good-looking do nothing at all for her? His blue eyes were a shade paler than the water, giving him an unearthly appearance, which suited, she supposed. According to Nik, he was an alien of some kind. "Yes," he continued. "His execution of those who took human lives made him an enemy of most vampires and in violation of the treaty, which is why his uncle could put a kill order on him."

"But Nik didn't know about the agreement."

Stefan smiled. "Yes, he's been kept in the dark about a lot of things."

She fiddled with the tie on the white cotton shorts his housekeeper, Bridgette, had laid out for her this morning. She swore she wasn't going to ask. That she didn't care. Still, she couldn't help herself. "Is he still at your place?"

He pulled his cell from his pocket. "According to security, he teleports in and out."

A teeny kernel of panic bloomed in her belly. Surely, he'd stay out of danger. "So what is my role in all of this?"

"Walk with me." Even his movements seemed inhuman as he effortlessly rose from his lounge chair.

She wrestled her way out of the wood and canvas contraption much less gracefully and collected her drink. The sand was soft and warm underfoot—the opposite of the snow she'd trudged through with Nikolai. Where was he now, she wondered? Was he looking for her?

Stefan glanced over and then stopped. "I don't know what manner of creature you are. I know Fydor desires this war and he wants you dead, so it stands to reason, you are—or he believes you are—the Uniter from the prophecy. The one to build the bridge and end the war."

"What war?"

The sea breeze blew his hair across his face. "There have always been factions of the Underveil that want to take over the human world, rather than protect it. Right now, with Fydor in power, that element has great strength."

Definitely like a horror movie plot, only weirder. She walked to the waterline and let the waves lap over her ankles. "Where does Nik fit in?"

Stefan joined her, hands in pockets. He stared at her with those pale eyes and smiled. It was a sad smile that tugged at her heart. "He fits with you…and he is in grave danger, Elena."

Her heart stopped for a moment. "Danger. Why?" She hoped it wasn't because of her. Because of the risks he'd taken by not killing her as ordered.

"There are two obstacles to Fydor's desire to lift the Veil and place humans at the immortals' mercy. First, is Nikolai Itzov. He's the rightful heir to the throne, but he abdicated to his uncle for unknown reasons. It was a big upset. Fydor was never considered a viable candidate to be ruler because he is unstable and volatile. Were Nikolai to take his rightful place as Slayer king, the Underveil would follow and desert Fydor instantly."

Whoa. Nikolai was supposed to be the king. "So you think Fydor will kill him to put an end to the divided loyalty." She picked up a rock and rolled it in her free hand. "Where do I fit in?" She pitched the rock out into the crystal water.

"I don't know. That's the other missing piece in the equation."

"Fydor believes I'm the Uniter from the prophecy. What's the prophecy?"

"Well, I can only tell you what the hieroglyphs on Itzov's body say, as I'm not familiar with the origin or mechanics of the prophecy. Time Folders are more like long-term observers than members of the Underveil."

"Spill it, Stefan."

He closed his eyes as if seeing Nikolai's body in his head. "His glyphs say, *'From the ashes of death, the Uniter shall rise. Awakened by warrior's blood to restore balance.*

With the power to dethrone tyrants and anoint kings.'"

As if the words themselves had power, a strange jolt rocketed through her, like the bolts of current when Stefan touched her. The phrase was familiar, but she knew she'd never heard it before. That weird need to search for something lost washed through her, and she pushed it down.

The Uniter would dethrone tyrants. *Riiiiight.* They had the wrong girl if she was supposed to be this Uniter person.

"There's more," he said. "The Uniter is also, *'Guardian of the bridge between species above and below the Veil.'"*

"What the hell does that mean? What bridge?"

"I assume it's metaphorical." He waited patiently while she processed.

This was a terrible and deadly game she'd been dumped into. And then it dawned on her that as kind as this man—or whatever he was—had been to her, she knew nothing about his motivations. She didn't even know what kinds of powers Time Folders had, other than that of the almighty dollar and an electric supercharge of some kind. Still, Nik seemed to trust him. Perhaps it was just that of all the evil in this new world, this guy was the least horrible option. "And where do you fit in all this? Whose side are you on?"

He shrugged. "I'm on the side that protects the stability of the planet I inhabit. Right now, that would be any faction that opposes Fydor."

"So, Nik's side."

"Ah." He folded his hands behind his back. "No. Not unless he steps forward and demands his throne back. As of now, he's self-absorbed, careless, and politically unmotivated."

A strange sensation surged through her at the slight to Nik. It was as if her frustration had pooled in her palms. "But only because he doesn't have all the information."

"None of us do, yet he just goes on blindly thrashing his way through the days, refusing to look into the dark places that sent him on this quest to begin with. My bet is on you. Whether or not you bring Nikolai Itzov into your wake as you destroy Fydor, is your business."

The sensation in her palms dissipated, and fear caused the fine hairs on her neck to prickle. How in the world could she destroy a Slayer like Fydor? Somehow, she felt like she was being manipulated again. She turned and strolled back toward the lounge chairs, sipping her daiquiri. "Nik is immortal. How can Fydor kill him?"

Stefan ran his fingers through his gold hair. "Being immortal doesn't mean living forever. Humans have a life expectancy of eighty-five or so years, though some die much earlier. Immortality is the same. Though Underveilers can live for hundreds and even thousands of years, depending on species, many are destroyed prematurely."

"Destroyed how?" She cupped her hand above her eyes to block the sun so she could see his face in the bright sunlight.

"All immortals have an Achilles heel. With many, like the

elves and shifters, a simple beheading with any weapon is enough. Vampires have to be burned. Poisons specific to species are fatal as well, like that poor woman in my building. But all of them, including Slayers, are subject to death from a sword of elven ore. Some species require a full decapitation, while others will die from a wound from such a weapon."

"Like Nik's sword."

"Yes. There are a limited number of them, thanks to Fydor. He imprisoned a light elf named Aksel, the only craftsman who could forge the swords. He locked him away centuries ago in some unknown location, in order to halt their manufacture. It wasn't until recently that I realized the significance. The fewer swords there are, the better Fydor's chances of survival. He had been planning this war for a long time—centuries before his brother died."

She strolled along the beach, trying to organize this new information in some kind of cohesive fashion. A week ago, she was studying blood cells through a microscope and analyzing blood anomalies. Wars, swords, and imprisonments weren't even on her radar, now she was supposed to be some Uniter person who could end wars. There had to be a punch line to this, but sadly, she doubted there was. "What about you, Stefan? What's your Achilles heel?"

A strange look crossed his face, and then was replaced by a slight smile. "I have none. I cannot be killed by any hand but my own."

She finished off her drink, studying his perfect face over the rim. "I guess that makes you your own worst enemy."

"Aren't we all?" Stefan's phone rang. "Excuse me," He turned away from her and answered. It sounded like a business call because he asked about the authenticity of something and then told the person on the other end to buy it regardless of cost.

Must be nice, Elena thought. She had struggled for years just to make ends meet. Now she was hobnobbing with Mr. Buy-A-Plane. She pulled some hair that had blown across her face out of her eyes and sighed. It was an overwhelming concept to wrap her head around that this man had unlimited funds and would live literally forever if he wished it.

His phone rang again. "Yes?" he answered. His eyes met Elena's. "I will bring her now. Thank you."

He took her hand, and she braced for the low level current she always felt with his contact. Instead, she felt nothing but his smooth, warm hand. He gasped and immediately withdrew. Then, he smiled. "Well, well, well. You are full of all manner of surprises."

"What?"

"You shocked me electrically when we touched. It's supposed to be the other way around. It's new, and honestly, a bit troubling."

Aw, crap. She didn't need any more troubling things in her life. "Why?"

He gestured toward the house. "I'll tell you over dinner."

"Tell me now. I'm not hungry." Which was troubling, too, because it was probably her true vampire nature kicking in. A lifetime of a blood-only diet would suck. Literally.

"You *are* hungry. You're simply depressed, which suppresses your appetite."

"I'm not depressed." *Freaked out, yes.*

"Of course you are. You have been separated from something you cannot live without." He struck out through the powdery sand ahead of her. She remained rooted in place for a moment while she reconstructed his words in her head.

"Wait a minute!"

He didn't even slow his pace.

"Hey, what can I not live without?"

Still striding on ahead, he didn't respond. *The jerk.* Glaring at his retreating form, she imagined herself standing right in front of him and just like that, she was there.

He stopped short of walking right into her, a surprised look on his face. Yeah, she could get used to this superpower stuff. "Stop screwing around with me, Stefan. Say what you mean, or just shut up."

His eyes narrowed. "You know exactly what I'm talking about, or you wouldn't be so agitated. You've both had adequate time to come to terms with what is facing you. It's time for you and the Slayer to put your petty differences aside and accept fate."

"I don't believe in fate."

"What a splendid luxury." He threw his arms up, exasperation in his tone. "What would I not give to be in your shoes? To have my perfect mate only a phone call away. To be able to hold her in my arms without it being a death sentence for us both!" His voice cracked on the last word.

Stunned, Elena watched him stride away. His phone rang as he climbed the porch stairs, but he didn't answer it. It stopped ringing as he disappeared inside the house.

He was wrong. She could live without Nikolai. She missed him, yes. But she didn't need him—anymore than he needed her. *Yeah, just keep telling yourself that, moron.* She took a deep breath and climbed the steps to the house.

"What are you doing here?" Aleksandra asked, lowering her sword.

Well, that answered Nikolai's question about the identity of the other Slayer who had visited Stefan's penthouse. He slid the sword back in its sheath, and she did the same. "I might ask you the same thing."

"I'm there to see the Time Folder."

"For what purpose?"

She strolled over to the wall of windows and stared out. Nikolai scanned her body, looking for signs of injury or abuse, but found none. Good. Fydor hadn't hurt her—at least not recently...or not where it showed.

The bastard. He'd kill him if he hurt Aleksi.

She faced him. "Where is the human? She's in extreme danger. So are you."

Nikolai stopped next to a glass and chrome table. "She's no longer human, and I have no idea where she is. I followed her here, and then the Time Folder took her to another location."

"Well, tell him to bring her back."

If only that would work. He was going mad without her. "It's complicated."

"Aw shit. Now you sound like a bad made-for-TV movie."

Nikolai crossed the room and grabbed her by the shoulders. "Why are you here, Aleksi? You didn't come looking for Elena or me because you had no way of knowing we'd been here. You seek the Time Folder. Why?"

She didn't answer, so he gave her a shake—a hard one.

She gasped, and then her eyes narrowed. "Remove your hands from me, Niki, or I'll slice your balls clean off."

With a curse, he released her and retreated to the other side of the room. He'd never used physical force on her before. What was wrong with him? Desperation—that's what. He'd searched for Elena everywhere he could think of, including her home and the hospital where she had worked. He was terrified for her safety and sickened that she had cut him off. But he had no right to take it out on Aleksi. "I'm sorry. I was out of line."

She slumped into a chair. "It's okay. We're both on edge."

He moved to a chair opposite her, and they sat in uncomfortable silence for a while.

"How bad is it?" he asked.

"What?"

"Your situation… Fydor?"

"Not nearly as bad as yours." She stood and paced the wall of windows like a large, lithe panther, her thigh-high boots silent on the carpet. "The shit is totally about to go down. Fydor's gone all comic book supervillain, complete with maniacal laugh and plans to rule the world." She stopped and met his eyes. "I'm scared, Niki."

He took a deep breath through his nose. In the centuries he'd known Aleksandra, he'd never heard her say she was scared of anything. "Why do you seek the Time Folder?"

"I believe all of this revolves around what happened between the two kings up there on that mountain ridge. I don't think they killed each other. I'm here to ask Darvaak to fold back to the fight again and see if he can figure it out."

Nikolai ran a hand through his hair. "He has already witnessed it. He, as well as the two other Time Folders. All of them say the same thing: the event has been masked."

"They missed something. There has to be a clue there somewhere as to what really happened."

"The real question is who masked it and why? There are only a handful of beings with magic that strong."

"The elves tell me there are only two: the twins Borya and Zana," she replied. "And both of them have gone missing since that day. One of them must have been there." She flipped her long, black hair over a shoulder. "A spell that strong requires proximity. Whichever one was there knows what happened because he or she cast magic that hid it."

Zana, Gregor Arcos' seer, was capable of great magic, but she'd never been involved with black arts or anything deceptive like masking a murder—at least not that Nikolai knew of. Borya was equally powerful, but worked freelance. Little was known about him other than the Itzov family had called on him from time to time. He'd only seen him once when he was just a boy. His uncle had called Borya for a conference while Nikolai's father was out negotiating with the wood elves. He shuddered at the memory. Dressed in flowing purple robes, Borya had looked at Nik with his jet-black eyes and ordered the boy removed. "He's dangerous. I will kill him if he so much as looks at me again," the sorcerer shouted, the ground shuddering in a magic-induced earthquake under his feet. To this day, he could still hear his uncle's laughter and taunts about the terrible, powerful seer being afraid of a smooth-faced boy.

"If Borya and Zana don't want to be found, you won't find them," he said, "And three Time Folders have gone back to the event and found nothing."

"They weren't looking for seers; they were trying to witness the murder."

He shrugged. "It's your money. Suit yourself."

She covered her face. "I don't have the money."

Of course she didn't. She'd been on a spending spree unlike anything he'd ever seen. A time fold cost one million dollars, nonnegotiable. "Then why are you here?"

"I was hoping to appeal to his..." She took a deep breath. "I was hoping he was a typical man and I could barter."

With her body, no doubt. Nikolai shot to his feet. "No. Absolutely not. Even if he weren't some kind of biological eunuch, I would forbid it."

"What on earth do you mean, 'biological eunuch'?"

"He only desires one person, and you're not it."

She turned back to the bank of windows. "I didn't know that. Pity. He's pretty."

He was sure his head would explode. "I suppose anything is preferable to Fydor."

She spun on him, crossing to come toe-to-toe, fists clenched. "Fuck you, Niki. I'm not discussing that right now. And I'm not a little girl you can intimidate anymore. That's what your human is for."

They glared at each other until he conceded defeat and looked away. She was right. That was what he had done to Elena. He had been an overpowering ass, which was why he was alone and miserable right now. He'd realized that over these last days. She wasn't like the Slayers and needed a different approach. And he needed her. More than anything before or perhaps ever again, he needed Elena Arcos.

Aleksi took a step back. "Do you know how to reach Stefan Darvaak?"

"Yes."

"Please do."

"There's a price."

"You sound like your uncle."

"And you act like a whore."

"How dare you!" Her punch to the jaw sent him reeling. "How dare you judge me for keeping you safe! Safe while you fuck a vampire! Who's the whore, Nikolai?"

He placed his hand on his aching jaw. "I did what I had to do."

"So did I," she shouted. "So did your mother."

He'd never seen her this worked up. She was usually unnervingly cool. It was as if he were watching a stranger. "What do you mean?"

"Do you really think she wanted to marry him? To…" She

shuddered. "She did it to buy you time to get your shit together and find the Uniter."

It had never crossed his mind that his mother had married his uncle for any other reason than it served her own purposes. For two decades, he'd convinced himself she had betrayed his father and turned her back on him. He'd looked at it through the lens of a selfish, self-righteous grieving son who had loved and lost his father. Not a man trained to lead his people. A sickening dread pooled in his gut. What else had he missed while he was off blindly slaying every rogue vampire he could find in order to alleviate his grief?

"She did what was best for her people. Now it's your turn. Pull you head out of your ass and help us. Fydor says your human is the Uniter. You said she's your fated mate. It doesn't get better than that, does it?" She ran her hands through her hair, moving it out of her face. "For fuck's sake, Niki. It's time to end this. We need to stop Fydor, and I need to uncover the truth about the murder."

Deep down, he knew the truth. Somehow, his uncle was behind the death of both kings. He'd just been too selfish and stupid to acknowledge it. Rather than take his rightful place as king all those years ago, he'd turned the throne over to the very person who least deserved it. He took a deep, painful breath. "What do you need me to do?"

"Other than make it right with your human so you can help her scrawny ass save the world? I need you to contact the Time Folder."

He collected the phone from the bar and dialed the only number entered. When no one answered, he left a message for Darvaak asking that he return to his penthouse as soon as possible.

Nikolai had no idea where he had taken Elena, but he

knew it would take a while for him to return since he couldn't teleport. Nikolai wondered if he would bring her with him, or if he had her at another safe house where she could remain hidden. He hoped she would come if for no other reason than he could see her. That alone would make him feel better. He had never needed anyone like he needed her—and not just physically, though *that* certainly kept him up at night.

He poured two glasses of Scotch and took one to Aleksi. She accepted it and sipped, studying him. They sat and for several minutes, remaining silent. He felt like such a prick. "I apologize," he said. "I had no right to say the things I said."

She shrugged. "I was out of line, too."

He set his drink down, stood, and opened his arms. She rose and stepped into his embrace. "I love you, Aleksi. I don't know how I'd live if something happened to you."

"Love is for humans and fools," she said, leaning her head on his shoulder.

"Call me a fool, then."

CHAPTER EIGHTEEN

Elena stared at the embracing couple in utter disbelief. Dressed in skimpy leather and wicked boots like something out of an S&M strip club, Aleksandra wrapped her arms around Nikolai's waist and leaned her head on his shoulder. His hand splayed across her bare upper back above her leather bra.

"I love you," he said to the Amazon in his arms. *Slayers don't believe in love*, is what he'd told her. *The liar.* "Call me a fool," he said against Aleksandra's perfect, silky, black hair.

Elena would call him a whole lot worse than that. Here, she'd been thinking maybe the Time Folder had been right and being apart from Nik—her destined mate, partner, whatever-the-hell-he-was-supposed-to-be—was wrong. What a crock. If he felt the same way, he wouldn't be playing grab-ass with She-Ra. She dropped Stefan's hand and growled.

"Uh-oh," Stefan said with a smile.

Uh-oh was right. And why was he smiling? Rage rolled through her, and she lifted her hands, focusing her energy on Nikolai. She had no idea what she was doing, but it felt right—as though all her anger had traveled to her palms. "Now," she whispered, imagining all that rage slamming into his big, strong, hot, worthless, womanizing chest.

Nikolai noticed her and made eye contact right before the bolt of energy knocked him on his ass.

Yeah! Better than teleporting. Elena refrained from pumping her fist in the air.

Aleksandra drew her sword and with a burst from Elena, found herself planted on the carpet right next to Nikolai.

She'd expected him to be outraged and furious, but instead, the look Nik gave her was one of awe. Then he grinned. "My God, you're magnificent."

Oh no. None of his flattering bullshit. "And you're an ass."

"I like her much better as an immortal," Aleksandra said, sliding her sword back in its sheath.

Stefan sat on the sofa, arms spread over the back as if he were watching a movie.

"Well, I don't like *you*," Elena said to the woman, before turning her gaze to Nikolai. "And I *really* don't like you."

When he crouched to stand, she raised her hands. "Don't."

His eyebrows cocked up, and he rolled back to a seated position. "She can channel," he marveled.

"She?" Elena took a step closer. "I'm right here. I'm sick of you talking as if I'm not in the room." Tears stung the back of her eyelids. No way was she going to let him see her cry. "Oh, wait, I can help with that. I'll just leave the room, and then you can talk about me all you want, because you won't ever be talking *to* me again. Have a nice life, Itzov." She met Stefan's amused gaze. "Call me when he and his…girlfriend are gone."

Before she could make it to the bedroom door, Aleksandra burst out in laughter. "Girlfriend? She thinks I'm your girlfriend? Is that what you told her?"

Elena wanted to send her crashing through the window, but balled her fists at her side instead. "I'm sorry. Did I use the wrong term? What do you want to be called? His lover? His fuck buddy?"

Nikolai remained seated with a look of genuine horror on his face as Aleksandra jumped to her feet.

"No blood on my carpet," Stefan warned.

Elena sent a massive charge to her palms as the woman approached in a walk that looked like a cross between stripper saunter and runway model strut. "Girlfriend? Lover?" Aleksandra snickered. "Fuck buddy?" She shot a look back at Nikolai, who dropped his face to his hands.

Elena's palms itched with the stored charge. *Come on, get closer and I'll knock you clear to the other side of the planet, bitch.*

Aleksandra grinned. "How about *sister?*"

The charge dissipated completely. Elena looked from Nikolai's covered face to Stefan's amused smirk to Aleksandra's shit-eating grin.

"Is this true?" Her voice was barely audible. Searching through all her memories of their interactions, she couldn't find evidence it wasn't.

"I'm afraid so," Stefan replied. "Allow me to formally introduce you to Aleksandra Itzov, Nikolai's sister."

"Then you're not... You haven't..."

"God, no," Nikolai said, lowering his hands. "I can't believe you even—"

"Oh, yeah, go ahead and blame me. You blame me for everything else." She was mortified and embarrassed and honestly, so mad at Nik she couldn't see straight. She thought about taking off to the island again but knew that Stefan needed a teleport back. She was stuck here, well, at least until their business was finished. She closed her eyes and imagined herself in the bathroom.

Nikolai let out the breath he was holding when he heard the bathroom door lock click. She was a channeler. Vampires couldn't channel. Only sorcerers could. Sorcerers didn't convert from humans by ingesting blood, though. And her eyes still had a red tinge, which mixed with the natural blue, made her irises almost look purple. "What is she?"

"I have no idea," Darvaak answered, "But she needs to be trained before she hurts or kills someone—perhaps even herself."

"What else can she do?" Nikolai asked, getting up from the floor.

"I'm not sure. The channeling is a new skill she's never exhibited before." Darvaak smoothed the tops of his linen pants. "And she seems to be gaining power as she becomes aware, sort of like a child acquiring speech. You should be careful, Slayer, she very well might be able to kick your ass." He turned his attention to Aleksi. "What did you need of me?"

She sat on the sofa next to him. "I need you to fold to the kings' battle again."

"I've told you there is a blank space where they would have been fighting. It has been, for all practical purposes, erased."

"Someone was there. The light elves strongly believe that the sorcerer who erased it had to have been there. Please go look for anyone who might have been close by. Go well before the battle and see if there is a person hiding in the forest."

"You know my price for this, yes?"

Aleksandra stared at her hands in her lap. "I don't have that much money."

He stood. "Then I'm afraid I have to decline your request." His phone rang, and he glanced at the screen. "Excuse me for a moment, please."

Aleksandra moved to her brother by the bar and brushed

the hair from his face. "You need to smooth this out with her. The Time Folder is right. She can't be just set loose to zap people at will. She should be trained. And if she's the Uniter, we need her."

Even if she wasn't the Uniter, Nikolai needed her. Seeing her had crystallized it. He had to get her back. He would earn her. Somehow, he would show her he was trustworthy and deserving of her. First, he had to get her to talk to him.

Darvaak's voice was just a low murmur from where he stood in the back corner of the room. His eyes were closed as the carried on the conversation.

"Fydor is planning something big," Aleksi said. "I don't know what it is, but the leaders of almost every faction have met with him at least once. Even the light elves."

"And Mother?" He leaned on the bar, trying to look more relaxed than he felt, knowing he'd misjudged his mother all these years.

"She hasn't left her rooms in over two weeks."

Nikolai closed his eyes and took a deep breath. This was his fault. His father had only been ashes for a month when she wed his uncle. And now Fydor had Aleksandra, too. It was as if there were a vise around his heart. He had to find a way to stop Fydor—to end this war, and Nikolai was certain the key to his uncle's defeat had just locked herself in the Time Folder's bathroom.

"He allows you to roam freely? Surely he doesn't know you're here."

She lifted her chin. "I'm a skilled actress. He believes I enjoy his…attention. And the guard he assigned to me is easily bribed to remain in my chambers when I teleport. I'm nothing but a vain, materialistic woman out shopping right now, you see. I will return with dozens of packages, many of which will be for the guard's mistress."

That explained where her money had gone. His stomach churned with worry. Fydor was not one to tamper with. If he found out, he'd… Nikolai didn't even want to think about what Fydor would do. He should never have turned the throne over to him. He should never have trusted him. His grief over his father's death had clouded his reason. "Please be careful."

Darvaak shoved his phone in his back pocket. "Three squads, one of tree elves, one of vampires, and one of shifters have attacked three of my properties. It appears your uncle has deduced my involvement with you." He walked to the center of the room. "Which of you will teleport me to the scene of the king's battle? It appears I need to evaluate it for my own interests. Four of my human employees were killed. One was a child. I will waive the fee. Take me there."

Aleksandra strode to him. "There is a kill order on Niki. I'll take you. Besides, he needs to smooth the feathers of his angry little ex-human."

"I wish you luck," he said to Nik. "You might be safer taking me, kill order or no. Elena's very hurt. Be gentle. Think, Slayer. This may be your last chance with her. Cord or no cord, neither of you will fare well if it ends badly."

Aleksi winked and put her hands on the Time Folder's neck. "In other words, little brother, don't fuck it up."

Elena splashed cold water on her face. The tear-induced splotchiness was even more dramatic than when she'd been human. "Oh, how lovely. Your hideous pink blotches bring out the creepy red hue of your eyes," she said to her reflection.

Aleksandra was Nik's sister. How had she missed that?

She hadn't. There was no indication they were siblings. This wasn't her fault. None of this was her fault. But in all fairness, it wasn't his fault either. He had never said he and Aleksandra were lovers. She had jumped to that conclusion.

The knock on the door made her jump. She didn't answer.

"Elena, please," Nik said from the other side of the door.

No freaking way. She was not going to make this easy. She had missed him terribly and she wanted nothing more than to rip open that door, but he wasn't going to get to rip open her heart again.

She teleported to the living room and leaned against the arm of the sofa to watch him through the open bedroom door.

He ran his hands through his hair. What would she not give to be able to do the same? "We need to talk. Things got all twisted around."

Yeah, no kidding. Like the truth, maybe?

He placed his hands against the bathroom door. "Just give me five minutes."

It probably wasn't a good idea to watch him like this. Obviously, from the heat rushing through her, her body forgave much more easily than her mind…or her heart. Her heart might never recover.

He bumped his forehead against the door and sighed. "I screwed up. I treated you terribly." He thumped his forehead against the door again "I need you, Elena. I'm sorry." He had said it too low to be heard through the door, but she heard it from where she sat. Even though the words weren't intended for her ears, he meant them. The fissure in her heart closed just a bit.

I'm sorry, too. She cleared her throat, and he turned and then smiled.

His eyes met hers, and the relief on his face sent a thrill up her spine. Then, a look far more predatory that made her toes curl crossed his features. "Clever girl."

"You've no idea."

He leaned against the door and crossed his arms over his chest. Big, sexy man. "Indeed, I do. You underestimate my estimation of you."

She fought back a grin. "How Dr. Seuss."

"I have no idea who that is, but playing doctor works for me."

Her heart slammed into hyperdrive. Sexuality at warp speed. *Whoa. Put the brakes on*, her mind said. *Captain, you've got the con*, her body shouted, dumping adrenaline and sending pulses to all the right places. All those places he'd touched and filled so completely that now felt empty and screamed for attention.

He simply stood there and grinned, as if he knew exactly what she was thinking and feeling. And his grin was beautiful. *Mmm. That mouth.*

No! She shook her head to clear it. It had to be the blood mojo that was making her horny enough to rip her clothes off there and then.

"Stop it," she said in an embarrassingly husky voice.

"Stop what?"

She gestured to him with one hand. "It."

"I'm not doing anything. I'm just standing here. Do you *want* me to do something?"

Yes. "No." *Yes.*

He walked toward her, and she held her breath. So hot. He was just so painfully hot and everything in her felt alive when he was near.

Stefan's words ran through her head. *You are separated from something you can't live without.* Maybe he'd been right. And perhaps he was right about setting the rules too.

"I'm not a possession," she said as he stopped only inches

away. "Or a subordinate you can order around."

Saying nothing, he stared at her with those gold eyes as if he were seeing into her very soul.

She squirmed under his scrutiny.

Light as a feather's touch, he ran his knuckles down her cheek. "You are so beautiful. Your skin, your new musculature, and especially your eyes." He placed his hand on her neck. "I didn't think it was possible you could be more appealing than you were when I met you, but you are."

His words threw her. She had to get back to the topic and not be sidetracked by his flattery and her body's impressive attempt to hijack her rule-setting agenda. "I don't like it when you order me around. You don't own me."

"No, I don't. But you own *me*, Elena Arcos. Whether you want me or not, I completely belong to you. Do with me as you will, but just give me another chance. We belong together and you know it. You feel it, too."

Her jaw dropped, and she just stared. Talk about a one-eighty.

He put his mouth to her ear. "But you *do* like it when I order you around."

She shook her head, trying to catch her breath.

"You like it when I tell you to open for me, or when I tell you to come. You love it." He ran his tongue over her ear, and she shuddered. "You crave it. Need it. Just like I need you. Our souls are fated to be together, and we are bound by my blood."

Hands on thighs, she was glad to be leaning against the arm of the sofa. If she weren't, there was no way she'd be upright. She'd have melted into a boneless puddle. She closed her eyes, trying to remember why she was supposed to resist him and came up blank.

He moved to her other ear. "You're wet, aren't you? So

ready. As ready as I am." He took her hand and placed it over the bulge in his jeans. "We are meant to be together. Even our bodies know it, don't they?"

She nodded.

He straightened. "Unfortunately, folding time doesn't happen in real time. He can spend several hours at the crime scene, but he returns to this dimension in only minutes. They will return any time now."

She held in a groan of disappointment. She shouldn't even be considering the things she was considering. They should be setting the rules for this relationship, not...

"But I have a plan." He slowly pulled the tie on her shorts loose.

"We need to talk," she said, hardly believing she could form words.

"And we will, after I tell you my plan." He nudged her feet apart with his, placed his hand on her abdomen, and slid it down inside her shorts. He met her eyes as he rubbed his fingers over her panties. "So wet."

She leaned back to give him better access, and he put his hand under the lace and slid a finger inside her. God, it felt so good. So good she might just...

His stilled. "Not yet. I need to tell you about my plan."

Her head cleared and the spasms subsided. *Shit.*

"Do you still crave blood?"

"No, but I'd like to make you bleed right about now."

"Good, then my plan is perfect." He began slowly stroking her again, sliding his long fingers in and out, and she closed her eyes. "Are you listening?"

"Yes." But barely.

"Then here's my plan. When we have more time, I'm going to bend you over a table and take you from behind."

Her whole body tightened at the image of his big, strong body standing behind her.

"That way," he continued, "I can rub you here"—he tweaked the most sensitive part of her and her breath caught—"while I slide in…" He pushed two fingers all the way inside her, and she groaned. "And out." He pulled his fingers all the way out, and she moaned. "And you will be in control and will tell me how hard and fast you want me to take you. And I'll obey your every command."

She was so close. The way he touched her. His smell. The deep rumble of his voice. All of it was just right. "Nikolai, I—"

He slid his fingers back inside and rolled his thumb over her, and she cried out despite her best efforts to remain silent.

He nipped her earlobe. "You don't have to tell me now. You can surprise me."

Right there. Almost there. No more holding back. Screw the rules. She needed this. She thrust against his hand, and he chuckled and struck a steady rhythm, bracing her lower back with his other hand. His mouth took hers at last, and she reveled in the minty taste and smell of him. Her angel of death was what she needed right now. And he said he was hers—that he belonged to her.

And now she understood why he'd said it. *Mine*, she chanted in her head as the stars gathered behind her eyelids and the pressure finally built until she couldn't stand it. *Mine.*

"Come for me, Elena," he ordered, and she obeyed.

CHAPTER NINETEEN

Nikolai wasn't surprised when Aleksi and the Time Folder appeared only moments after he had removed his hand from Elena's shorts. He was grateful they hadn't appeared a minute or so earlier, because he believed he'd gained some ground with her. One orgasm was worth a million words at that moment. It had been foolhardy, though. Before he had touched her, he should have thought to move her to the bathroom or another location. He needed to take Darvaak's advice and start thinking. Her culture wasn't like his. She would have been embarrassed to have been discovered. Now that she was receptive, he didn't want to blow it. He'd reached her body and soul, but now he needed to appeal to her mind. That was what stood between them now, and it was a substantial obstacle. She was smart. Brilliant, in fact. And he loved that about her.

"News?" he asked once the two had solidified from teleporting.

"Yes!" Aleksi said. "Both of the sorcerers were there. We just need to locate one."

Darvaak walked to the bar. "Drinks, anyone?"

When Aleksi strode to the bar, Nikolai caught Elena's eye and placed his fingers in his mouth and licked them. She gasped and he winked. That would get her going—that, and the idea he had planted earlier. By the time he had her alone again, she'd be ready for anything. Everything. And Nikolai wanted everything.

"I'd love a glass of wine," Elena said. "Red, if you have it."

"That sounds good to me, too." He put his mouth to his ear and whispered, "You taste much better, though."

She trembled with desire and he laughed.

Darvaak opened a bottle of wine and set it on the counter. "We need to give it a moment."

"So you saw both of them?" Nik asked, running his fingers down Elena's spine.

"Yes. I'd never thought to look for them before. They were hiding a distance from the site. They were not there at the same time. Borya was there before whatever occurred. Zana showed up at the end. I can't tell what happened while they were in the erased area, but I could see them outside of it."

"Erased area?" Elena asked.

He spread his hands out on the bar. "Yes, in the past, it looks like a bad Photoshop job. You see the men talking, and then they are rubbed out until the blur dissipates and they are dead in the snow. The area around the fight scene is clear and intact. I can't even walk into the erased area. It's blocked by some spell. If we can break it, we can see it. That would involve finding the one who cast it or ordered the spell, and convincing him or her to lift it."

"Or killing the one who cast the spell in the first place." Aleksi grinned. "I like that option best."

The Time Folder didn't react. "We must find one of the seers."

"Impossible," Nikolai said.

"Theoretically, very little is impossible, Itzov. Well, other than making you a decent, civilized being." He crossed his arms over his chest.

"I'm perfectly civilized."

He took in a deep breath through his nose, then arched a brow. "Not quite, but better."

Smartass Time Folder and his creepy bloodhound nose.

"It's my understanding that Gregor Arcos was almost never without his seer. Surely at some point, Elena saw Zana, Could maybe even give us a clue where she is now," Darvaak said, pouring four glasses of wine.

Elena strode to the bar and collected two glasses. Nikolai was mesmerized by her fluid, sure steps. Her immortality had changed her gait. What was she?

"What does Zana look like?" She handed Nikolai one of the stemmed glasses. He intentionally rubbed his fingers across hers and grinned when she met his eyes. She was thinking about his plan. He was sure of it.

"Zana is gorgeous," Aleksandra answered. "Drop-dead beautiful. Dark red hair down past her waist and skin like snow. I used to pretend to be her when I was a little girl. I even had a doll with red hair named Zana. Well, until my little brother beheaded her."

Nikolai lifted his glass in toast. "I was practicing for my career as a Slayer."

"You're lucky I didn't give you like punishment."

Elena's brow furrowed as she took a sip of her wine. She shook her head. "No, I never saw anyone like that. Dad never brought anyone home, and I never went to work with him... well, obviously."

"No one ever came to your home? No friends, no visitors?" Darvaak refilled Aleksandra's glass. "Because it would go a long way toward saving lives if we could find her."

"No. Well, no one except for my aunt, but believe me, she's

not a redheaded knockout. She's a middle-aged, crazy, eccentric cat lady."

"What exactly do you mean by 'cat lady'?" Darvaak asked.

"Um, an old lady who has no family, so she has a lot of pet cats."

"Shifters?" Aleksandra set her glass down. "Under the Veil, Zana had a whole cult of shifters at her disposal."

"Could be." Darvaak leaned closer. "Is she an aunt on your father's side?"

"I have no idea who she's related to. I don't think she's really my aunt. She's always just...been there." Elena's brow furrowed. "She lives next door and looks in on me a lot and..."

She drank the rest of her wine in two swallows. Nikolai knew she'd connected the dots.

Darvaak refilled her glass. "And?"

"And she's always been a little weird. Well, really weird, actually. She seems to know what's going to happen before it does."

"Because she's a seer," Aleksi said.

"And she talks to her cats. Not like, here, kitty-kitty. I mean full conversations."

"Because they're not cats," Darvaak and Aleksi said in unison.

"Holy shit. Aunt Uza's been deceiving me this whole time." Elena took a sip of wine, then muttered, "Why, that witch."

"Technically, a sorceress and seer, but witch will do," Darvaak said. "She must have a glamour in place to hide her true appearance."

Nikolai placed his empty glass on the bar. "No glamour. I saw her, and there was no trace of one on her. No magic aura at all. She just looked like a human—but then, so did Elena—to me anyway."

The Time Folder crossed his arms and leaned back against

the cabinets behind the bar. "Aunt Uza, you say?"

"Well, she has me call her Aunt Uza, but her name is Uzana."

"Zana!" the four of them said together.

"We might actually be able to stop this war." Aleksi sighed with relief.

"Here's to crazy cat ladies," Elena said, raising her glass.

Nikolai clinked his glass to hers. "And tables."

Aleksi and Darvaak exchanged confused looks, shrugged, then joined the toast while Nik enjoyed watching Elena flush the most arousing shade of red.

E lena had never noticed how many tables were in Stefan's condo before. Dining table, end tables, occasional tables... the coffee table. It was like she was under an I-spy-a-table spell of some kind, and invariably, every time she glanced at one, Nik was watching her. Then, he'd grin like crazy, and her face would get hot.

"Shall we?" Stefan said, holding out his hand.

"Shall we what?" She set her wine on the bar.

"Teleport to your home to talk to Zana."

Aleksi placed her wineglass next to Elena's. "I have to go buy some things and get back to the fortress before the guard gets antsy." She touched her brother on the cheek. "I wish you luck, Niki." Her gaze shifted briefly to Elena, then back to him. "Keep her safe. Keep us all safe. Especially yourself."

He pulled her into his arms. "Give Mother my regards."

She nodded, stepped away, then chanted some foreign words. Before a tear could breach the rim of her eye, she disappeared.

"Heaven help her if Fydor discovers her treachery," Stefan said.

"Heaven help Fydor if he harms either her or my mother," Nik replied.

Stefan clasped his upper arm. "You are doing the right thing. Going in there now would jeopardize any hope at all of stopping this war. You have to focus on keeping Elena out of his reach and yourself alive until you have a clear picture of the entire situation."

Nik nodded, pain clear in his face. And then Elena understood. Love was love, whatever his species chose to call it. This man was as capable of love as any human.

He took a deep, shuddering breath. "Let's go."

Elena's house looked just as it had when she left it: drab and out of date. Stefan was the first outsider other than Nikolai to set foot in it. The few men she had dated always met her out somewhere. She flipped on the living room light. "So you're sure Fydor's goons aren't going to come busting in here again?"

"Not likely. They can't track me though the dagger anymore."

"This is your father's house?" Stefan asked, walking to the fireplace to look at framed photos on the mantle.

"Yeah. I plan to fix it up, but haven't gotten around to it." More like with the bills and student loans, she couldn't afford to on her researcher's salary, but a time-folding Daddy Warbucks would never understand that.

Stefan gave Nik a pointed look, the meaning of which flew right over Elena's head.

"What?" she asked.

"Nothing," Stefan responded, picking up a photo of Elena's mother. "It's just not what I'd expected."

She put her hands on her hips. "What did you expect? Coffins and vats of blood?"

Nik coughed and Stefan laughed outright. "No. I expected a palace, or at least a mansion. Your father was one of the wealthiest men on this planet…next to me, of course." He gestured to the faded navy blue velour sofa and love seat. "This makes no sense at all."

"Maybe he wanted his daughter to have a normal life if she turned out to be human like her mother," Nik said, sitting on the sofa.

"The mother did survive undetected a long time. Perhaps that was it. Hide in plain sight." Stefan put the photo back on the mantle. "So you mentioned your Aunt Uza lives next door?"

"Yeah. Ordinarily, I'd call before going over, but I don't have a house phone, and I haven't seen my cell since the hospital. She won't pick up if I use yours. She's anti-stranger." She strode to the kitchen and the two men followed. "I hate to do this in the middle of the night, but I guess we'll just go on over, though she's always asks me not to do that."

"I can't imagine why." Stefan's droll tone made her chuckle.

Over the low fence, she noticed that cats seemed to come out from under every bush as the three of them neared the gate connecting her yard with Aunt Uza's. They'd always greeted her with ankle rubs, mewling, and purrs before. This time, they eyed her in silence from a distance, eyes glowing in the security light from her porch that shone into Uza's yard.

She pulled up on the latch and opened the gate. The cats tensed. It wasn't until Nikolai followed her into Uza's yard that they crouched and began to growl.

"Maybe we should wait over in Elena's yard," Stefan suggested, backing up several steps.

"They're only cat shifters," Nikolai said. "We can take them."

The closest cat growled low in its throat and then made an eerie howling sound. Two cats closest to the porch of the house slunk over and flanked him. Elena nearly screamed when they stretched and contorted, human skin visible in swatches between openings that popped in the fur.

Stefan grabbed Nikolai's shoulder. "There are ways other than violence. Let Elena make contact. We are strangers."

Nik shook him off as if he'd been shocked. "Fine."

She looked from the now half human/half cats in front of her to the street and back. *Holy shit.* The neighbors would call the cops for sure. Thank God it was nighttime.

"Calm down, kitty cats," Nik said, after retreating back to Elena's yard and closing the gate. "We're just looking for someone."

The first guy stood erect, pieces of cat pelt sloughing off his naked body. Yep. The neighbors were going to freak out for sure. She expected to hear sirens at any minute. Two more naked men emerged from their cat forms.

"Uza," she managed to say. "I need to talk to Aunt Uza."

"You were not announced," the center guy said.

She kept her eyes on his face, trying not to check out his thin, muscular form. God. She knew this cat, too. He was the calico that always sat in her lap when she and Aunt Uza watched *Dr. Who* reruns. She repressed a shudder. "I lost my phone."

The taller one closest to him spoke next, pulling the remains of the Siamese pelt from his shoulder. "You brought enemies."

She stared at the man's face. This was the cat that always rolled over to have its belly scratched. Unable to help herself, her eyes dropped to his ridged abdomen and then flitted back to his face. Yep. That belly. God, this was so messed up. "They are not my enemies, which means they are not Aunt Uza's enemies. Please tell her I need to talk to her."

"She is not in," the third one said. She recognized this one from the longhaired, bright pelt shreds at his feet. He was the big, blond Persian cat that cried to be fed all the time. He had a golden beard and was much stouter than the other two.

"Hi, Elena!" her neighbor, Mrs. Prescott, called from the sidewalk in front of the house, little dog in tow. She approached the chest-tall fence and placed her forearms on the top of it. "Isn't it lovely weather tonight?"

Holy crap. There were three naked men in her aunt's yard, and this woman wanted to chat her up about the freaking weather?

Ah. The cat boys were under the Veil. The women couldn't see them. But she could see Elena. Why? She was immortal now. "Um. Yeah the weather's great."

The small white dog at the woman's feet yapped, and she picked it up. "Was just giving Chester his last potty call before bedtime." The dog growled low in its throat at the men, and one of them hissed. The dog fell silent. "Your aunt and I are going to the Friends of the Library meeting tomorrow afternoon. Do you want to join us?"

It was bizarre to see all these powerful men put totally on hold by this woman wearing a terry cloth bathrobe and baby-blue Crocs. "Thanks for the invite, but I can't."

The dog growled again, and she set it down. "Uza needs to try to keep some of these cats indoors. The neighborhood committee has received a couple of complaints. She's only allowed to have four pets. And they need to be neutered and have their rabies tags, too."

The murderous expressions on the cat shifters' faces were so comical when Elena looked back she laughed out loud. "Yeah. Neutered for sure. I'll tell her."

Ms. Prescott nodded and wandered back across the street to her house, and the big shifter with the gold beard took several steps closer, growling low in his throat.

Nikolai's sword made a *shing* sound as he pulled it out of the sheath on his back. "One more step, kitty, and I'll neuter you here and now."

The man opened his mouth to speak but was interrupted by the slam of the front door.

"Well, run me down and call me road kill! Ellie baby is back." Aunt Uza grinned from her porch. She threw both arms up in the air. "And hallelujah, she brought a hottie along."

Elena looked over her shoulder and saw only Nik, and then Stefan straightened from where he'd been crouched behind the fence.

"Woo!" Aunt Uza wolf whistled. "Two hotties! You go, Ellie!"

At her puzzled look, Stefan shrugged. "I'm visible in both planes, but I cannot cloak myself under the Veil. I thought it best to conceal myself from the neighbor."

"Oh, speaking of concealing... We don't want Fydor's flying monkeys to swing in, now do we?" Uza raised her arms over her head and shut her eyes. A rumbling sound like the echo of thunder rolled in Elena's head. "There. You're undetectable in your house for a while. Didn't have juice for much else."

The shifters lost their hostile stances and relaxed, acting like it was normal to be standing naked in the yard. Maybe it was. Normal for Elena was a moving target these days.

Aunt Uza shuffled in her housecoat and slippers through the side yard toward her. "Why don't you sweet kitties go on inside and I'll be with ya in the span of a flea hop."

The one in the center nodded, and they followed her instruction, including the ones still in cat form lurking in the bushes and on the porch. As Uza passed the thickest one with the beard, she patted him on the backside, and Elena swore she heard a purr. *Holy crap.* Elena shook her head to clear it.

"Figured you'd turn up soon," Uza said, passing her and

opening the gate between yards. Stefan held it for her. "Ah, a foldy hottie. Good company, Ellie baby." She winked at Stefan, who gave a shallow bow.

Uza stopped and stared at Nik for a moment. "Mercy. I might melt." She grinned at Elena. "He's like birthday and Christmas dipped in Nutella and rolled around in powdered sugar, huh?"

Elena was too stunned to respond. Her aunt had always talked in terrible colloquialisms, but never about men before. It was a bit shocking, actually.

Winking, Uza patted her bouffant hairdo. "Is he as good as he looks?"

She could only gawk soundlessly.

"Better," Nik answered.

Uza laughed and shuffled to Elena's side door. Stefan rushed past and opened the door for her. "Good boy," she said with a chuckle. "Well, don't stand there with your mouth open catching flies, Ellie. Let's swill some bubbly."

Nik and Stefan followed her into the house, and Aunt Uza had them sit at the tiny dining table. She rummaged in the fridge and pulled out the cheap bottle of champagne Elena had bought last New Year's Eve. After her ex stood her up saying he had a family obligation, she had shoved it to the back of the fridge, and there it sat, just like her love life. Until now. Well, it was more like a lust-life with Nik, but there was always hope. His apology had been remarkable. He was remarkable. They just needed to find a way to make the differences between them acceptable.

Uza plunked four champagne flutes on the table and shoved the bottle toward Stefan. "Open 'er up, foldy hottie. The smokin' Slayer might break it with all that pent-up frustration."

"Your appearance is markedly different from the last time

I saw you, Zana," Nik said.

"So is yours." She winked. "The centuries have suited you."

The cork eased from the bottle with a pop. Stefan filled the first glass and handed it to Uza.

"What happened to you?" Nik asked.

Stefan passed a glass to Elena.

Aunt Uza smiled. "I hope for Ellie's sake you're better in bed than you are with polite conversation, little Niki, or I'll be regretting my decision." His eyes narrowed and she laughed. "Well, she's immortal and unbound. Obviously, you were able to pull off the minimum necessary, so lighten up, hottie-totty, it's all gravy from here." Uza held up her glass. "To the Uniter," she said. Then her brow furrowed, and she set the glass on the table.

Her eyes met Stefan's, and then his phone rang.

"You need to get that," she said when he made no move to answer it. "It's important."

He pulled his phone from his pocket. "Yes?" He closed his eyes and took a deep breath. "As always, your service is impeccable and appreciated. I'll return immediately. Tell Bridgette I will bring Aliana there as soon as things are cleared up, and I am satisfied she will not flee." He listened for a moment. "Thank you."

He put the phone back in his pocket and lifted his glass. "Where were we?"

Uza tilted her head and studied him. "You are an odd hottie. I figured that news would have you skedaddling faster than a kitty on hot coals. We were toasting the Uniter."

"So we were." He gave Elena a sad smile. "I wish you luck, love, and long life, Elena Arcos. You as well, Nikolai Itzov." He clinked his glass to Uza's. "To the Uniter." He downed the champagne in one swallow and set the glass down. "You know what I need, yes?"

"Of course I do," Uza replied. "Hottie needs are my specialty." She closed her eyes, and the air changed and charged with current, and then the glasses in the cupboards rattled, and with a crack, Stefan disappeared, just like that.

Uza turned her attention to Elena and Nik. "Well, I'd better go back and tend my kitties while there's a lull in the action. We're all about to be as busy as one-armed wallpaper hangers."

She stood to leave.

"Wait," Nik said. "We have questions."

She grinned. "And I have answers, but can't share. The knowledge is mine. The discovery is yours." She shuffled toward the door.

"Why can't you share with us?" He gestured to Elena. "This girl loves you."

"And I love her, but I don't love being in this form. If I breach the rules of silence, the curse will be unbreakable."

Nik blocked her way. "What is she?"

"She's a miracle. The joining of a vampire and any other species rarely yields offspring."

"Yes, but she's not a vampire."

Uza shook her head. "She most certainly is not. But you are a smart hottie. Figure it out."

"You know what happened to my father."

"So do you," she said.

"Did you cast the masking spell?"

The plates in the cupboards rattled again. "The one with the most to lose commissioned it. I don't deal with losers. Kill the one who ordered it, and the spell is broken."

"Fydor."

"For my Ellie's sake, I hope that tongue of yours is good for more than stating the obvious, hottie." She shoved him to the side. "You have about twenty-four hours before all hell breaks loose. Use your time...and tables wisely."

CHAPTER TWENTY

The look on Nik's face when he turned to Elena was nothing short of predatory. Thrill shot through her, and she flared with heat as if lit with a blowtorch.

Had Uza really said that? *Really?*

"Pick a table." His voice was just over a whisper—more like a growl.

With one sentence, he had bypassed any need for foreplay. She'd been picturing his "plan" ever since he'd whispered it in her ear.

"We still need to talk," she said so unconvincingly she didn't even believe it herself. The last thing she wanted to do was talk about his bossy, caveman ways.

"And we will. Later. Suffice it to say for now, I need you, and I want you, and the time I spent away from you was painful. I don't want to be parted again, and I'll do whatever it takes to keep that from happening."

"Shouldn't we be preparing for battle or something?"

He ran a hand though his hair. "We don't know what's coming. We have no way to prevent it or prepare. Zana told us we have a twenty-four-hour pass before something happens, and as much as I'd like it to, this won't take that long. Now, while

Zana's spell is still in place, pick a table."

Stefan had been right. This man was the thing that had been missing, and clearly, he felt the same way. Right now, her immortal body was screaming for them to do something with their mouths other than talk.

Her eyes shot to the small, round, pedestal breakfast table where he had just laid his sword.

He chuckled and shook his head. "Closest, certainly, but too fragile."

No. Not fragile. Not for this round. Trying not to appear overly eager, she picked up her glass of champagne and took a sip. Nik lowered the blinds over the sink and locked the door.

"Take off your clothes," he said.

Ah, back to bossy. Well, that was okay to a point. She picked up his champagne glass and handed it to him. He reached for her, but she backed away, grinning. She took another sip of her own drink and set it on the counter.

They were equals now. No more leash. No fear. Twenty-four hours of each other. Power surged through her, and she reveled in the hum and buzz and heat filling her from head to toe. He needed her. Longing was written all over his face. He would do whatever she wanted. And she wanted him to do everything.

The blouse skimmed across her skin like a whisper when she pulled it over her head. Nik took a sip of champagne. Slowly, so very slowly, she loosened the tie on the shorts he had masterfully untied earlier, but she didn't slide the shorts off. Instead, she took another sip of champagne and met his eyes directly. She didn't lower her gaze from his, which became more heated as she pushed the shorts over her hips and let them slide down her legs to the floor.

After stepping out of the shorts, she walked to the table to pour herself a bit more champagne, then topped his glass off as well. This time, he made no move to touch her. He simply smiled and clinked his glass to hers. "To the Uniter," he said. "And Stefan Darvaak's taste in lingerie."

When she'd first slipped on the sheer, pearl white lace bra and panties, she'd been slightly uncomfortable, but was glad of it now. She wasn't used to skimpy underwear, but could certainly appreciate its appeal. She felt sexy and powerful, and obviously, it appealed to Nik, who was rubbing his hand over the bulge in the front of his pants, smiling like a starving man at a feast.

She loved it when he touched himself. His unabashed sexuality was painfully appealing. And so was his plan. She strolled into the living room in search of the perfect table. The room was fairly dark due to the closed curtains and no lights being on. She flipped on a lamp. This time when he touched her, she wanted to see him. No more darkness or being cold. No cord or fear.

He had paused in the doorway to watch her. Reveling in her power, she ran her fingers over the sofa end table, pretending to consider it. She put some weight on it and jiggled it. "Mmm. Nah. I want something…bigger."

The low rumble of his chuckle made it hard to breathe. She paused and collected herself, then moved to the coffee table. She met his heated gaze and shook her head. "Too low. I don't want you on your knees…yet."

Nik groaned, took a sip of champagne, then, to her absolute surprise, dropped to his knees. "I'm already there."

She strode to where he knelt in the doorway and stopped right in front of him, then handed him her glass. "Don't spill." He grinned and held both glasses out to the side.

With deliberate slowness, she unlatched the clasp between her breasts but made no move to take the bra off. Nik groaned as she stood within inches of him, breasts at his eye level. He blew on her nipple though the lace, and her breath hitched. Her skin was so sensitive even his breath across it set her on fire. Through the thin fabric, he caught her taut skin in his teeth and ran his tongue over the tip of her nipple, causing her knees to almost buckle.

"You have a little current to you now, you know," he said, lips still against her. "You can channel energy."

Earlier today, Stefan had drawn back when he took her hand. She shifted from foot to foot. "Am I shocking you? Does it hurt?"

"Not at all. It's like you are charging my battery. Stand still."

She grabbed the doorframe for balance as he caught the edge of the clasp in his teeth and peeled the bra from her breast, then opened his mouth and took as much of her as possible in and sucked, rubbing his tongue over her at the same time. All day, she'd imagined his tongue on her—had relived their moments in bed in the cabin in her mind in thrilling detail. He'd made her feel amazing, just as he was right now. Unable to stand it, she ripped the bra off and presented her other breast, and he repeated the procedure until she pulled away, head reeling.

"I didn't spill," he said, handing her glass back.

Clutching the fragile stem of the flute, she fought for control. His pupils had expanded, almost pushing his gold irises to the edge. Forever, he stared up at her face, and she couldn't peel her eyes away. This man. This beautiful, immortal being wanted her, and she wanted him, too. Like nothing she'd ever experienced.

"Find a table, Elena. Now. Before I die like this on my knees."

Now. Yes. She was dizzy with need. The oak dining table was at the far end of the room in a darkened nook. No darkness this time. She flipped on the chandelier above and walked a full circle around it slowly, skimming her fingertips across the surface while Nik watched from his knees in the doorway.

She stopped and pulled the chair away, then slid her panties down and kicked them off. He stood, but made no move to come closer. Turning her back to him, she leaned over the table. "This one," she said, reveling in the power of her invitation.

Never, not even in his most vivid fantasies, had Nikolai imagined this scenario. Strong, bold, and borderline defiant, Elena had driven him wild as she played along with him. Now, she bent over a table completely naked, inviting him inside her. It was enough to make a grown man weep. But he didn't. He crossed to her and ran his hands over her beautifully presented body instead.

Her breaths came in fast puffs. It was clear she was ready and so was he. Hardly believing his good fortune, he ran his hands up her back and back down, sweeping his fingers through the seam of her ass and running them through her wetness. As he stroked down the insides of her thighs, then back up to her heat again, she shivered and made an odd noise somewhere between a moan and a sigh.

"Don't move," he whispered. "Stay just like that."

He tore his shirt from his body, then stripped out of his pants in record time. His urgency troubled him. He needed to stay under control. This was their first real time together with no agenda or ulterior motive, and he wanted to make it the best experience she'd ever had.

He nudged her legs farther apart and leaned over her. Like a homing device, the head of his cock found her opening and nudged against the wetness. She groaned and pushed back against him.

"Not yet." He pulled back slightly and ran his lips over the soft skin at her nape. "I want you to come first, so you are completely relaxed and ready."

"I *am* ready," she practically shouted. "God, Nik. You're killing m—"

Her protest was cut off short when he slid two fingers inside her in a hard thrust. "I'm sorry," he said. "I didn't catch what you said." He thrust again and she groaned. "Oh, you said you like what I'm doing and you want me to continue?"

She laid her cheek against the table and closed her eyes. It was so hard not to fuck her right then and there, but this was about her. About their future together. He would make sure she didn't regret giving him another chance. And when he was done, she'd have no doubt as to their bond.

He pulled his fingers out and dropped to his knees. He'd never seen anything as beautiful. And she'd turned the lights on purposely. He parted her with his thumbs and gently stroked his tongue across her. She groaned.

"Stand up straight, Elena," he said. Using her hands to push up, she stood. "Now, turn around and sit on the table, please." She did. He placed her feet wide apart, then slid her to the edge of the table, parting her knees. "Now, relax and watch me."

He touched the tip of his tongue to her, and she groaned. So receptive and responsive. She was perfect.

Elena gasped when Nik touched his tongue to her again. She leaned back a little more to give him a better angle, and he took full advantage of it, using his tongue and fingers to take her higher. The lights from the outdated, vintage sixties chandelier reflected off the crystal prisms, casting little rainbow shimmers across her pale skin as he worked to bring her more pleasure.

"I missed you," he said. "I looked for you everywhere."

She cried out as he thrust his fingers inside her and met her gaze directly. "I would have searched forever, you know." He ran his thumb over the top, and she writhed as a tremor shimmied through her body. Then he replaced his thumb with this tongue and set a rhythm that he knew would take her over the edge. She groaned and muttered some incoherent encouragement as her orgasm built.

"Don't close your eyes. I want you to watch me so you know how much I enjoy doing this."

Her eyes met his, and that was it. With almost frightening intensity, her body came apart in what he knew was a nmindless blast of pleasure. On and on it went while he slid his fingers in and out, pressing hard against the top of her with his other palm.

"Yes," he said. "Keep going. Say my name, Elena."

"Nikolai," she said, waves still rolling through her.

"Again," he whispered, pressing into her deeper.

"Nikolai."

Fingers still inside, he stood, and his mouth met hers, causing one more intense contraction to pass through her, leaving her limp and loose jointed.

Before the tiny ripples signaling the end of her orgasm had stopped, Nikolai pulled her from the table and bent her over it, gently laying her down, pressing her breasts to the cool surface. He skimmed his fingertips of one hand over her back while he rubbed the head of his cock against her opening. "Tell me when, Elena. Then tell me how."

"Now," she said, "Now, Nik."

Pushing just part of the way in, he reveled in the tightness of her body. Her contractions began again, just not to the level of a full orgasm.

"Mmm, you're still there. I feel you tightening around me," he said. "You don't have to wait for me. You can go whenever you want to, you know. Make the most of this immortal body you have. See what it can do."

She gasped as he pushed farther in and waited for her body to accept him. Hands on her waist, he pulled out and then pushed in deeper.

She moaned and pressed back, making it almost impossible to not simply give in to his body's instinct to take her hard and fast. *No.* He took a deep breath and calmed his heart. She deserved more.

"I need you," he said, barely in control.

He retreated several inches and looped his arm around her to where he could touch her. Then, he pulled out until only the head of him was inside her. "Don't ever leave me again." His voice was strained. "It almost killed me."

A shudder passed though her. "Nik, please."

He rubbed his finger over her, and she gasped.

"Yes," he said. "Come again. I want you to come again. And then I'll do what you want." He made tiny thrusts in and out as he rubbed circles over her most sensitive part, making her writhe and strain under him. "What do you want, Elena? Tell me how you want me to take you. Slow and gentle, or hard and fast?"

"Hard," she managed to say, voice and body tense.

"I was hoping you'd say that." But he continued with the shallow pulses and circles until she was gasping for breath. "And I'll comply as soon as you come again for me." He increased the speed of his circles and thrusts and then, without warning, pushed all the way inside in one hard thrust, sending her tumbling over the edge again.

"My God, Elena," he said, grabbing her waist. "I've never…"

And the man who was usually all talk was rendered speechless as her body squeezed his cock, nearly making him lose his hard-won control. "Now, Nikolai," she whispered. "Hard. Now."

And Nikolai was happy to comply. Again and again he slammed into her as she cried out with pleasure. She repositioned and gripped the edge of the table, her hair fanning in a gold sheet to one side as she laid her cheek against the wood, allowing him to see her expression on her face. An expression of desire that made him want to last all day for her.

"Yes?" he asked, nipping her shoulder blade as he slowed his pace in order to calm down.

"Yes. Nik. Yes."

He liked the familiar form of his name. It was like she had taken a bit of him as her own. Leaning over her, pressing his chest to her back, he reached down under them and ran his fingers around where his body entered hers. He groaned and flicked her clit, and she writhed. He did it again and then pressed against her as he moved in and out.

"More," she groaned. "Faster."

He maintained pressure with his fingers and increased his thrusts until she screamed and he was almost screaming with her. When her muscles contracted, he rocked into her even harder. So hard, the table scooted forward with each slam of his body into hers.

"Now, Nik! Go with me."

Before they shoved up against the wall, he did as she asked and came harder than he ever had in his very long lifetime. And as he lay sweaty and slick over her back, gasping for breath, he realized her request was much more far-reaching than she had probably intended. He'd go with her anywhere. His heart and soul were hers.

He reached up and entwined his fingers with hers over the lip of the table. And they lay there for a while, catching their breaths.

"Well, that certainly lived up to the hype and expectations," she said with a smile.

He slowly pulled out as she gave a disappointed whimper. He kissed her cheek. "Glad I didn't disappoint." He stepped back, giving her room to straighten up.

"Ha! Disappoint?" She turned to face him. "I've had more orgasms today than I had in the entire time I dated my ex-boyfriend." She took his hand and pulled him toward a door off the living room.

"Who is he? I might have to kill him."

She led him into an outdated bathroom with pale blue tile, pulled back the shower curtain covered in colorful fish, and turned on the water. "Don't bother. He's not even worth the effort."

Nikolai smiled, not only at her words, but at her demeanor. She was totally at ease even after the mind-blowing sex. He followed her into the shower and enjoyed watching the spray ricochet off her body and run across her skin in rivulets.

Then he noticed the angry bruises across her pelvis and upper thighs from where he had slammed her body against the table, and dread prickled through him. "I hurt you."

She picked up a pink bath pouf. "You're kidding, right? I was the one saying 'harder,' and 'faster,' remember? Turn around."

He wanted to purr like one of Zana's cat shifters when she rubbed the soapy sponge over his back. Then she scrubbed lower, taking her time and driving him mad…again.

"So, how long were you with this guy?" he asked, surprised by his level of interest in her affair with a human. Maybe it was because he couldn't imagine a woman this responsive not finding fulfillment with even a novice human lover. Maybe it was because he needed to know she valued him over this human. Certainly that wasn't it. He couldn't be jealous. He was a Slayer. Jealousy was for insecure weaklings.

She scrubbed down his legs. "On and off for two years."

He almost choked. "Two years?"

"Yep. Turn around."

She ran the sponge over his chest, studying him as if memorizing his body.

"Two years…" he mused. "Less orgasms than you've had with me today."

"Definitely. He sucked and I mean that figuratively." She ran the sponge lower, then systematically scrubbed the rest of him efficiently and effectively, and by the time she was done, he was so hard it hurt. "Rinse time," she said, taking the hand-held nozzle from the wall and rinsing his body. "Now, my turn."

He thought he just might die when she began lathering her body as if it were the best feeling on earth. She rubbed the sponge in circles over her breasts, and her eyes drifted shut. She even moaned when she scrubbed between her legs. By the time she rinsed, he was a total wreck. "Now, Mr. Itzov. You had me eye spying tables and crossing my legs all morning after you told me your plan, so here is my retaliation." She stepped out of the shower and wrapped in a towel. "I make plans, too, you see." She pulled a towel out of the cabinet and handed it to him. "Because we have a limited amount of time, and even though we don't know what 'all hell' is, we know it's going to break loose around this time tomorrow, I think we need to maximize our time together."

Nikolai couldn't agree more. Nor could his aching cock straining against the towel around his waist.

"So, while you had me thinking about tables, what I want you to think about is my tongue, okay?" She leaned forward and swirled it around his nipple. As difficult as it was, he kept his hands at his sides. This was her show, and he needed to give her the floor.

He swallowed hard as she unwrapped the towel around his waist. "So, I'm thinking after we eat something—because when all hell breaks loose, we don't know when we're going to get to eat again—I could use my tongue here, kinda like this." And she leaned over and circled the head of him with her tongue, but pulled away after only two passes. He groaned.

After securing the towel around his waist again, she pulled a brush from a drawer and drew it through her hair. "Yeah, like that, and then I'd see how much of you I can take in my mouth because that's a real consideration, seeing how large you are. Not that I'm complaining or anything."

"No, of course not," he said in complete disbelief as she strolled out of the bathroom.

"So, what do you think of my plan?" her voice called from the hallway.

"I…um. It's a very sound plan. I like it."

She leaned against the wall. "I'm a little sore still, but I guess being immortal, that will pass soon. Look, the bruises are almost gone." She opened her towel and showed him the fading marks along with the rest of her lovely body. What hadn't faded were the glyphs under her collarbone, and those turned him on almost as much as the red in her eyes or the thought of her mouth on his body.

Her gaze dropped to the bulge in his towel. "Are you thinking about my plan?"

"I am."

"Are you hungry?"

"Not for food."

She grinned. "Too bad. I am. Get dressed and let's go. I'm craving pancakes." And with that, she left him all alone in the middle of the hallway wearing nothing but a hard-on and a bath towel.

CHAPTER TWENTY-ONE

Elena shook her head. "You can't take the sword to breakfast. You'll scare people."

"We're in danger. I won't go without it," he said. "I should never have had it out of arm's reach this whole time. We're lucky no one found us." He tightened the strap one notch and checked the location of the hilt. "I'll put it under the Veil. I can put my whole self under it if you'd feel better, but I'd rather not leave that kind of signal and trail."

"No. I want a real date. Like two regular people going out." It was probably silly and maybe just an attempt to hold on to the last vestiges of being human, but she needed this affirmation.

"Let's just get something to go."

"Look, Nik. I don't know why it's important to me, but it is. I just want one more normal human experience before whatever is going to happen tomorrow happens. We've never done anything remotely natural or normal together."

"We've had sex."

"Was that normal, really?"

"It was natural."

"It was freaking *super*natural." She sighed when he grinned. "Please."

"It's nonnegotiable. Sword under the Veil. Normal date."

She shrugged. "Okay."

Then it dawned on her that she didn't even have her car anymore. It had probably been towed from the convenience store when she'd been shot. She sighed. That seemed a lifetime ago. They'd have to teleport. So much for a normal date. She held out her hand, and Nik took it.

"May I?" he asked. "I know an excellent all-night diner. I think you'll like it."

She grinned. "Sure."

He placed his hands on either side of her neck and chanted. Her mind rushed back to the first time they'd ever done this. She'd envisioned herself straddling him, and he'd been furious. She chuckled. No way would he have that reaction now. This time, she just emptied her mind and enjoyed the buoyancy that came with her molecules shifting for transport, then the slam of reconfiguration as they reached their destination. Nearby, a car honked. The warm air was scented with exhaust fumes and the faint taint of sewage. When she looked around, buildings towered on all sides. The sun was not even up yet, and already, the sidewalks buzzed with people.

"Where are we?" she asked as they stepped out of the tiny alley onto the sidewalk.

"New York City. You said you'd never traveled outside of your home state. I thought I'd put a spin on your normal date."

She took his hand, thrilled by this adventuresome, romantic side of him. "Cool."

"Cool," he repeated, grinning.

As they strode down the street hand-in-hand, Elena's heart soared. She was actually spending time with Nik like a normal person. Well, sort of. They *had* teleported well over a thousand miles in seconds, and the god of a man holding her hand had an ancient sword strapped to his back, used to kill immortal creepies. But still, since the convenience store, normal was relative.

The diner was fantastic. For fleeting moments, she could almost imagine "all hell" would not break loose in less than a day. That she and this beautiful man could just enjoy their pancakes and coffee without the fate of the human world hanging in the balance.

But it did hang in the balance. Since seeing Uza's cats transform into human form, Elena could no longer deny this bizarre, invisible world was as real as her feelings for this man. Real and dangerous.

"Are you okay?" Nik asked, finishing of the last of his scrambled eggs.

"Yeah. I just…"

The curvy brunette waitress refilled their coffee and grinned at Nik. He ignored her completely and took Elena's hand. "You just what?"

The waitress moved to the next table, and she tried to untangle her thoughts into a coherent thread. "I just wish we had more time."

"We have forever."

She resisted the urge to roll her eyes at what would have been a totally cornball sentiment had he not meant it literally. "No. I mean before whatever Uza alluded to happens."

"Ah." He wove his fingers through hers. "Well, I've learned to plan for the future, but to also live in the present."

She looked down at their entwined fingers. Hers looked so tiny and delicate laced through his. "I wish we could stay here, like this, forever in the present, not thinking about the future, but I really think we need a strategy or plan."

"We don't know what will happen. Planning is futile," he

responded.

"You didn't get where you are without planning and training. Because of your experience, you can adapt to handle any situation." She took a deep breath and realized she was trembling. Nik placed his other hand over their entwined fingers. "When whatever horrible thing is coming happens, you'll be able to act on instinct and training, while I only have ignorance. Everything is new to me. I need help to learn how to fight whatever is going to come along. If I'm really this Uniter person, I need to stay alive."

"I'll protect you," he said.

"What if you're injured or we get separated?" She pulled her hand from his. "I have some wacky superpowers now, and I need to know what to do with them."

The waitress returned and dropped the check on the table. Nik picked it up and retrieved a roll of cash out of his pocket. He slid some bills from the roll, put them with the check, and handed it back to the waitress. "No change," he said.

The girl's eyes widened. "Wow! Thanks. Thank you so much." Then she scampered off super quick, probably thinking he had made a mistake and would catch it.

"I won't let anything happen to you, Elena. You're too important to me."

Her heart skipped a beat. He cared. "Then you'll train me and get me ready?"

He stood and held out his hand. "I will." She placed her hand in his and stood. He pulled her against him in an embrace. "I want to show you something first."

"What?"

He looped his arm around her waist. "Well, you've never been to New York City before, so I thought I'd show you Times Square. It's only a short walk from here."

She adored this side of him. It felt so human to stroll from the restaurant arm in arm. The streets were buzzing with people rushing to work.

He guided her to the end of the block and turned left.

Then she saw them—three creatures walking in a huddle directly ahead. She froze, jerking Nik to a stop. "It's some of those things," she said with a shudder.

"What things?"

"The ones on the snowmobiles."

"Wood elves, here, in New York? That's impossible. They can't tolerate urban areas."

"Well, they've developed a tolerance, look." She pointed to the three creatures crossing the street one block up with a large group of people. They stopped halfway up the block from them, crossed the other side of the street, and looked into a luthier shop with stringed instruments hanging on display in the window. "Don't suppose they're musical, huh?"

"Not at all," Nik said, tensing. "Something is up."

Then, one of the glowy creatures like she'd seen in the forest with Nik exited the shop.

"And a light elf, too," Nik said. "Very strange."

The light elf saw the three wood elves and basically lost it. She screamed at them so loudly everyone within a mile radius should have heard it, but no one reacted. Obviously, the creatures were under the Veil. They spoke a funky language Elena couldn't understand, but pissed off was pissed off in any tongue.

Elena covered her mouth to prevent a scream as one of the wood elves pulled out a gun and shot the light elf in the chest. The creature shrieked, fell to the ground, and disappeared.

"Oh my God," Elena whispered. "They killed her."

Nik took her hand and pulled her back against the building. "No. She'll be fine. She teleported back home to heal. They just wanted to get rid of her. If they killed her, the light elves would eliminate every wood elf from the planet. They have some kind of pact that goes way back."

The oddest thing about all of this was that the people on the sidewalk continued on as if nothing had happened. They hadn't heard the gunshot. They hadn't seen the woman fall.

"So, has shit like this been going down my whole life, and I just never saw it?"

"Yes," he answered, never taking his eyes off the men as they headed down the sidewalk. "We should follow them. I find it odd they're here, but odder yet they're wearing human disguises. They plan to lift the Veil, and when they do, they are in violation of the code. I will have to take them prisoner."

She punched him in the shoulder. "Hey, big guy. Stop thinking like a cop. Who will you turn them over to? Fydor? I think your Slayer duties have been suspended."

"I can't let them harm humans," he said. "I wouldn't be able to forgive myself."

And this, she realized, was why she was so attracted to him. He was a good man who longed to do what was right, and something in her had recognized that from the moment of their dubious first meeting.

He placed a hand on her shoulder. "I guess your training starts now. Do you know how to cloak yourself in the human Veil?"

She shook her head. "I don't know how this Veil business works at all. I need a full tutorial."

"We need to follow those wood elves, so abbreviated lesson for now. If you're like the rest of us, you simply wish it so. Try it now. Wish to not be seen."

I don't want to be seen, she thought, and her body hummed for a moment, then returned to normal. "Did I do it?" That seemed ridiculously easy. She must have done it wrong.

"Test it. See if humans interact with you."

She approached a man speaking on his phone at the corner. "Excuse me," she said. The man did not acknowledge her. "Hello!" she shouted, waving her arms in front of him. Still no response.

"It appears you are successful," Nik said. "Let's go." The three wood elves had taken off and were about to turn the next corner.

She broke into a run to keep up with his long strides. It turned out that the creeps shot the block, and blocks in NYC were big. As they followed them around to the street that ran in front of the luthier shop, one of them looked back and met her eye to eye. *Shit.*

"Slayer," he called to the other two. One pulled a sword out from under his full-length jacket. The blade was much smaller than Nikolai's but equally ornate.

"Shoot him," the one with the sword ordered. Nik pulled a dagger out of his boot and shoved Elena behind him. To her horror, the man pulled a gun out of his coat pocket, but before he could raise the muzzle, he was sporting Nik's dagger in the middle of his chest.

An old man walked out of the luthier shop, and the elf with the sword went blurry for a moment, then solidified.

"Fuck. He lifted the Veil." Nik bolted toward them, but got there too late to save the poor human, whose head separated from his body with one quick slice from the elf.

The elf handed the sword to his companion and shouted, "Kill them both, and then find the cello," and sprinted away down the street at full speed.

Nik withdrew his sword, and before Elena knew what had happened, he freed the remaining elf's head from its body in a black, sticky mess.

Nik leaned down to retrieve his dagger from the first elf's chest right as his body disintegrated. He picked it up, and it was clean of the black blood. So was the sidewalk. In fact, there was no trace of the elves anywhere.

The poor human was another story. A crimson pool crept across the pavement from the headless body and oozed into the street. People screamed and shrieked all around. And then a woman came out of the shop. A young woman about Elena's age, wearing an apron, clutching a violin.

"No! Uncle Frank!" The young woman shifted her weight foot-to-foot, anguish filling her cries. "Not you, too. No, no…" She threw her body over his, violin crashing to the pavement and splintering into pieces.

"Take us to the Time Folder, please, Elena," Nik said, pulling her several feet away. He placed the wood elf's smaller sword in her hand. "We need to get there quickly, and you can teleport us much faster since I used so much energy getting us here. They saw us, and others will arrive right away."

She pried her eyes from the gruesome scene, took his hand, and pictured Stefan's living room.

Nik sighed with relief when he reformed in the Time Folder's place, holding Elena's hand. They had made it out safely. He knew he should have called first, but had they waited, the elves certainly would have come with reinforcements. Darvaak emerged from the bedroom wearing rumpled clothes and a furious expression.

"It's a bad time, Slayer. Zap out now," he ordered.

"We can't," Nik replied. "The wood elves just executed a human on a busy New York City street. Elena was seen. They will hunt her now."

"They are hunting her anyway," he said, looking over his

shoulder toward his bedroom.

Nik's radar immediately blipped. Something was wrong here. Darvaak continued to talk quickly. "Fydor has activated troops all over the planet. There's a huge bounty on Elena's head. Big enough to tempt even me, so get the fuck out of my house."

He'd never seen a Time Folder rattled before. "What's going on?" he asked, concerned that perhaps an enemy was in his bedroom. Hell, he could even be a hostage, as weird as things had gotten. "Who's here?"

"Stefan?" A woman's voice called from his bedroom. "What's up?"

He ran his hands through his gold hair and took a deep breath. "Put the swords away. She's frightened enough."

"Stefan?" the voice called again.

"Some friends are here. I would love you to meet them if you are so inclined." He shot a warning glare at Nik.

Elena, sword still in hand, lowered it to her side. He held out his hands, and she relinquished it to him right as a drop-dead beautiful woman wearing tattered clothes and way too much eyeliner appeared in the bedroom doorway. Nik knew immediately who it was. It was the Time Folder's mate.

Darvaak cleared his throat. "Aliana, I'd like you to meet Elena Arcos and Nikolai Itzov, friends of mine. Elena has just come across this antique sword and wanted me to appraise it for her."

Still barely inside the room, she nodded. She seemed skittish, which struck Nik as odd, especially since she was dressed all badass, like a heavy metal rocker. Something about wasn't quite right, and the Time Folder was way too edgy. Nik's adrenaline kicked up a notch in response.

"I have no need for this kind of relic. I suggest you try

museums. Thank you for sharing it with me. We are late to meet someone. I hate to toss you out, but we really need to leave. Thanks for letting me see the sword, Elena." He pressed his palm against the panel next to the door, and it swung open. "I'll just see them out, and I'll be right back, Aliana."

After the door closed, Darvaak took a deep breath. "I'm sorry. Your timing is awful. I had to extricate her from her hiding place among the humans earlier than I had planned. She is only just now aware of what she is, and that's bad enough without revealing there is a whole dimension she didn't know about as well. She's a bit angry and a lot frightened."

Nik got that. Elena had been terrified when the Underveil was revealed to her. "Well, finding out you're a space alien would throw anyone off her game."

"Wow, that's your life-mate?" Elena said.

He smiled. "She is. I need you to go away, now."

Hanging out with his chick was not nearly as important as what was happening under the veil. "They have begun to murder humans," Nik said.

Darvaak ran his hands down the front of his dress shirt to smooth the wrinkles. "My sources have been hearing buzz about this hit for a while. Elderly human male in New York, yes?"

"Yeah, but why would elves kill a human?" Nik asked.

"I believe it's the result of the grudge match between the elf factions this human's family got in the middle of generations ago. The kill order did not come from Fydor and is not part of the war initiative." He glanced at his watch. "You should seek out Zana again for guidance, rather than delay me further. Please leave now." He met Nik's eyes directly. "Losing this girl would be losing my life. I'm sure you understand."

Well, Darvaak was undoubtedly a dead end for now.

Hopefully, he would get whatever shit was going on settled so he didn't really end up dead. Poor bastard made it sound like his woman was in jeopardy. These alien freaks evidently would self-destruct if they lost their mates. Nik nodded. "Good luck."

"Thank you. And I might call on you, Slayer, to return the favor of my housing Elena earlier. Aliana's life is in danger. The threat is not immediate, but present, nonetheless. I believe I can solve it solo, but please keep my phone on you in case I need backup."

"Done." Nik held out his hand, and Darvaak took it, delivering a jolt of current that made his head buzz. He winced and withdrew, then rubbed his hand.

Darvaak grinned at Elena. "I've still got it." He clapped him on the shoulder. "Sorry, Slayer. Being near my mate kind of charges me up." Then his expression grew serious. "The intel rumblings are that something big is about to occur. No one is clear on exactly what is in the works. I sincerely suggest you seek Zana's counsel."

"We will," Nik replied.

The Time Folder placed his hand on the black pad outside the door, and it swung open again. "You both look well. Accepting fate suits you. I wish you good choices, Elena Arcos." Something in the way he looked at her led Nikolai to believe he knew more than he was revealing. "And you, too, Slayer. Think before you act. Appearances can be deceiving."

Yep. He definitely knew more than he was letting on, but before Nik could say a word, the metal security door swung shut. Conversation over.

CHAPTER TWENTY-TWO

"She's not answering," Elena grumbled, pacing the worn-out vinyl flooring of her kitchen for the zillionth time. She'd called Aunt Uza repeatedly for twenty minutes using the phone Stefan had given Nik. "She always answers my calls. Maybe it's because it's a strange number."

"Maybe she's herding kittens," he suggested from where he leaned casually against the refrigerator. "I still think we should simply go over there."

Uza's number rolled straight to voice mail this time. *Dammit!* Why wasn't she answering? A sickening dread coiled through Elena's stomach. What if something had happened to her? What if she *couldn't* answer? "Okay. You're right. Let's go."

She led Nik through her back door and stopped short at the gate leading to Uza's yard. Cats stared at her from everywhere: from the bushes, the lawn, the roof, under the porch, and even from inside the house. Gold, blue, and green eyes glowed and followed her from the windows. So many. Too many. The back of her neck tingled. There was a threat or some kind of danger here.

One of the closer cats growled low in its throat. Elena slipped the latch from the gate, and the beast crouched lower and twitched its tail. The growl got louder. It was going to pounce.

Nik stilled her hand on the latch. "They fight like their shifter animal even in human form. They will bite and scratch. They can leap great distances in either physical manifestation. Don't let their looks deceive you. Even unshifted, you're not dealing with house cats here. They're dangerous. You must be careful."

Well, crap. That's not what she needed to hear. She used to cuddle and pet these guys.

He leaned closer. "They won't be expecting you to channel. Zap a few and they'll back off. Cats don't like water or electric shock. Go get 'em."

The cat closest to them hissed, and Elena flinched. "Wait. Where are you going to be?"

"I'll be watching from here. You wanted training. Well, here it is. Hands- and claws-on training." He slid the latch all the way open and swung wide the gate. "You're on!"

Holy. Freaking. Shit.

The cat closest didn't even wait for her to move. It launched into the air the moment the gate stopped swinging.

Perhaps it was her new immortality affecting her reflexes, or maybe it was just being in a fight-or-flight situation where dozens of creatures with sharp, pointy edges were determined to shred her flesh, but for some reason, the entire scene seemed to clarify and divide itself out into a threat-based hierarchal schematic in her brain. She could anticipate who would come at her and from where... And it was awesome.

As the first creature flew at her in its feline form, she held up her tingling palms and sent it launching back halfway through the yard with an invisible pulse. It rolled with the impact and righted itself, no worse for wear.

Two more came from the left and three from the right, all

meeting the same fate as the first. That thing about cats always landing on their feet? Total myth.

She progressed into the center of the yard, fending off attacks from all sides as if she had Uza's ability to see the future. *Wait. That might be it.* Maybe she had some kind of wacky premonition ability or something, like when she'd seen herself teleporting before it happened. As a test, she closed her eyes, and to her amazement, she could see them coming before they launched.

And then it dawned on her; this felt right. Fighting and zapping combatants was, in some freakish way, fun. *Oh shit.* What a difference a little bit of immortal blood made.

"Enough," a male voice shouted from Uza's porch.

The cats fell back, and Elena opened her eyes and straightened from her fighting crouch. It was the thick guy with the beard who doubled as a gold Persian.

"That's enough." He sauntered toward her, completely nude, and stopped a few feet away. "My mistress cannot see you right now. And, had her guardians not been forbidden to shift, you would not be standing unharmed to receive that news."

Nik laughed from where he leaned against the fence. "I wouldn't be so sure of that. She was just getting started."

"Why can't I talk to Uza?" Elena asked. "Why were they told not to transform?"

The bearded cat guy glanced over his shoulder at the house, then jerked his chin in the direction of the porch. The dozens of cats filed toward the front door. When the yard had cleared, he looked around again as if not wanting to be overheard. "She's in a trance state. She cannot be bothered until she comes back to us. She is at her most vulnerable when like this. Our transformation to human form leaves a significant signal that can be detected by our enemies." He gestured to her house. "It is why we rarely shift at this location. You need to leave now. Your little electric show surely caused enough disruption to alert those hunting Zana. We will need to relocate her now. For your own safety, you should leave, too, before they attack."

"Who would attack?" Nik asked. "Who are your enemies?"

The man took a deep breath and shook his head. "Everyone is an enemy. All but the Uniter."

Nik's stance changed, and his hands formed fists. He spoke slowly and distinctly. "You must tell me this. Who hunts Zana?" When the man didn't answer, Nik took a step closer and pulled the front of his shirt open so that the shifter could see his markings. "It is my charge to protect the Uniter. Tell me now."

The man's eyes widened as he studied Nik's chest. "The Slayers." The man seemed transfixed by the markings. "And the Time Folders."

"You lie," Nik said, wrapping both hands around the man's throat. "The Time Folders have no stake in our affairs."

"I must go to my mistress. I must protect her," the man croaked. Then, he twisted and blurred in Nik's hands until he dropped free of his grip in the form of a golden cat with long hair. After a hiss and a flip of his tail, he sprinted to the porch and disappeared around the front of the house.

"Fuck this," Nik grumbled, stomping after the cat.

"No, stop," Elena said, suddenly dizzy. She needed to sit down. "Not now. Let's go back to my house."

"He's lying. The Time Folders are not a part of this war. They don't give a shit about anything other than themselves. We need to talk to the Seer."

She took his hand and led him to her side of the fence, finding it difficult to balance. "Uza will call when she's done… doing whatever it is she's doing." He was still offering a bit of resistance, so she tugged hard. "If memory serves, we had a plan before we left for lunch. I don't want to spend our time with a bunch of naked men and my crazy aunt."

"No naked men, huh?"

She was relieved when he fell into step behind her. "Just one." When she looked over her shoulder, he was smiling.

Hardly able to make the steps to the house, she sighed when she finally closed and locked the door behind them.

Nik's eyes narrowed. "Are you okay?"

She leaned back against the door. "I'm not sure. I feel totally drained, like my battery has run out of charge or something."

"All magic and power have a price. It's why Slayers rarely invoke the teleportation spell. It drains our energy. You've teleported today, and used a huge amount of energy fighting off Zana's guardians. It's good to know what kind of toll it takes before you actually do battle. I had hoped that whatever you are, you'd be more immune to the energy drain than other species."

She slumped against the door and slid the floor. "Evidently not."

He sat next to her and rested his palm on her thigh. "Vamps recharge though feeding. Do you feel a need for blood? Would it help?"

A tiny spike of desire shot through her at the thought of when she'd drunk his blood in the wagon. Her heart rate picked up and her breath caught.

He kissed her neck. "It would be very convenient for that to be a rejuvenating source. Slayers have to rest to restore energy, and it takes time." He took her earlobe between his teeth and gave a gentle tug. Her body tightened with desire. "If you can get energy back from my blood, that would be nice to know and exceedingly useful—not to mention fun. Let's find out."

"I suppose it's worth a try," she whispered, feeling oddly shy. She'd done so much with this man. Biting him again shouldn't give her butterflies.

He put his big hands around her waist and pulled her across him so she sat astride his lap, facing him. She wound her arms around his neck and kissed him. It was a gentle meeting, but it filled her with a surge of emotion. This big, powerful man was so tender and giving. "Nik, I…" *Love you*, she finished in her head. The timing was wrong. She was practically delirious with exhaustion. She would wait for a better time to say the words out loud. He tipped his head, exposing the pulsing vein on the side of his neck, and she felt her teeth elongate.

Mmmmm. It came from her throat involuntarily as she ran her lips over the side of his neck. She felt him growing hard beneath her.

"Yes, Elena. Do it."

And she did. Sweet, rich blood filled her mouth as he groaned and thrust up beneath her. Elena almost came then and there.

"That's it," he said, running his hands under her shirt. "Anything you want. Just tell me." He placed his warm palms over her breasts. "I need you, Elena," he whispered so quietly she barely heard it above the blood pounding in her head "I need you and want you with me always. Forever. I've fallen in love with you." With a jerk, she pulled away.

Breathing hard, she stared into his eyes. His pupils almost filled his iris, leaving only a tiny bit of gold visible. Had he really just said that? Before she could catch her breath, he kissed her so hard she almost fainted.

The phone at her knee rang. She wound her hands tighter in his hair.

He pulled away and turned the phone over. "It's Zana." His voice was ragged and deep.

"Ignore it." She leaned in and kissed him again.

He chuckled. "I can't believe I'm actually saying this, but

you must take this call. We need to meet with her to find out what's going on."

She glared at the offending phone as it continued to pulse with what was possibly the most irritating ring tone in history.

"Your timing sucks, Aunt Uza," She growled into the phone. Nik ran his tongue down her neck, and she shuddered.

"It does suck," Uza answered. "I might actually be too late. Now listen to me, Ellie, honey. You've gotta get out of that house lickity split. Don't dawdle. Some baddies are gonna swoop in and open a can of whupass."

Images flickered behind Elena's eyelids. She rose to her knees and then stood, too horrified to even speak as flashes of images filled her head. Nik was in a jail cell of some kind, chained to the wall. "No," she whispered "No."

"Now keep it together, Ellie darlin'," Uza's voice called through the phone. "You've gotta zap yourself to the place where your daddy took you on the weekends. I'll come join you as soon as the coast is clear."

Nik stood and took her by the shoulders. "What is it?"

Uza continued speaking. "Don't tell the hottie where you're going. They will torture him to find you. They might have a mind reader. It will be easier on him if he doesn't know."

Images of blood running down Nik's face flickered through Elena's mind. His whole body was broken. She shook her head to clear it. "No," she said again.

"Ellie, I'm not shittin' ya. Poof now or else this will all go wonky," Uza said. "You can't save him from this. You need to save yourself. You're too weak to take him with you. Honey bear, you may not have enough juice to make it there yourself. If you die, so do millions. They are more valuable than the one. Do it now."

Millions could die because of me.

"Elena…" Nik cupped her face in his hands. "What's going on?"

A helicopter thrummed close enough to make the dishes in the cabinet rattle.

"Shit," he said. "I can't get us out in time. The spell takes too long. You've gotta get us out of here."

"I'm so sorry, Nik." She took several steps back from him, breaking their contact. She could barely see through her tears. "So very sorry. Please forgive me."

Hoping she had enough energy to make it to the designated meeting place, she envisioned it. Before her body totally broke apart to teleport, two huge Slayers in combat gear broke through the door of her kitchen. Nik was so distracted that one was able to kick the sword from his hand. The other grabbed Nik by the hair and held a knife to his throat while the first reached for what remained of Elena, only to get a handful of empty air.

"Where did she go?" she heard the man demand as if in an echo chamber. "Tell us or you will die here and now."

"I have no idea where she went," Nik's voice answered from far, far away. "Hopefully, she's gone straight to hell."

CHAPTER TWENTY-THREE

It took forever for Elena's body to reconfigure. For a while, she thought she'd be stuck in a noncorporeal, molecular limbo forever, which honestly, might have been preferable to the pain that crushed her heart when her body solidified at last.

I don't wish to be seen. Taking a shaky breath, she wondered why Uza would pick this place to meet up. The sound of children's laughter and the calliope music from rides echoed in her head, mixing with the memories of the last time she had been here. Fortunately, the human Veil appeared to be working; no one around seemed to notice her standing in the middle of an aisle on the carousel with tears running down her face.

She slumped down onto a bench seat flanked by fiberglass swans and clutched her aching chest. Nik's voice in her head overrode the cacophony of amusement park. *"I've fallen in love with you."* She took a gulp of air as his last words he'd told his captors bounced through her brain. *"Hopefully she's gone straight to hell."* He thought she'd betrayed him. He believed she'd turned him over to his enemies.

And she had.

The relentless twirling of the carousel, mixed with the carnival music and pulsing lights, made her feel like she was caught up in a whirlpool. If only she could truly drown, rather than be suffocated by her own sorrow and regret. A sob racked her body, and she curled up on a ball on her side on the carousel bench. She willed the images of Nik to return, but none did.

She had nothing now. When her parents had died, she thought she'd suffered the greatest loss possible. Now she knew that wasn't true. This was as bad. Worse in some ways. It was like losing part of herself that could never be retrieved. "Nik," she choked out between sobs. "I'm so sorry."

She didn't know how long she'd been on the carousel. It had stopped and started with new riders many times when a loud pop came from somewhere nearby. "Well, howdy-doody, Ellie baby. Glad you had enough juice to not get lost in space."

She sat up and scraped the hair out of her face. Another pop sounded, and Aunt Uza appeared on the carousel swan bench facing her. She rubbed her eyes and did a double take. Uza's hair was so big that it looked like it had been teased all the way to the ends, and she wore a mu-mu covered in cats. No way was this woman the uber hot sorceress Aleksandra described.

"Peppermint Park," her aunt said, smoothing the front of her dress. "You used to love this place. Your daddy brought you here all the time."

Yeah, great. Just when Elena thought she couldn't hurt more.

"You know why, now, don'cha?"

What on earth was she babbling about? Elena shook her head.

"The sun! Vamp-daddy could stand rays, but didn't like it. Most vamps become crispy-critters with prolonged exposure to the sun, you know. Those movies get some things right." She gestured wildly with her arms. "Just look at this place. An indoor amusement park. Isn't it the cat's meow?"

The ride stopped and Elena's stomach lurched. She sprang to her feet and jumped off the carousel. No. It was not "the cat's meow." It was horrible. Nik was somewhere being tortured while she was in an amusement park with a sorceress wearing a cat mu-mu, speaking in ghastly colloquialisms. It was screwed up beyond belief, and she had to do something about it. Tears stung her eyes as she stormed for the front door.

Pop!

She slammed right into Uza, who appeared out of nowhere. They glared at each other for a moment, and then she heard it.

"Oh my God. Is that your outfit meowing?"

Uza grinned and stroked all the way from her neck to her thighs. "Mmm hmm. Couldn't just leave 'em." She winked and whispered, "I like my kitties. Girl's gotta get some tail, right?"

Shit. Her mu-mu was purring. "Stop it," she shouted. "This isn't a joke."

"Oh, so are you ready to get serious now?" Uza put her hands on her ample hips. "Done screwing the hottie and ready to save the world, are ya?"

"I wish I could screw him! I can't very well do that while they're torturing him, now can I?" And at that, she totally broke down. "He thinks I set him up."

Aunt Uza put her arm around her shoulders and led her to the snack bar. "Now, just set yourself down. You want a blue Slurpee? You used to love those things."

"No!" Elena plopped down on the wooden bench of the picnic table. Her chest ached so bad that she was sure her ribs were disintegrating. Again, she searched her mind for a vision of him, but came up blank.

"How do you know they are torturing him?" Uza asked.

"I saw it. I had a vision or dream or something."

"When?"

"Right before the Slayers came."

She tilted her head and studied Elena. "Were you doin' the

hanky panky?"

"What? No!"

"Don't get your panties in a bunch. There had to be a catalyst. What were you doing right before you had the vision?"

"Well, I… It's none of your business."

The entire building froze. The rides stopped, kids froze mid-giggle, and all around them, time had seemed to stop. Uza put her face within inches of Elena's, and her eyes flickered between black and the faded blue that was customary. "Now you listen to me, Elena Arcos. Without me, you would not have a fortune, a future, or even the shitty existence you've experienced so far. Every breath you take is my business, and if you get defiant with me, life's gonna suck so bad you'll wish you had kicked the bucket in that convenience store."

"I already do! I've lost him, don't you see?" She felt like the little girl she'd been the last time she was here.

"Watching millions of humans and immortals die will make losing your lover look like a trip to the amusement park. Joke intended." She nodded her head, and the world spun back into motion. Kids giggled from rides while their mothers continued to brag and gossip at the tables around them.

"You can stop time?"

"No. I can speed us up so fast it seems that way. It takes a lot of energy, though. Were you impressed?"

"Uh, yeah…"

"Good." She pulled a wad of cash out of her pocket and shoved it into Elena's hand. "Try to stay in the human realm. It uses less energy for you. Only use the Veil when necessary. You are part of both realms, but your natural place is above the Veil. Now get yourself together so you can save the world…and that hottie of yours. He's too yummy to waste if you ask me."

She took a deep, ragged breath and studied the cash. "What

is this for?"

"You'll figure it out. Now, answer me straight. What were you doing right before you had the visions?"

"I bit him."

Uza grinned. "Like father, like daughter." She winked. "Body fluids are the most common catalyst for seers." A loud purring emanated from her dress.

Elena covered her ears. "Ugh. Just stop."

"What did you see?"

"He was chained to a stone wall. He was bleeding and hurt."

"But alive."

Elena shuddered.

Uza shook her by the shoulders. "But he was *alive*, right?"

She nodded.

"Well, then. You need to get it together quick-like, because I didn't see him dead, either, and I would have if it were a done deal." She gave Elena another shake. "You are made for this. It's what you do."

"What do I do? What am I?"

Uza grinned. "You hunt baddies. You snuff 'em. You're a Dhampir."

"What is that?"

"Half vampire, half human—or in your case, half *almost* human. You're a mix."

"Wait. My mom was human."

"Sort of. Her great-great-grandmother had a little tooky with an immortal. It's why your mom could get knocked up by a vamp—they're the least compatible with humans, you know."

"What kind of immortal did my great-great-grandmother...?"

Uza looked away and patted her hair. "That's irrelevant."

She was hiding something. "No, it's not. I've been taken

prisoner, starved, frozen, and I'm not going to be lied to anymore. Tell me."

"You've been starved, frozen, and taken prisoner, but you've also been whoopied until you couldn't see straight by a scorchin' hottie, lucky girl, and you're immortal, too. You can thank me anytime now." She patted her hairdo again and smiled.

How on earth was she supposed to respond to that? She shoved the cash in her front pocket, crossed her arms over her chest, and clamped her jaw shut.

Uza shook her head. "You have all the pieces. Figure it out. I'm under a spell, missy, and I'm not going to be stuck lookin' and talkin' like this because I flap my yapper." She smoothed some hair behind Elena's ear. "Not even for you, Ellie Baby."

Elena's emotions were a tangled mess stuck in her throat. "Help me. I don't know what to do. I don't even know what I am."

"You're the best kind of immortal in the whole shebang. Dhampirs look and act like humans, but they can see beneath the Veil without being under it. In the good old days, every village wanted one because they weren't dangerous to humans and could spot and kill vamps."

"I'd never seen freaky stuff before I met…" She swallowed the lump in her throat. "Until recently."

"Yeah, that. Well, you had to kick the bucket first. That's the vamp side of you."

"So, you knew this was going to happen."

"Yep."

Elena digested this for a while. What if it wasn't fate, but instead, the machinations of a crazy old witch. "So, did you manipulate things? Did you send him to me?"

"No. Fate did that. I saw it coming, though. And coming, and coming, and coming…"

"Ugh. Shut up!"

Uza laughed, and her mu-mu purred.

"But you did this to me." She pulled her neckline of her shirt down to expose the top of the strange markings on her chest.

"It was part of a spell. Yes. As were the hottie's markings."

"So, he was only with me because of a spell."

"No. He was marked because of a vision. Because of his destiny. He was yours before I ever became involved or before you were born."

"I don't believe in destiny and fate."

Her eyes narrowed. "Then we are all screwed ten ways from Sunday because it's your destiny to save us. And I suggest you stop jawing and get moving."

"What do I do?"

"You use that analytical brain for more than feeling sorry for yourself and figure out where your hottie is and how to save his finely formed fanny. Start there. You should be recharged by now."

And without so much as a good-bye, Aunt Uza vanished with a loud pop.

Elena stared out over the tiny amusement park, and for a moment, she could almost hear her father's laughter. She had to succeed. For her dad, for Nik, for herself. A fleeting burning sensation flitted across her ribs and abdomen, then subsided.

A little boy squealed and ran by her, clutching a huge puff of cotton candy. Hell, she had to succeed for everyone. And just to think, only a short few weeks ago, her biggest concern was paying her electric bill.

Chapter Twenty-Four

The cab smelled like sweat and cheese, but Elena wasn't going to waste precious energy teleporting unless she had to. She'd gotten around the old-fashioned way for twenty-six years, and money wasn't an issue. Uza had handed her plenty of cash to live on for a long time.

"Should I wait for you again this time?" the driver asked, pulling up in front of the sporting goods store.

"Yeah, I'll only be a few minutes."

She dashed into the store and ripped warm-up pants, a running shirt, and fleece from the racks. Then, she grabbed a pair of running shoes and a ski jacket with a hood. A backpack, a huge box of protein bars, and a pair of fleece-lined Gore-Tex boots, and she was set. She wasn't going to freeze or starve this time, she told herself at checkout.

"Okay, now to the airport, please."

"Terminal?"

"International flights," she answered.

Then her stomach flipped. Well, crap. She hadn't thought this all the way through. She didn't want to teleport to the Slayer fortress in the Carpathian Mountains because it would use a ton of her energy, but she didn't have a passport or even her driver's license. She could call Stefan! She still had his phone in her pocket… No. That wouldn't work, either. He was right in the middle of some crisis himself, and besides, she was a bit leery of him since the cat guy said Time Folders were Uza's enemies.

How could she get on that plane? And then she grinned. She grinned so wide it almost hurt. She would cloak herself under the Veil to get through security and then onto the plane. Surely that wouldn't use that much energy. Certainly not as much as teleporting thousands of miles.

After sliding off her flats and replacing them with the new running shoes, she stuffed the protein bars and warm clothes into the backpack. She also zipped the phone and most of the cash into an inner pocket. The remainder of the cash was divided between her pants pocket and the pocket in the lining of her coat along with a couple of protein bars. She had no idea what she was getting into, but she wasn't going to be unprepared this time.

She stepped out of the cab, certain that Nik was alive. She just knew it, and if all went well, she'd have him free soon. And when she did, she was going to tell him how she felt. He'd said he had fallen in love with her. No matter how mad he was right now, once he found out she hadn't really betrayed him, he'd come back around… She hoped.

First, though, she needed to navigate the huge, intimidating airport. She scanned the boards and found a flight landing in Bucharest. Even with a direct flight, she'd be stuck on the plane for thirteen hours—a waste of precious time, but at least she'd be fully charged when she landed. The thought of Nik being tortured, like in her visions, made her want to teleport, but she knew she had to play it smart. She hadn't seen him dead, and she had to hold out hope that she was truly seeing his future, horrible though it was. He was immortal and would heal.

Before she approached the security gate, she ducked behind a support beam and wished herself to not be seen. The same buzzing she'd experienced when she cloaked herself in New York hummed through her bones. This time, she was certain it had worked, but out of an abundance of caution, she stepped out from behind the column and cleared her throat as a man with a briefcase and wearing a suit walked by. He didn't even look her way. Just to be sure, and because she was buzzed with adrenaline, she lifted her shirt like a spring breaker at Mardi Gras. As expected, the man kept on striding toward the security line. Not that he'd have gotten a real shock; she had on a sports bra, but there was no doubt in her mind now that she was invisible to humans.

"Very nice," a familiar voice said from behind her. She lowered her shirt, forcing her fingers to unclench from the hem.

"Going somewhere, yes?"

Shit. "Hey, Stefan." She pivoted to face him, every hair on end.

His gaze shot over her shoulder and then back to her face. She fought the urge to turn around. "Where is Aliana?"

"She is in Greece. She…" He took a shuddering breath, and his brow furrowed. "She is with the others of my kind."

Nik had said there were two others on the planet. That they could not be parted from their mates. "Why?"

"To save us—me. It is complicated. But none of it will matter if you fail. I have come to be sure that doesn't happen." When she didn't respond, his eyes narrowed. "Please remove the human Veil. I live in the human plane, and though I can see under the Veil, I can't cloak myself. Right now, it looks as though I am speaking to the air." She didn't respond or comply. "Please. I am here to help you."

She didn't budge.

"You have lost trust in me." He took a deep breath and ran his fingers through his hair. "I have no intention of hurting you. I do not play games and am unable to lie effectively. Conserve your energy. Step behind the column again and lift the Veil."

He was right about using up energy. She might need it to defend herself sooner than she thought. She stepped behind the column so no human could see her remove the Veil and did as he asked. "How did you find me?"

"You carry my phone, yes?"

"Yeah, but you said it was untraceable."

"By others. Not by me." His expression was smug and unnerving.

She backed up a couple of steps. If she screamed, one of the security guards would surely respond.

He put his hands up as if he were calming a frightened animal. "I have an interest in your success, Elena Arcos. My own existence depends on it."

Aunt Uza's shifters said the Time Folders were enemies. "I don't trust you."

"As well you should not. Trust no one but your own instinct. But know this: were I the enemy, you would have been dead the first time you appeared in my home." He glanced over his shoulder, and this time Elena looked, too. The woman from his condo, Margarita, was there with a tall, well-dressed man with jet-black hair wearing sunglasses.

From the way people stared as they passed, she knew they were not under the Veil. Stefan gestured for them to approach, and as they got closer, her heart raced. If she were taken captive or died now, Nik didn't stand a chance. She focused on concentrating electricity in her palms just in case.

Margarita smiled. "I'm happy to meet again, Elena Arcos.

Good to see you converted to your true form." She gestured to the man next to her. "This is my brother, Ricardo."

This was the rebel leader—the one who had picked up her father's cause after he died. The man slid off his sunglasses, and she met his piercing, blood-red gaze. "An honor," he said. His voice was as smooth and slick as his appearance.

She stared at him in awkward silence, waiting to find out what their objective was in coming to intercept her. The charge in her palms tingled.

The man searched her face with his unnerving crimson eyes, then took her chin in his fingers. She stood stock still as he stared into her eyes. "Fascinating," he said. "There hasn't been a Dhampir born in at least a century."

"There are others?" she asked, barely above a whisper as he continued to study her eyes.

"Not anymore. The Revolutionists slaughtered every last one."

"The Revolutionists are the factions of immortals who want the war in order to take power over the human world. They are Fydor's followers, though that is a bit simplistic," Stefan supplied.

Ricardo released Elena's chin and put his sunglasses back on, then turned to Stefan. "You say she is Arcos's offspring, but have no proof, Darvaak. It's clear she's a Dhampir, but I need evidence she's truly the Uniter before I rally my people."

Stefan remained very still and calm. "I told you she bears the mark."

"Look, guys. I hate to cut you short, but I need to catch a plane right away...like yesterday." She took off toward the security lines. Ricardo grabbed her by the arm. She placed her hand on his shoulder and released the current stored in her palm. He recoiled but made no sound.

Elena expected him to charge her, but instead, he just

rubbed his shoulder. "Conserve energy. I'm not your enemy," he said.

"Don't grab me again."

He nodded.

"Please, Ricardo," Margarita said.

"Not until I see it."

"My word isn't good enough?" Stefan asked from where he leaned casually against the column.

"No. You could be like the others of your kind. No one's word is good enough."

"Oh, shut up," Elena said. "I'm kind of in a hurry, and your squabbling is holding me back. What is it you want to see? The markings?"

Ricardo nodded.

Elena tugged at her T-shirt neckline, but it was too tight to show much of anything. Damn. She wished herself cloaked in the Veil, hoping she'd done it right. If not, she'd be giving some travelers and tourists something to write home about. She slid the backpack off and set it at her feet, then ripped off her shirt. "Yeah?" she asked.

"Yeah," Ricardo answered. "Almost."

Almost? *Oh. The sports bra.* It covered a majority of the glyphs. Damn.

Human modesty," Stefan said with a shrug and a half smile. "You had seemed to have gotten over it when I first arrived."

After she scanned the area, it was clear from the men and women walking by without a glance that she was truly invisible because a shirtless woman in a hot pink sports bra would probably draw at least a little attention. Fine. She needed to put an end to this so that she could save Nik. She pulled off the bra and gritted her teeth when her breasts bounced.

Ricardo took off his sunglasses and made some kind of

appreciative, growly sound. If it had it gone on any longer or been any louder, she would have shocked him into the next county. "Well, you are right, Darvaak. She is without a doubt the Uniter."

"Isn't that interesting?" Stefan said, circling to face her, eyes sweeping over her chest.

Yeah. My boobs are real interesting, asshole.

"Look down, Elena."

She did. *Holy shit.* There were more of the odd shapes. They now expanded across her ribs and down to her navel. She gasped and met Stefan's clear blue eyes. "What the hell?"

"What, indeed," he remarked, still studying the markings.

She leaned over and grabbed her bra from the floor and yanked it on. "Spill, Stefan."

He lightly ran his fingers over the markings across her ribs, and a grin crept across his face as he traced them to her navel. His touch wasn't sexual, but affectionate. Reverent, almost. He splayed his hand across her abdomen and spoke in a strange language.

"Stefan! What the hell is going on?"

He opened his eyes and took her face in his hands. "Sweet girl. I am asking the powers that be to protect the child you carry."

CHAPTER TWENTY-FIVE

Elena rolled the words written on skin over in her head. "Guardian of the bridge between species above and below the Veil." The child she carried was the "bridge," Stefan had explained. Evidently, the meaning was clear in whatever freakish tongue the glyphs were written. She may be the Uniter who was prophesied to dethrone tyrants, but the child was the key to long-term peace.

She shook her head in disbelief. This was a real game-changer. She couldn't just go blasting in there and risk her life to save Nik. She had to be careful now.

From her seat in the back of the plane, she pressed her palm to her stomach. Margarita patted her hand. "It is a good thing. A miracle."

Yeah, no shit. Miracle was right. She wasn't supposed to be able to get pregnant with someone from another species. Like cats and dogs, right? If she lived through this, she had a few words for Aleksandra and her absolutes. She rolled her shoulders and took a deep breath. And then, in spite of herself, she smiled. Nik's baby. She'd never really thought about having kids—she'd never met anyone whose kids she wanted to have… until now. Her heart stuttered. Nik's baby was growing inside her right now. And that was *awesome.*

Stefan and Ricardo were in the cockpit. Had Stefan not laid this little bit of news on her, she would never have agreed to let him fly her. She would have done this on her own and owed a debt to no one. Somehow, that didn't matter anymore. What mattered now was keeping this baby safe while rescuing Nik, offing Fydor, and ending this war, regardless of how many favors she'd owe when it was over.

Stefan walked back and joined them in a seat facing across a table.

"Who's flying this thing?" Elena squeaked.

He smiled and relaxed against the back of the seat. "This plane practically flies itself. We are over the ocean on a straight course. Relax."

Planes didn't fly themselves. "I don't like this."

"You are immortal. You would survive a crash, though that will not happen, I promise. I only want to speak with you for a moment."

"Could we talk with you back at the controls?"

"If you would feel more at ease, then, yes. Please join me."

He held out his hand, and she took it. He squeezed. "You still have a charge in your palms. Do you feel threatened?"

"No." She followed him to the cockpit. Not threatened. Just terrified. Terrified of everything. Of failure. Of losing Nik. Of somehow losing this baby.

She perched on the little jump seat behind the two pilot chairs, probably intended for a flight attendant or assistant of some kind. The panel had tons of controls and knobs that would be impossible to keep straight. "What did you want to talk about?"

"Fuel."

"Oh God. Do we have enough?"

"Not for the plane. Fuel for you."

"Oh no. I'm great. I have a whole box of protein bars. Thanks."

Ricardo turned in the copilot's chair to face her. "You know exactly what he's asking. I'm not nearly as polite and polished as the Time Folder, so allow me to clarify. You are a Dhampir. You don't need blood to live, but it fuels your powers. You need as much power as possible before we land. We don't know what you will face at the fortress."

Oh God. There was no way she could do this. She wasn't some superhero Uniter thingy. She was just a woman. One frightened, confused woman who was powerless to face a foe she didn't even understand.

"You are far more than that," he said. "You may be confused, but you are far from powerless, and you absolutely can do this. You are the Uniter destined to stop the war."

Holy shit, could he read her mind?

"Yes, I can."

Fuck.

"I can do that, too." He laughed, and despite herself, she laughed along with him. It felt good to laugh. Stefan smiled, shook his head, and stared out at the blank nothingness through the windshield.

"Okay then, what about fuel did you want to tell me?" she asked.

"You need some," Ricardo answered. "You need blood. You need mine."

Wait. No. She couldn't. She went all horny and practically dived into Nik's pants the last time she drank blood. "I can't."

"It won't be that way with me. I'm not your mate." He waited for her to calm down a bit. "It was his blood that changed you. No one will hold the same appeal for you. You've nothing to fear."

Stefan shifted uncomfortably in the captain's chair and cleared his throat.

"Well, someone doesn't agree with you."

Ricardo glared at Stefan, and she knew it was true. Something was up.

"Nothing is up," he said. "The Time Folder is not worried about you. He's worried about me. I'm the one likely to lose control. I don't have a mate, and vampires are not like elves and Time Folders. We have multiple options. Like humans, our mates come by choice, not destiny, though once we make our choice, it is firm."

"Why not Stefan?"

"He's of a race not even of this world. It won't fuel you."

"Margarita?"

"She is centuries younger, and her blood is not as fortifying."

She took him in from his Italian designer shoes to his perfectly tailored suit, to his blood-red shirt that matched his eyes and his jet-black jacket as dark as his hair. What, she wondered, would happen if he lost control?

"I would bite you back. In a bloodlust, I would react much the same way you react with your mate." He grinned, showing perfectly white, straight teeth and sharp fangs. "I would…how did you so eloquently put it? Ah, 'go all horny and practically dive into your pants.'"

Uh-oh.

"Yes, exactly. But there are measures we can take. And I really need to teach you how to block your thoughts."

"Can't you just cut yourself and put it in a glass or something?"

"Straight from the vein, or it has no potency at all."

Before long, Ricardo was strapped to a chair in the cabin and bound with netting Stefan said was used to secure loose items being transported. It all seemed a little excessive to Elena, but all of this was new to her, so she just stood back while Margarita tied one last knot in the rope around the vampire's arms, then put a large silver cuff over each wrist. Stefan sat on the edge of the seat facing them.

"The neck is the best location. The fastest. And do me a favor," Ricardo added. "Think of something awful. Something other than your mate or me or what you are doing. Think of paint drying or something utterly boring, okay?"

"Can't you turn the mind-reading thing off?"

"Sadly, no. But I can't read everyone's mind. Time Folders and Slayers for example, are immune."

"But you can hear me all the time?"

"Like a bullhorn in my brain, baby."

Shit.

"Exactly. Now, let's get this over with."

His voice was tinged with a Spanish accent that was appealing. And as she got closer, she noticed he smelled like starch and clean linen.

"Stop it. You hate my voice, and I smell bad. Like horse manure."

And soap and shaving cream. The blood pulsed just under the surface of his skin, and her body approved with a sharp pulsing of her canine teeth.

"I am so screwed," he groaned.

She leaned down, but for some reason, despite the aching in her teeth, she couldn't go through with it.

"Do it now," he ordered.

Nik. She would do this for Nik. She had to be strong to save Nik and the baby.

"And your people," Ricardo added. "And stop thinking

about him. Think about drying paint and do it."

She bit down hard and he gasped. His blood didn't taste like Nik's. It was more metallic. Still, it felt amazing as it charged straight to her veins. This couldn't be right. She didn't want to be unfaithful to Nik. This was wrong.

"No. Don't stop. You're not cheating. You're not fucking me. You're getting strong so you can save the guy you want to fuck."

He had that right. Boring thoughts... Drying paint. Being stuck in traffic. Logging entries in the research journal. Looking at slides through a microscope. Vacuuming the blue velour sofas. Folding clothes.

His body relaxed, and she kept monotonous thoughts running through her head. And then, the visions started. Nik was chained by his ankles and wrists to a stone wall like out of some medieval horror movie, being questioned by a huge Slayer wearing black leather. The Slayer held a club like the kind cops used. She couldn't hear anything, like watching TV with the volume turned off, but the man would talk, and when Nik didn't answer, he would hit him in the head with the club. Over and over and over, he slammed the club into Nik's head until blood ran from his nose and mouth and his body went limp. Then he turned to talk to someone else in the room.

"Enough," Ricardo whispered from far, far away. "Stop now, Elena."

Like an app being closed in her brain, the images stopped. Still latched on to his neck, her current reality replaced the horror she had just seen. She pulled away and her canine teeth retracted. "I'm so sorry."

"Are you okay?" he asked. "Your thoughts were a jumble. All I got was no, no, no."

She stared down at the bound vampire, still horrified by what she'd seen in the vision. Before her eyes, the marks on

Ricardo's neck closed and faded. Nik was immortal. His wounds would fade, too, if she could get there in time.

"She has visions. She saw him beaten," the vampire said, obviously hearing her thoughts. "Only seers can see the present or future. It is not a Dhampir ability at all. What the hell is she?"

The two men exchanged glances.

"What did you see, Elena?" Stefan asked in a calm, soothing voice across from where Ricardo was bound to the seat.

"They are torturing him." Her voice was so low she wasn't sure she had said it out loud.

"Of course they are," Ricardo said. "That's not helpful information. What else did you see?"

"Nothing. Only another Slayer—huge with long, black hair. He was beating him." Elena shuddered. "And there was someone else in the room. Someone I didn't see."

"He will survive a beating. He has many times," Stefan said, taking her hand.

"Let me out of this chair. I need to teach her how to mask her thoughts. I have a suspicion of who the third person was. Let me out now!" Ricardo demanded. Margarita removed the silver cuffs, but left him tied down. He stared at Elena for a moment, then disappeared, leaving the empty net and ropes intact.

She spun around to find him sitting up in the cockpit. What the hell? He could have teleported out of the bindings at any time.

"No," he answered. "The elven cuffs kept me from teleporting. And the bindings prevented me from grabbing you and biting you back—because I would have. I did my duty so that you can do yours," he said over the hum of the motors. Then he said something else, but she couldn't quite hear him.

"What?"

He motioned for her to approach. She did so, tentatively.

"That is exactly how it works. Extra noise blocks the words. It's like humming in your head. Hell, you can really hum if you want to. It will muffle your thoughts. Try it. Think of something specific while you hum and let's see if I can hear it."

Stefan slid into the pilot's seat. She started humming, then thought of how she needed to change in to cold weather gear before they landed in Romania.

He turned in his chair to face her. "Excellent. I only got humming and a couple of syllables. Get in the habit of doing that now, before you get there. Soon, you will not need to hum out loud, but for the time being, it's safer that way. You can sing, too, if you want to. It jumbles all the thoughts you transmit."

She settled back in her chair next to Margarita, but he continued staring at her. "Thank you," she said.

"You're welcome."

He smiled and turned back around. He was terribly handsome, and with that accent, Elena was sure he had the choice of any woman he wanted. He shot a look over his shoulder at her and arched a brow.

Shit. She immediately began to hum "Row, Row, Row Your Boat."

She didn't remember drifting off, but Elena awakened to the plane motors growing louder and louder, and then the plane pitched hard to the right as it banked into a turn. Something was wrong.

"He's landing at a small, private landing strip in the mountains," Margarita explained. "Nothing is wrong."

"Can you read minds, too?"

She shook her head. "No. It's a very rare talent. Only the

oldest and strongest vampires can do it. Less than half a dozen, probably."

Her brother didn't look older than thirty. "He's one of the oldest vampires?"

She smiled. It was clear she was proud of her brother. "Ricardo is special. He was born with the gift."

"I bet that made it tough growing up."

She grinned. "A pain in the ass. But I effectively block him all the time now."

The plane banked even harder, and Elena checked her seat belt. In the cockpit, Stefan seemed calm and collected. Maybe this *was* normal.

"I can hear you," Ricardo shouted to her over the increasing motor noise.

Elena hummed an indistinct tune as the wheels roughly touched down and she bounced in her seat several times. The engines roared, and the plane slowed to a roll.

Stefan's phone rang, and he put it to his ear. Elena couldn't hear what he was saying over the plane noises. Eventually, they came to a stop, and she unbuckled. "I need to put on cold weather gear," she said. "Being so cold sucked beyond belief, and I'm not going to let it happen this time." She unzipped the bag and pulled out the warm clothes and jacket she had bought. While Stefan finished his phone call, she pulled the gear on over her clothes. Sliding on the Gore-Tex boots, she thought about how much better it would have been to be outfitted like this when she was in the cabin with Nik. If only she could have those moments back. A smile pulled at the corners of her mouth as she remembered their time together. The long conversations, the incredible things he did to her with...

"I can hear you," Ricardo practically shouted. "If you don't learn to mask what you're thinking, they could discover what he means to you. That he's your weakness and you carry his child."

"It's too late," Stefan said, sliding his phone back in his pocket. He unfastened his seat belt. "They already know she's here. And they're waiting for her. She can't disembark. None of us can. The entire airport is full of Underveilers of all kinds. Someone tipped them off."

Ricardo shot from his seat, and crouching to not hit his head, stormed toward his sister, whose eyes grew huge. "It's that asshole weasel you work for. You told him where you were going, didn't you?" He grabbed her by the throat with one hand.

She appeared calm. "No. I called in sick. He doesn't know anything."

"If you have compromised us, I'll kill you, Margarita. You know I will." From the rage on his face, Elena knew he was dead serious. "Let down your guard and allow me into your mind, or your life ends right now."

Elena had never seen anything as terrifying as Ricardo's eyes. The red from the iris had spread all the way out into the whites. She shrunk back into her chair, praying Margarita was telling the truth. Stefan gestured her to the front of the plane, and she gladly put distance between herself and the enraged vampire.

"Is he going to kill her?" she whispered, sliding into the copilot chair.

"If she lied, yes." Stefan seemed eerily calm.

She peered out the tiny windscreen of the plane and gasped. It was dark out. The tarmac was covered in beings with torches and... *Holy crap*. Torches, weapons, and big tools, including pitchforks. It was like they'd landed in the middle of a Dracula movie shoot. "Oh my God."

"The situation is less than optimal," Stefan said, gaze never leaving the brother and sister locked together in the first row in the plane. Both were stone still with their eyes closed. Then,

Ricardo broke away and moved to the seat across from her.

"You didn't betray us."

"Of course I didn't." Margarita didn't seem angry, which surprised Elena.

"Oh good. No blood on the carpet," Stefan said, face expressionless.

There were crazy people waiting outside the plane with torches and deadly farm tools, a vampire was ready to kill his own sister mere feet away, Nik was being tortured in a cell somewhere, and this asshole was worried about blood on the carpet? "I can't believe you!"

He gave no reaction whatsoever to her outburst.

It felt like her head would explode. "How can you be so cold?"

He shifted only his eyes in her direction. "Actually, that was a clearly unsuccessful attempt at humor. Though I truly am relieved to not have to replace the carpet. It would have been messy."

Elena clasped her fingers together in an effort to consciously not store a charge in her palms, which happened every time she got angry. "I just don't get you."

"When you are several centuries old…no. *If* you live to be several centuries old, you will understand completely. There is nothing I have not seen and very few things I have not done. I try not to get invested or tangled up in other people's business unless it affects my own."

"So you don't really give a shit whether I live or die."

A smile crossed his lips. "You are absolutely wrong. I care very much about your fate. I will do whatever I can to facilitate your success. Mine depends on it." He indicated Ricardo and Margarita with a nod of his head. "So does theirs." Then he gestured with one hand to the crowd that was closing in around the plane. "And ironically, theirs as well. We all need you to succeed."

"So if Margarita did not tip Fydor off, who did?" Ricardo asked, looking out the tiny, round window next to his seat. "They appear to be primarily shifters."

Stefan touched Elena's hand to draw her attention back from Ricardo. "Other than us, who knew Itzov was taken and that you were coming to Romania?"

"Only Aunt Uza."

"No one overheard your interactions with her? You didn't tell anyone where you were going?"

"No."

Stefan ran a hand through his hair. "Odd. Uza would not have sabotaged your success unless it will be better for the outcome. Well, this certainly changes our plans. Angry mobs are historically not my thing, and though they cannot kill me, they can slow me down. We also can't risk losing Ricardo yet."

Yet? Like losing him at all was an option.

"I can hear you," Ricardo called from behind her. "And, yes, I'm expendable."

She couldn't believe it. Anger prickled up her spine. "No one. Absolutely no one is expendable."

Stefan fired the motors, and they roared, causing the few brave…whatevers that had moved closer to the plane to back up. "The frightening part of this is that you really believe that."

"Damn right I do."

"I think I'll move us a bit away. What do you suggest as a new plan, Ricardo?" He made the engines roar again, then turned the plane slightly to the left and drove it forward on the pavement. "Clearly, my flight plan has changed. I need to call it in." He picked up the intercom mouthpiece and spoke so low Elena could only hear what sounded like the teacher from Peanuts cartoons. Mwa mwa, mwa mwa, mwa mwa.

"How are you feeling, Elena Arcos?" Ricardo asked. "Powerful?"

Scared. She was freaking terrified. "Yes."

Stefan put the intercom mic back. "Well?"

Ricardo took a deep breath. "I think she needs to go in alone. None of us have been to the fortress, and vampires can't teleport very far anyway. We had planned to drive, then hike, but we'll never make it past the mob out there. You'll have to teleport, Elena, and taking all, or any, of us would drain too much of your power. You're going to need that energy to fight and get the royal family out, if need be."

They had planned to come with her. She felt suddenly ashamed of being so rude to Stefan. "I'd never planned on anything but going in alone. I…I appreciate you guys wanting to help." She grabbed her snow jacket and zipped it on, then strapped the sword they had taken from the wood elf to her leg using a leather sheath Stefan had supplied. The Time Folder had serious organizational and planning skills. She was glad he was on their side, whatever his reasons. "And thanks for getting me this close. I'm sure thousands of miles less teleporting is going to help a lot." She pulled the hood over her head and drew the cord so that it tightened around her face. She turned her attention to Ricardo. "And thanks for… Well, you know."

Eyes still full red, he smiled. "You are more than welcome. I wish you good choices."

Stefan made a disgusted grunt. "They are actually trying to set fire to my tires. Hang on, everyone." The motors roared, and he turned the plane back in the direction of the runway and taxied to the end of it. "We will fly to Sibiu Airport to refuel." He turned back and looked at Elena. "This is as close as I can get you, sweet girl. Good luck." His gaze traveled down to her belly, then back to her eyes. "To both of you."

CHAPTER TWENTY-SIX

Nikolai remained perfectly still as consciousness returned with more pain than mental clarity. After the previous round, he had jerked awake with a start, alerting the guard, who promptly retrieved his uncle, and the interrogations, or rather beatings, had begun immediately. He needed to buy time. He knew Elena would come, and he needed to be as whole as possible to help her when she did. Broken bones and a fractured skull would not enhance his fighting ability.

He cracked his eyes open fractionally. Night had fallen and his cell was dark. What was taking her so long? He'd expected her to teleport in soon after he arrived. Maybe something had gone wrong or she'd decided not to come. No. She would come. Like a moth to the flame, he knew she'd be drawn to fulfill her destiny. He just hoped her destiny included him.

A loud snort came from the other side of the cell, no doubt his bear shifter guard. Nik held his breath and remained motionless. Another snort, then a regular rhythm of snores followed. He cracked his eyes open a bit more and dared to lift his head. Enough moonlight spilled in through a window high in the wall to reveal the hulk of a bear shifter slumped in his chair, sound asleep. This would be the perfect time for Elena to arrive. Most of the fortress was asleep, and he was as healed as he had been since he first got here. Honestly, he was surprised Fydor hadn't just used his Slayer sword and killed him outright when he refused to swear allegiance. Obviously, he needed him for something.

His stomach churned at the memory of Elena's agonized face right before she teleported out. He knew why she'd done it. She didn't have enough power to take him with her. He just hoped she hadn't heard what he'd said to the Slayers taking him captive. If she had, then she would think he truly hated her, which would explain why she hadn't come yet.

A haunted scream sounded from somewhere nearby. Then another. It was Aleksandra. The bastard was torturing his sister. His muscles tightened as his instinct to kill kicked in. He had to lure Fydor away from her, even if it meant suffering more injuries or making promises he would never keep.

He straightened and stretched his aching body. "Where's my uncle?" he shouted, waking the bear shifter from his sleep with a jolt.

E lena flattened against the side of the building outside Aleksandra's bedroom. Trembling, she refused to look down at the moat or snowy forest beyond. Nik had said teleportation wasn't possible inside the fortress, so she'd followed his example and landed on the wall, just as he had. Another horrifying scream came from inside, followed by pleading.

"Scream again," the male voice urged. "It's why I opened the window. Let him hear you. I want him to suffer so that he agrees to publicly swear allegiance to me."

Elena wiped the snowflakes from her nose and maintained her calm.

"He'll never join you. Let him go," Aleksi sobbed.

"He will join me to save you and his mother."

"He's too strong to give in to you." She screamed in pain again and Elena cringed. Whatever he was doing must have been terrible. Her palms itched with current. She needed to conserve energy, so she consciously willed the charge to recede.

The screaming subsided and he practically growled. "I will bring him to you, and you will convince him. You will either convince him or kill him."

"He's done you no wrong, Fydo—" The thud of something solid hitting flesh cut her off, and she groaned.

Elena exhaled in a white cloud, hands buzzing with re-newed current. She wanted to go in and just zap the sorry bastard. There were too many variables, though. He could have others in there with him. He could have an order to kill Nik if he doesn't return. She blinked against her tears.

"If you do as I ask," Fydor said in a sickening sweet voice, "the pain will stop, love. Convince him or kill him, and you will be free."

"It will never work." Her voice was weak.

A knock sounded on the door, cutting Aleksandra's next scream short as he abandoned her to answer it. There was the murmur of male voices, and then a heavy door slammed shut, causing Elena to flinch. She pressed her back harder against the outer wall of Aleksi's bedroom. Through the lead mullioned windows to her right, she saw the man from her visions, club in hand, and another giant man storming through a hallway toward a round turret section jutting from the other end of the wall she was standing on. It had only one window up high. Perhaps that was where Nik was being held.

No sound came from inside Aleksi's room. Surely he hadn't killed her. Nik had said Slayers could only be killed with one of those special elf-forged swords, and he didn't appear to be carrying one. She patted the one strapped to her thigh, then gingerly swung the window several inches wider so that she could peek inside. No one was in the room except Aleksi, who was on the bed, motionless. The coppery smell of blood was powerful, but didn't affect her like it had when Nik was injured.

Just as she had with Nik the first time she was here, she silently entered the room, pulling the window shut behind her. Willing her heart to stop hammering, she leaned against the sill and took in the scene. Aleksi was bound to the bed with metal chains. Why hadn't she simply teleported out?

"Aleksandra?" she whispered, sneaking closer. Feet from the bed, she stopped short and covered her mouth to trap the scream threatening to erupt. What she had thought was a dark sheet thrown over her was actually blood. Her entire body and bed were covered with it. The aborted scream turned in to the urge to vomit. She'd been tortured for a long time. Maybe being immortal wasn't a good thing in some cases.

Calm down, Elena told herself. *Nik needs you.*

Staring down at Aleksandra, she remembered Nik's broken body from her visions, and then his angry words wishing her to hell ran through her head. She couldn't blame him really. He thought she'd turned him over and abandoned him.

"Who's there?" Aleksi asked.

Elena wanted to touch her for encouragement, but was worried about shocking her because of the residual current still buzzing in her hands. "Hey, it's Elena. It's okay, Aleksandra. I'm going to get you out of here."

"Niki," she whispered.

"Yeah, him too. Where is the key for these chains? Please don't tell me Fydor has it."

Her voice was raspy and weak. "No. He likes to keep it

where I can see it. It makes it worse to see freedom and not have it. It's hanging on my dresser."

Sure enough, a skeleton key hung from a big round ring looped over her drawer knob. She grabbed it and made quick work of the cuffs holding her ankles and wrists. "Why didn't you teleport to safety?"

"I couldn't. Can't teleport in fortress. Plus, backup: elven-forged chains."

Like the cuffs Margarita had used to keep Ricardo from teleporting. Maybe it was a good thing this Aksel guy was locked away so he couldn't make stuff anymore. So far, she'd seen nothing good come of his handiwork, from these chains, to the sword that had beheaded the old man in New York, to the cord that had bound her to Nik.

Aleksi groaned as she sat up. "Shit, it hurts. I think he broke everything this time. Lock the door. It won't keep him out, but we'll hear him coming at least."

"You need to get out of here." Elena locked the door, then pulled the key off the huge ring and slipped it in her sports bra. She didn't want that asshole to be able to lock anyone else up in those cuffs and chains, and it took the key to close them as well as open them.

"I can't teleport yet. Too weak. Besides, I need to help Niki."

Elena went to the washstand and poured water into the bowl next to it, just as Aleksi had done to clean up Nik's blood. She dipped the washcloth in it and handed it to her. "I'd help, but I might shock you accidentally."

"Yeah, been there. Done that. No thanks. Keep that to yourself, girl." Her voice was a little stronger already. She wiped the blood off of her face and wrinkled her nose as she examined it. "He usually doesn't touch my face."

"Usually? He's done this before?"

A half laugh, half gasp escaped, and she grabbed her ribs. "Uh, yeah. He's not one of the good guys, sweetie."

Shit. What had she gotten into? How on earth could she face a monster like that alone? "Is there anyone here who *is* a good guy?"

She winced as she shook her head. "He exterminated those who he couldn't threaten or blackmail to join his side." Taking a deep breath, she stretched as if working out a cramp. "Mother, Nik, and I are the only ones he doesn't own. And the only reason we are still alive is because he needs the royal family alive to give the appearance of being respectable and the rightful king. It almost killed my mother to marry him, but she did it to protect Niki and give him time to get his revenge on Arcos's offspring, find the Uniter, and return to the throne." She rinsed the rag and rubbed it over her neck. "Fydor would have killed him years ago if she hadn't married him. We kept hoping Niki would change his mind and step into the place of king while he searched, but he was so crazy with grief over Father's death and completely consumed with revenge, he didn't see what Fydor was doing." She wiped the blood on her forearms and rinsed the rag in the now red water. "I didn't either, at first. Not until I heard Mother screaming at night. Then I figured it out. That's when I started..." She covered her face. "Doing my part to distract him. To relieve Mother and give Niki time to find and kill you. But then you turned out to be the Uniter as well, and things got complicated."

Elena was horrified.

She took a ragged breath. "Well, now you've been found." She dipped the rag in the water again. "And Niki's time is running out. What do you plan to do? You're supposed to be the answer to the problem. The cure. The miracle. The *Uniter*."

Elena's chest felt like it was being squeezed, and she

couldn't get a breath. She had no idea what she was going to do. Hell, she didn't even know what she *could* do. This family had suffered so much. And Nik was probably suffering right now. She had to stop it. "How many men does he have?"

Aleksi pulled a bathrobe out of her wardrobe. "Thousands. Tens of thousands. He commands my father's army and the Slayer Elite Forces in addition to the armies of other species he has blackmailed and bribed into submission."

"No. I mean how many people here, right now in the castle that would defend him."

"Most are only loyal out of fear. If he's on the losing side of a battle, they will follow the winner. If Nik took the throne, most would fall away from Fydor immediately to follow him. My uncle only holds them through ill-gotten power. And I know he's behind the death of my father. I just can't prove it. If I could, this would all be over."

"How many?"

"Thirty tops. Maybe ten at this time of night."

Elena thought about Uza's cat shifters and how she had fended at least thirty off. How her body had sensed where they were and when they would strike. Right now, her best hope was that she could do that again with tougher opponents and much higher stakes. And she felt strong, too. Nik's and Ricardo's blood had made her powerful. She could do this.

"Is Nik in the tower opposite this one?"

"Probably. The dungeon is under the building, but the tower is where Fydor likes to work. He calls it his rec room."

A plan began to formulate. "Who is in the dungeon?"

Aleksandra took a large towel and wiped off her chest and abdomen. "Fydor's enemies. Well, the ones that he hasn't killed yet because they might become useful. Ow. Shit." She patted at a nasty-looking gash over her ribs.

"How many guards?"

She leaned down to wipe her legs. "At this time of night, two in the front hall, one will be in the rec room if that's where he's holding Niki, one outside my mother's room, and two in the dungeon."

"Do people know about the prophecy of the Uniter?"

"Everyone does. Everyone is waiting. If you reveal yourself as the Uniter, some will fall away from Fydor's hold just because of the prophecy."

Perfect. "Will they recognize the symbol of the Uniter?"

She smiled. "Of course. Nik bears the whole prophesy, but every Slayer bears the symbol. They appeared on our skin at the moment of the kings' deaths. Fydor says it is black magic. A curse. Probably because he doesn't bear the mark."

"Awesome. Are you feeling up to a fight tonight?"

Aleksandra's smile was huge. "I will be. Just need some more time to recoup."

She smiled back. "I have a plan, but first I need to borrow some clothes, and I want you to tell me everything you know about your uncle."

CHAPTER TWENTY-SEVEN

Fydor paced the far end of the cell. Nikolai knew there was no way in the world his uncle was going to buy this sack of lies. No way in hell. Nobody was that stupid. He wiggled his fingers to keep them from going to sleep. The cuffs chaining him to the wall were not tight, but they kept his hands above his shoulders.

Fydor stopped pacing and faced him, hands behind his back. "So, you will agree to stand on the balcony and swear allegiance to me in front of witnesses and a gathering of subjects?"

Maybe he *was* that stupid. "Yes."

He struck out pacing again, which was out of character. Fydor usually remained unreadable and still. Right now, he was agitated to the point of being twitchy. Slayers were trained from birth to be calm in the face of adversity or danger to promote concentration and effectiveness. If his physical life were an accurate indication, his uncle was highly ineffective right now. Good.

"Get out," Fydor shouted at the bear shifter guard lurking in the doorway.

The huge hulk of a man lumbered away from the cell, leaving the door open behind him.

His uncle came within inches of him. So close, Nik could smell the elven elixir on his breath. Fydor had been hooked on it since the death of Ivan Itzov. A sickening churn rolled through his gut. This was his fault. He had been so selfish and consumed with revenge, he'd allowed this weak-minded, drug-addicted sadist of a man to destroy everything his father had built. He had to stop him. Elena had changed everything. He saw clearly now. His duty was here, to his people. Hopefully, he wasn't too late.

"I will need you to prove yourself before I allow you any kind of freedom again," his uncle said, still right up in his face.

"Of course." He would say whatever it took to get out of these cuffs so he could kill the bastard.

"You will lead the first massacre."

Fuck. "What massacre?"

"The only way to let the humans know that fighting us is futile is to make a bold opening statement when we lift the Veil. I have an army ready to invade. Until that happens, you will remain captive."

No fucking way was he going to let that happen. "When?"

"When I'm given the command." His face paled when he realized his slip.

Finally, a foothold. "Who commands you?"

Fydor stormed to the other side of the cell. "No one! No one commands me."

Whether it was the drug in his system or fear, something had his uncle rattled. Nikolai just needed to find out how to exploit it. Only one person could hold that kind of power over the Slayer king.

"The sorcerer Borya," Nikolai said.

Fydor stopped pacing and closed his eyes.

"Borya holds your strings and uses you like a puppet."

"No one uses me!" he shouted. "I am the king!"

If only he were not chained to the wall. With his uncle this agitated and out of control, Nikolai knew that even injured, he could take him down with his bare hands. "You are nothing but his tool. A pawn in his game."

Fydor pulled a vial of purple liquid out of his pocket, uncapped it, and drained the contents into his mouth. Never looking at Nikolai, he leaned against the wall and closed his eyes. After a few moments, his shaking subsided and he opened his eyes. "I answer to no one." He dashed the vial on the stone floor like a spoiled child. "My offer no longer stands. You will be executed at midnight tomorrow."

"You'd better get permission first," Nikolai shouted at his back before the door slammed shut.

Fuck. Not good. Not good at all.

Elena pulled the cloak tighter around her as she descended the stairs to the dungeon. The guard at the top had been no problem at all. One zap from her palms and he was out cold.

As she neared the bottom of the narrow, uneven stairs, gold candlelight flickered across the pitted bricks of the wall and floor, making them appear to move like scales of a slithering snake. She stopped and closed her eyes, hoping for a vision of how Aleksandra was faring, but received nothing. She ran her fingers around the short sword strapped to her thigh and took a deep breath. She'd only need it if she ran out of electrical energy or if she had to really kill someone…or something. She hoped it didn't come to that.

"Who goes there?" a man's voice called.

Rounding the corner, she readied herself, allowing charge to build in her hands. The man looked up from where he sat behind a table and scanned her head to toe, then gave a dismissive wave of the hand. "Nobody's allowed to see the leach. Take your fantasies elsewhere."

She simply stared at him, trying to figure out what he meant. His dark hair and gold eyes indicated he was a Slayer, but she didn't see a sword. He wore a dark blue military outfit of some kind.

He shook his head. "Oh, yeah. Play dumb. We get girls down here all the time wantin' a look at him. It's not permitted. Off with ya. Shoo."

"She's with me," Aleksandra said from behind Elena's shoulder, nearly causing her to launch out of her skin.

The guard stood, removed his cap, and bowed. "Lady Aleksandra. I apologize."

She was wearing a long, hooded cape that obscured her face, so he must have recognized her voice.

"No apology necessary. You were doing your job, Claude." She ran her finger from his throat to his waist. "Very well, I might add. Please unlock the door."

Sweat beaded on his forehead. "I...I... I'm sorry, Lady Aleksandra. Nobody goes in without a pass, not even the royal family."

"Since when?" she asked.

The man's discomfort was evident by his nonstop shuffle from foot to foot. "Since this morning. King Fydor said no entry without a pass until after day after tomorrow."

"What happens day after tomorrow?"

"Well, uh, they're evidently going to execute the leach and the other prisoners. All the surrounding villages know about it, so he didn't want any escape attempts or interference."

"A public execution?" she asked.

"Yes, my lady. Burned on the stake."

Elena was amazed how unaffected Aleksi seemed by the news. "Does he plan to kill the elf?"

The Slayer nodded, clearly shaken. "Not so sure that's a good idea, but yes." His eyes narrowed as he studied Aleksandra. "How did you get past the upstairs guard? He wasn't supposed to let anyone pass."

"Claude, how long have you known me?"

"Centuries. Since you was a little girl."

"And you knew my father."

He crumpled his hat in his hands. "Yes, miss. Of course. King Ivan was a great man."

"And you are really wondering how I got past the upstairs guard?"

His gaze flitted between Aleksi and Elena.

Aleksi's voice was as smooth as honey. "Open the gate, Claude. We're in a hurry."

"I can't, my lady. You need a pass or he'll kill me, too."

"Open it, Claude."

"Oh, please, Lady Aleksandra. He'll kill my wife and children." He shook all over.

Elena's anger flared hot in her chest at the suffering these people experienced at the hands of Fydor. Aleksi said all Slayers would recognize the mark of the Uniter. She hoped this guy was really a Slayer and was fed up enough with fear to react according to expectations. "I have a pass," she said, untying the cloak from her neck.

The man's eyes grew huge in the candlelight as he stared at her chest. The leather top she had borrowed from Aleksi was so low cut it left the entire mark exposed. The part about the baby was below her ribs and well concealed. She was pretty sure that Stefan was the only one in modern times who read the "old language," but she didn't want to run the risk.

"Ah, I…" He met her eyes and then stared at the mark again, then recited the opening of the prophecy in a slow monotone. "From the ashes of death, the Uniter shall rise."

"Yeah, yeah. From the blood of a warrior, I awakened. Now open the freaking door so I can go dethrone a tyrant, will you? We're running out of time."

Aleksi took the key from his shaking hand when he produced it and unlocked the heavy wooden door. The stench of unwashed bodies was oppressive and made Elena's nose burn.

The man followed them in, carrying a candle. In the dim, flickering light, she could make out cell after cell on either side of a wide hallway. The bars were too close together to get a hand through.

"How do they feed them?"

Aleksi laughed. "They are immortal. Why waste the money? They can't starve." She moved farther down the hallway.

"But they can suffer," she muttered, more to herself than anyone else.

Aleksi spun to face her. "Don't go soft on me now. I'm in way too far to back out without landing myself a starring role in that execution day after tomorrow, and I'd rather not go to that party, okay?"

"Were it not for me, Slayer, you'd still be chained to your bed, doing the backstroke in a pool of your own blood."

"You have a point." Aleksi stopped at the cell at the end. "Hello, Vlad, baby. You hungry?" It was too dark to see into the cell, but the low, rumbling chuckle that came from it made Elena's hair stand on end.

She took the candle from the guard and moved closer to the cell. The circle of light crept across the floor until it lit a huge, red-eyed hulk of a man in tattered clothes. A gorgeous, red-eyed hulk of a man in tattered clothes.

He chuckled again.

The lack of light was maddening. "I wish we had a flashlight," Elena grumbled. Her palm burned like crazy, so she waved it by her side and the entire room was enveloped in light.

"Shit, girl," Aleksi said. "What else can you do?"

"I've got something she could do," the vampire in the end cell said in his deep, rumbly voice.

Her palm was throwing off flecks of light like a sparkler. Certain it used too much energy, she willed it to dim, and it did.

At least she could see now, but what she saw filled her with horror. Every cell had an occupant chained by heavy cuffs to the wall. There appeared to be one of every kind of immortal there, like a zoo of exotic, sentient, humanlike creatures. Some cringed at the light, while others snarled or simply stared. The vampire, however, leaned his long body against the wall to which he was chained, looking amused. She decided he was the most dangerous force down there. No matter how you sliced it, this situation was not amusing.

"Okay, listen up, losers," Aleksi shouted. "We're going to bust you out of here, but only on the promise that you will help the Uniter. Once Fydor is defeated, you can have your lives back. We're going to send you to your people to spread the word. You must commit to follow her before we free you. If you renege, you will die."

"Follow *her*?" the vampire asked quietly with a smirk. "You should hear her thoughts. Following her is suicide unless she gets herself under control." He moved as close to the bars as he could, stretching the chains binding his arms and legs tight. "But you're right about one thing, little Dhampir. I'm the most dangerous force down here."

"You're a Dhampir?" Aleksi said conversationally, as if the guy wasn't all doomsday creepy. "That kinda kicks ass."

What Elena wanted to do was kick the big vampire's ass.

He busted out laughing. "Much better!"

She hummed a round of "Respect" to mask her thoughts, and the vampire laughed even louder. "I take it back. She may be worth following after all."

"So, here's the choice, my lovelies," Aleksi announced to the creatures in the cells. "Either you help us, or we leave you here."

"What's in it for us?" a guy in the cell behind Elena asked. She spun to come face-to-face with a wood elf.

"I'll tell ya," Claude shouted. "Fydor has a mass public execution planned for day after tomorrow. One of every creature of the Underveil will be burned alive in a show of power intended to secure his place as ruler of the Underveil. The inhabitants of this dungeon are the lucky representatives chosen for sacrifice."

Elena placed the candle on the floor and then raised her arm to make the light from her palm spread farther into the back of the cell next to the wood elf. Crouched in the corner was the most delicate, beautiful creature she had ever seen. Dainty and feminine, its white-blonde hair was matted and its clothes torn and filthy.

"What are you?" she asked.

The creature only stared with enormous, dark eyes.

"She's a light elf," Aleksi said. "Fee, the Alchemist, sister of Aksel the Forger. The shackles dampen her light and render her mute."

"Unlock her," Elena ordered the guard.

Claude unlocked the door and flung it open with a bang. The tiny elf flinched and shuddered. "I only have a key to the cell, not the shackles. Fydor keeps the only key," he said.

The heavy bands around the creature's tiny limbs had a keyhole on top that looked exactly like the ones on the bands

Fydor had used to restrain Aleksi. Elena reached between her breasts and pulled out the key she'd taken from Aleksi's room, unable to contain her grin.

This time she sang out loud to keep the vampire out of her head. *"R-e-s-p-e-c-t. Find out what it means to me."* She inserted the key into the keyhole on an ankle band and laughed out loud when it popped open.

She unlocked the band on the other ankle. *So, I hold the only key to your freedom. What do you think of me now, asshole?* she taunted in her head.

"I think I love you," the vampire called from his cell.

She laughed and hummed another chorus as she unlocked the elf's wrists. The minute the last shackle dropped, the creature glowed brighter than her hand on high-power mode. No need for glowy palm anymore. Elena concentrated on sucking the power back into her body from her hand, and it dimmed to appear normal.

She passed the key to the guard. "Unlock all who you think will be loyal. Do not free the wood elf or the vampire."

The vampire laughed and her skin prickled.

The glowing elf reached out with a slender finger and traced the glyphs on Elena's chest. Then, she touched her under the collarbone in the same way as the elf in the woods. Her voice was beautiful. So entrancing, in fact, Elena stopped humming to listen. "Drink me."

"Don't do it. She's toxic," the wood elf in the cell next door warned.

"Not to you," the light elf said in a high voice, barely above a whisper. "You have blood of a vampire, human, seer, and Slayer in you. You need an elf."

No seer. Only vampire and Slayer...well, and human if her mom counted.

"She lies," the wood elf shouted.

"Focus, Dhampir," the vampire said. "Trust your instincts; they never lie."

She hummed out loud. Her instincts may not lie, but they also didn't have a basis in real life. Everything was new. Everything was scary and threatening.

A cell opened down the hall as Claude set about unlocking another prisoner under Aleksandra's watchful eye. "Stand against the bars," she ordered whatever creature they had released. "Move and you're dead."

The elf came even closer to her, way inside her personal space bubble and tilted her head. She was so bright it hurt to look at her. Then, she rubbed her tiny, glowing fingers over the hilt of Elena's sword. "My brother made this. My people make beautiful things. We do not destroy. I am not toxic."

"Her people are murdering butchers," the wood elf yelled.

"Shut up, bark boy, or I'm going to use you for kindling," Elena shouted back.

The vampire chuckled.

The fact that he could be so cool and amused when he was scheduled to be the main event a barbeque soon made no sense at all. She stormed out of the light elf's cell and stood outside the vampire's bars.

"Let me out of here! My people are harmless," the wood elf shouted.

Harmless? She'd seen his people behead an unsuspecting old man. Elena shot a bolt of energy at him, knocking him completely unconscious. Then she turned back to the vampire in the end cell. "Okay, Mr. Badass. What's your story?"

His voice was infuriatingly nonchalant. "I've been alive thousands of years. I don't think you have time to hear my story. Besides, Fydor just discovered the lovely Lady Aleksandra is missing."

"That's bullshit. Vampires can't read Slayers."

He leaned forward. "Where did you learn that?"

She rubbed her burning palm on the front of her pants. "From a friend."

"Ah, the vampire you drank from. Did he taste good?"

Ricardo's blood had tasted metallic and powerful, not... good. Not like Nik's.

"Ah. It was Ricardo. Good choice. Not as good as me, though." He winked—a particularly unnerving act with those red eyes. "And you are correct; I can't hear Fydor, but I can hear the bear shifter who is with him."

She had to get these guys free and out of here before she was discovered. She had to protect Nik and their baby.

"Oh dear," the vampire said, in a lazy drawl. "Someone has a secret."

Shit, shit, shit.

"Leverage is time sensitive. Your little secret is safe with me...for now," he whispered so softly she was certain no one else had heard.

Everything brightened as the light elf moved to stand next to her, and Elena got a good look at the vampire. He was even more attractive than she had originally thought, with thick, auburn hair, strong features, and blood-red eyes. He smiled when her gaze drifted to his mouth, revealing long, sharp fangs. "Like what you see, Dhampir?"

"Drink from me," the elf said. "Do it quickly."

"What is your take on this, vampire? Is she toxic?" She didn't hum so he could read her thoughts. *What would you advise?*

He arched a brow and tilted his head. "I will only answer direct yes or no questions." Then he stepped back to his bench and sat, arms over chest, completely silent.

Aleksi stood on her other side. "He's smokin' hot, huh? Makes my mouth water. Too bad he's a vamp."

Elena turned to stare at the immortals lined up in the dungeon hallway.

"Fydor is searching the west wing for you, lovely Slayer," the vampire said.

"Fuck Fydor," Aleksi growled.

"No thank you," he said. "I'd rather kill him."

Elena spun to face him. *Is the elf lying?*

"No."

Will her blood make me stronger?

"Infinitely."

"Unlock his cell but keep him shackled," Elena ordered the guard. She handed her sword to Aleksandra. "If I die, cut off his head."

"No. Don't trust him. You're playing Russian Roulette, only you're holding a gun to the whole world. You die, we all die," Aleksi said.

Humming, she looked from Aleksi, to the elf, to the vampire. It all boiled down to instinct. Her instincts told her he was telling the truth. Her death wouldn't benefit him, since he was scheduled for execution.

The elf tilted her head, offering her neck and shoulder. "Time is short. Become stronger. Elves' blood has properties unlike that of any other species. It is my people's gift for rescuing me."

Elena's heart hammered in her throat as she rested her hands on the elf's shoulder and placed lips against the delicate flesh of her neck. She sucked in a huge breath through her nose as her fangs elongated, and then she bit down. Sweet, floral tasting blood flooded her mouth, and she swallowed only a tiny bit. It had an aftertaste like jasmine tea, her favorite. Power so great she could hear it in her head roared through her veins like a freight train. She buried her hands in the elf's hair, tilted her head more, and bit down harder. The elf whimpered, and she forced herself to slow down and then release her. Power rushed through her in a heady mix of adrenaline and light.

Head reeling, she leaned against the bars of the vampire's cell, catching her breath. "I'm so sorry. Are you hurt?"

The elf shook her head. She rubbed her fingers over her neck, closing the wound.

She took the creature's hand in hers. "Thank you for your gift."

"That was very exciting to watch, ladies, but Fydor is leaving the west wing of the fortress. The bear shifter with him is in significant distress," the vampire warned. "You should take your prisoners and go, Dhampir."

She shook her head to come out of her blood high and focused on his face. "They are no longer prisoners." But *he* was, along with the wood elf. She should free him, but something told her that might be a mistake. He *was* the most dangerous thing here.

"Yes, I am." He smiled and his wicked fangs showed.

"Let's go," Aleksi said, striding to the front of the line of immortals. "We're going out the back of the great hall to the stables. Stay together until I dismiss you to go report to your people." She held the sword up. "Any funny business and heads will roll, literally."

Elena turned to follow, but couldn't seem to make her feet move when she reached the stairs. Something felt off. She turned and faced the vampire watching her from the far end of the dungeon, barely visible in the flickering light from the candle on the floor.

Claude rushed to her side and pulled on her elbow. "We need to hurry before Fydor finds us here."

"You'd better run along, Dhampir," the vampire said casually. She couldn't. Something was wrong. She closed her eyes and focused. Blood in the past had been the catalyst for her visions. Maybe the elf's blood would work that way. *Yes*. Behind her eyelids, she saw the elf, wrapped in shiny fabric, pass her a small object. But before she could figure out what, the vision faded. A faint flicker of something else fluttered just out of reach. She took a deep breath of the stale dungeon air and concentrated harder. The image solidified enough to let her see the vampire dressed in clean clothes, all black, holding her in a tender embrace with her head against his chest. Her eyes flew open to find him studying her.

The guard pulled on her again. "Fydor'll kill us if he finds us."

The vampire had said he was thousands of years old, but he looked no older than thirty as he stretched his long, shackled legs in front of him and smiled. "Make good choices, Elena Arcos."

He knew her name and used her father's words. "Who are you?"

"The most dangerous force down here. You said so yourself."

He was a lot more than that. She closed her eyes again and saw nothing. The seer effect of the elf's blood had worn off.

Loud voices came from somewhere above their heads. "Fydor now knows you are in the fortress," the vampire warned. "The guard you shocked is conscious and telling him what happened... Oops. Now, he's dead."

"I need to know who you are." Elena pushed.

"It's too late."

"Do not kill the Arcos female under any circumstances.

I want her alive. Are we clear?" Fydor's voice bellowed from above. "Bring her to me when she is secured."

The vampire gave a defeated shrug. "The dungeon is lined in metal mixed with elven ore. You cannot teleport out of here. I'm afraid you did not make a good choice in remaining behind, Elena Arcos."

She pulled the key out from between her breasts and placed it in his hand. "I think I did." She closed his cell door so it looked like he was locked in and whirled to face the stairs.

CHAPTER TWENTY-EIGHT

Nikolai felt like his rib cage had exploded at the last strike from Fydor's club. "I don't know," he said again.

"If you don't tell me what Elena Arcos is, and what her powers are, I will find your sister and tear her limb from limb in your presence. That Arcos bitch shocked a guard into unconsciousness, somehow freed all but two of my prisoners, and took another guard hostage. She escaped capture by shocking a bear shifter and two other Slayers to the point they can't even talk." He shook his head in disbelief. "She broke prisoners out of my dungeon. Nobody ever escapes my dungeon." Fydor raised the club again. "Last chance."

The guy was all kinds of crazy, and keeping him in the dark about Elena seemed the best tactic. "I can't tell you what I don't know. I could make shit up if you want." Nikolai's vision blurred red as some blood trickled into his eye. "You told me she was a vampire, but she was human. She escaped from me, and right as I located her at her home, your goons came in and grabbed me, letting her get away. It's your fault she's on the loose, not mine."

Fydor circled the room, tapping the club in his hand. Nikolai studied his every move, hoping for a clue as to how to defeat him, which looked pretty fucking remote while chained to a wall. Still, Elena was in the building and Aleksi was alive, or Fydor wouldn't be using her as a threat. Things could be worse.

"You don't need him anymore," a familiar voice said from outside the room.

Okay. So, now things *couldn't* be worse.

Nikolai gritted his teeth as the sorcerer Borya entered the room. His black-eyed gaze flitted over Nik dismissively before he turned to his uncle. "He's useless."

"Perhaps, but I enjoy him."

The sorcerer took a step closer to Fydor, who flinched visibly. "Enjoy someone less dangerous. Enjoy someone who does not have a legitimate claim to the throne you like so much, King Fydor. Someone who is not tied to the Uniter, who I understand is in this building."

"It's rumor only," Fydor sputtered.

Borya held his staff in front of him, and what looked like a lightning bolt shot from the knob on the handle, straight into Fydor's chest. His face froze in a mask of pain and terror. Borya's voice was barely intelligible over the crackle of the bolt. "Do not ever lie to me again, Slayer, or you will feel pain like this for the rest of your immortal tenure."

Fydor gasped and slumped to the floor in a heap after the bolt sucked back into the staff.

"Are we clear?" Borya asked.

Unable to speak, Fydor nodded.

The sorcerer gave Nikolai another glare before returning his attention to Fydor. "I want you to find the escaped prisoners, and I want them, along with this one, executed for treason tomorrow night. The Uniter will burn on a stake next to him for all to see. Do you understand, *King* Fydor?"

Still racked with pain on the floor, he nodded. "Yes, yes. I understand. It will be done."

"When I return next," Borya continued, "I want to see nothing but ash smoldering around burning posts and all the factions bowing down to your terrible power."

It was a long time after the sorcerer left before Fydor finally rose to his feet.

"He's playing you, Uncle," Nikolai said. "Murdering a member of each faction will not make them fear you. It will make them hate you."

Obviously still in pain from the bolt that knocked him down, he picked up the club from the ground. "Hate and fear are intertwined and powerful."

"No. Fear and respect are the most powerful combination."

"Ha! Respect. You sound like your father." Fydor's hold on the club tightened.

"Borya wants chaos. He has no intention of letting you rule. You are no more than a puppet. A pawn in his game."

Nik braced himself for a blow, but instead, Fydor threw the club at his feet like a child who'd just lost a game of jacks before storming from the cell.

Thank goodness Claude knew where the stable was because Elena was certain she'd have never found it. The thick, predawn fog made the air seem liquid and the grounds surreal, which reflected her whole situation. It felt like any moment, she'd shake off sleep and wake up from this nightmare.

An animal shrieked from somewhere in front of them, and they both stopped short from their full-out sprint.

"The barn's right ahead. The sound came from there," Claude whispered between gasps for breath.

"Owwww!" It sounded more human than animal this time.

Elena recognized Aleksi's voice immediately. "Shut up, or

I'll give you something to really scream about."

She nodded to Claude, and they crept forward, and then she gently pushed the barn door open enough to peek in.

Aleksi was kneeling in the hay next to a bony woman whose head twitched side-to-side in swift, jerky movements. The only other creatures in the barn were two boys who looked no older than thirteen or fourteen, sitting on a bench in the corner. Well, sitting wasn't really the right word. They were both balanced barely on the edge of the seat as if they would leap to their feet at any moment. Both appeared too well-fed and healthy to have been prisoners in the dungeon.

"This is a terrible idea," the woman said in a shrill, nasal tone, rising to her feet. "Fydor will surely look in here."

"Then shut the fuck up so we can find the plug and get out of here." Aleksi yanked her back down by the shirt, which tore with a loud ripping sound. The woman hit the ground with a thud.

Both boys jumped to their feet at the same time. "Someone's here, Lady Aleksandra!" one said in a breathy tone, pointing at Claude and Elena lurking just outside the door.

"Yeah. You told us to warn you if we saw or smelled somethin'," the other added.

She met Elena's eyes, nodded, then turned her attention back to the whiny lady next to her. "Lie on your stomach. Based on your racket, it's in the back of your right thigh."

"We did good, huh? Me and Iosif did right, didn't we, huh?" one boy said while the other ran in a circle. "We told ya like you asked." Their goofy grins were contagious, and Elena almost found herself smiling at their exuberance.

"Iosif and Simion. Sit!" Aleksi commanded.

Both boys dropped to their butts on the floor instantly, still grinning.

"Dog shifters," Claude said, opening the door wide enough for her to pass through. "Still pups, but they make good stable boys."

"You don't have X-ray vision or any such cool superpower, do you, E?"

Elena liked Aleksi's pet name for her. E beat the hell out of parasite. "Sadly, no."

Aleksi ran her palms over the back of the woman's thigh, and she let out a glass-shattering screech, arms flapping in the hay.

"Hey, what kind of bird are you, a chicken?" Aleksi rolled her eyes. "We don't have time for this kind of thing. You're absolutely right. This is not the safest place. Now lie still unless you want to be a roasted hen day after tomorrow at midnight."

Elena moved farther into the barn, and Claude closed the door behind them. "What are you doing?"

"I'm removing a piece of elf ore implanted by one of Fydor's witches that prevents Underveilers from using magic. In this case, it keeps her from shifting into her alternative form."

"Where is the elf?"

"Ack!" the bird lady squawked.

"Bingo! Now hold still because it's gonna hurt like a—"

"Eeek!" The woman covered her mouth as Aleksi pressed her palm to her leg.

"Yeah. Ripping that piece of metal back out is probably worse than putting it in there. Hold still." Aleksi kept her hand over the woman's leg but looked up at Elena. "I sent Fee back to her people to get them on our side. An army of enraged fey will scare the crap out of Fydor. You just don't screw with those guys." A grin spread across her face. "I take that back. You *do* screw with those guys. Elves are wicked in bed."

Elena was glad she didn't have Ricardo's mind-reading

abilities at that moment. She was pretty sure she'd know way more about elves than she wanted to know.

"Owwwwww. Ow." Blood splotched the back of the bird woman's pants below Aleksi's palm. She pulled her hand away from the woman's body, sat back, and relaxed. "All done. Fly away."

The woman jumped to her feet in a startling, inhuman burst and shook her leg. A slender, bloody metal dowel the length of Elena's thumb and the diameter of a pencil slid out of her pant leg into the hay. "Thank you."

"No problem." Aleksi waved her off. "Go bring back some bird badasses, okay?"

Even knowing she was a bird shifter, and being prepared for the transformation, Elena gasped as the woman crumpled and morphed into a hawk of some kind, human skin sloughing off in sheets like the cat pelts had in Aunt Uza's yard. This sort of thing was just too freaky to take in stride. She'd never get used to it, no matter how long she lived. *If* she lived. She rubbed her hand over her belly. "We need to get Nik out of there."

"It may be best to leave him for now," Claude said. "Going in and getting caught would be bad. Lord Nikolai would be the first to die if trouble started."

"He's right. We need to buy time to let the factions organize," Aleksi said. "Besides, Fydor expects you to go back in after him. It would be suicide."

This helplessness sucked. "I can't just leave him there."

"You risk everything if you don't."

She really wanted to talk to the vampire from the cell. Something in her believed he'd know what to do. "Who is the vampire in the dungeon?"

Aleksi patted the hay next to her, and the boys rushed to her side. "I call him Vlad," she said, "but no one knows his real name. He used to live in the old Poenari castle before he was captured by my uncle."

"Yeah, but who is he?"

"Don't know, but he's delicious, isn't he? If he were anything but a vamp, I'd so do that." Aleksi reclined back on her elbows between the two young teens, who squirmed with excitement to have her near. "I understand abandoning the wood elf, but why did you leave him in the dungeon?"

"I...I had to." She was hesitant to mention she could see glimpses of the future, even though she was certain everyone in the barn was an ally. "I just kind of know stuff sometimes, and I knew I had to leave him there." Hopefully, her vision was accurate and he had not been killed after she escaped. *Where are you?* She called to him in her mind. *We're in the stable.*

The other vision, the one with the elf, was as puzzling as that of the vampire. "Tell me about the elf."

"Oh, Fee the Alchemist? Not much. I've never even seen her before."

"Why 'Alchemist'?"

"Elves don't have surnames. They use their talents as identifiers. Her brother is Aksel the Forger, her mother Leione the Weaver, her father is Dalra the Warrior, which is why it was a fucking stupid move for Fydor to pick this particular elf to kill. Dalra puts the bad in badass, and he keeps his daughter under close watch ever since his son disappeared. I have no idea how Fydor pulled off capturing her."

That was not exactly what she had meant. "So, Aksel makes the swords and stuff from enchanted metal. What does Fee do specifically?"

"She deals with infusing the metal with properties that bind powers. The elves are all about making money off other species. She also helps formulate multiple elven elixirs that are sold by intermediaries to Underveiler dealers."

"So she's a drug dealer?"

"Sort of, only under the Veil, most everything is legal as long as it doesn't involve humans. I guess from your perspective, light elves are the weapons dealers and drug lords of the Underveil, but it's not a bad thing, so stop thinking like a human."

God, she hated being told that. "She makes the elixir your uncle is hooked on. The one you told me about?"

She put her arms around the boys' shoulders. "Maybe. Several elves are Alchemists."

It would explain how Fee had contact enough with Fydor to catch his eye and to get caught by him, perhaps. The image of her from her vision popped to mind again, and a sparkle of hope shimmered in Elena's heart. She couldn't beat Fydor using brawn or nonexistent fighting skills, but she just might be able to play on his weakness and outwit him. Grab him by the Achilles heel Stefan talked about.

"Okay, you two know what to do, right?" Aleksi ruffled the boys' hair in a sisterly way.

The larger one nodded. "Simion and I are going to run to the castle and tell everyone the Uniter has teleported to the elves' forest with Lady Aleksandra and Mr. Claude as hostages."

She smiled. "Right. And then?"

"Then we're gonna run home and not tell anyone anything else or you'll cut off our testicles and use them as marbles," the other one said, grinning ear-to-ear. If he'd had a tail, he would have wagged it.

Elena shook her head. "Niiiiice."

"Visual imagery works. Easy to remember, motivational, and highly effective." Aleksi stood, brushed off the hay, and flipped her black hair over her shoulder.

Elena remembered the hostile reception Nik received when

he asked the elf for help in the forest. She was pretty sure there was no way that was their destination. The story the boys were to tell was a red herring. "Where are we really going to go?"

The door slammed open, knocking Claude down, and two huge men stormed into the room. Not Slayers, Elena noted immediately, based on their dark brown eyes and brown hair. "Where are you really going? You're going to the dungeon," one growled.

"Bear shifters," Aleksi said, pulling her sword from the sheath on her back. "Slow moving. Strong. They claw and bite."

Still in human form, one charged her while the other one stalked toward Elena, making a low, grumbling sound in its throat. Aleksi brought her sword down on the huge man's shoulder, nearly severing his arm when he got within reach. "And they're stupid."

The one closest to Aleksi shifted into a huge bear with black claws and fangs as big as the head of a claw hammer, while the one nearest Elena remained in human form. He grabbed Claude by the collar.

"She took me prisoner!" he shouted. "She's dangerous. Release me!"

The guy let him go and spun to face Elena right about the time the bear stood on his hind legs, towering over Aleksi, who remained in fighting stance, sword in both hands in front. The bear roared, and both boys shifted into dog form.

Keeping her eyes on both the bear and the man stalking toward her, Elena sent a charge to her hands. Very little energy was building up. She must have used it up zapping the guard on her way into the dungeon or maybe lighting the cells with her palm. She slipped the sword from the sheath on her thigh.

"We're not supposed to kill 'em," the man hollered to the bear. "Jus' maim 'em."

The bear made a swipe at Aleksi, and she ducked, spun, and buried the sword in the beast's chest. It roared in pain, right as the second bear man grabbed Elena by the hair, knocking the sword out of her hands. One of the dogs launched itself at his neck, but missed, biting and latching on to the man's shoulder instead. Immediately, he shifted into his bear form, and before Elena had built up enough power to deliver a shock, he sunk his fangs into the dog's neck, ripped it loose from his shoulder, and flung it across the barn, where it slammed into the wall with a yelp and a sickening crack. When it turned its enormous head back to Elena, she shoved her palm against its nose and released all of her current into the beast. His human-looking eyes widened, and soundlessly, his body went rigid and tremors jerked through his huge form. When his eyes glazed into a blank stare, she released him and he collapsed to the floor, bear skin sluffing off to reveal the man again.

Completely drained, Elena was mildly aware of the sounds of struggle going on behind her, but could focus only on the boy in a heap on the floor where his body had landed, limbs sprawled at unnatural angles.

As if someone had turned the volume up on the television, the sounds of fighting behind her came back into focus, and she spun to find the bear swinging wildly at Aleksi, Claude, and the other boy, still in dog form, barking and biting at the enraged animal. She had no charge left. In fact, she was having trouble standing at this point.

Claude picked up a pitchfork, hefted it over his head, and slammed it down right between the bear's shoulder blades. It gave a roar and rose on its hind legs, towering over Aleksi, sword still in her hands. The dog bit its heel, and as it dropped to all fours, Aleksandra thrust up with her sword into its chin, driving the blade all the way through the beast's skull and out the top of its massive head.

Elena turned away, unable to watch the transition as it turned back to a man, but what she saw instead, was the dog shifter resuming his human form, then throwing himself over his friend's body. She closed her eyes, surrounded with the smell of blood and the faint whimpers and whines of the surviving boy. Was this the world she was condemned to live in now? A world of violence and hate?

Shouting came from outside. "More are coming," Aleksi said to the surviving boy. "Shift and run, Iosif! Get out of here."

"No, Lady Aleksandra. I will fight for you. For Simion."

"Now. Dammit. Obey me. Out!"

Iosif shifted into a dog and loped to the back of the barn and squeezed under a board at the back of a stall.

"You should have teleported out," Aleksi said, scooping Elena's sword from the ground and handing it to her. "Claude can't and I'm not healed enough yet." She wiped the blade of her sword off on the bale of hay beside her. "Why did you stay?"

The shouting grew louder as the new enemies approached. "It never dawned on me to teleport out." Everything was still too new. Stefan was right; she needed to stop thinking like a human. Though, she would not have left them to fend for themselves against two of those creatures. She would have remained regardless.

"They're in the barn!" a gruff voice shouted.

"Fuck. I'd know that voice anywhere," Aleksi said. "That's Commander Mihai."

A quick glance at Claude confirmed this was bad news. "Leader of Fydor's Elite Slayer Force. We are as good as dead."

No. They were not going to die. "Not yet." She hadn't seen this ending here. If the visions were correct, she still had to hug the vampire and take an item from the elf. "Whatever happens,

I need you to remain here. You must go back to the fortress and act like you were against me. I have a plan."

The first three Slayers, swords drawn, filled the wide opening at the front of the barn. Backlit by the rising sun rendered a dramatic silhouette effect, like something from a horrible second-rate action movie. Only this was real.

"Get out, E!" Aleksi whispered from behind her.

"I'm too weak to teleport," she answered under her breath, standing perfectly still.

"In here," one of the Slayers shouted over his shoulder.

There was no way they could fight off the Slayers. Their only hope was to buy some time. "Overtake me," Elena whispered. "Act like you're my hostages and are turning the tables." Not a great plan, but it was all she had since she had no clue how she would get out of this.

"Move and die, parasite!" Aleksi said, yanking Elena back by the hair and placing her sword blade against her neck.

Claude caught on to the ruse and pointed the pitchfork, still slicked in the bear's blood, at her chest. "Tell Fydor we've got Arcos," he shouted to the Slayers. "She killed the bear shifters and the boy."

"You should consider a career in acting, there, Claude," Aleksi murmured.

Heart hammering, Elena closed her eyes and searched for a vision showing her how the hell she was going to get out of this one, but came up blank. If only she had freed the vampire and had him come up here with Claude. *Stupid mistake.*

"Not stupid." The deep, rumbly voice behind her caused her to flinch. "What was stupid was broadcasting your location by calling out to me in your mind with Borya in the fortress. It's how they knew to come here. He is telepathic, too. Now, hum."

She did. It was a shrill version of "We've Gotta Get Out of

this Place," and the vampire actually chuckled as if they weren't facing Slayer Armageddon.

"Send word that the vampire escaped the dungeon!" one of the Slayers shouted.

"They already know," he replied calmly. "Well, those I left alive, anyway."

Aleksi pulled Claude close and whispered in his ear.

When the first three Slayers began to advance, swords raised, the vampire moved within inches of Elena. "Touch me. Do it now. You must choose to come, or it doesn't work."

Without hesitation, she did as he instructed, and the moment her fingers met the cool skin of his arm, everything blurred and the pressure of teleportation wrapped her body like a cocoon. She had no idea where the vampire was taking her, but wherever it was, it beat the hell out of a barn full of angry Slayers.

Chapter Twenty-Nine

Elena solidified from teleportation with more discomfort than usual. Her knees buckled, and the vampire caught her before she hit the floor—the very elegantly appointed floor covered in an Aubusson rug.

"Nadia," the vampire called. A square-shouldered woman with high cheekbones and full lips rushed to them from across the huge stone room. They appeared to be in the great room of a castle or fortress of some kind. Expression neutral, the woman called Nadia stood silently as if running over to wait for his command were a normal thing. "Please escort our guests to rooms and provide them with baths."

Guests? Elena swung her gaze around to find Claude on the other side of the vampire, still clinging to his tattered, filthy shirt. The vamp was a fine one to order baths when he had the dungeon grunge working. She met Claude's gold eyes. "You were supposed to stay behind with Aleksi."

"This wasn't my doing," he replied. "Aleksi ordered me to stay with you."

"Nadia, they are not to leave their rooms until I return, are we clear?" the vampire said. "I have work to do."

"Yes, sir." She took Elena by the elbow, grip firm, and

started to lead her away.

Jerking her arm out of the woman's grasp, she suppressed the urge to zap her. "Wait a minute. I need to do some things. You can't just lock me up, Vl... Whatever your name is."

Dozens of people had entered the cavernous room, servants or friends perhaps... Did creepy vampires even have friends? Most of them wore hooded capes in a dark brown, leaving their faces only partially visible. None of them reacted to her outburst; it was as if someone had flipped an emotional off switch on the entire population of the place.

The vampire moved close. So close she could see the variations in the shades of red in his eyes. "Keep your voice down and your emotions in check, and never again tell me what I can or cannot do in my own home. I can do whatever I wish. I can slaughter every living creature in this castle in the matter of minutes, and no one could do a thing to stop me. Not even you, Elena Arcos." He calmly turned and strolled toward the gaping mouth of an archway at the other end of the room where several women wearing long, drab dresses stood in a cluster. "At least, not yet," he added over his shoulder. At the snap of his finger, the women stood shoulder to shoulder, and he pointed to the tallest of them. She smiled and approached him, no fear evident in her features despite his ominous threat to butcher everyone in the castle.

Stopping right in front of him, she appeared totally relaxed as he removed whatever held her silky brown hair in a tight bun on the back of her head. He ran his fingers through the strands, fanning them out over her shoulders in an affectionate caress. "It has been so long," he murmured, brushing the hair to one side to reveal her neck and bare shoulder. "Too long." The woman, still showing no fear, tilted her head to expose the bare column of her long neck. "The things we do for love," he said as he ran his fingertips over her skin and she closed her eyes.

Surely, he wasn't skeevy enough to bite that poor woman, no matter how willing she appeared, in front of all these people.

His rumbling chuckle stalled her heart for a moment. "Skeevy is not a word with which I'm familiar. And, yes, I *am*… not skeevy, based on context, but planning to bite her. Stop thinking like—"

Like a human, yeah, I know.

"And hum or sing in your head when you don't want your thoughts to be heard. In fact, for my benefit, do so now, so that I can concentrate on refueling rather than refuting."

Too bad his personality and manner weren't as good as his looks.

He straightened and glanced over his shoulder at her, a wide, cocky grin exposing his fangs.

Shit, shit, shit. She launched into the chorus of the old Carly Simon song her mom used to play when she cleaned house, "You're so Vain," and he chuckled again before returning his attention to the woman in front of him.

Still singing the song in her head, she took in the reactions—or lack of reactions—from the others in the room. They watched him bite the woman's neck with complete detachment. The only ones who reacted were the vampire, who made a yummy sound, the girl who moaned as if being bitten were pleasing, and Claude, who turned away in disgust.

The woman he'd called Nadia took Elena's elbow and pulled. Another person, a guy much taller than Claude, did the same to him, and they were led through a doorway at the opposite end of the room. When the girl made a louder, clearly erotic moan, Elena sang out loud, wishing she remembered more than just the refrain.

She and Claude were taken to separate rooms off the same hallway, and she took note of where he'd been taken in case she'd misjudged the vampire and needed to find Claude in a pinch. Nadia entered the room with Elena and locked the door behind them, then slipped the key into her pocket.

"You cannot teleport in this wing of the castle, so don't waste your time or energy."

Elena gave the woman her best "screw you" glare, but it had no effect whatsoever.

"Please assist Miss Arcos with her bath," Nadia said in a clear voice. No one else was in the room, at least no one visible.

The click of the tumblers seemed unnaturally loud as Nadia left and locked it from the outside. She was a prisoner. *Again.* Nik was being tortured in the Slayer fortress, and the thought of that made her want to vomit. She had to get out of here somehow.

"You asshole!" she shouted to the vampire, hoping it was as loud in his head as it was in the room. "I have things to do! You can't just lock me up. I'm the reason you're free at all, you ungrateful, bloodsucking..."

The sensation of being watched crawled over her neck like a spider, and she spun to again, find no one.

"Who's here?"

A scratching drew her attention to the corner. She almost screamed when a tiny gray mouse lifted its head high, whiskers circling as it sniffed the air.

Surely not. Not even in this messed up world.

The mouse recoiled when she narrowed her eyes to a glare, and then it scurried under an armoire.

"You can't just lock me into this vermin-infested hellhole, Vlad!" she shouted.

"I can and will." The voice was deep and menacing, and *close*—right behind her. His breath ruffled the hair on the back of her neck, but she didn't flinch or react at all other than to ball her fists at her side as he continued to speak. "Keep your voice low and level in my home, please. And maintain your control."

"It's a little hard to control myself when I'm a prisoner."

He rested his hands on her shoulders and kept his voice a bare whisper. "You are not a prisoner. You are a secured, temporary guest. I have something I must do. It is important and you will wait here."

She shrugged off his hands and faced him, then took a step back because he was way too close for her comfort. "Why? So you can go make some other poor girl moan while you drain her blood?"

He gave a long-suffering sigh. "I wish that were my mission. I could do with more fuel after being starved for months. I could do with a lot of things." His crimson eyes scanned her from head to toe, and ended on her lips.

"Screw you," she said.

"Are you offering?"

She took a step back. "No." He wasn't someone to trifle with, yet here she was provoking him.

"Good, because it would be a tremendous conflict of interest for me and I have things I need to do."

"I need to save Nik." And possibly the entire human race.

"My mission is more important at this juncture. You will wait here until I return."

Bossy jackass.

"See she bathes," he ordered the empty room, just like Nadia had.

There was that bath thing again, coming from Mr. Dungeon Dweller. "Maybe *you* should bathe."

"I fully intend to. I, however, do not smell of fear and bear blood. You will upset my household. Please do as instructed."

God, she hated controlling men. And ever since the

convenience store, that's all she'd encountered. Maybe that's all there was in the Underveil...that, and people who turn into animals and kill boys. Her heart constricted as she thought of the poor little dog shifter who died in the barn.

The vampire reached out, as if to comfort her, then dropped his hand, blurred, and disappeared. Evidently the teleportation block wasn't in place here, like it was at the fortress. Well, good. She had no intention of allowing Mr. Bossy Pants to keep her prisoner. She'd freed herself from the cord that bound her to Nik, and there was no way she'd let herself be held captive again. Even if he *had* saved her from the Slayers in the barn.

Nik needed her. She had to get to him. Focusing all her energy, she imagined the wall outside Aleksi's room. Her body went warm for a moment, then returned to normal, still in the same room.

Maybe this part of the fortress really was teleport proof. Again, she closed her eyes. This time, she focused on the room where she had just been. Nothing.

"Shit!"

The hall outside the door. Nope.

The bed across the room. Nada.

"I hate this place. I hate vampires and shifters and every damn freaky thing that lives under the Veil. You all suck!" she shouted at the top of her lungs.

Covering her face, she slumped to the floor, legs folded under her. Before getting shot in the convenience store, she'd just gone along with the ebb and flow of life, never fighting fate's current. Now, she felt like she was constantly struggling to swim upstream—like those salmon that fight and fight to reach some place at the top of the river, only to breed and die. She rubbed her hand over her belly. Well, she sure as hell wasn't going to be one of those salmon. If being part of this freaky existence had taught her anything, it was to be proactive. Being helpless and going with the flow was as much of her past as her humanity.

Pushing to her feet, she took in her surroundings. It looked like one of those museum castles she'd seen on television. The walls were stone, as was the floor, with heavy, rough-hewn, wooden support beams overhead. A small, ornate four-poster bed with emerald damask curtains tied back with gold cords stood in the center of the room, the only furniture other than the armoire. A door on the opposite side of the room stood open with a view to a modern bathroom.

A skittering sound drew her attention back to the armoire where the mouse peeked out at her. "You're not really a mouse, are you?"

It shook its head, which should have creeped her out, but didn't. Maybe she was adjusting finally…or maybe she was just tired.

The mouse moved out from under the armoire and rose up on its hind legs, still studying her.

"Go ahead," Elena said, crossing her arms. "It's nothing I haven't seen before."

Even so, the mouse stretching and a full-grown woman morphing in that spot was still unsettling. The woman was completely naked, the tiny, discarded mouse pelt in a ball at her feet. Wordlessly, she opened the armoire, pulled out a simple frock, and pulled it over her head. "Shall I run a bath, Miss Arcos?"

Be proactive. "Nah, I've got this." She tromped to the bathroom, turned on the faucet in the enormous claw-footed iron tub, and held her hand under the water until it turned warm. "What's with the bath anyway? I'm not as grimy as he is."

"Our master will wash when he returns."

"Where did he go?"

"It is none of our business. Our job is to trust, learn, and obey."

Like hell.

The water had reached a good level in the tub, so she turned it off and reached up to unfasten the leather halter she'd borrowed from Aleksi. She paused and arched a brow at the mouse girl.

"Go ahead," the girl said, in a fairly good imitation of Elena's tone earlier. "It's nothing I haven't seen before."

Touché. She unzipped the soft leather at her neck and back and pulled the halter off. The pants and boots followed. Mouse girl, despite her words, was transfixed by the markings on Elena's body. She stepped into the tub. "Who are the people in the big room? No. Better question is *what* are the people in that room?"

"Some are shifters, but most are vampires. They are the Master's students."

"What are they studying?"

"Pacifism."

And here she'd been thinking it couldn't get weirder.

She lowered herself into the warm water. "Pacifist vampires."

"Yes. It is a special order. They are all empaths."

"Including your...Master?" The word rankled. Nobody should be a Master. She felt like she'd been dumped in the middle ages. She dunked under, wetting her hair.

The mouse girl picked up a small bottle and poured some of the gold liquid in her hand. "No. He took over the job for someone else. He is telepathic with empath tendencies. The previous master was an empath." She rubbed the shampoo into Elena's hair, and despite her desire not to, she found herself enjoying it. It seemed so wrong to be here, in a tub big enough for two people, being pampered while Nik was in a cell, enduring torture.

"Where is the previous master?"

"He was murdered."

So much for pacifism. "What is your name?"

"Lilian. Rinse, please."

Elena slipped under the water and ran her hands through her hair, removing the shampoo and resurfacing. "I need to get out of here."

"I am truly sorry, but I cannot help you."

Elena stood, washed her body, then sat back in the warm water. "Have you ever been in love, Lilian?"

A faraway look crossed her face, her brown eyes going unfocused for a moment. "Yes."

"I'm in love. And the man I love is in danger. I must go to him."

"Only at my Master's wish will it be so."

"Are you afraid he'll kill you if you help me?"

She held out a towel. "It is my composition to be fearful. The instincts of my animal form carry over. It is why I remain in my animal form most of the time. My fear in human form disrupts the comfort of the students. Most of the shifters here are bovine. They are much calmer."

So, the vamps in the hoods were empaths, which probably meant they read emotions, while Vlad and Ricardo were telepathic, which meant they could read minds. *Damn.* There needed to be a guidebook for all this craziness. And Big, Bad Vlad kept a herd of human cattle. *Aw, crap.* "Why are there bovine shifters here?"

"In the Underveil, each species assume the jobs for which they are most suited. Slayers are law enforcers. Elves create. Shifters use their unique attributes to their advantage. I move fast. Bovine shifters… Well, they are calm, and the Master…" Her voice dropped off.

The hackles stood up on the back of Elena's neck. Bossy *and* bigoted. She thought back on all the shifters she'd met. Yep. Bears were guards. Dogs were stable boys. Mice were servants, and cows were...*food?*" Nuh-uh. No way. Elena grabbed the towel and wrapped it around her body with shaking hands. Rage billowed inside her like flames as she thought about the poor boy in the barn, his life taken so young. "No!"

Lilian scampered back a few steps. Elena hadn't meant to scare her, but damn, she was mad. That bastard had locked her up and taken off like nothing mattered but himself. "That's it!" She grabbed her clothes from the floor and ripped her pants on. "He's not keeping me here." This level of anger was not normal for her, but somehow, it felt empowering and liberating. She'd saved his ass. After fastening the halter on, she leaned against the side of the tub and pulled on her boots. "Unlock the door, Lilian."

Shaking her head rapidly, hands wringing, she backed up. "I'm sorry, miss. I can't. I won't." She froze and closed her eyes. "Kill me now if you must."

Holy shit. Elena couldn't kill someone. Well, unless her life was in danger...or her baby's...or Nik's. Did she look like a killer? A glance in the mirror confirmed she did. All in black leather with crazy wild markings on her skin and her newly acquired lean muscle and red-tinged eyes, she looked like a killing machine. Horrified, she slumped into a stool in the corner.

A howling sound came from outside the door. The girl immediately morphed into a mouse, leaving a horrifying pile of human skin behind, and scampered under the armoire. More howls. Then screams.

She had to get out of this place. Rescue Nik, displace Fydor, end this war or whatever was brewing, and try to break free of this untenable existence. She couldn't live like this. No one could. Human cattle, dead boys, oppressed women. Just, no. She gripped the door handle right as another howl sounded, and she froze. It was a human sound, but animal also.

She felt more than heard a change behind her. He was back. She didn't even have to turn to know. "What is out there?" she asked, leaning her forehead against the door.

"Your rage."

Now, she did turn. The vampire stood in the middle of the room, covered in blood from his chin to his waist. She shuddered.

He pointed to the bed. "Sit."

Like the dog shifters in the barn at Aleksi's command, she obeyed.

"This is not your fault. It is mine. I should have explained. So much in our world is taken for granted, and I failed to see the implications from a human perspective—a downfall from living too long as an immortal. We forget what it's like above the Veil. How short sighted and prejudiced you can be."

"Short sighted and prejudiced?" She leapt to her feet, and he held up a palm.

"If you lose your control again, I will have to kill more of them, so please refrain. I've grown fond of them, despite their shortcomings."

What an ass.

"Not really. When you lose your temper, the vampires housed here feed off your emotion and react accordingly. They have been isolated from inciting forces until their training is complete and they can either be released or destroyed. All here were slated for destruction."

She gestured to the blood on his chest and face. "What happened to you?"

His smile was bittersweet. "The better question is what happened to them."

No. No, no, no. He did not just kill the vampires she saw in the big room when they arrived.

"Indeed, I did. Not all of them, though. Some passed the test, which was unexpected."

"Are you telling me my anger got them killed?" Her insides roiled and she covered her mouth.

"No. Their lack of self-control got them killed. You simply helped me along. I was in that dungeon so they had not been tested a second time yet. It should have happened long ago." He took a deep breath. "Do not let it trouble you. I will explain it after I clean up. Please, I beg of you, remain calm until I return." He disappeared without a trace or sound.

Oh yeah. Stay calm. He just slaughtered people in his own home because of her. No biggy. Welcome to the Underveil, the freaking gateway to hell.

CHAPTER THIRTY

Nik stretched his back and wiggled his fingers to bring them back to life. Fydor and Commander Mihai had been conferencing for what felt like hours, right outside his cell door. The bear shifter guard growled when he flexed his fingers again, and he growled back. The first thing he planned to do when he was free from these bindings was kill that fucker.

"If we're lucky, Borya is wrong and the vampire will kill her. If not, we know she'll come for me in order to fulfill the prophecy." Strain was evident in his uncle's voice.

"She can only get in via three places. Lady Aleksandra's window, which is how she got in before, the back door, where she escaped with the hostages to the barn, and the front door itself. We have guards stationed all over the perimeter of the building," Mihai said.

Nikolai had never really liked him. A little too self-serving for his taste, but that was probably because he was trying to stay alive in the regime of King Fydor, who should never have been given power in the first place. Chalk up another point in the guilt column. Oh, wait. He was out of room for even one more point. He swallowed against the bile taste in his mouth. He'd been chained to this wall for so long that his focus was slipping a bit. He had to get free soon.

"I would like to personally stand guard in Lady Aleksandra's room," Mihai said. It was no secret he'd always had a thing for her.

"Wouldn't you just?" Fydor snapped. "No. She says she wants to take the Arcos bitch down herself. Aleksi has great pride and needs to avenge wrongs herself." Nikolai could hear the smile in his uncle's voice. "It's one of the things I like most about her. Her need for revenge. You will stand guard at the front door."

He could only hope his sister got her revenge against the bastard who had really hurt her: Fydor. And he would be only too happy to help.

"Yes, sir."

"Stay alert. She's coming. Borya has seen it. He's also seen her burning at the stake. We just hope she shows up sooner rather than later."

No shit, Nikolai agreed. And as for that burning at the stake bit. No fucking way was that going to happen. Fate was a bitch, but even *she* wouldn't deal the world that bad a hand. She had to leave someone standing to screw over.

The vampire looked like a completely different person when he unlocked Elena's door and gestured for her to follow him. Dressed all in black, he could have been a model or movie star playing the part of a special ops soldier, complete with weapons strapped to his chest, waist, and legs. His state of combat readiness should have been frightening, but it was anything but.

"Hum, Elena Arcos," he warned as she followed him down the hallway. "Your thoughts, though flattering, are not helpful to anyone."

"Finding you attractive doesn't mean I want you." She loved Nik, pure and simple. No one would ever appeal to her the way he did. "Looking and doing are two different activities."

"Thank you for your insight."

Jackass.

"Much better."

She was seated at a long table to his right, and gobs of fantastic food were placed in front of them. An empty plate sat across from her. "Where's Claude?" She hoped he hadn't been hurt when the vamps went nuts.

"He will be here shortly." He took a bite of fish from his plate and closed his eyes, savoring it.

"I thought vampires didn't eat."

"You thought wrong. We don't have to eat. We like it, though."

She placed her napkin in her lap. "Sun allergy?"

"Partially true. The younger the vampire, the more sun sensitive. We never fully overcome it, though, and can be in direct sunlight only for very brief periods. Our skin burns off easily. It won't kill us, but it hurts like hell and takes a long time to grow back. Bright light also hurts our eyes."

She looked around the room, and there were only two people. A man and a woman, and both appeared nervous.

"They are. It was a bad day here. I lost all but three pupils. Fortunately, none of the shifters had been killed when I arrived to put an end to it. I released all but these two and the cook for some time off."

All because she had defied his orders and had lost her cool. Her stomach dropped to her feet. If only she could go back in time like Stefan and fix it.

"Your remorse is unwarranted. You know Stefan Darvaak?"

"Yes."

His only reaction was to stare at her face for a moment, and then he went back to eating. "Friends in high places. Just like your father. That's a good instinct."

Yeah, only it hadn't been her instinct. Nik had introduced them. Her whole body ached just thinking about what he was going through. She had to get him out of that cell.

"I know."

She fiddled with the napkin in her lap. "I really hate that you can read my mind."

"Then keep me out."

She hummed an indistinct tune in her head, and he nodded. "You are still angry over what you perceive to be injustices distinct to our world under the Veil."

"Real, not perceived." She picked up her fork.

"Human reality."

"My reality."

"Fair enough. Were we at liberty to spend time exploring this, I would act as the Ghost of Christmas Past in that Dickens story and show you how wrong you are."

She rolled her eyes, still humming, which was good because she was calling him names inside her head she wasn't even aware she knew.

"I could hear your tirade from the forest. You are upset at the death of the shifter pup." He cut off another bite of fish, his manners impeccable. "The killing of children is not unique to the Underveil. Human children are killed in wars all over the world and in gang battles in your own city."

He was right there. Teens were caught in gang crossfire and the victims of horrible murders. She'd seen it on television way too often.

He took a sip of wine, never taking his eyes off her. "The loss of young life is tragic, despite species. Which is the real issue here: *species*. Humans have only one. We have many. Do you think your world would deal with this kind of diversity better? Is everyone in your society slated to be CEO, president, commander, or king, or do they need a skill set, education, connections, or a birthright, just as we do?"

Again. He had a point. She turned her attention to her food.

"We have shifters in our leadership and all jobs in the Underveil, though most pursue careers that best suit their skills or animal nature, sticking with their flock, pack, or herd by choice. They are not oppressed or excluded, unlike in your world where females of your species were not even allowed to vote until the current century. Recall how hard it is, even in your own country in modern times, for different races to accept one another. And that is only skin color or mild differences in features within a single species. Imagine how hard it is to integrate different species. We've done well." He set his wineglass down. "Adjust your thinking, Elena Arcos."

The delicious fish turned to tasteless mush in her mouth.

"As for the brutality that occurred here today. Empath vampires are dangerous, not only to the Underveil, but to humans in particular. They react off emotions rather than logic. This castle functions like a prison psychiatric unit in the human world. They are kept away from civilization and receive treatment in the hopes they can go out in the world and live normal, productive lives. Those who can't are destroyed in order to save the innocent. You did not cause their destruction, Elena. They met the end they were destined for. It just wasn't on today's schedule, and it put the shifters at unnecessary risk. It turned out fine. Lesson learned."

Elena set her fork down. His words made sense, but her heart still ached to think she'd been culpable in any way.

"We are not barbaric or any more bigoted than the human

race. Sadly, as you saw today, we are more violent, as necessitated by nature itself. We deal with long, sometimes *overly* long lifespans, which alters our outlook as well."

Yeah. Stefan had said almost the same thing.

"The Time Folder is wise. And far more neutral than most. He will keep you safe."

"What about you?" Elena recalled how he looked all covered in blood and feared he was a representative of the darker, more violent side of the Underveil.

The door at the far end of the hall burst open, and Elena jumped to her feet. Claude stumbled in, looking around frantically. "Where are they?"

He was in his slayer uniform still, but clean-shaven with his hair slicked back from his face, making his gold eyes even more prominent.

The vampire nodded to the man standing near the door at the other end of the room, and he exited. "Please sit down and join us, Claude."

He remained just inside the room. "No…no. I was told they were here. I…"

"Daddy!" a little boy shrieked as he sprinted through the door where the man had disappeared. He jumped up into his father's tight embrace, no fear whatsoever of not being caught. "Come see Mommy and Sasha. We have a *huuuuuuge* room with the biggest bed I've ever seen. Mommy says we can all stay there together."

Claude approached the head of the table. "I don't even know what to say. I never thought I'd see any of them again. Thank you."

"Go be with your family. Thanks aren't necessary. Just be ready to fight for Nikolai Itzov when the time comes."

He set his son down. "Absolutely." The little boy tugged

him by the hand furiously toward the door. "How? How did you know where to find them? You can't read Slayer's minds."

"I was captive at that fortress for quite a while. You have several friends among the shifter guards. They worry about your family. You must be a good man to warrant such concern. Go."

Claude, eyes bright with unshed tears, allowed his son to lead him from the room.

Completely surprised, Elena returned to her seat. "Your important task was to get his family?"

"An elite force had already been dispatched to execute them all. 'Big, Bad Vlad' couldn't let that happen."

She smiled at the name she'd called him in her rant. "What is your name, really?"

"Oddly, my real name is Vladimir Dalca. Please call me Vlad."

"You're shitting me."

"No, if I ever did such a thing as shitting someone, that is not what I'm doing right now."

It was hard to believe such an act of kindness after the horrors she'd seen. He hadn't even told Claude what he was doing. Maybe he was right and she needed to judge this world differently. But now that he'd returned, it was time to get back to business. "I need to go get Nik."

"I know."

"I don't have a plan. I don't think I'm strong or smart enough to do it without help."

"You are highly intelligent, Elena Arcos. You simply are not familiar enough with our world to navigate it successfully yet." He sat back in his chair considering her. "You have mentioned that you see visions of the future. What is the catalyst? Sex or blood?"

"Blood."

"Well, that's a relief in more ways than one."

That made no sense at all.

He took her hand. Surprisingly, his was not cold like a corpse, just cooler than she was. He chuckled. "I *do* metabolize. My heart beats and pumps blood, albeit much more slowly than a human's. The movies are all fictional." He patted her hand.

"Now what?"

"Well, now you need a vision. I'm relieved it's blood induced because although you are highly appealing, you are bound to another, and he'd kill me if he survives were we to have...an encounter, regardless of my intentions."

"Yeah, besides, you're old enough to be my great-great-grandfather."

He threw his head back and laughed. "No. Nikolai is old enough to be your great-great-grandfather. I'm off the chart. And you are lucky to have a blood catalyst. Nothing kills the mood better than a doomsday vision."

Now it was her turn to laugh. "So who do I bite? Let's get this done."

He nodded to the woman at the end of the table, and she approached. Elena looked into her warm, calm, brown eyes. No fear at all. "So, I got power from Nik, Ricardo, and Fee. What will I get now?"

"Only enough energy to teleport and hopefully a vision of what to do when you arrive."

She stood, and the woman smiled, tipping her neck. It should have felt awkward or wrong, but it didn't. She just detached herself emotionally and bit down. The woman was silent. Her blood almost tasteless. When Elena pulled away, there was no wild buzz of power like she'd had before, only a warm hum. She closed her eyes and waited for the vision. Nothing at first, then only two brief images: She was biting Vlad. And then she was studying a picture of the area where Nik was being held. Her eyes shot open and met his.

"I was afraid of this. Uzana as much as warned me—something about sharing Kool-Aid and not making you wacko."

Clearly, he'd read her mind as she saw the visions. "You know Aunt Uza?"

"Everyone knows Uza."

"What did she mean?"

He placed his napkin on the table. "With all power comes great risk. In my case, you might pick up some of my gifts—or curses. In order to pick up any of my talents, you already have to have them present to some degree. I hear other's thoughts. That won't transfer because you do not hold that power at all. What I'm afraid will transfer is my ability to see the past."

"Why is that a problem? We all have memories of the past."

"Which is exactly why I think it would transfer. Elena, I don't just see the past, I see it with absolute clarity and from everyone's perspective. It makes events entirely different than originally perceived. It could drive the strongest person mad."

This situation was crazy enough. She really didn't need a dose of mad. "What's with the paper in my vision?"

"That's my other gift. I can teleport to a place I've seen, rather than only places I've been. It is extremely rare. I only know of one other who could do it."

"My father."

"Yes."

She remembered how compassionate her father had been. How he seemed to know exactly what she was feeling without her having to tell him. He just seemed to know when she'd had a bad day, or when something made her happy. Putting that with what Lilian had said, she was getting a clearer picture of the man she thought she knew, but really didn't. Not even a little bit. "My father was the empath vampire who used to run this place,"

"He was. His ability to feel others' emotions made him a powerful leader."

She stood. "I have to bite you, Vlad. I need to go to Nik as soon as possible, and I can't do it without your ability to teleport to places based on pictures."

"I know."

Heart hammering, she approached his chair. "Do you need to be restrained like Ricardo?"

He crossed his arms over his chest. "No. I am much older and have far greater control than Ricardo Juarez."

"So you do this a lot?"

"I have never let another take my immortal blood before, Elena." He took her face in his hands. "I am not kidding when I tell you this is dangerous. I am hopeful the effect will be temporary, but seeing the past with absolute clarity is not a gift. You will not like it. Please be sure this is correct."

She closed her eyes, and the image of her biting him came up again. He was in the chair where he sat now, hands wrapped around the seat under him. Eyes closed, face relaxed. "Yeah, I'm absolutely certain. Will I see your memories?"

"Possibly, but only while you are drinking. After the physical connection is broken, they should all be your own. I hope they are more pleasant than mine."

She stood over him and studied the vein pulsing in his neck just below the skin, and her fangs elongated with a sharp twinge deep in her jaw. Vlad showed none of the anxiety or tension Ricardo had, only calm resignation.

"The comparative study does not help. Leave the research scientist behind, Miss Arcos. Bite me."

And he smelled different than Ricardo, too. Like the

outdoors after a rain. Natural and fresh.

"Hum, please," he said, barely above a whisper.

She struck up with the "Hokey Pokey," her father's favorite when he'd danced in the living room with her, and Vlad laughed.

His blood was cool and thick. The power hit her like a body slam, and she pulled back with a gasp.

"And you were worried about *me*," he said with a smirk. "That wasn't enough. Go all in, Elena. You have to save the world."

"Will it hurt the baby?"

He actually looked offended. "Absolutely not."

Knowing what to expect this time, she braced herself for the power rush. What she wasn't prepared for were Vlad's memories. She saw him with her father laughing, then smiling as he willingly went with the Slayers to the dungeon. He'd allowed himself to be captured on purpose because Uza told him he would need to save her. Then she saw the horrible slaughter in the fortress as he fought his way from the dungeon preceding his arrival at the barn, and then the scene in the great hall after the vampires had gone wild. Blood was everywhere and so were broken bodies. She shuddered, and a tear slid down her cheek. She kept on, hoping to get another glimpse of her father, but none came, only Vlad's voice telling her to stop. Strong, cool hands shook her shoulders, and reluctantly, she opened her jaw, releasing him.

He steadied her, and after a moment, she opened her eyes to find him staring into her own as if searching for something. "Now sit," he said. "Then focus on the future. Do not think about what you saw."

Dizzy and body buzzing, she collapsed into the chair next to him, but found it almost impossible to concentrate as the vampire's memories jumbled together with hers.

He leaned closer and whispered in her ear. "You must only look to the future until you fulfill your destiny as the Uniter."

Just as he'd predicted, his memories faded, and her own moved to the forefront.

"Leave the past behind," he said. "We all need you to succeed. If not, we all die. Including Nikolai Itzov and your unborn child."

And with that, images of the future flooded her head like a fast motion slide show. Her eyes flew open, and she grinned. "I need Claude. And then, I need someone to get a message to Fee the Alchemist. Oh, and please return the key I gave you in the dungeon. I believe it's in your back right pants pocket."

He leaned back with an amused smile. "Anything else?"

"Yeah, do you have a superhero cape around here anywhere, because I'm feeling badass."

"Save the badass for Nikolai Itzov, please."

Chapter Thirty-One

Nikolai fought hard to remain optimistic. Elena *would* come for him. It had only been hours since Fydor was telling Commander Mihai to keep on the lookout for her. It was crucial to remain patient and positive. Some things were hard to brush aside, though, like what the hell was Aleksi up to swearing revenge against Elena? It had to be a ploy. Nikolai knew in his heart she'd never side with his uncle. Just like he knew Elena hadn't betrayed him back at her house. She was just doing what she had to do. They all were.

The shifter was snoring like, well, a bear again. At least it kept Nikolai from falling asleep. He wanted to stay awake for when Elena came. How odd that the weak little human he spared in that store and took prisoner was the very person he now relied upon to free him from captivity. But she was different now. They both were. And he loved her. That was what had been his biggest incentive since his capture: a future with Elena Arcos. During the beatings, when the pain was at its worst, he had eased his mind by imagining what their children could have looked like had he and Elena been compatible species and able to reproduce. Strong, black-haired, gold eyed, sometimes. Other times, he'd see them with her coloration. Gold curls and purple eyes. Maybe even blue, like when she was a human. Yes. Blue. He'd like that.

His stomach rumbled. Being immortal, he couldn't starve to death, but that didn't keep him from suffering hunger and thirst. And he was weakened considerably. Hopefully, she'd come soon, before he could no longer walk on his own.

The first things he wanted to do when he got out of here were eat, shower, and sleep. If he got out of here. No. He could not let negativity cloud his reasoning. Slayers were trained to focus and have positive visualizations. When negativity was allowed in, resolve would be weakened, like his uncle's.

The sorry bastard. At least he'd lost interest in using him as a living piñata since Borya left. Most of his wounds had healed, though some food and rest would speed the remaining injuries along. Willing his body to heal itself, he shut his eyes in attempt to relax, using the meditation techniques his mother had taught him as a boy.

A faint buzzing and a grunt roused him from his meditation. He opened his eyes to find Elena with her hands on either side of the guard's face struggling to keep him in her grasp as she channeled power as effectively as a Time Folder. A couple of times, it looked like the big bear shifter would break away from her, but ultimately, she kept contact long enough to win the battle.

"Fancy meeting you here," she said, abandoning the unconscious hulk of a guard and sauntering toward him in a skimpy leather halter and skintight leather pants like something out of a fantasy. "You come here often?"

"First time. You?"

She pulled a key out of her cleavage and inserted it into the cuff at his left wrist, pressing against him in the process, causing his body to roar to life. He may have been starved and in pain, but his body knew his fated mate. She pulled back slightly as the cuff fell away.

"First and last, I hope. Not a big fan of the ambiance." His limp arm dropped below shoulder height for the first time in days, and painful tingles shot from shoulder to index finger. She unlocked the cuff on his right arm, then his ankles, and stepped back, checking him out from head to toe. "Mr. Itzov, if you don't mind, I think it best we take this party elsewhere."

Shouting erupted outside the chamber.

She shot a look at the door. "I suggest you hang on to me right now, because I'm about to give you the ride of your life. Pun intended."

"Pun appreciated," he said, wrapping his arms around her. "Get us the hell out of here."

Nikolai had never thought reconfiguring after teleporting felt good, but this time, he reveled in it because when he solidified, Elena was in his arms.

"Welcome to Castle Poenari, King Nikolai," a familiar voice said from behind them, right as he was about to rip Elena's clothes off—well, right as he was about to *try* to rip her clothes off as best he could with no feeling in his hands. Maybe the interruption was a good thing.

"Vladimir Dalca. To what do I owe the honor?" The vampire had been tight with his father and was Elena's father's right hand man. He'd been at the fortress many times. But this was the first time Nikolai had been inside Castle Poenari.

"To your lovely mate. She insisted on saving you, and being generous, I allowed it."

A door across the room flew open. "A message came for you, Miss Elena." The last person Nikolai expected to see in Vlad's castle was Claude Ungur. But lo and behold, there he was in

Slayer uniform, no less, looking better than he had in years.

She pulled away to retrieve the scrap of paper. After scanning it quickly, she grinned. "Excellent. Everything is working perfectly so far."

"Yes, everything," Nikolai said, realizing his bad innuendo had failed because his hands really weren't working right. He shook them, and the tips of his fingers stung. Looking down, he realized what a horrible state he was in. He'd been beaten to the point of human death repeatedly and his body, and surely his head and face, were coated in layers of dried blood. He must have looked and smelled like death. "Is it possible to for me to get a shower and a change of clothes?"

"And food and rest so you can heal before we have to go back to the fortress? Yes," Elena said. "Come with me."

The room was sparse, the only feature being a bed with green curtains and yellow ties. Sleep. How long had it been? Days. He'd lost track of how many.

A steaming tub of water was waiting for him in the bathroom. As he brushed his teeth, he mused that he'd gone from hell to heaven in just a matter of minutes. And he was safe here. Fydor would never think to look for him here. No one hated vampires more than Nikolai; his uncle had seen to that. Even if he did think to find him here, he'd never penetrate this castle. Colonies of Vlad's reformed empath vamps were scattered all over the mountain. No one had ever successfully reached the castle alive that he didn't bring here himself. Which brought up a whole host of questions...

Elena unbuttoned his shirt.

Questions that could wait...

Then, she pulled down his pants, and he stepped out of them.

Yeah. Questions that could wait a long time...

And ran her hands down the outside of his thighs.

A really long time…

She trailed her hands back up to his waist again.

…What questions?

"Step in," she said, picking up a bottle of soap.

The warm water lapping over his skin was heaven. So was having his hair shampooed by possibly the most beautiful woman in the world. With unguarded appreciation, she helped him soap his entire body, and then after he rinsed, she drained the tub and refilled it with fresh, clear water. "How are your hands?"

"What hands?"

Her gaze trailed down his body, pausing at his cock, which had been rock hard since she appeared in his cell. "Yeah, what hands?" she repeated.

They stared into each other's eyes for a moment, and her brow furrowed.

"Nik, I didn't abandon you to—"

"Stop. We'll have centuries to talk about this. Right now, I need your hands on me. If you don't touch me, I might go mad."

Turning her back to him, she untied the halter, which slipped to her feet, exposing her pale skin. His cock pulsed and he groaned. There were moments in that cell, when weakness would prevail and he'd contemplate never seeing her again— never hearing her laugh or touching her smooth, soft skin. But, just before he would allow the negativity to pull him under, he'd remember just how strong and smart she was. Somehow, he always knew she'd find a way to free him, and together they'd defeat Fydor.

She slipped off her pants, and it took all he had not to touch himself to relieve the ache at the sight of her round, perfect ass—an ass he needed to get his hands on immediately, now that they had feeling again. Then she turned, and his breath caught. A fresh set of markings ran from under her breasts to her navel. Mesmerized, he couldn't take his eyes off the new hieroglyphs. "What do they say?"

"They say, I need you inside me right now, Nik. That my body is on fire for you." She pulled the drain on the tub and stepped in, with a slender foot on either side of his waist and crouched over him. "That I missed you." She took him in hand and positioned him, and in one movement, pushed down, taking him fully inside her body. His entire world tilted. The overwhelming heat and tightness of her—the *rightness* of her—took his breath away.

Gripping the edge of the tub, he almost came on the spot. Simply being inside her made all the suffering of the last days worthwhile. Remaining absolutely silent, he took a shuddering breath through his nose and stared into her fascinating purple eyes.

"You are very, very quiet, Nik." Her teasing grin made him even harder. "Bear got your tongue?"

"Empaths," he whispered.

"All gone." She put her hands on his shoulders and rocked forward, then back, taking him even deeper. Then did it again. "Vlad relocated them for a few days. Feel free to shout my name at any time now." She increased her speed, and he placed his hands on her thighs, loving the feel of her muscles flexing as she rode him.

"My God."

"Elena is sufficient." Faster still, she moved, breasts bouncing as her body slapped against his in the wet tub. "Missed you," she said in a strained voice.

Missing her didn't begin to cover it. He loved her. Needed her like he needed air. She threw her head back and ground against him even harder until he was barely hanging on by a thread, his whole body humming with energy and pleasure. Nothing could be this right. "Need you to come," she whispered.

No problem there. When he felt the waves of her climax begin, he grabbed her ass and pulled her down against him, driving up as hard as he could, joining her. And, yes, even shouting her name.

E lena popped another grape in her mouth while Nik finished off his second steak. "Nothing like room service," she said.

Obviously, if he had thought she'd betrayed him, he was well over it based on his reaction to her and his repeated promises to make love to her all day and night until they returned to the fortress to take on Fydor.

His color had returned, and the injuries were fading to white scars. As she lay on the bed next to him, it was hard to recall her life before he entered it. Her memories of it since were frighteningly clear, though. Vlad had been right: perfect recall was more of a curse than a gift. It was much easier to justify actions when bias was involved. When she recalled Nik taking her prisoner now, she no longer saw it with the self-righteous indignation of a human being ripped from her life; she saw his side, too. A confused, betrayed Slayer wanting revenge for the death of a man he loved. He had never hated her. He had hated vampires—a gift from his uncle.

Part of her hoped this ability would fade soon. Another knew that as Uniter, it would serve her well to see all sides. It was like mind reading, actually… just after the fact.

"Your thoughts are far away," he said, standing to place the tray on the floor next to the bed.

"Right here with you." He needed rest to heal completely.

"You should sleep."

The look that crossed his face made her toes curl. Obviously, sleeping was not on the agenda, which suited her just fine.

"Lose the towel before I lose my mind," he said, completely naked, staring down at her from the other side of the bed. She pulled it off and pitched it on the floor, marveling at his beautiful, chiseled body. Even after extreme abuse in that cell, it had bounced back to its original, powerful, drool-worthy form. Wide shoulders, narrow hips. Mmm…

He scanned her body, stopping on the markings on her ribs and belly. "What do they say?"

She wanted tell him, but the timing was wrong. There were too many variables, and seeing backward had given her clear insight into his motives. She now knew that all those times he'd acted like an overbearing ass, he'd only been trying to protect her. Keeping her safe had been his top priority, and would continue to be. If he knew about the baby, he'd be so distracted by protecting her and his child that he'd be less effective. In order to defeat Fydor, he needed to be in top form. So did she. Telling him about the baby would have to wait. She needed his blood, so she needed him rested and strong.

"I'll tell you only after you're a good boy and get some sleep."

Like a powerful predator, he climbed onto the bed and loomed over her. "I'll show you good." He grabbed her and pulled her to the center of the bed, pushing her to her back. She giggled. "I'll show you *great*," he said, pinning her arms over her head.

She didn't fight him, but simply watched in amazement as he took total control. No snow, no cord, no fear—other than a tiny tinge of anxiety over his reception to her news. But that could wait. Right now, she needed this and so did he.

"In fact, I'll show you stars, Elena Arcos." Arms still pinned above her head, he shoved her legs apart with his knees and settled his body over hers. His weight felt amazing as it pushed her into the soft mattress. She was completely pinned and possessed, and she loved it. She loved *him*.

"Nik, I—"

He cut her off with a searing kiss that took her breath away. No gentle lead in. He angled his mouth over hers and was relentless, coaxing, stroking her tongue with his, nipping her bottom lip, all the while his body rocked in a rhythm letting her know exactly what he planned. But not yet.

"I'm going to kiss you all over your incredible body, and after you come at least twice, I'm going to fuck you so hard we both have to sleep in order to recuperate."

"Using only your mouth or your hand this time?"

A cocky smile caused his dimple to show. "Baby, this time, I'm going to use my whole body."

Her mind and her newly immortal body rejoiced, anticipation zinging through her, as he moved down, kissing a hot trail from her breasts to her navel to the place where she needed him most. And after she'd come twice, as prescribed, he finally covered her body with his and pushed his hard, hot length inside her, filling her completely, but only making the longing stronger.

"Yes," she murmured. "Nik, please."

He lowered onto his elbows and took her earlobe between his teeth. "Tell me what the markings say."

No. Not this. Not now. She wrapped her legs around his waist and angled up to take him deeper and fill the ache. He reacted with a gratifying thrust. She groaned, and he did it again. Soon, he was pumping into her in a rhythm that was sure to put her over the edge, their sweat slicked bodies sliding against each other as he twined his fingers into her hair. She unwound her legs from around his body and dug her heels into the bed, meeting his thrusts, and right as she reached that edge, he stopped.

What the hell? She thrust up and he didn't react. Opening her eyes, she found him staring down at her. Sweat beading on his forehead, expression grim.

"Tell me," he said, voice strained.

"After you sleep."

"Now."

"After we finish."

"Now."

An involuntary tear trailed from the corner of her eye down her temple. He brushed it away with his thumb. He deserved to know. Maybe they could take up where they left off later, depending on how he took the news. "I'm pregnant." She straightened her legs, half expecting him to pull out. Instead, he remained perfectly still, hard and hot inside her.

His brow furrowed. "Are you sure?"

"Yes." When he didn't respond, she added, "You don't look happy."

"I'm confused. This is physically impossible. How do you know?"

"Stefan read the glyphs…and I'm late."

When he still didn't react, her heart ached like it had shattered. She didn't know what she had expected, but this wasn't it. She felt helpless pinned beneath him, his body still inside hers. She needed to get away.

And then he moved: a long, slow withdrawal, followed by a strong push back to bury himself deep inside her. A beautiful, brilliant smile lit his face. "You have just made me the happiest man on this planet. Or any other, for that matter."

Her head reeled. The man never failed to surprise her. Good thing they had centuries, so she could get a chance to figure him out. "Really?"

He thrust again, harder this time. "Really."

Twining her fingers in his hair, she pulled him down for a kiss, and he increased the tempo of his body and kissed her like he'd die if they stopped. She raked her nails down his back, and he groaned, then froze. "I can't hurt you, can I? I mean, the baby and all."

She almost laughed, but bit her lip instead. "Only if you stop."

"Well, we can't have that, can we?"

She dug her heels into the mattress again and met him thrust for thrust until the bed creaked like it was going to break apart.

She needed more. Something else, but he needed rest.

"Do it, Elena, I can't hold out much longer. Bite me."

He knew. Her fangs elongated, and she arched up, burying them in his skin, his rich blood filling her mouth, and she came instantly. He'd made good on his promise to make her see stars.

"Yes," he groaned. His body stilled as he pulsed inside her, riding his own waves of passion while her orgasm seemed to stretch on and on, pulling her fear and anxiety away with it as it started to fade.

"Nik," she whispered, tremors finally easing.

"Yes, say it again."

"Nik."

"Once more."

"I love you, Nikolai Itzov."

His gold eyes seemed to glow as they bored into hers. "And I love you, Elena Arcos."

He rolled off and pulled her against his hard body. Never had she felt this relaxed and complete. This man, this child, this world. If they survived the next few days, they had a real future. "I thought Slayers didn't love."

"So did I."

CHAPTER THIRTY-TWO

The woman in the vision had black hair and gold eyes. Her face showed no fear whatsoever as a man in a uniform like Claude's lit the wood piled beneath and around her. She didn't struggle against the chains, nor did she cry out as the flames danced all around the stake to which she was bound. "Forgive me, Queen Tatiana," the man said, backing away.

Shit. It was Nik's mother.

Elena rolled over in the bed and ran her hand over Nik's smooth chest, and he smiled. "Again, so soon? You're relentless." He shifted to face her. "I like it." His smile faded as he studied her. "Something's wrong."

"Yes, I…" How do you tell someone his mother is going to be burned alive? She swallowed and took a deep breath. *By being straightforward and putting it out there.* That's what she would want were the tables reversed. "I had a vision. Your mother's name is Tatiana, right?" He didn't react, but she already knew the answer. "She is going to be…" It was harder than expected. "Fydor is going to…" Another breath. "I saw her burning at the stake. I'm so sorry."

Deliberately and slowly, he sat up and swung his feet over the side of the bed. "I must go."

She mirrored his motions. The floor was cold under her bare feet. "I'll come with you."

"No!" His response was so immediate and forceful that she flinched. "You will stay here where you're safe."

His reaction didn't surprise her, but it rankled just the same. Charge tingled in her palms. She closed her eyes and willed the current to subside. Seeing the past with Vlad's "gift" had given her a much better understanding of his Slayer mentality, and she knew the best way to deal with him was to not strip him of control.

Without arguing, which was a close to impossible feat, she padded to the bathroom and pulled on her clothes. He couldn't stop her from going, so feuding with him was a waste of time and energy.

He was still naked when she returned to the bedroom, pacing like a caged lion. Leaning against the doorframe, she watched him until he stopped abruptly and ran his hands through his hair. "I need your help," he said.

Well, what do you know? He came around to reason a lot faster than expected. "Okay."

"I need you to go find me some clothes. Mine are destroyed for the most part."

So much for reason. "I'll do it if I can come with you and help you get your mother out of there."

"No." He opened the door and disappeared into the hallway.

Well, that worked great. Yeah. Awesome. Way to be reasonable, Nik. She sighed and followed him. No sign of him anywhere, but as she neared the great hall where she had first arrived, male voices fell silent, and in an old-fashioned gesture, Vlad stood. Two men dressed in brown, hooded cloaks seated at the table also rose. Empath vampires. She intentionally calmed her emotions. Surely Nik wouldn't teleport out to save his mother naked.

"One would hope not," Vlad said.

"Do you know where he is?"

He closed his eyes, then after several moments, shook his head. "None of my staff have seen him… Oh, wait." He smiled and opened his eyes. "My cook thinks he has a nice ass."

She wasn't sure whether to be amused or jealous, but she knew to keep her emotions in check. "So, he's in the kitchen?"

"Was. Would you like to join us?" He gestured to the two men at the table, who like him, were still standing.

"No, thank you." She didn't want to join them. She wanted to join Nik before he zapped out on a suicide mission to rescue his mother.

He gestured to the chair to his right. "Please sit. What we are discussing involves you." When she hesitated, he held his hand out. She could totally see him fitting in centuries ago in a more formal society. "Please, Elena. He cannot 'zap' anywhere without me. The entire mountain is secured to where no one can teleport without possessing something of my person."

And what the hell did that mean? "I teleported to go get him out of that cell."

"Yes, you were in possession of something of my body."

His blood.

"Yes." He wiggled his fingers and she placed her hand in his. With a gentle tug, he pulled her to the chair next to him. Once she sat, the others did, too, which was weird, but oddly flattering.

"Several of the Underveil factions have already mobilized. Sending the dungeon prisoners as emissaries was an excellent idea."

It had been Aleksi's idea. Elena wondered how she was faring. Her chest ached when she thought of how she'd found her tied to the bed, coated in blood. That memory, though, didn't present an alternative interpretation of Fydor's character thanks to Vlad's gift of seeing the past with unbiased clarity. Nothing but rage and fear of Borya colored Fydor's actions, which in some ways helped. Discovering any sympathetic or redeeming traits in the man would make it harder to do what she had to do.

"Most of the Underveil factions have mobilized and will be poised to strike once it's dark," he continued. "The wood elves and some of the shifter groups are still siding with Fydor's revolutionist movement, but the rest have taken up arms for the resistance."

"Have we heard from the light elves yet?" the hooded vampire to his left asked in a monotone, expressionless voice. Her father had been an empath, but he was always charming and animated—at least around her he had been.

"No, but I've known Dalra and Leione for over six centuries. They will join us."

The other empath spoke with the same odd lack of expression. "They have always remained neutral and apart from the rest of the Underveil factions. Don't you expect they will simply avoid the conflict altogether like they have in the past?"

Vlad leaned back in his chair, arms folded across his chest. "No. There is too much at stake this time." Then he smiled, fangs barely visible. "Besides, Fydor made a very stupid mistake where the elves are involved." His smile broadened into a grin, exposing his sharp, deadly fangs, and Elena shuddered. "He kidnapped and imprisoned Dalra the Warrior's only daughter. The light elves' days of being passive, uninvolved observers are over. Taking Fee was declaring war. Had he destroyed her, the Slayers would have been obliterated."

Nik, wearing something that looked like a monk's tunic,

burst into the room. "Let me out of here, Dalca." His gaze flitted to Elena and stopped on the two vampires to Vlad's left. Immediately, his shoulders dropped to a more relaxed stance as he reigned in his emotion. "Please."

"Join us, Nikolai. We were discussing strategy for tonight. The factions are converging on the Slayer fortress at this moment and plan to launch an attack sometime after dark."

"I plan to launch an attack right now," he said, not moving. "How do I teleport out?"

Squawking and racket from the other door cut off Vlad's response. The bird lady from the barn trotted into the room and stopped short, out of breath. "The avian flock is joining the battle on the resistance's behalf. So are the light elves," she said. "And Fee the Alchemist requests a key to teleport."

Pose still relaxed, Vlad arched an eyebrow. "For what purpose?"

The woman's jerky, nonhuman movements made it hard for Elena to take her seriously. "She has business with the Uniter." Now *that* she could take seriously. Maybe this crazy plan would work after all.

Vlad plucked a hair from his head and gestured her over. "Deliver this to Fee and thank your flock leader. Tell him King Nikolai is honored by her decision."

The woman left immediately without words of parting.

"I am not the king," Nik said.

"Yes, you are. Fydor usurped the throne by committing a crime, and we all know it."

"I abdicated. He obtained it rightfully because of my mistakes."

"Yes, Nikolai. You made errors, but only because your father was brutally murdered along with his best friend. *My* dear friend. His claim to the throne was illegitimate. It's time for you to make things right."

"Which is exactly what I plan to do. Let me out of here."

The cloaked vampires shifted in their chairs, clearly uncomfortable. Vlad clasped one on the shoulder and gave a reassuring squeeze. "You are not in the mindset to do this at this time, Nikolai Itzov."

"Fydor plans a human massacre. A large-scale one. I fear it will be initiated today."

"Doubtful, if he plans to execute the queen tonight."

Nik's brow furrowed. "How did you know that?"

"He can read my mind," Elena answered, rising to go to him. Which also meant Vlad knew what she planned to do to stop Fydor. So far, he was keeping that to himself, which was good.

She met Vlad's amused gaze. *Sneaky devil.*

"Just so," he said, with a wink.

He pulled away from her. "This can't wait. A surgical strike on Fydor and the rescue of the queen is critical. I can do this and prevent the human massacre and a full-scale attack on the Slayer fortress by our resistance." He stood very still, tension practically rolling off him in waves from his dark hair to his bare feet. His attempt to hold his emotions in check had him close to cracking.

"Take the Uniter with you," Vlad said.

He answered without even considering it. "No. Absolutely not. If you can read her mind, then you know exactly why. There is too much risk for her."

"You underestimate her."

"You underestimate *me*," Nik answered.

"How about letting me weigh in on this?" Talking about her like she wasn't in the room was infuriating.

"No," Nik snapped.

Hands on hips, she collected herself for several reasons. Not only did she not want to set off the two empath vamps, she didn't want to set Nik off, either. He'd just been through a horrible ordeal, and he was being asked to give up control and concede he needed help, neither of which were easy for him.

"She doesn't need your approval. She has her own powers and can go without you," Vlad observed.

"I won't allow it."

Enough. Elena gripped the edge of the table. "Is Chauvinism 101 a required course for all Slayers, or is it reserved for royalty?"

Both of his dark eyebrows shot up. Other than that, he remained still.

"I can teleport out of here any time I want, Nik, but *you* can't. I'll give you half an hour to make up your mind whether or not you want me to take you when I teleport to the fortress." With that, she marched out the door to go get her sword from her bedroom.

Her vision blurred through the tears she refused to shed. She was trying, she really was, but he needed to meet her halfway. When he was ready to treat her as an equal and stop acting like a royal ass, she'd be more than happy to talk to him. As soon as she got what she needed from the elf, she was out of here, with or without him.

Nikolai knew he was being a prick, and possibly giving Elena cause to hate him, but couldn't risk losing her or his baby. Just thinking about her carrying his child made his heart beat faster . No. She would stay here with Vladimir Dalca where they both were safe.

"I would like some more suitable battle clothes if available."

The three vampires didn't respond, not that he expected the two empaths to do anything. Freakish creatures, but invaluable in battle. They fed off the opponents' fear or fury and were unstoppable. Sadly, that carried over into everyday life, so they had to be contained to this mountain where their interaction with other species, especially humans, was limited.

Dalca reached for a goblet on the table in front of him. "You spoke of mistakes you'd made. You are about to make the biggest one of your existence."

"I can't allow her to put herself and our baby in harm's way."

"Which is exactly what would happen if she remains here. We will all be in harm's way. She's the key to ending the war."

Part of him knew he was right, but the other part wasn't willing to take the risk. "I couldn't bear to lose her."

"Based on her thoughts, you very well might have lost her already." He took a sip from the goblet and put it back on the table. "Your markings do not say that the Uniter will rise from the ashes of death by a warrior's hand, only to be locked away for her own good, thereby denied the ability to dethrone tyrants and anoint kings."

"This is bullshit."

"Yes, it is." He closed his eyes and then stood. "Evidently, there is some unusual activity in the forest on the south side. You two are needed to see your units secure the castle. Go now."

Both vampires stood and wordlessly left the room.

With a crook of a finger, Dalca signaled to the woman in the corner. Without hesitation, she crossed the room to stand before him. His eyes darkened, and she smiled as he loosened her hair and ran his fingers through it.

"It's a funny thing about fated mates. I've never had one, so I can only relate what I've heard from those who have been more fortunate than I." He unbuttoned the woman's blouse and slipped his hands inside, but his gaze was on Nikolai. "One's weakness is the other's strength." The woman moaned, and he whispered something in her ear that caused her to moan again. "Your strengths, Nikolai Itzov, are bravery, honesty, and fighting skill." He sat in a chair, pulling the woman into his lap. "Elena Arcos's strengths are compassion, intelligence, and an uncanny ability to think analytically."

The woman reached for the button on his pants, and he stayed her hands. "Together, you and Elena are a formidable team, making up for each other's deficits. Her brains, your brawn. Think about it." He released the woman's hands and brushed her hair over her shoulder as she worked his zipper open with a zing. "But please think about it somewhere else, Nikolai Itzov. I think my castle is about to be under attack, and I have something to do first."

When Nikolai was a few yards from the door of the bedroom he'd been sharing with Elena, female voices brought him to an abrupt halt.

One was Elena; the other he didn't recognize. "Thanks for putting it together so quickly," Elena said.

"I owe you my life. This was my honor."

Nikolai peeked in to find Elena with a female light elf. The elf handed her a vial of purple liquid that looked to be the elixir his uncle was addicted to. No. He wouldn't allow Elena to even sample that shit.

He consciously unclenched his fists. "Hello, ladies."

They turned to face him, but didn't act the least bit startled. In fact, Elena held the vial up to the light as if it were a jewel. "Fee just gave me a gift."

He shot the elf what he hoped was a warning glare, but based on her lack of reaction, clearly it was ineffective. "How…

nice."

"Prenatal vitamins," Elena said.

From down the hall in the great room, Vlad cut loose with a burst of laughter.

Vitamins. He looked from the elf to Elena's smiling faces. What an ass he was. An overbearing, shortsighted, completely head-over-heels-in-love ass. "Thank you…"

"Oh. This is Fee the Alchemist," Elena said.

"I've heard of you often. I'm sorry about your brother."

"Thank you. I am certain we will be bringing him home soon. My father thinks we are close to locating him."

"I hope so."

"I must go," she said. "Be careful. I'm not sure how quickly the vitamins will take effect, but I am confident they will have the desired result." She wrapped her slender arms around Elena, and they held one another like sisters. Clearly, lots had happened while he was chained to the wall in Fydor's "rec room."

The elf disappeared, leaving no trace except the floral scent common to all light elves.

Elena slid the vial into her pocket and pulled her hair back, tying it up with a leather cord she gathered from the bathroom counter. "I'll see you later, Nik."

"Wait!"

She lifted a perfectly formed eyebrow, which made him feel more chastised than any words ever could.

"Look, I…" *Fuck. This shouldn't be so hard.* He loved this woman. Needed her. Still, asking someone for help was hard, but going against every instinct he had to protect his mate was almost incapacitating. And he was about to ask her to risk her life—probably a Slayer first. "I'm sorry I was such a prick. You're right. I need you to go. Not only are you a better planner and strategist, you are the Uniter, which means this is your show. I'm just there to wield a sword and keep you…" He was pleased when she let him approach and run a hand over her belly. "Keep both of you safe. Allow me that." He brushed his lips against her jaw. "Please."

A knock sounded on the door, and then it was thrown open by Dalca. "I brought some clothes for Nikolai, along with this, since he arrived without a weapon."

Nik stared at the all too familiar sword in the vampire's hand. "That was my father's."

"It was. I took it from Ivan's body before Fydor arrived. I couldn't bear the thought of that worm even touching it." He passed it to Nikolai and handed a stack of clothes to Elena.

Nik's vision blurred as tears stung his eyes. He blinked them away. Slayers never cried. "Thank you. I'd thought it was lost forever."

"No. Just in safekeeping until you were ready to receive it." He patted him on the shoulder. "You're ready now." He took the pile of clothes from Elena and passed them to Nik.

"And as for you, Elena Arcos. I wish Gregor were alive for more than one reason, but right now, I wish it so that he could see you. You are magnificent and he would be proud of his daughter."

He opened his arms and she stepped into his embrace. "I wish you luck," he whispered into her hair. "Make wise choices."

CHAPTER THIRTY-THREE

Sword drawn and with "Happy Birthday" running in her head to mask her thoughts, Elena pushed the window open to find Aleksi's room empty. Nik followed her in silently and closed the window behind them.

"My mother's apartment is just down the hall," he said.

Dammit. Where was Aleksandra? None of this would work if she couldn't get the elixir to her. "I need to talk to your sister."

"It will have to wait."

No. It couldn't wait. Nothing was more important than this. Not even his mother. "Go on. I'll stay here in case she shows up." Which she hoped to hell happened soon. Everything hinged on this. "I will only get in the way." She pointed to her head. "I'm the mastermind. You are the trained swordsman." Yeah, some mastermind. *Happy birthday, dear whomeveeeeeerrrrr. Happy birthday to yooooooooou.*

He ran his hand over her bare back. "When this is over, I'm buying you a dozen of these halters. I love seeing your markings...among other things." He ran his fingers down her cleavage, and she trembled. Lips replaced fingers, and she had to concentrate to keep singing as his warm breath fanned over the exposed swells of her breasts. Behind the leather, her nipples hardened. *Happy birthday, dear...*

He moved his lips up her neck and whispered in her ear. "I want you close. Come with me. Leaving you here alone feels wrong."

It sure did. But she needed to see Aleksi. "I..."

The door burst open, and Aleksi stormed in, then slammed the door behind her. "Asshole! You've got it wrong, Mihai. I've never been anything but loyal to Fydor."

"You were not supposed to leave your room until the danger had passed," a deep voice said from outside the door. "You promised to defend this entrance to the castle in case the Uniter tries to gain access this way again."

She jumped but made no sound when she discovered Nik and Elena in her room. "Okay, fine."

"Aleksandra, you know how I feel about you. I would never —"

"Fuck off, Mihai. Just go."

After many long minutes of silence, she took a long breath. "Ballsy move coming back here, Niki baby. Fydor has been in a rage since you were "stolen" from him."

Nik sheathed his father's sword and pulled his sister into his arms. "Did he hurt you?"

She shook her head. "He's been too high to do much of anything since Borya left."

"Borya was here?"

"Yeah. He locked Fydor in the rec room with him for a while. Fydor has been fucked up since. Said something about a vision Borya had about Mom proclaiming you king or something. Really shook him up. Well, that and the quality one-on-one time with Borya."

"Are there any other mind readers here?" Elena asked, still singing in her head.

"No. There are no vampires or sorcerers. They are the only ones with that power. And not all vamps at that."

Thank goodness for small favors. She stopped humming and reveled in the silence in her head.

"I'm here for Mom," Nik said. "Elena saw her burning at the stake. Where is she?"

"Her apartment, I guess. She never leaves anymore."

Pulling Elena close, he leaned down, his familiar minty smell folded around her like a warm blanket. "Say it," he whispered. "I need to hear it."

"I love you, Nikolai Itzov."

"Aw, shit. Don't make me barf," Aleksi teased.

Nik's lips met hers, and she wrapped her arms around his neck, sword still in her hand. He ran his warm palm down her back and pulled her against him, then gave her butt cheek a squeeze, which made her whole body flush hot. She'd never get enough of this man. Good thing they'd live forever… Well, if they made it past tonight. "Wait for me. I'll be right back," he said against her lips.

He stopped just inside the door. "I can't wait to introduce you to my mother." And with a gorgeous grin, he slipped out the door and out of sight.

Focus. She shook off her lusty haze and pulled the vial out of her pocket. "Here's the plan. You need to get it into Fydor's stash somehow and make sure he takes it sometime before midnight tonight."

"He takes that shit all the time. Mom got him hooked on it by calling it medicine. He thinks it makes his thinking clearer. Getting him high won't work."

"This 'medicine' won't make him high. It will kill him."

For a moment, her eyes lit up, and then she slumped down onto the bed. "Impossible. He won't let me anywhere near. He's on a bender and says he knows I'm in with you somehow. It will never work."

"Who is he letting close?"

"No one. He just broods alone in his room. The entire place and everyone in it is on lockdown. Including me." She buried her face in her hands.

There had to be a way. She turned the tiny bottle in her fingers. Always another answer. She'd spent her time in graduate school troubleshooting potentially hopeless problems. She just needed to step back and think about it logically and analytically: goal, obstacle, solution.

First, define the goal. Well, that was easy. Get Fydor to drink the replacement elixir, which meant getting it into his possession in such a way he would ingest it today.

Define biggest obstacle. Easy as well. Lack of proximity and access.

Discover solution. Not as simple. She had to get someone close enough to sub that vial into his supply, but he had closed himself away.

There's always an answer. Always a way… She paced the room and stopped short dead center. Adrenaline surged through her in a prickly wave. The solution was obvious as well. Her stomach sank. Nik was not going to like this. Not at all. "What is the one thing your uncle wants to get his hands on more than anything else in the world right now?"

Aleksi raised her head from her hands. "You."

Nikolai peeked around the corner to find only one bear shifter standing guard outside his mother's apartment. Wrapping his hand around his father's sword handle, he slid it from the sheath on his back and took a deep breath. The sword felt warm and alive in his hands, and for a moment, he could almost feel his father's presence. *For you, Dad. I'll free her for you.*

The guard's head was separated from his body before the beast had even registered the danger. The door was locked, but it was easy enough to find the key on the guard's ring. Careful not to track blood into his mother's room, he paused inside the doorway. "Mother?"

No answer came in return. He shut the door behind him and crossed the room he had spent so many hours in as a child. Still decked in white and gold, the airy space reflected his mother perfectly: classic, elegant, understated—so unlike his uncle.

"Hello? Mother?"

Sharp, stinging pain erupted on the back of his neck, like the time he was stung on the ear by a wasp when he was seven. He slapped his hand over it, plucking the insect off.

His uncle's voice sounded far away. "I knew you wouldn't be able to resist coming here."

He opened his palm to find a feathered dart. *Fuck.* He'd been poisoned or drugged. The edges of his vision blurred. "Human tricks."

"Yes." Fydor moved closer, but not close enough to grab. Nik tried to lunge, but ended up face down on the floor.

The image of his uncle waved like ripples on the surface of a pond as he leaned down and pulled his father's sword from his hand. "And shortly, I'll have *all* of the human tricks, just as soon as we lift the Veil."

Nikolai had never experienced helplessness like this. Unable to move or even talk, he could only listen as his uncle spoke from far away. "I'm so glad you dropped in. Your mother will be delighted to see you."

Fucking bastard. He tried to lift his head, but couldn't even open his eyes.

"Uncle Fydor! I have something for you," Aleksi said from behind him somewhere.

Surely she'd see and help him. Any second now, she'd liberate Fydor's head from his body.

"Oh. I see you found Niki."

No.

"What is your surprise?" his uncle asked.

"You are going to love it."

She sounded so far away. Using all of his strength, he cracked his eyes open to see her rubbing against him. Hands all over his body. She slid her hands into his front pockets, and he groaned.

No, no, no, no, no, no.

"I brought you the Uniter. She came in through my window."

"Where is she?"

"Mihai has taken her to the dungeon."

"I want her in the rec room."

No...

"She can teleport. The dungeon was the only place secure enough."

"Call one of the witches. I'll arrange to get rid of this."

Nikolai heard the thud and knew it was his uncle's foot connecting with his rib cage, but he felt nothing other than the ache in his heart knowing he had failed. All his training and power couldn't help him now. And he'd never see Elena again. Never hold his child. Never...

Elena brushed the hair from Nik's forehead. "I have no idea what they drugged him with, but he seems to be coming around." He groaned, and she took his hand. "Nik, I'm here. So is your mother."

The oppressive darkness of the dungeon made it almost

impossible to see the woman sitting on the other side of the tiny space. Unlike the wood elf in the next cell, they weren't chained.

"What goes around comes around. You should have let me go," the elf taunted through the darkness. "Then you wouldn't be here as a prisoner, too."

Actually, being a prisoner beat the hell out of the other possible scenarios. "Shut up."

Nik groaned again and covered his mouth and nose. "The smell."

"You're in the dungeon," she explained. "It appears you were drugged."

He sat up with a groan and pulled her into his arms. "Never thought I'd…" She couldn't make out his face well enough in the darkness, but it sounded like he'd choked up emotionally.

Knowing how Slayers admired the strong outer appearance, she took his face in her hands to ground him and bring him back. "Hey. You're okay. We are all alive, and we need to hold it together to get out of this with our lives. Lie back and heal, because we're going to need your strength soon."

The door at the entrance to the dungeon creaked, and several sets of footsteps descended the stairs. The cellblock door flew open with a bang, and Elena squinted against the light of the torch carried by the big Slayer called Commander Mihai. With him was a hideous woman with tangled hair, wearing a filthy dress of sorts. It looked more like a burlap sack with armholes and a hole for the head.

He unlocked the door and grabbed Elena, yanking her out with him, then slamming the door shut. Nik tried to rise to his feet but couldn't get past his knees. Having seen her memories from his perspective, she knew how hard this was for him to be helpless. It broke her heart to see him struggle.

"It's okay, Nik. Recover. They are not going to kill me right now. I know what I'm talking about." And she did. She'd seen his mother bound to a stake. What she hadn't told him was that the point of view of the vision was from a stake right next to her. She'd at least live long enough to be burned alive.

The big Slayer pulled her into the cell where she'd first met Fee. He pointed to the stone bench at the back of the cell. All the surfaces undulated in the flickering light of the torch, giving the cell an eerie fluid quality. Not wanting to cause a scene and agitate Nik, she sat on the bench.

The old woman got right up in her face, but didn't look directly at her. Her weird, cloudy eyes stared straight ahead. She ran her fingers over Elena's face and grunted. Then she placed her palms flat over the markings on her chest and grunted again. It was all Elena could do to sit still while the old woman ran her hands over her breasts and down her ribs. She gasped when the woman shoved her hands under the front of the leather top, laying her palms on her belly. "No." she said. "Not going to do it."

Mihai shifted uncomfortably. "You have orders."

"No."

He pulled out his sword, and the old woman cringed. Holding the torch in one hand and his sword in the other, he looked fierce. Too fierce. Charge built in Elena's hands, and she nailed him in the chest full force with a bolt of electricity.

"Elena!" Nik yelled from the cell across from her. She grabbed the key ring off the unconscious Slayer and inserted it into the keyhole of the cell where he and his mother stood just inside the narrow bars.

Before she could engage the tumblers, a *tsking* sound came from the entrance to the cellblock followed by a sharp sting in her arm. Almost immediately, she ripped the dart out, but not soon enough. Her vision blurred within seconds.

"You will now insert that elf ore in her body, witch, or I will kill every man, woman, and child in your coven. Are we clear?" Fydor said.

"Y-yes," the old woman answered, pulling a wicked-looking medical instrument from a bag slung over her shoulder.

Nik looked ready to roar in anger, but she shook her blurry head. "Let them," she slurred. "S'okay. Heal. Trust."

His mother put a comforting hand on his arm as Elena sunk to the ground, too dizzy from the drug to stand.

Too bad it hadn't been enough to knock her out, she thought as the woman placed the instrument against the inside of her bicep. Yeah, really too bad, she lamented as the steel penetrated her flesh with an intolerable breath-stealing sting. The woman, hands shaking, depressed the plunger that inserted the metal plug of ore that would dampen her powers, leaving her one step short of human again. She gritted her teeth and held in a scream as the procedure was completed and the instrument removed. No anesthesia, no sterilization of the instruments, not even a freaking Band-Aid. She pressed her palm to her arm to stop the flow of blood from the incision sight. Welcome to the Underveil.

Several Slayers entered the dungeon, swords drawn.

"Showtime!" Fydor said.

CHAPTER THIRTY-FOUR

Dread, fear, rage, regret—Nikolai's emotions had run the gamut by the time he was bound with elven chains to one of four stakes. The execution site had been fabricated on top of a raised stone platform on the enormous fortress balcony overlooking the open field below. He hadn't even fought the men he thought at one time were friends because Elena had asked him not to. She wanted him to save his strength. For what? So he was in top form when they fucking burned them all alive.

Below, armies from numerous Underveil factions gathered. Just like Nikolai, they were helpless to do anything. Borya had put some kind of enchantment on the fortress that was like a force field bubble. Even arrows bounced off it.

Fydor, looking more unstable and nervous than Nikolai had ever seen him, was decked out in the typical Slayer black leather, but wore the king's crown. His father's crown. What should have been *his* crown if he hadn't fucked everything up. Fingers twitching, the man he'd allowed to have power, stood on the platform only feet in front of Nikolai, staring down at the crowd while servants piled hay at the edges of the giant pile of wood.

He relaxed his head against the heavy pole. To his left, the wood elf whimpered and Elena, on his right, remained calm and stoic. Beyond her, his mother ascended the stairs to the top of the stone platform. At the sight of the queen being secured for execution, the angry shouts from the warriors in the field below became deafening.

"Have you had a vision as to how we escape?" he asked Elena.

"No."

"Any visions at all after this?"

"Only the one I told you about at Vlad's castle."

Oh, yeah, the one where his mother was surrounded by flames. Fucking perfect.

Focus. Buying time was the ticket at this point. "So, Uncle. What do you think is going to happen when your protective bubble is gone?"

He shrugged.

"I know what will happen," Nikolai said. "They will storm the castle and kill every living thing inside."

Fydor pulled several vials from his pocket, selected one, and shoved the others back. His hands shook as he loosened the top and gulped the contents. "Borya will leave the protective spell in place then, of course."

A volley of arrows soundlessly hit the magical barrier well over Nikolai's head and fell away. "Then you will starve," he said. "I warned you, though, didn't I, Uncle? You are nothing but a puppet in his plan to create chaos and lift the Veil. And now, you're not even going to live to see the chaos you have helped create."

"Shut up!" Fydor yelled, pressing his palms to his head. "Light the fires."

"Not yet," Borya said, as he reached the top of the platform.

Nikolai clamped his mouth shut, not wanting to incite the

sorcerer to hurt Elena as he picked his way over the piled wood, stopping right in front of her. She didn't seem to notice and had a glazed look on her face. "Stop that!" he ordered.

She grinned. "Would you prefer I sing out loud?" At the top of her lungs, she belted, *"When I dance, they call me Macarena, and the boys they say que estoy buena!"*

With the back of his hand, he struck her across the face, and Nikolai roared, straining against his chains.

But instead of crying or showing fear, she simply started singing again. *"Hey! Macarena, M-M-Macarena, M-M-Macarena."*

The sorcerer, still clutching his staff, wrapped his other hand around her throat. Nikolai, unable to look away, nearly vomited at the prospect of watching his mate die. And his child. He swallowed the lump of dread in his throat and prayed they lit the fire soon if the bastard killed her.

"What's up, Borya? You don't like to dance?" she said. Nikolai held his breath as her face went red from the constriction of her throat. "Do it," she squeaked out. "It beats the hell out of being barbecue."

With a growl, he released her. Nikolai gave a silent shout of gratitude as fear's choke hold on his heart lessened.

She gulped air. "Chicken."

"Light the fires," he ordered the Slayers surrounding the platform after he had cleared the wood and straw.

Nikolai noticed their hesitation. Slayers never hesitated or disobeyed orders, yet none made a move to light the stack of wood.

Fydor held his arms out, and the crowd below shouted in anger.

"God help you, Uncle, when that protection spell is lifted. You'll wish you had a death as easy as mine. I imagine the elves will enjoy torturing you for centuries, maybe millennia, depending on Aksel's fate."

Fear flashed across his uncle's features, something Slayers never allowed. Good, his will was cracking. Now, if only the bubble keeping the warriors out would crack.

The overwhelming roar from the furious mob below rang in Elena's ears.

Speak, King Fydor," Borya urged from the bottom of the platform stairs.

Still singing in her head, Elena caught her breath and straightened up, relieving the bite of the chains. At least Borya had backed off, leaving the show to Fydor, who seemed pretty strung out. She was disappointed Fydor hadn't taken the poison when he chugged the elixir earlier. Not that it would have stopped the execution, necessarily, but at least the bastard would be dead.

Fydor held one arm up, palm out, and the mob below fell silent.

"A puppet," Nik called to his uncle. "He's pulled your strings, and now you must say what he directs."

"This is the beginning of a new era for the Underveil. We will rise together to the power we deserve."

No reaction from the gathering of weapon-toting creatures below. Elena had no idea there were this many.

"Tomorrow morning we will lift the Veil, forever changing the face of the planet," Fydor yelled. "I ask for your help and loyalty."

Still, silence. Commanders had their arms up at the ready. They were waiting for something. A signal to advance. A hope fluttered in Elena's chest. They knew something.

"I told you to light the fire," Borya shouted to the Slayers around the platform. Obviously, they didn't want to torch their queen. When they didn't move, he lifted his staff and a bolt shot from it, knocking a Slayer off to the stones below.

They needed more time. Something was going to happen. *Stall.* "Do it yourself, asshole," Elena challenged. "Or are you too weak?"

He once again climbed over the pile of wood and got right in her face. "I would, if I could. And I'd enjoy it, too. The problem is, Elena Arcos, I can't destroy my own blood or it weakens my power." She held completely still, heart slamming against her ribs like a captive animal as he kissed her on the cheek. "Goodbye, my sweet granddaughter."

Holy shit. Aunt Uza had mentioned her great-great-grandmother hooking up with an immortal. It was Borya.

He backed away and pointed his staff at the Slayer Elena remembered from her vision. "You will now do exactly as I wish," the sorcerer ordered.

Clearly against his will, the Slayer moved. Fighting his own body that was controlled by Borya, he lowered his torch to the straw at their feet. "Forgive me please, Queen Tatiana." The straw caught fire with a whoosh.

"These prisoners have been convicted of treason against the king," Fydor shouted. There was an odd void of reaction from the crowd below. "And sentenced to death by fire."

For the first time, Elena truly doubted they'd make it out alive. She'd seen the last of her visions unfold and had no idea what would happen now. If Aleksandra had been successful in putting the tainted vial with his others, at least Elena could die confident that Fydor would not live to lead that massacre tomorrow morning. She strained to look at the crowd inside the fortress behind her, but didn't catch a glimpse of Aleksi.

And then, there was the baby. She closed her eyes at the sting of the smoke. The precious baby Nik had given her. The bridge between worlds. A tear rolled down her cheek as the ache in her chest became intolerable. The heat from the flames was increasing, and in moments it would spread enough to ignite the wood at her feet. This was it. Still careful to hum so Borya wouldn't hear her thoughts about the baby and the poison, she knew it was time for good-byes. "Nik?" He met her eyes, calm and relaxed. "I'm glad you found me in that convenience store."

"I love you, Elena Arcos," he said.

"I love you, too, and I'll see you wherever we end up after this lifetime," she answered.

He cleared his throat. "Thank you, Mother."

"You are an excellent son and Slayer," she answered.

The wood elf said nothing. He trembled all over, black eyes wide with horror in his rough, gray-skinned face as the flames spread and grew, getting closer to the center every second.

A twinge of sympathy pricked Elena's chest. He had no one to comfort him. "I wish you well, elf," she said.

He closed his eyes and nodded.

The heat built as the flames crept closer, and Elena switched from "The Macarena" to "The Hokey Pokey," in honor of her dad, who maybe she'd see soon, if there really was an afterlife. Sweat beaded on her forehead, and she bid her unborn child a silent good-bye.

So close. They'd almost done it.

"Woo hooooooo!" someone shrieked, and Elena opened her eyes to see Uza, still dressed in her cat mu-mu, solidify with a pop on the platform just outside the flames. "Let's get this party started, dudes!"

Uza turned in a circle, hips swaying like she was on the dance floor. Once back around to face Elena, she swept her arms in a wide circle, puckered her lips, and blew, looking even crazier than usual. A huge gust of wind followed, blowing cinders and flaming straw around like flash paper. "I'll dance the Macarena with you, Ellie Baby." She blew again, and the rest of the fire went out like candles on a birthday cake, leaving only tiny smoldering embers. "*And* the Hokey Pokey."

Watch out!" Elena shouted as Borya raised his staff.

Aunt Uza turned and held her palms out to him, blocking the bolt he fired off, causing it to ricochet back, nearly hitting him.

"Now, kitties, you know what to do." She brushed her hands over her mu-mu, as if dusting off hay, but instead, dusted off her shifter companions, who hit the ground as full-size house cats. They immediately sprang into action, lining the perimeter of the platform as if daring anyone to try to come light the fire again.

"Behind you," Elena shouted as Borya raised his staff again.

Uza rolled her eyes and met his bolt with her palm, shooting it back at him, this time directing the energy right back at him, setting his robes on fire. "Liar, liar, pants on fire!" She giggled. "I've always wanted to say that for realz."

Borya raised his staff over his head, and an amazing thing happened. Clouds formed and rain poured down, but only on the balcony. The cats howled and hunkered down as any remaining cinders were doused along with Borya's robes. That rumor that cats don't like water? Totally true. Pretty much simultaneously, they busted out of their pelts and stretched into rain-slicked naked men.

"Oh, hallelujah," Uza squealed, deflecting a bolt from Borya. "Almost as good as mud-wrestling. Huh, Ellie Baby?"

The shifters maintained defensive stances toward the Slayers stationed around the platform, who made no move to advance.

As Uza and Borya exchanged lightning bolts, Fydor climbed off the platform and slunk out of sight behind them. Elena strained to see behind her, but was bound too tightly. Where had he gone, and where the hell was Aleksi?

She relaxed slightly, relieved that at least for these few moments, the Slayers were making no offensive moves. Still, the cat shifters remained crouched, ready to strike. Except one. The big guy with the beard who doubled as the gold Persian broke ranks and approached them, long claws out. Maybe he was going to try to unbind him.

As he passed Elena, she heard a low, rumbling, predatory growl, and her fight-or-flight instinct flew in to full flight mode. Something was wrong—well, more wrong. Wrong was relative when tied up to be burned to death.

He stopped when he got to Nik and raised his razor claws to throat level.

"Uza!" Elena shouted.

"Bad kitty!" She zapped him, and he crumbled to a ball, writhing in pain.

The remaining shifters hissed and growled at him as he muttered about rising up, picking the wrong twin to worship, and the pitfalls of serving ugly old bats. Well, that answered the question about who had tipped off the creatures that met them at the airport.

"We have to get free," Nik said. "Who, other than the Slayer that bound us, has the key? Where's the one you used to free me?"

The Slayer Borya had zapped was the one who'd locked the shackles, and he was unconscious, out of reach. Her key was probably at Vlad's castle. Once she'd used it to free Nik, she'd forgotten about it. It was probably lying on the floor of the bathroom or something like a discarded bath towel. "I don't know."

He closed his eyes and thumped his head on the post behind him.

"A-3! Direct hit!" Uza shouted. Borya howled and clutched his charred arm. "You're doing it wrong, brother, you're supposed to say, 'You sunk my battleship!'"

Like a dropped glass bowl, a fissure opened in the protective shield, probably as a result of Borya's injury. Below, the gathered armies shouted and mobilized.

Screaming came from somewhere in the building below as Vlad, along with Ricardo, Stefan, and Fee materialized on the top of the wall in front of the platform.

"Sorry we're late," the vampire said with a wink. "Traffic was a nightmare."

More screaming below.

"You forgot something, Elena." Vlad held up the key, and she slumped against the post with relief. They might live through this after all.

He inserted the key in the lock of one of Tatiana's shackles. "Ladies first," he said.

While Borya and Uzana duked it out, blasting each other and yelling insults, the cat shifters kept guard on the platform, the Slayers stood completely still, Ricardo climbed off the platform, and Fee approached Elena.

Her movements were fluid and graceful. Elena took a deep breath through her nose. The floral scent was intoxicating. "I brought you something," she said.

"You're next Elena." Vlad was unlocking the only remaining shackle on Queen Tatiana's ankle.

Still, no one made a move to either attack or defend. It was a stand off for something nobody really wanted—a cause no one believed in. This was Borya's and Fydor's war. Not a war of the Underveil.

Fee held up a vial of green liquid. "This will react to my blood in your body. It will make the elf ore useless against your powers."

"You mean the plug they put in my arm?"

She uncapped the bottle and held it to Elena's lips. "Yes. And the chains as well." She poured the liquid in Elena's mouth. "Swallow."

It was bitter. She shuddered as Fee took a step back. Concentrating on the spot next to her, Elena attempted to teleport out of the shackles. "It didn't work."

While Stefan escorted Queen Tatiana off the platform, Vlad unlocked the first cuff.

"Unfortunately, there is a delay," Fee explained.

"How long?"

The second cuff fell away, and she rubbed her wrists while he worked on her ankles.

"I don't know. It's new." She smiled. "I made it special for this event."

The screams and shouts from below grew louder.

Vlad handed her the key. "You free Nikolai. I need to join Ricardo below." And with that, he pulled a dagger from the sheath on his hip and climbed down the platform stairs.

A sizzling sound filled the air as Uzana's and Borya's lightning bolts met each other and twisted and tangled.

"Give up, brother," Uza said. "Your odds of beating me are about as good as a one-legged man in a butt kickin' contest!"

"The revolutionary vampires, bear shifters, and wood elves did not join the resistance," Fee explained. "They are attacking from the back of the fortress, while the resistance enters from the front. My father is in charge of the resistance forces and will defeat the opposition as they enter the great hall."

The smile Nik gave as Elena unlocked his chains brought

back memories of the last time she freed him and what followed. Her face got hot at the notion that sex would even cross her mind right now. Clearly, it was crossing his mind, too.

"Aren't you glad you saved your energy and didn't waste it fighting the guards?" she asked.

He pulled her against him with his free arm, and her body heated. "Yes, when this is over, I'm going to need lots of energy. So are you."

When the last of the chains fell away, he kissed her fiercely, then looked around. "I have to find Fydor. And I have a feeling I know exactly where he is." He splayed his fingers over her belly. "Please stay safe."

Placing her hands over his, she pulled back slightly to meet his eyes. "You can't kill him."

"Fuck that. He's a dead man."

She tightened her grip. "Listen to me. This is really important." When she was sure she had his focus, she continued. "His blood cannot be on your hands if you plan to lead effectively."

"I'm a Slayer. We are charged with meting out justice."

"I'm the Uniter. My charge is burned into your very skin!" She waited until she was sure he'd completely processed her words through his Slayer instinct for revenge. "Skin I want to spend the rest of my life touching and kissing."

His expression softened, and his gaze dropped to where their hands were joined over their unborn child. "What is the best course of action, then?"

"I am going to stay here until the sorcerers have concluded their duel, and then I'll join you."

A quick glance confirmed Aunt Uza was still going strong, pausing for an occasional victory fanny shake when she had delivered a particularly strong jolt. Borya's energy bolt was dim, and it was clear he was losing.

"I think this is close to over. Find Fydor and keep him secure. Beat the shit out of him if it'll make you feel better, but do not kill him. Wait until the royal family and leaders of other factions are present and a consensus can be made. Prove you are a rational leader who favors peace over violence."

"I am."

She rose on tiptoe and kissed him. "I know."

She watched him until he disappeared inside the building. *Please stay safe, Nik.*

First things first. She needed to get a grip on what was happening around her.

Borya and Uzana, electric bolts still tangling, were duking it out with no interference from anyone else. Good call. Getting in the middle of that wouldn't end well.

Fee was still at her side, and the cat shifters were defending the platform against…no one. A glance behind her let her know that the Slayers had formed a defensive ring around the queen, who was conferring with…Aleksi!

Right now, this was the place to be. The safest for sure.

"Stop before I make you a crispy critter," Aunt Uza said. "I'm stronger than you and always will be."

Borya grunted in response, long, black hair matted to his sweaty face.

"You and I both know you've lost this round. Because you're blood, I can't deep-six you, bro, but one of these hotties can, so skedaddle. Go lick your wounds and plan your next futile attempt at world domination." The bolts crackled. "Somewhere else." She growled, and her bolt got brighter as his flickered, then disappeared completely, allowing her bolt to nail him in the chest. He disappeared instantly.

"Woo, Ellie Baby! Did you see that? It'll take him a century to heal from that!" Aunt Uza hollered from across the balcony.

"Hated to let him go, but we're gonna need him down the road."

Need him?

Aunt Uza pointed at her head. "I see stuff, remember?" Then she burst out in laughter. "Yippee! New Year's fireworks right in his chest. Yeah! I'm hotter than asphalt in August." She danced in a circle singing "The Macarena," and Elena laughed—something she didn't think she'd ever get the chance to do again.

There was a gentle touch on her shoulder. "What about him?" Fee gestured to the wood elf still bound to the post.

He kept his eyes down, certainly expecting to be abandoned there. She searched through her memories of their first meeting in the dungeon, hoping her new ability to see the past objectively would help. *Fear.* Incapacitating fear and something else colored his view of the scene. Confusion. Hatred—but not of the others in the cells. It was self-loathing. This pitiful creature hated himself.

The air smelled of wet ash and rain. From the floor below, shouts and the sounds of metal clashing and scraping rang out. With any luck, this was the end of the old regime of hatred. Her job was to unite. What better place than right here to begin change?

She inserted the key into the wood elf's shackles.

CHAPTER THIRTY-FIVE

Nikolai knew exactly where he'd find Fydor. Hopefully, the fucker hadn't teleported out already. Forging a direct path through the battling warriors, which consisted of wood elves, bear shifters, and some rogue vamps against everyone else, he paused to snag a crappy sword from a dying wood elf. The resistance was crushing the poor fools fighting on behalf of his uncle, so he didn't even bother helping out as he shoved and pushed his way to the door of the "rec room."

Fydor was standing perfectly still in the middle of the large, round space, his brother's sword clasped point down in his hands and the crown on his head. The chains and shackles hung limp and empty from the wall where Nikolai had been bound and beaten by this monster of a man he'd once trusted.

"I knew you'd come," Fydor said, broad back to him.

"I assumed you'd teleport out and flee."

He turned. "I tried. We are locked down, evidently." Fydor pulled a vial out of his pocket, popped the lid, and downed it. "Aren't you going to try to kill me, Nikolai, like I killed Ivan Itzov and Gregor Arcos?"

There it was. The admission he thought he'd never hear. "Deathbed confession time, Uncle?"

"Just figured you should know the truth before I kill you." He raised the sword in a ready stance.

Nik held out his inadequate "borrowed" weapon. "Hardly a fair fight, Uncle."

"Didn't your father ever teach you that life's not fair?" He swung a wide arc with the sword, missing Nik by only inches.

"He taught me to level the playing field in the interest of fairness." In one burst, he leapt and slammed his uncle's hands with a roundhouse kick that sent the sword careening into the wall, then clanging to the floor along with the crown. He threw his own sword to the opposite wall. "Now it's fair."

Fists raised, the men approached each other.

Nikolai wanted to kill the bastard, but kicking the shit out of him would just have to do for now.

"Ooo, honey, c'mon over here and let me check ya for ticks!" Uza shouted at a tall light elf pulling a sword out of a bear shifter's torso. "Dang, those elves are hella fine, aren't they, Ellie?"

"Yeah, fine," she answered, ducking to avoid being whacked in the head by a wood elf's club. Stefan reached out and gave the elf a zap to the head.

"Timber," he called as it fell over.

"Ha! Good one, hottie," Uza said, clearly enjoying herself as they pushed through the waning battle in the great hall. Only a few of the revolution fighters were standing.

"I hope Fydor didn't teleport out," Elena said, tripping a wood elf that was trying to sneak up on a vampire. She would have electrocuted him, except she still didn't have any powers.

"No way, Ellie. I put a roach motel spell on this place."

"I'm sure I'll regret this, but what is a roach motel?" Stefan asked, stepping over the body of a bear shifter.

"Mercy," Uza said, pushing some hair back in place. "Haven't you seen the ad on TV? 'The roach motel! Roaches check in, but they don't check out!'" She did a little shimmy and giggled. "My spell allowed folks in, but not out. Get it?"

"Got it." Stefan retrieved a dagger from the floor.

"You asked," Elena said as they stopped outside the round room where she rescued Nik. Sounds of struggle came from within. Grunts and smacks of fists on flesh.

"Open it," Uza urged. "This is exciting, like getting a present. Open it!"

Stefan turned the handle and pushed the door open. Both men were bloody, Fydor more so than Nik, mainly on their fists and faces. Elena's chest felt tight. He'd followed her request rather than his instinct. They were both alive.

Nik grinned and gave Fydor a hard shove into the wall. "Took you long enough."

Dazed, blood running from his nose, Fydor slid down the wall to a crouch.

"Sorry, we had to check out the scenery on the way in," Uza said. "Nothing like a little elf tushie to improve your circulation."

"My dear uncle has been clearing up many things for me." Nik wiped his mouth with the back of his hand, smearing more than wiping away blood. The smell of it made Elena's jaws ache. As soon as this was over, she had plans for King Nikolai.

Aleksi and Tatiana entered, along with Fee.

"Well, Uncle, now that we are all here, why don't you share with them what you told me?"

It was just a flick of his eyes to the sword, nothing more, but Elena knew what Fydor planned. "Ni—"

Before she could even get his name out, Fydor lunged,

picked up the sword, and shoved it through Nik's thigh. When he doubled over in pain, Fydor put the blade at his throat and pulled up, causing Nik to stand upright to keep from being decapitated—which would end his immortal life.

Stefan and Aleksi had weapons drawn, but had not gotten there in time.

"Don't do anything stupid, or he's dead," Fydor said. "Close the door, drop your weapons, and move back against the wall."

Elena's heart tried to leap out of her chest as she pushed the door closed and weapons clattered on the stone floor.

"This is your fault." His eyes twitched as he glared at Elena. "All your fault."

"Calm down, my love," Nik's mother said in a soothing tone. "You need a dose of your medicine so you can focus."

"Yes. Medicine. It's in my pocket."

Tatiana's eyes flitted to Aleksi as she walked toward him. She knew! Aleksi must have told her on the balcony. She reached into his front pocket while he kept the sword at Nik's throat and removed two identical vials of purple liquid. Again, she looked at Aleksi, who shrugged. "How about taking two this time?"

"No. I need to focus. Only one. Now. I'm in pain."

"Of course you are," she said, brow furrowed as she studied the vials.

"Now."

Eyes closed and body relaxed, Nik grunted as Fydor jerked the sword against his throat.

Tatiana pulled the stopper out of one of the bottles and poured it into Fydor's mouth. Elena held her breath, hoping he'd keel over right then and there. Nothing. It must be the remaining vial.

"I killed him, you know," he said, still shaking. "I killed them both. I had to." He closed his eyes and took a deep breath through his nose. "And then the markings started appearing." His eyes flew open, and his now-steady gaze landed right on Elena. "The markings saying you were coming for me, on the bodies of every Slayer under the Veil. So, of course, you had to die."

A bit of blood trickled down Nik's neck where the blade scored the skin as Fydor tightened his hold.

They needed to stall, possibly through enough time for him to drink that other vial of liquid. She had to keep him occupied. Damn, she hoped the elixir Fee gave her really rendered the ore in her arm inert. She focused on sending charge to her hands and felt a tiny buzz. Hardly anything, but maybe she'd charge up fast once it took effect.

"I have a deal for you, Fydor," she said.

"No deals."

"You'll like this one." She moved to stand right next to him. "It's me you want. An even trade. Let Nik go and take me."

"No!" Nik's voice was strained and harsh. Desperate.

"Why would you do that?"

Yes! She had him now. "I love him. Would rather die than watch him die. Plus, you might be able to get my aunt to open the sunroof here so you can teleport if you use me as a bargaining chip."

"Smart girl. Lie down on your back right next to my foot, hands behind your head. If any of you move, I'll run her through. That's all it takes to kill a Dhampir."

"Truly, it's okay," she said, hoping the others would realize she had a plan. "Everyone do as he asks." She lay on her back on the floor.

Fydor, in a smooth maneuver, stepped back, lowered his sword, and shoved Nik with his foot on the backside. He then stood over Elena, foot on either side of her thighs, sword tip at her throat. Nik, with his injured leg, lost his balance and fell forward.

Man, oh, man, she hoped that elixir to restore her powers was working or this was a really bad plan. A look of pain crossed Fydor's face. He shook his head and held the sword steady. "Kill the spell, Uzana, or I kill her."

"Nope. Sorry. No can do, dude," Aunt Uza said from near the door. "Roaches check in, but they don't check out."

"Let him go! He's not worth it," Nik said, struggling to his feet, blood coating his thigh.

"Sorry, hottie. Gotta think of the greater good and all."

Fydor dragged the tip of the sword from her throat down between her breasts in a stinging trail of fire. "I can make her death slow and painful."

"No!" Nik shouted, shuffling closer.

"Move and I kill her, nephew." His gaze drifted down her body. She could feel the cool air over her belly button. Her shirt must have ridden up. He lifted the bottom edge with the tip of the sword and nudged the leather up. "What's this?" He blinked hard and made another grimace. "What the fuck is it!" he shouted. "Answer me, Uzana, or I'm slicing her open."

"Go right ahead."

Elena couldn't believe her reaction. What was she about?

"Folder. You can read this shit. What does it say?"

Stefan didn't answer.

"I know Time Folders can't lie. Tell me or I'll choke her with her own intestines."

"It's another prophecy."

Clutching his stomach, he winced. Elena's breath caught. Maybe he had drunk the poison, and this would work after all. She bit her lip and tested her power. Still, only a vague buzzing. *Shit. Relax. Will your power to increase.*

He straightened and held the sword hilt above his head,

point down, just as her death angel had done in the convenience store, only this time, she didn't welcome death. Not at all. She had way too much to live for.

"Tell me what it says, Time Folder."

"It says she's carrying a baby that will be the bridge between worlds."

"Not a chance in hell will I let that happen."

Just as it had when she battled the shifters in Uza's yard, things seemed to move in slow motion. It started with a guttural yell from Fydor, followed by a battle cry from Nik who lunged right as Fydor plunged the sword toward her abdomen. Before the tip came within range, Elena envisioned herself standing behind Fydor. She'd picked a close distance, hoping she had enough juice. Right as she felt the blade touch her skin, her body buzzed and reconfigured exactly where she'd envisioned it, just in time to see Nik take Fydor to the ground.

It had worked!

Nik wrestled the sword out of Fydor's hand, both men gasping in pain. Nik struggled to his feet and swung the sword up in position to decapitate his uncle.

"No!" Elena shouted. He froze. "Please." After long moments, in which she knew he fought a vigorous internal battle with his Slayer nature, he lowered the sword.

She looked around the room at the horrified faces. Well, all except for one. Uza was grinning ear to ear, stroking her purring mu-mu.

Fydor groaned again and convulsed.

Fee's shoulders lowered, and she took a deep breath, relief clear on her face. Aleksi, too, relaxed a bit, brow arched as she watched in fascination.

Gasping, Fydor rolled to his side in a ball. "Tatiana, help me," he groaned.

"I'll help you like you helped my husband." She crossed her arms over her chest, face expressionless, and stood still.

It didn't take long after that for him to die. Elena had a suspicion it happened far too fast for Aleksi and Tatiana, who had suffered at his hands for years. Once he stopped convulsing, no one moved for a while.

Nik took a step back and slid his father's sword into the sheath on his back, and then his eyes met hers. Her heart soared as they stared at each other, and everything else seemed to fade away. He held out his arms, and she ran to him, loving the feel of being folded against him. "It's over," she said. He pulled her even tighter and kissed the top of her head.

"Not quite." Tatiana calmly felt for Fydor's pulse. Then she picked up the crown, strode to the door, opened it, and entered the great hall.

Nik wasn't bleeding anymore, but he had a slight limp still. His leg would heal. So would the cut on her chest. Unwilling to let each other go, they held hands as they followed his mother.

"Fydor Itzov is dead," she shouted. The room fell silent, and all turned to look at the queen. From the looks of it, the battle had all but ended.

"All hail King Nikolai," she said, holding the crown high over her head.

"All hail King Nikolai," an exuberant chorus of voices responded from all around the room as Tatiana placed the crown on her son's head.

"Eternal life to the Uniter. Bringer of peace. Protector of the bridge," Vlad shouted from the back of the room, bloody dagger held high.

"Eternal life!" the crowd repeated.

"Well, my work here is done," Uza said from behind them. "Getting you two together was slower than molasses in January.

Don't screw it up." She disappeared with a pop.

"And now your work really begins, sweet girl," Stefan whispered in her ear. "Good luck keeping him in line."

Ricardo's red eyes met hers from several yards away. "I wish you good choices, Elena Arcos."

She grinned up at Nik, whose bruised, bloody face was the most beautiful thing she'd ever seen. "Loving you was the best choice I ever made."

He put his lips against her ear. "That was not a choice. That was inevitable. I'm irresistible."

He was. And as soon as they were alone, she'd show him just how irresistible she found him. Every part of him.

He placed his palm over her belly. "I love you, Elena Arcos."

"Love is a myth, remember? Slayers don't love."

"This one does."

EPILOGUE

"Leather. No respectable Slayer nursery is decorated any other way. It has to be done in black leather," Aleksi said.

"I guess this room will just not be respectable, then." Elena held up two wallpaper samples. "Planes or puppies?"

Aleksi groaned and plopped down in the rocking chair sent as a gift from the bird shifters. It was striking and ornate with carved raptor talons gripping the rocker rails.

"He's only half Slayer. The other half is vampire and human with some seer thrown in."

"Puppies, since he'll be a mutt."

Elena ran her hands over her abdomen. She wasn't showing yet, but the day before he returned home, Stefan flew a doctor in from Belfast with a portable ultrasound, and they now knew for certain it was a boy. She was pretty sure she could have just asked Aunt Uza to get that information, but nobody had heard from her or Borya since the day of the battle.

Children's laughter rang out in the hallway as Claude's kids pushed each other in a wagon, pretending it was a human car. Mihai had stepped down as Commander of the Elite Force, and Claude had taken his place, moving into the fortress with his family. A happy squeal was followed by giggles.

"Thank you," Aleksi said. "You did this."

She closed the wallpaper book. "What?"

"This." She gestured to the door. "Laughter. There hasn't been laughter in this building in twenty years. Now it's everywhere. Niki laughs all the time. So does my mother."

"What about you?"

She smiled. "Yeah, me too." She sighed. "You've brought love here. We always had it, but we covered it, like we cover our fear."

"Love should never be covered up or hidden. It should be used and savored and screamed from the rooftops."

"Kinda like you screamed last night?" She winked.

Heat raced up Elena's neck and over her face. Their bedroom was all the way at the end of the hallway, for goodness sake. She picked up a teddy bear Ricardo had sent when he got back to the States and pitched it at Aleksi's head. Nik had made her scream all right. More than once.

Her body hummed all over at the memory. Time for a change of topic. "We're going to name the baby Ivan Gregor Itzov, after both of our fathers."

"I think that's a fantastic idea."

"It was Vladimir Dalca's idea."

"Mmm. Vlad." She ran her fingers over the teddy bear's ears. "Too bad he's a vamp."

"Yeah, too bad." Elena grinned and went in search of Nik. It wasn't much of a search, actually; she knew exactly where he'd be: the rec room. Which was now truly a rec room, complete with wet bar, huge flat-screen TV, multiple game consoles, and oversize—or Slayer-sized—comfy leather sofas. And at that moment, her oversize Slayer was snoozing on one of those sofas with a rugby match playing on the television. She picked up the remote from his chest and switched it off.

"I was watching that," he said, not even bothering to open his eyes.

"Ah, men and their sports," she said, climbing over his body to straddle him. That got him to open his eyes…and grin. "I have a sport in mind. It involves a lot of practice." She leaned down and kissed him.

He put his hands on her thighs. "I hope it's a contact sport."

"It is." When she reached over to put the remote on the coffee table, two wrapped packages caught her eye. "What are the boxes for?"

"For you."

"Really?"

"Yes." He wrapped his hands around her backside. "But what about our sport?"

"Well, we're taking a brief time-out." She turned the smaller of the two boxes over in her hands, but found no card. It was wrapped in shiny gold paper. He released her backside and rubbed his hands up and down her thighs, gorgeous smile on his face. She swatted his hand. "You're distracting me."

"You don't say." He put his hands behind his head, soft T-shirt stretching over his muscled chest and upper arms.

She slid her fingers under the wrapping paper, revealing a velvet box. A ring box. Her gaze shot to his, and his smile broadened. Heart fluttering, she opened the box and gasped. It was a ring with a blood-red stone surrounded by diamonds.

"The ruby was your father's. He wore it in a pinky ring Vlad collected when he retrieved my father's sword. I had it reset," he said. "I had wanted to give it to you on the day we married, but it took much longer than expected."

She looked down at her plain gold band he'd given her at their wedding. "This works fine."

He took the ring out of the box and slipped it on above the

gold band. "Yes, but this one suits a queen. And the mother of my child. And the love of my life."

Wow, how far they'd come since that day in the convenience store. Nothing on earth would tempt her to go back to her old human life.

"Thank you. It's amazing." She picked up the other box, wrapped in plain brown paper. "What's this one?"

He propped up on his elbows. "I assume it's from your Aunt Uza because it was addressed to *Queen Ellie Baby's Baby care of King Hottie-Totty.*"

"Well, that certainly narrows the possibilities." She tore the paper and read a note scrawled on the lid. *"I made these myself. Nimble fingers/nimble mind, as they say."* She lifted the top and peeked in. "It appears she's taken up knitting?" She pulled out two booties of entirely different sizes made out of the oddest yarn. It was soft, but uneven… *Surely not.* She turned one over in her hand and…

"Cat hair!" she and Nik said simultaneously. She busted out giggling as he grabbed the booties, box, and wrapper and tossed them over his head.

Then he rolled her under him. "Time-out is over."

"Yeah?" Her voice was breathier than she'd expected. "I'm thinking this game might go into overtime if you're lucky."

"Baby, count on it. I'm the luckiest man alive."

ACKNOWLEDGMENTS

Getting Love Me to Death to this point has been an absolute delight, thanks primarily to the team at Entangled, especially Liz Pelletier, who believed in this book from the start.

Huge hugs to the whole gang in Camp Clarke for cheering me on and getting the word out, especially Shawna, Lucy, Nicole, Mariela, Tabatha, and Allison. Pass the marshmallows!

Love to Patrick McDonald at QueryTracker for always listening and making those website changes with a moment's notice.

And of course, I would not be able to finish a page without the support from my amazing husband, Laine.

Also by Marissa Clarke

SLEEPING WITH THE BOSS

Claire Maddox is off to see the world, but first, she needs quick cash. A temp job at Anderson Auctions seems perfect, especially with the unexpected benefit of the hottest man she's ever laid eyes — or hands — on. William Anderson's military training makes him the perfect man to flush out the spy undercutting his family business, but no amount of time in the Marines could prepare him for the suspicious — and sexy — new temp. Desire lands them in bed…but duty may cost him his heart.

Looking for more strong heroines and to-die-for heroes?
Try these Entangled Select novels...

WINNING LOVE

by Abby Niles

Cage fighting helps Mac "The Snake" Hannon manage his demons, but it doesn't take away his pain. Gayle Andrews chases tornadoes, determined to save others from experiencing loss like she has. Her new neighbor, Mac, intrigues her, but his tragedy means he can't deal with Gayle courting disaster at every turn. When a raging tornado puts Gayle's life in danger, Mac's head tells him to walk away, but his heart pulls him into the eye of the storm. But will it be too late for Gayle and Mac to have their happily ever after?

DYED AND GONE

by Beth Yarnall

When Dhane, a dynamic celebrity hairstylist, is found dead, Azalea March suspects foul play. Her friend Vivian confesses to the murder and is arrested, but Azalea knows there's no way she could have done it. Vivian's protecting someone. But who? Now Azalea and Alex, the sexy detective from her past, must comb through clues more twisted than a spiral perm. But the truth is stranger than anything found on the Las Vegas Strip, and proving Vivian's innocence turns out to be more difficult than transforming a brunette into a blonde.

TANGLED HEARTS

by Heather McCollum

Highland warrior Ewan Brody always wanted a sweet, uncomplicated woman by his side, but he can't fight his attraction to the beautiful enchantress who's stumbled into his life. He quickly learns, though, that Pandora Wyatt is not only a witch, but also a pirate and possibly a traitor's daughter—and though she's tricked him into playing her husband at King Henry's court, he's falling hard. As they discover dark secrets leading to the real traitor of the Tudor court, Ewan and Pandora must uncover the truth before they lose more than just their hearts.